INSTRUCTIONS FOR BRINGING UP SCARLETT

INSTRUCTIONS FOR BRINGING UP SCARLETT

Annie Sanders

WINDSOR
PARAGON

First published 2011
by Orion Books
This Large Print edition published 2012
by AudioGO Ltd
by arrangement with
The Orion Publishing Group

Hardcover   ISBN: 978 1 445 87260 5
Softcover   ISBN: 978 1 445 87261 2

British Library Cataloguing in Publication Data available

Printed and bound in Great Britain by
MPG Books Group Limited

To our mothers.
We miss you and your wisdom.

Chapter 1

18 May 1994

'This isn't going to work.' Virginia slumped back in her chair and ran her fingers through her hair.

Alice took her feet off the table, sat up and peered at the little diagram Virginia had been poring over. A page of carefully drawn circles with names written and crossed out beside them in pencil.

'Bloody hell! That looks like an air traffic controller's nightmare.'

'It feels like it.' Virginia got up and put the kettle on again. 'I think we're heading for a mid-air collision, and even if I make this work, you can bet someone is going to pull out in the next week.'

Alice looked out of the window at the small garden and a couple of birds dancing about on the terrace. 'It's still not too late to elope, you know.'

'No kidding. I've practically packed my bag already.' Virginia poured hot water into the mugs and brought them over to the table.

'Perhaps we should have settled for a buffet, it would have been so much easier,' she sighed. Alice patted her knee, a bit at a loss to know how else to help.

'So long as it's boy-girl-boy-girl, does it really matter? And so long as I'm not on the children's table.'

'You don't know the half of it. The Waverley family are like the Kennedys, and Mother-in-law has given me a spreadsheet of which family members can't be put together or there will be fighting in the aisles.'

Alice scooped out the tea bag with a pencil and dropped it onto the empty biscuit plate. 'They sound more like the Borgias. It's at times like this that I'm glad I'm an only child.'

'If only it was as simple as just one family. The problem is merging the two, and there is no way I am putting any of my relations with the Waverley lot. Can you imagine? We'd have a high court judge next to my cousin Sharon, who's a sales assistant in a shoe shop. Where's the common ground there?'

'Well . . . we all wear shoes . . . ?'

'Nice try, Alice. Nice try.'

They sat in silence for a moment. The last two hours had been spent trying to make the wedding table plan work, and Alice felt frankly useless. Seating their university friends had been a breeze, but she didn't know enough about either Virginia or Piers' families to be able to make a useful contribution. She furtively looked at her watch. With a bit of luck they could start getting ready soon. She'd arranged for the hen night to start about seven and the sooner the better. Virginia needed a break from this.

'At least you've got the top table sorted. You'll look like that painting of the Last Supper.'

'They only had one table to worry about that night!' Virginia laughed. 'Oh God, look. I've put the vicar next to that friend of Piers who works for the whisky distillery. Would that be sacrilegious?'

'Some of the best clerics drink. We had a priest at school who was permanently pissed. Isn't it called the Holy Spirit? Listen, Gin, I think you might be trying too hard. It's *your* big day and everyone will be there to see *you*. They can bloody well put up with who they sit next to.'

Virginia let her shoulders drop. 'You're right. I suppose I'm just feeling a bit pressurised by Judy. She's the world authority on party organisation and she keeps reminding me how perfect Barney's wedding was.'

'Yes, but she's the mother of sons and so she's never actually had to organise one herself, has she? And you said yourself that Barney's wife was posh enough for two and Judy loves all that. Your problem is that you want everything to be perfect. It'll be fine. They'll love you just the way you are, whippets and all.'

Virginia rubbed her eyes. 'My job is a breeze compared to this. No wonder people have to be engaged for two years—you need that much time to organise it. Perhaps a six-month engagement was too short after all, but I'm damned if I'm going to give Judy the satisfaction of being right.'

'Frankly, I think you'd have shot her if it had been any longer.'

The front door of the flat opened and was slammed shut. 'Hello?' Piers called from the little hallway. 'Is it safe to come back in yet?' He walked into the room and dropped his sports bag by the washing machine before leaning down and kissing Virginia lingeringly on her upturned face. 'Hello, how's my gorgeous bride?'

'I don't think I'm any further on than when you left,' Virginia groaned. 'You should have made them row another few miles.'

'The boys were knackered. Thank goodness it's nearly half-term. And how's the gorgeous bridesmaid?' He leaned down and kissed Alice on

3

the cheek. 'What time did you get here?'

'About eleven. Getting through Hammersmith was a complete nightmare as usual, but a nice relaxing session of wedding planning has eased the tension a treat.'

They all laughed and Virginia threw her pen down on the scrawled plan and stretched. 'I've had enough for one day. Come on. Let's have a drink and start thinking about tonight.'

'Aha!' Alice put down her tea and pulled a carrier bag from her overnight case. 'As officer in charge of the hen night, I have your costume right here.' With a flourish she produced the swag. She'd been having so much fun choosing the bits, she'd been late for a meeting, and with unashamed glee she now laid it out on top of Ginny's table plan: pink sashes for all eight of them (Virginia's emblazoned with 'bride-to-be' in sequins), pink devil hairbands (the fluffy horns bobbing about suggestively) and, for Virginia alone, fishnet tights, a pink satin bodice and matching tutu.

Virginia gasped and put her hands over her face. 'No. Way.'

'Yes way!' Alice responded. 'It's the law.'

Piers picked up the tutu and the tights. 'Ooh, darling, I like the look of this. Can you keep them on for the bedroom later?'

Virginia's face was a vision of embarrassment. 'If I've got to walk down St Giles in this lot, I'm gonna need that drink,' she squealed. 'Just promise me, no photos.'

Alice raised an eyebrow. 'I'm promising nothing.'

Saturday, 25 May 1994

'Don't turn around yet.' Alice put up her hand and adjusted Virginia's veil on her shoulder, then appraised her. 'We've got to have you looking absolutely perfect before you see the result.'

Virginia could feel a bubble of anticipation rise in her stomach. The organza silk of the dress felt cool and unfamiliar against her legs. At the fittings it had all seemed such fun. Standing here now, groomed and cleaner than she'd ever felt before, rigid in case something creased, her nerves began to push to the fore.

'Relax, honey,' Alice cooed. 'You can blink, you know!'

'It all feels a bit odd and precarious.'

'That bloke in the salon has put so much hairspray on you, you'll have to snap your hair loose this evening so I wouldn't worry too much about it falling down out of that bun thing.'

'I think the proper word's a chignon,' Virginia laughed.

'Whatever it is, it's beautiful, Gin.'

Virginia's head hurt. She knew the second bottle of champagne last night had been a mistake, but Alice had insisted they celebrate her 'last night of freedom' properly. With Virginia's mother safely in bed in her room, and her sister Rosie having tottered off too, and after a few more glasses than was really sensible, Alice had ordered another bottle of Lanson from the barman. They'd then worked their way down the bottle, Alice reminiscing as if tomorrow Virginia would change personality altogether and nothing would ever be the same again, and Virginia assuring her, in an increasingly slurred voice, that she'd be the same person as she always was, even if she did have a ring on her finger.

Yesterday afternoon had been fun as well. Rosie had arrived at the hotel in her little car with their mother, Cameron and Kerry, in time for a cup of tea before they all headed off to the church for the rehearsal. Despite complaints about the Friday traffic on the M6 and the children's fights over a bag of Hoola Hoops, Rosie hadn't been able to hide a measure of excitement at their arrival. Virginia was fairly sure she'd hardly ever stayed in a hotel, and certainly not one as good as this one, and after some huffing and complaining, she'd surrendered her bags to the porter and there had been a glint of pleasure in her eye as he threw open the door on the king-sized bedroom Virginia had allocated to them.

She tried to imagine where Piers would be now. Would he already be greeting guests outside the church with his usual ease? He'd stayed at the flat last night with his best man after a civilised Waverley family dinner at a favourite restaurant in the middle of Oxford. Her experience of family get-togethers since she'd met Piers told her it would have been a noisy affair, and it felt odd not to have been there with them all. Instead, Virginia's last night of spinsterhood had ended with her and Alice lying on the enormous bed in Virginia's suite, giggling hysterically over nothing in particular.

The room was now filled with summer sunshine and the scent of flowers from an arrangement Derek, her boss, had had placed there with uncharacteristic generosity. He'd given her an unbeatable staff discount on the wedding reception and rooms too. Working in the hotel business had its perks.

'Can I have more paracetamol please?'

'Nope.' Alice snapped briskly and stood back. 'Absolutely nil by mouth. You'll smudge your lipstick. Ooh, Gin. You look perfect.'

Virginia felt a mixture of pleasure and a strange embarrassment at being scrutinised so closely. 'You don't look too shoddy yourself. In fact,' she took in the pretty deep-red dress in Virginia's favourite shade and Alice's hair, scooped up by the hairdresser earlier and held with combs they'd found in a vintage shop in Camden Market, 'I've never seen you look so ... *normal*. Where's the haphazard, thrown-together woman I know and love? I think you'll steal the show.'

'Oh, I don't think so.' Gently Alice placed her hands on Virginia's shoulders and turned her around to face the full-length mirror. For a moment they both stood there speechless.

'Gosh, who's she?' was all Virginia could eventually manage, and then she smiled in disbelief. The dress was indeed perfect. She'd never been the sort of girl who fantasised about weddings and dresses, always being more at home in sports kit and comfortable jeans, but looking at herself now, the delicate pearls on the bodice catching the light and the fresh pinky-white of the dress emphasised by the deep red of the roses in her bouquet, her hair and make-up flawless, she barely recognised herself.

There was a tap on the door, and, as Alice opened it, Rosie and their mother scuttled into the room, Rosie wearing a pale-blue dress and small pillbox hat, and Elizabeth in a familiar floral shirt-waister and the only hat she possessed, that had made outings as long as Virginia could remember. She'd refused all offers from Virginia to buy another outfit for the occasion with a 'this one is perfectly serviceable'. Her hair had been 'done' though and she was immaculately turned out.

'Sorry we're a bit late—oh, Virginia!' Rosie stopped and put her hand to her mouth. 'You look like a princess.'

'You look lovely too.' Virginia smiled as a stab of something—was it guilt?—shot through her. Today, all this fuss, the dress, was the kind of day Rosie had always dreamed of, had planned for from about the age of six, but which life had conspired to rob her of.

Rosie came over and pretended to look more closely at the dress. 'I lost Mum again,' she whispered so only Virginia could hear. 'Found her in the hotel kitchen chatting to the chefs. It's getting more and more frequent, this wandering off.'

Virginia glanced over at her mother. Alice was chatting to her and straightening her hat. 'I know. It's worrying. Let's talk when Piers and I get back, hey?'

Rosie nodded. 'Right,' she clapped her hands. 'Kerry and Cameron are in the hall with the porter and I daren't leave them a second too long in those bridesmaid and page boy outfits or there'll be a disaster. I've already taken Cameron to the toilet three times! Are we ready to go? The cars are here.'

'Yup.' Alice scooped up her small bouquet from the bed. 'Let's leave the bride for a minute to

8

compose herself and we'll go on ahead as planned. OK, Gin? Ready, Elizabeth?'

'One moment, dear.' From her clip bag Elizabeth brought out a small box and with fumbling fingers she opened it and took out a brooch in the shape of a swan. 'It's not much, but I wore it at my wedding and I think my mother wore it at hers. It's for you today, sweetheart.'

Virginia took the modest little trinket from her mother and pinned it to the front of her dress, then kissed her mother's powdery cheek. Elizabeth's eyes were watery with tears and, pulling out a tissue from the box on the dressing table, Virginia dabbed them. Did she know that she was getting worse, Virginia wondered, wretched with sadness. Did she realise that she would need constant care very soon? Would she even remember this day?

'Thanks, Mum,' Virginia said quietly. 'It's beautiful.'

Alice mouthed 'love you', then the door shut behind the three women and, for a moment, everything was silent. Virginia turned back to the mirror. In the reflection she could see the bed in which she'd slept fitfully last night, too excited— and drunk—to sleep deeply, and in which she and Piers would sleep tonight. Even after just one night apart, she missed him, his warm body beside her. She couldn't wait to see him again, so with one last check that she didn't have lipstick on her teeth, she left the room.

Dominic, in dark morning suit and a red rose in his lapel, was standing at the bottom of the wide staircase as she made her way down. A few hotel guests were milling around the hallway on this busy Saturday afternoon in May and they stopped and looked at Virginia. Dom's face was wreathed in smiles.

'I won't kiss you or I might smudge something,' he laughed in his immaculately pronounced voice so like Piers', 'but all I'll say is that my brother is a bloody lucky man and he'd better look after you.'

Unable to speak in case she cried, Virginia slipped her arm through his and they made their way out to the vintage Rolls-Royce parked outside the front doors, bedecked in ribbon, pausing only for the photographer to bob about and take pictures. Virginia had a sense of being in a carapace of unreality as the car pulled away from the kerb for the short journey to the church, and found herself waving royally out of the window at the people watching.

'I feel like the Queen!' she giggled.

'Only much better-looking!' Dom replied, then moved uneasily in his seat. 'Look, I know I've said it before, Ginny, but I feel deeply honoured that you asked me to give you away. I know that you no longer have your dad and all that, but I'm sure you could have mustered up an uncle or something.'

'There aren't any, I'm afraid,' Virginia laughed. 'And the only cousin I have would have been so overwhelmed by you Waverleys that he'd have staggered up the aisle with me on a wave of Dutch courage!'

'I guess we are a bit much en masse, aren't we? Especially dear Mum.'

'For simple northern folk like me, you are.' Virginia laughed, hamming up her accent, then patted his leg. 'Having you with me is brilliant, Dom. Thanks.'

'I bet your dad would have been so proud.'

10

'Don't make me cry! My mascara will never recover!' Then, to distract herself from the large missing piece of the jigsaw, she went back to watching the shoppers out of the window, wondering how they could be going about their day so normally when it was the most fantastic day ever and surely everyone should be enjoying it as much as she was.

There was a commotion around the church door as they arrived, Alice trying to corral Cameron and Kerry who, overcome by the gravitas of the moment, were hiding their faces on Rosie's skirts, but as Virginia and Dom made their way up the blossom-strewn path, they were distracted by the image of her in her dress and veil, and Rosie was able to extricate herself and slip into the church door, giving a thumbs-up of support and approval to Virginia as she did so.

The church bell was pealing out in the spire above her as Alice and the children moved on ahead of her towards the door through which she could make out a sea of people in hats and finery, and for a moment Virginia's ears felt muffled and she was in a place entirely alone. This was it. Too late to go back, though that was the last thing she could imagine wanting to do. This was their future, hers and Piers', to be cemented now in front of all these people. Everything she had ever wanted. Slipping her arm through Dom's, she squeezed it for support.

'Come on then,' he laughed. 'Let's make you a Waverley,' and he led her into the church. As the organ burst into life, Piers stepped out from his seat at the top of the aisle and turned to look at her as she made her way slowly towards him. He looked strong and so handsome in his morning suit, his eyes never leaving her face, his smile the widest she had ever seen in her life.

Chapter 2

Summer 1995

With no regard for who might hear, Virginia trilled in high-pitched accompaniment to Celine Dion on the car radio.

She had seen *Titanic* about four times already and Piers had bought her the CD for her birthday. He sighed tolerantly every time she put it on or it came on the radio, and she adored bellowing out the chorus as she drove. Today, with the windows down and the May breeze blowing her hair, it fooled her into thinking for a while that she was confident and on top of things.

Natasha had asked her to come for coffee this morning when the four of them had met for dinner the week before—Piers and Virginia, Natasha and Sebastian—tucked away chummily in a booth in a favourite local gastropub. Both older than her by ten years, Sebastian ran a logistics firm just outside Oxford and Natasha worked part-time as a receptionist for some medical consultants, with hours that fitted around the kids and lunch parties. And, presumably, coffees with the newish wives of her husband's friends.

Virginia slowed and squinted at the road sign. Woodstock was uncharted territory for her and, even though Natasha had been fairly detailed in her instructions, Virginia still wasn't sure where she was going. 'You sort of bear left' wasn't very specific, but then people are generally hopeless directing others to a place they know too well.

Even before she pulled in through the gate, Virginia knew the sort of thing to expect. A pretty stone house smothered in wisteria with a wide drive in front and a substantial car—no doubt Natasha's—and a smaller hatchback parked neatly by beds teeming with flowers that Virginia couldn't name. She sighed. She'd have to reciprocate the invitation or, worse, offer to have them for dinner, and her hands felt clammy even now at the prospect.

'Virginia, how lovely to see you!' Natasha was at the door in jeans and a floaty shirt. Her face was freckled and tanned and her reading glasses were pushed on top of her head, holding back healthy, well-cut hair. Virginia kissed her cheek briefly, then pulled away quickly. She wasn't quite sure about the protocol of social kissing and had never been entirely comfortable with it. Alice had tried to explain it to her, but she always seemed to get it wrong. At home, growing up, they'd hugged each other briefly if they hadn't seen each other for a while, and when she saw mates like Alice greetings usually involved a squeal and a massive embrace, but since meeting Piers she'd had to negotiate a whole new minefield. Did you simply make contact with one cheek, or did you go for both? And what noise did you make? It seemed ridiculous to fake a 'mwah' sound, but nothing at all seemed a little ... flat. Whenever they met with friends, usually Piers', she tried to watch what everyone else did before stepping forward and, more often than not, there would be an awkward moment as she was left leaning forward, cheek half-proffered, or she'd pulled away before realising the other person was expecting more. Piers' mother, Judy, barely even made cheek contact and simply left Virginia in a haze of Van Cleef & Arpels.

'Gorgeous garden,' Virginia offered, hooking her handbag up over her shoulder.

Natasha waved a dismissive hand. 'Terrible mess I'm afraid. That rain the other night has decimated everything and I haven't had a chance to tidy up. We have a chap who helps, but he's gone on a fishing holiday or some such thing. Come on in.'

Virginia followed her through the half-glazed front door, painted in the olive green so favoured around these parts, and into a large, airy flagstoned hall. Coats were hung randomly on brass pegs, and the floor was strewn with walking boots and wellies. An enormous bouquet of flowers appeared even bigger as it was reflected in the overmantle mirror behind it and Virginia picked up the heady scent of lilies. Natasha led on through to a spectacular and even larger kitchen, with French doors along one entire wall giving way to a patio, probably called a 'terrace'. Virginia could see a long teak table and chairs and wide cream parasol and, beyond, a lawn and garden twice the size of the one in front.

It was all perfect and effortless. Just right. Just what the magazines said comfortable middle-class life should look like. Quality and taste oozing out of every handmade cornice and Corian worktop, with the haphazard details of family life—children's drawings on the fridge, papers and magazines piled up on the central island—that smacked of days well spent and successful, attentive parenting.

14

Virginia swallowed hard.

'Coffee?' Natasha started to bustle with a percolator and Virginia knew that asking for a cuppa wouldn't be the right thing to do at all. She found real coffee made her feel a bit sick but she had battled on and had even bought a machine for home. Well, everyone else had one. As Natasha made up a tray with pretty mugs and a packet of Hob Nobs, a youngish woman walked into the kitchen. At first Virginia thought it must be a child of Natasha's she didn't know about—she was fairly certain their eldest was only about twelve—until she saw she was carrying a basket containing furniture polish and dusters.

'This is Alessandra,' Natasha introduced her in the patronising, overfriendly way people keep for foreigners or domestic help, or both. 'She's a marvel—looks after the kids and keeps us all in order. How did you get on with Ollie's room? Did you find the floor?' Alessandra smiled and shrugged, perhaps missing her meaning. Natasha raised her eyebrows exaggeratedly.

'Kids! Spend your whole time cleaning up after them,' She picked up the tray and headed out of the French windows. Virginia hesitated and smiled at the young girl, feeling rude walking away, then, unable to think of anything to say, followed Natasha through into the garden.

'You've got all this to come, haven't you?' Natasha laughed, putting the tray down on the teak table. 'Just you wait. Ruin your life they do, and wreck your house. Are you going to have a brood? Piers comes from quite a big family, doesn't he?'

'Yes, yes he does.' Virginia sipped on the scalding coffee, realising she was sounding much more

15

reticent than was normal for her. 'Four boys. We're still enjoying it just being the two of us, to be honest.'

'And you? What about your family?'

'A younger sister. She has two kids, a boy and a girl.'

'Does she live close by? Always nice to have family close by. Mine are in bloody Suffolk which is a nightmare to get to.'

'No, Stoke. That's where I grew up.'

'Oh right.' Natasha seemed stumped for a reply. Clearly Stoke was not on her radar and she was at a loss to make any social connections.

They chatted on for a while, Natasha sticking mainly to the safe subject of her children who went to the best private day school in Oxford, where Piers taught history. Private school was something Virginia knew nothing about but which Piers, having been steeped in them since birth, had explained the workings of to her. He'd even taken her back to his Alma Mater in Hampshire early on in their relationship and proudly shown her pictures of him sitting straight-backed in rowing team photos, but it was another time and another place. And another world. He talked of quirky traditions and odd names for things understood only by pupils and old boys. He recounted tales of being a fag or getting 'chits' for misdemeanours and she'd laughed at the quaintness of it all, utterly at a loss to comprehend it.

'Be great if our kids came here,' he'd sighed as he put his arm around her and they walked across the quad.

'Christ!' she'd gasped. 'We'll both have to get another job if we're going to afford it!' But they knew full well that there was no way any child of hers was coming to a place like this.

Natasha had now moved on to house prices. 'You are so sensible to stay in town. I spend a fortune on petrol going to and fro but you and Piers can just nip down the road for dinner or the shops.'

Virginia thought about their flat, so totally different from this house with its country views and huge garden. 'It was all we could afford really,' she explained and Natasha sighed.

'I know what you mean. Sebastian has hocked us to the eyeballs for this place and I *love* it, don't get me wrong, but you should see the bills. And that on top of everything else!'

After a bit more of Natasha talking and Virginia listening, and what seemed like a polite length of time, Virginia glanced at her watch and picked up her bag. 'I'm afraid I have to go, but thanks for the coffee. Delicious.' She stood up and Natasha ushered her back through the kitchen where Alessandra was mopping the floor. She didn't look up as they negotiated around her bucket.

'Usual Eastern European charm,' Natasha whispered once they were in the hall, and Virginia wasn't sure how to reply.

'At least you get the floor cleaned,' she said lightly, hoping Natasha would take it as a joke, but deeply uncomfortable.

Natasha kissed her briefly. 'I know you're busy, but do come again, won't you? It's been lovely and we'll get those two men of ours on the golf course too.' She folded her arms and stood in the doorway as Virginia reversed out of the gate carefully, not daring to attempt turning in the driveway in case she drove over the flowerbeds or pranged Natasha's car. She didn't drop her shoulders and relax until she was a mile or so down the road and heading back to the safety of home. It hadn't been lovely at all. It had been a strain trying to do the right thing and not make a gaffe.

She was sure she must have come over as boring and she could imagine Natasha and Sebastian discussing her as they tucked into a perfect macaroni cheese at the kitchen table later that evening. Natasha would recount it all and they'd agree she wasn't as much fun as Piers.

As she headed back towards Oxford, she wondered why she kept getting it wrong. She observed closely, studiously in fact, the way this circle of people operated—their casualness, what they drank, even the language they used—but somehow she kept falling short of the mark. Perhaps Alice was right—she was trying too hard and worrying too much.

Passing the playing fields for St Edward's and Keble College, she turned off the Woodstock Road and pulled into a space just down from the flat. The road was cool and shady, the parked cars covered in blossom like confetti and, at last, Virginia felt safe.

Slamming shut the front door of the flat, she dumped her bag and clicked on the kettle, throwing open the windows as it started to heat up and knocking over a couple of anniversary cards on the windowsill. Then she opened the French window that looked onto the small square of garden dominated in the centre by the gnarled apple tree she refused to let Piers cut down. The fruit it produced had been small and shrivelled, and its blossom was now patchy like an old lady dressed up in the last vestiges of finery, but it was the only

18

tree they had and to lose it seemed like a step backwards.

Taking her tea into the garden, she sat down at the table. Not nearly as impressive as Natasha's and considerably cheaper. The chair wobbled and nipped her thighs painfully through her shorts. Even though it was her day off, she had a report to write, but it could wait. She dialled Rosie.

'llo?'

'Hello, Kerry? It's Virginia.'

'Auntie Ginny?'

'That's the one,' Virginia laughed, imagining her niece's serious little frown, so like her mother's. 'Mum there?'

'She's just gone down the shop to get something for our tea.'

'Are you on your own?' It wasn't her problem, she kept reminding herself, but it bothered her that Rosie left the kids alone even for a second. Virginia had never mentioned it, but she knew Rosie struggled with the logistics of children and chores. Virginia had even teased her that she was making it sound as if motherhood was something someone had foisted on her without her permission!

'Tell her I'll call later.'

'Bye-bye, Aunty Ginny.' Kerry put down the phone. Virginia smiled at the abrupt end to the conversation and picked up her mug again, pulling up her leg so that her foot rested on the chair. She was halfway through the month's marketing report when Rosie called back.

'Can't talk for long. Kerry needs new shoes but God knows how we're going to afford them.' Virginia let that go.

'Have you seen Mum?'

19

'Only managed a short time with her yesterday. Kerry, take that off Cameron, can you? Kerry! When you coming up?' Rosie said back into the phone. 'I can't—'

'Yes, Rosie, I know.' She stemmed the flow before it got going. 'I'll try and get up next week but we're really busy at the moment with new brochures and a hotel opening in Harrogate so—'

'OK. Whatever.'

Rosie ended the conversation almost as abruptly as her daughter had and left the smell of guilt hanging in the air. Virginia sighed.

By the time she heard the front door open though, and Piers' call from the hall, she had finished writing her report and stretched her stiff back as he came through the kitchen and out into the garden.

'Hello, beautiful.' His height and build filled the room.

'Hello, gorgeous. How was your day?' She leaned her head back and he kissed her lips.

'Dull. Yours?'

'OK. I've made good headway with the monthly report and it's steak for tea.'

'Ey up, lass,' he laughed, washing his hands at the sink. 'I'll just go and check on ferrets.'

'Sorry, your lordship. *Supper.*' Piers had tried to tease her out of calling it tea pretty early on in their relationship and she had worked hard to remember to call it 'supper', especially when they went to visit his parents. Supper was in the kitchen and usually involved something baked in one dish, like cottage pie or fish pie. Dinner was in the formal dining room with the straight-back chairs and dark-red painted walls, and often involved the women

20

leaving the table after dessert in some archaic tradition. No, not dessert, *pudding*. Dessert, Piers said, was non-U, like serviette or lounge, and she'd tease him back and call him a toff.

'Sounds good. But until then, I've got something important to do.'

Virginia tried to hide her disappointment. 'Oh right. What's that then?'

'Something I've been thinking about doing all day.' He pulled round her chair and scooped her up then, kicking the chair out of the way, headed through the house towards their bedroom. Lying her on her back on the bed he started to undo her buttons. 'Screwing my wife. Any objections?'

She reached for his belt and laughed. 'None whatsoever.'

Chapter 3

May 2010

The alarm clock shrilled insistently on the bedside cabinet and Alice reached out from under the quilt to swipe at the snooze button. Again. This time she missed, but her flailing arm sent it tumbling to the floor from where it continued, mercilessly.

'Oh arse,' she groaned and slumped back defeated, burrowing as deeply as she could into the pile of pillows that cocooned her. But not even the goose down was enough to block out the noise and, after a few minutes, she gave in and sat up. Rubbing her eyes, she turned pointedly away from the curtains around which brilliant sunshine was attempting to force its way, and scrabbled around on the floor.

'There you are,' she said accusingly, plucking the alarm from among the chaos of her newly unpacked suitcase. 'Shut up!' At last, silence spread blissfully through the room. Ten thirty-five according to the red digital display. Still fairly early. What would she have been doing in Seville now? Alice smiled nostalgically at the memory and huddled back under her quilt to try to replicate the morning heat of the Spanish summer she'd been enjoying only yesterday. She'd probably be getting ready to leave Ana's fourth-floor apartment to go out for the first coffee of the day or meeting up with Daniel or one of the other American language students she'd befriended to share a plate of hot, fresh churros sitting in the sunshine out on the square.

And now she'd have to make do with a pot of PG Tips and whatever Ana had left behind for her at the end of their house swap. 'Welcome home, Alice,' she croaked and headed for the kitchen. She had arrived back at the cottage so late the previous night that she'd missed the supermarket in Lewes and the taxi driver had taken her straight home. Without even bothering to look in the fridge she'd gone to bed straightaway and had instantly fallen asleep.

Alice's fridge now revealed the makings of breakfast. Milk, some kind of funny yoghurt, chorizo, eggs, freshly squeezed orange juice. Exotic fare, by the standards of Ulvington. Ana must have ventured further than the village shop to get a stash like that. In the breadbin there was the end of a rather more prosaic white sliced loaf. As she waited for the kettle to boil, Alice finished unpacking her

22

suitcase, loading the washing machine as she went. With the first wash on, a cup of tea and a stack of toast and Marmite on a plate, she abandoned the unpacking and went to sit at the table by the front window to sift through the neat pile of mail and plan her day. She started on a list:

groceries
washing x 3
book haircut and roots
call Ginny
finish typing up notes and send to
  Andy
bank
go to gym?

She was tapping the pen thoughtfully against her teeth when she heard the front gate creak and she peered out to see the chairwoman of the PCC, Wendy Harcombe, stumping up the path. That was quick. Clad, as ever, in an odd assortment of garments, Wendy was looking critically at the unkempt flowerbeds and tubs on either side of the path. No doubt she'd have something to say about them. Alice sighed heavily. No use pretending to be out—she was clearly visible through the window— so she got up slowly and picked up a piece of toast in the hope that Wendy would take the hint and not keep her talking too long.

True to form, Wendy was speaking almost before the door was open, bombarding Alice with cheery questions without waiting for the answers. 'Hello there. Hope I haven't got you out of bed? Have you only just got back?'

'Yes, late last night,' Alice broke in. 'I've been in

Spain, working.' She wasn't quite sure why she felt the need to add that.

'Oh yes?' Wendy handed over a homemade flyer. 'Well, it's that time of year again and the fête.' She tried to look apologetic about something that was clearly the highlight of her year. 'I know you are terribly busy and don't want to get involved in these things, but I thought I'd let you know anyway. It would be lovely to see you there—and if you had a moment to bake a cake . . .'

Alice had never tackled one in her life, so she quickly took a large bite of toast to avoid answering and pretended to notice her watch. 'Good heavens, is that the time? Look, Wendy, I'm really sorry, but I'll have to dash. I've got a conference call with my publisher and I can't miss it.' She waved the flyer in her hand. 'I'll pop it on the mantelpiece so I don't forget . . .' She trailed off non-committally.

'Lovely.' Wendy gushed. 'Enjoy your breakfast.' And she wobbled back down the path.

Alice shook her head ruefully as she closed the door. Even after nine years, she was still convinced she wasn't cut out for village life. She'd only bought the cottage because it was cheaper than town and close enough at the time to her parents in Newhaven. With them long gone, and even with a small legacy in the bank, she hadn't got round to going back to London. Anyway, she travelled so much, it hardly seemed worth it.

With another cup of tea, she returned to her list. Groceries were not a priority, thanks to Ana— she'd email her later to thank her. The washing was already underway and she was well ahead with the updates to the book; the gym, realistically, was not going to happen, but her dark roots wouldn't wait, and neither would a chat with Ginny.

She pulled the phone towards her and dialled the number. The answerphone picked up and Alice listened, disappointed, to her friend's message, frowning slightly, as she always did, at the telephone voice Ginny adopted. It didn't sound like the Ginny she knew and loved.

'Hello! You've reached Piers, Virginia and Scarlett. I'm afraid we can't take your call at the moment. Please leave your message after the beep, or call us back. Bye!'

Alice swallowed her mouthful of toast. 'Hi, Ginny—it's me. I'm back. Had a brilliant time, but I'll fill you in on that later.' She paused, not wanting to say anything that might corrupt the innocent ears of eleven-year-old Scarlett. 'I met some—er—very interesting people and I've got loads to tell you. Gimme a ring when you can. Love you! Oh, and love to Scarly and the P-man.'

She hung up and redialled for the hairdresser, making the first appointment she could, then sat back in the bucket chair by the window, tucking her feet under her. Ginny was really the only person she could tell about Daniel. Although she was pretty sure they wouldn't be in touch again, he'd been a lovely diversion and flatteringly keen. She wanted to indulge in a bit of unrealistic mooning about him and who better than Ginny to be on the receiving end? Over the past twenty years, they'd shared all of their secrets, romantic and other, but Ginny never disapproved of her adventures, the way Alice's other married friends did.

'Ooh, I envy you,' she'd sigh. 'I don't know where you find the energy for all this lust. I'm happy in my flannelette nightie with a good book.'

25

'No place for complacency,' Alice had teased back. 'You're lucky you have it on tap. I have to keep looking for it!'

Alice looked at her watch now. If Ginny was at a meeting or another hotel today, she'd certainly make sure she was back by the end of school to be there for Scarly, as she always was, so she could call then. But it wouldn't be the kind of chat Alice craved. Never mind. They'd catch up eventually. They always did. She stretched luxuriously. Not even midday yet. A nice long bath was just what she needed, then she'd think about going to the gym. Maybe.

Chapter 4

September 1996

Judy and Bill arrived at the flat on the dot of twelve, and hearing them come up the path sent Virginia into a panic. Where the hell was Piers? He'd said he'd be back from the training session by now but he must have been held up. He could have bloody phoned.

She'd been half way through unloading the dishwasher, but in her flurry loaded the dirty breakfast things in with it, and went to the door.

'Lovely to see you.' Bill embraced her warmly in his signature West Indian Limes cologne, and Judy proffered her cheek. Unsure whether she should offer coffee or a glass of wine, Virginia made small talk about the journey as she fussed about and, perhaps sensing her unease, Bill put his hand on her shoulder.

'I didn't have time to buy a paper this morning before we set off, dear. Would you mind awfully if I popped round the corner and got one? Anything else you need while I'm there? You girls can stay and have a nice chat without an old buffer like me around.'

The door closed behind him and there was silence for a moment.

'Does Piers often work on Sundays?' Judy asked. Virginia glanced at the clock again. Should she put the macaroni cheese in yet?

'No, he popped into school to take a training session. There's an important head of the river race next weekend and he needs to get them on top form, apparently. Coffee?'

Judy sighed as Virginia filled the machine with beans. 'Such a lot of pressure on him, and such a good rowing school too. Bill and I follow their progress, of course. He's turned that team around. They're lucky to have him.'

'He loves it,' Virginia shouted over the grinder. 'Never happier than standing on a towpath bellowing his lungs out!'

'Yes, but he doesn't really get to do it for pleasure any more, does he? And it's such a good sport for a man.'

'Well, neither of us gets much of a chance anymore what with work and stuff.' She poured the fragrant coffee into a thin china cup for Judy. 'The days just fly by.' She glanced at the clock again. Where *was* he?

'You might think me old-fashioned,' Judy smiled as she took the cup and perched elegantly on the edge of a kitchen chair, 'but I really don't think a married woman should work full-time.' Virginia

27

gritted her teeth and turned to the cooker. 'Don't get me wrong. It's nice to have a little job and if a girl's a doctor or something, like Maggie is, I can see one would want to use one's training—at least before one starts a family. But I was never going to set the world of work on fire,' she laughed self-deprecatingly. 'I thought my main job was to be there for Bill, and I always had the supper on and a Scotch waiting for him when he came back from chambers.'

Virginia gripped the counter, her knuckles white. 'I have to keep a roof over our heads somehow!' She chopped up the lettuce for the salad a little too violently. 'Teachers' pay is pitiful.'

'I expect his book will sell terribly well when he finishes it, though I can't imagine how he finds the time! His history teacher at school always said he had so much promise. That he'd go far.'

He'll go to blazes if he doesn't get home soon and save me, Virginia thought desperately, and sighed almost audibly as she heard Judy's next sentence.

'If he is going to write, you'll need a bigger place than this little flat when the babies come. He'll need peace and quiet.'

'We've no plans for babies at the moment,' Virginia lied. 'I'm far too busy enjoying myself,' she added for good measure.

'That's a teeny bit selfish though, isn't it? I know Piers is longing to have a family—and soon. He told me so himself, and you're not that young. Perhaps you need to slow down a bit.'

Virginia looked at her mother-in-law quizzically. Where was this heading?

'Only, he did mention that you were having a few

28

problems in that department.'

'Did he now?' she asked, her hand holding the knife suspended over the cucumber.

'Well, I asked him outright, dear. You've been married a while now and Bill and I would so love more grandchildren.'

At that moment Virginia heard the key in the lock and Piers' cheery voice, followed by Bill's.

'Ah, lovely. Here are the men now,' Judy smiled, and, letting the knife drop violently, Virginia hacked the cucumber in half.

*   *   *

A couple of days later, Virginia put the phone down on the call from the surgery and looked out of her office window. The trees were beginning to turn and the leaves on the pavement were fluttering in a dance whipped up by the wind. Autumn was taking everything in its clutches.

She'd made the appointment with the doctor only because of vague feelings of disquiet that things weren't progressing quite as they should. She knew that getting pregnant wasn't always something that happened immediately, and even Rosie had told her it could take time—though she'd managed to hit the jackpot slightly too easily with two different men. But the call had filled her with relief. The news was good.

There was a tap on the door and one of the receptionists stuck her head around it. 'Virginia? Sorry to bother you, but that journalist from the wedding magazine has arrived for a show-round. Want me to take her?'

Virginia glanced at her watch. 'It's OK thanks,

Elaine. I'll take her in a minute. Can you make her a cup of coffee and I'll be right with you?'

As Elaine closed the door again, Virginia picked up her mobile and nibbled at the end of her pen as it connected. She didn't normally call Piers at work—as a rule he couldn't answer anyway—but it was break-time now and worth a try. His deep, familiar voice answered.

'Hello, you,' she smiled down the phone.

'Hello, you, back.'

'I've had a call from the doc. They've said I'm clear. They had a peek at my ovaries on the scan and I seem to be popping out the eggs OK.'

'That's great, darling.' She could hear the scream of children in the background. 'So where does that leave us exactly?'

Virginia leaned back in her chair. She'd been asking herself the same question all morning. 'Not sure. They keep harping back to the fact that I managed to get pregnant last year.'

It had happened far too soon after they were married. She'd missed a period and had dived for the testing kit, but after a week of shock and panic at the prospect of parenthood, they had just been getting used to the idea when she'd miscarried. It was disappointing, of course, but they had both been quietly relieved. They felt they'd been given a reprieve until they were really ready for the responsibility of a family.

'They say they will do more tests,' she went on, '. . . on both of us. See if you've got plenty of swimmers.'

'Eeek,' Piers laughed uncertainly. 'Have I got to toss myself off into a pot?' he whispered.

'Something like that, probably.'

'Will you be there to help, nurse?' he asked quietly.

'I'll buy you a dirty mag if you like.'

'Look,' he was suddenly serious. 'I'm a bit short of time for the next few days. Can I do *it* at the surgery?'

Piers was registered at a different surgery from Virginia's, an arrangement that went back to where he'd registered when he first moved to Oxford and lived on the other side of Summertown. They'd never bothered to change it. 'I don't see why not. Are you OK to make an appointment?'

'Yeah. I'll try and get there later this week.'

'Gotta go . . . I've a show-round. Oh, and don't forget we're away this weekend for the Classic English Hotels Conference.'

'Another free night away in luxury?' He sighed dramatically. 'Well, if you insist.'

Virginia smiled. 'Bye, you fool. Love you.'

Chapter 5

March 1997

'How's she been?' Virginia sipped scalding tea and watched Rosie make sandwiches for the children's packed lunches.

She'd arrived late last night, only able to get away from Oxford after a sales meeting that ran predictably late and, by the time she'd pulled up outside Rosie's house, it had gone ten. They hadn't bothered chatting beyond a 'how was the journey?' and Virginia had taken a cup of tea upstairs with her and crawled exhausted into Kerry's narrow bed, her little niece relegated to her brother's bedroom next door. She'd been shocked by the fatigue on Rosie's face when she'd opened the front door last night, and this morning she didn't look much better.

Virginia hadn't stayed with her sister for a while and the state of the house shocked her. The little semi seemed like Rosie's view on life; tatty, messy and chaotic. Left alone after her boyfriend had found the delights of an old schoolfriend more appealing than Rosie and two very small children— one not his—Rosie seemed defeated and resentful. She tried hard, but occasionally a bitterness snuck under the façade and pervaded the atmosphere.

The children, who'd been all over Virginia first thing and had only been pacified by the bars of hotel chocolate she'd managed to grab as she left, had lost interest now and gone into the lounge to watch TV before school. Rosie, too thin in shapeless jogging bottoms and hooded top, was turned away from Virginia as she threw crisps and chocolate bars into matching *Toy Story* lunchboxes.

'Not much change,' she said, expressionlessly. 'She got an infection in her waters and they had to give her antibiotics intravenously. She cried a lot but I managed to quieten her down.' She paused as she snapped two cartons of juice from a pack. 'I don't take the kids in to see her now.'

'I can imagine,' said Virginia.

'No you can't. You really can't.' Rosie turned to her abruptly, spitting out the words. 'You hardly ever see her!'

Virginia reeled at the attack. 'How can I, Rosie? I come as often as I can, but I have a full-time job and it's not always that easy to get away.'

'Well, it's not all that easy for me either,' she clicked the lunchboxes shut. 'But I do it.' Over the last few weeks, Virginia had noticed an increasingly hostile tone to Rosie's phone calls. Their mother had always said Rosie was the touchy one, a resentful streak never far below the surface. Their wedding had been a case in point. Virginia had been so busy at the reception negotiating the bridge over the social crevasse—Piers' family on one side in morning suits and neat dresses sipping champagne paid for by Piers' father, knowing the protocol exactly. Her family on the other; uncles and cousins uncomfortable in lounge suits, the girls in strapless dresses that showed too much flesh in church. It wasn't until the disco had swung into action that she had noticed Rosie slumped in the corner of the ballroom, her hair and lipstick awry. Her mood descended with each glass of champagne as she reminded Virginia over and over again just how lucky she was.

'You have no idea what a strain it is,' Rosie went on now. 'As if the children weren't enough trouble and Keith never visiting. I have a job too, you know, and if I'm not at work, then I'm over to the nursing home every second. When do I get a break?' She slammed the fridge shut. 'Cameron! Kerry! Here! We're going to be late.'

'I'll be gone by the time you get back,' Virginia said weakly, wincing under the weight of Rosie's diatribe.

'Whatever,' Rosie called over her shoulder as she corralled her children into the tiny hall and out of the front door.

The pervasive aroma of mince hit her as soon as she pushed through the glass doors of the care home an hour later. It wasn't the best in Stoke, though they'd looked at enough, but it was the best they could afford on Virginia's salary and the proceeds from the sale of her mother's house. In the hallway were uncomfortably upright chairs that Virginia had never seen anyone actually sit in, and in the centre of a conservatory-style wicker, glass-topped table, a bunch of artificial freesias.

She went to Reception and rang the bell. No one came for a while and Virginia was about to ring it again when a plump woman in a short blue overall and black trousers wheezed down the stairs.

'Hi, I've come to see Elizabeth Russell.'

'Come to do an assessment?' The woman walked behind the reception desk.

'No, she's my mother.' Virginia swallowed hard. 'How is she?'

The woman looked up at Virginia. 'None of them get any better, love, but she's no worse than the others. We just try to do the best we can for them.'

'Right,' Virginia nodded. 'Thanks. I mean, thanks for everything you do. I work in Oxford, you see, and it's hard to get up here enough.'

'No, love. I can imagine.' At this, she turned away and went into the back office.

Virginia followed the passage to her mother's room and knocked gently. The door was ajar so she pushed it open. The room was even more cluttered than she remembered. A whole house worth of knick-knacks and memorabilia was shoe-horned into one small room. Almost every inch of the walls was covered in photographs: pictures of grandchildren, and her father and mother from their courtship until just a few months before Stan's death; photos of Virginia and Piers' wedding; toothy images of Virginia and Rosie at school, Rosie younger and sweeter, Virginia older, taller and more gauche, told by the photographer to put her hand unnaturally on her sister's shoulder.

Sitting on a chair watching the TV blaring in the corner was her mother. Virginia stood and looked at her for a moment before her mother became aware that she was there. Her hair needed cutting and was lank and wavy, greyer than last time she had seen her. Virginia didn't recognise the pink candlewick dressing gown. Perhaps Rosie had bought it.

Virginia picked up the remote control from the low table in front of her and turned down the volume.

'Mum?' she asked gently.

Her mother started and peered round the wing of the chair.

'Hello?' Her eyes fell on Virginia but there was no recognition in them.

'It's me, Mum. Virginia.'

Her mother frowned slightly. 'Yes, of course, dear. Have you brought me my tea?'

'No. No I haven't, but I can get you some, if you like?'

'Yes please. One sugar, just how you usually do.'

Not sure where to go to make it, Virginia turned towards the door but a younger carer was coming down the corridor towards her, her smile wide and friendly. 'My mother would like some tea. Where would I go to . . .'

The carer brushed past her and entered her mother's room. 'No tea, darling,' she said brightly, puffing up the pillow behind her mother's head. 'Remember what the doctor said?' She turned back to Virginia and said, 'She keeps getting infections so they want to keep her on plain water as much as possible.'

'Oh I see. Sorry, I didn't know.'

'Of course you didn't,' the carer said gently. 'Don't tire her, will you?'

'No I won't, I promise.' Virginia put her bag down on the floor and pulled up the other chair as the carer left the room. 'Mum, it's me. How are you?'

'Virginia, is that you?' she looked hard and myopically at Virginia, her gaze clear and seeing now. 'Darling girl, where have you been?'

Virginia smiled broadly. Maybe she wasn't as bad as Rosie had said after all. 'I've been working hard, Mum. At the hotel, you know? The owners are looking to buy another one so that will keep me busy.'

'And your husband . . . ?' Her mother frowned with irritation.

'Piers. He's fine. He's busy too, with school.'

'Is he at school?'

Virginia sighed a bit. 'Yes, Mum. He's a teacher, remember?'

'Yes, dear. I was a teacher, you know. Where's Rosie?'

'Rosie's at work, Mum. I thought I'd come on my own today.' Virginia could feel things slipping away.

'She works too hard. And that man of hers is no help. Her father wasn't like that. Always making a fuss of me and making me feel special.' She looked at the walls, trying to find his picture.

'He was good, Mum, wasn't he?' Virginia had a vision of her father coming in from work, covered in oil from the cars he'd been mending, and within moments he'd have a brew on.

'Did you know him then?' her mother asked, her eyes twinkling.

'Of course I knew him!' Virginia laughed, thinking she was joking.

Her mother didn't reply to this but sat back in her chair for a while. Virginia thought she had dropped off until she leaned forward again. 'Can I have some tea?'

'No, Mum. The lady said the doctors don't want you to have tea.'

'Is that Virginia? Where have you been?'

Virginia grasped at this chink of clarity, and took her mother's cool hand. 'Yes, Mum, it's me.'

Her mother looked hard into her eyes again, her unplucked eyebrows set in a frown that reminded Virginia of tellings-off as a child. 'So it is.'

'I brought some nail varnish with me. I thought you might like me to do your nails. You always used to like having nice nails, remember?' Desperate to keep the moment, Virginia scrabbled in her bag and pulled out a bottle of dark-pink varnish and a nail file.

'That would be nice.' Her mother held up her hand, wrinkled and liver-spotted, but still long and elegant. Her nails though were too long and misshapen. Carefully, Virginia took her hand and gently began to file them one by one. Her mother didn't resist and, for a while, she just watched as Virginia chatted on, not really caring whether her mum was listening or understanding. She seemed to be watching what Virginia did intently.

'I always like to keep my nails good,' she said eventually. 'Always wear . . .'

'. . . rubber gloves when cleaning the bath!' Virginia finished her mother's famous phrase, and they both laughed.

'That's it,' her mother nodded. 'Always wear rubber gloves!' She snorted with glee, then went quiet again as Virginia applied varnish to the last nail.

As she finished, her mother held up her hand and admired it. 'Where's your husband?'

'He's working, Mum. I'll bring him to see you again soon.' Her mother nodded.

'And your children. Where are your children, dear?'

Virginia could feel her throat tighten. 'I don't have any children, Mum.'

Her mother looked affronted. 'No children? Everyone should have children. What's the point, otherwise?' She rested back in the chair. 'Now, turn the television up again, will you, before you go? I was watching that.'

Virginia stood up and did as she was told. It wasn't until she was back in the car that she let the sobs engulf her.

Chapter 6

May 2010

It was as if Alice had never been away. And not in a good way. She had caught sight of herself in the *feng shui* mirror she'd been persuaded to buy when her friend Krissy had returned from yet another 'lifestyle' course. At least it hadn't been as mad as that one on crystal healing. 'It's as though it was always meant to be,' Krissy had breathed in awe. 'Kris and crystals? See? Maybe I should even change the way I spell it. What do you think?'

Vince had managed to stand firm against being *feng shui*-ed—nothing was going to mess up his carefully planned and painstakingly coordinated decor, but Alice didn't have any such excuse.

The lighting in the bathroom was kinder, but reflected in the cheap-looking octagonal mirror with its frame of painted red dragons, she wasn't looking great. Over the last few days since she'd been back from Spain, her tan had dulled to a sort of grimy yellow and, with another week to wait for her hair appointment, the dark roots were starting to dominate the blonde streaks, now dry and frizzy at the ends. Thank goodness she worked from home. At least she could lie low and avoid being seen by anyone—anyone that mattered, at least— until the damage was repaired.

Still in her pyjamas, Alice threw herself into the chair by the window. She'd moved all the furniture back to where it had been before Krissy had given her the make-over, but always remembered to shift it back before she came to visit to avoid offending her. Krissy meant so well, but like all her fads, this one would wear off. Fortunately, Ulvington was just that bit too far from Brighton for her to drop by unannounced and Alice always had time to close the lid of the loo seat (to prevent positive chi escaping down the u-bend) or move the lamp back to the health corner before Krissy arrived.

Ginny would actually have roared with

uninhibited laughter if she'd seen the red silk cords, 'to keep them safe', encircling photos of Piers, her, and Scarly on the shelf that formed the 'family corner'. They were the closest thing to family that Alice had now, with both her parents gone and her cousins misty figures encountered only at weddings and funerals, and in the yearly exchange of non-committal greetings cards. 'Family of choice', that's what they called it these days, apparently.

She had a sudden urge to call Ginny—she might even suggest a girlie weekend away if she could extricate her—but she checked her watch. Damn. No point calling now—she'd be on the school run and she never remembered to check her messages. Time for a bath, maybe? The day stretched ahead, pleasant and stress-free, and Alice smiled to herself as she selected the bath gel to match her mood.

With cucumber slices on her eyes, face mask carefully applied and the scent of grapefruit wafting up from the warm waters, Alice jumped when the phone rang, but decided against getting out to answer it. If it was important, they'd call back. She wondered, for a moment, if it might be Daniel. He'd sent her a few emails and texts since she got back but nothing very promising. Alice suspected she was just something to brag about to his friends—a cougar affair. She groaned and slid under the water, feeling the cucumber slices float away.

As the water cooled, Alice hauled herself out, wrapped herself in a bath sheet and tissued off the mask. That was better. She turned her face from side to side and prodded at her cheekbones experimentally. She still had it! As the water gurgled away, she checked the phone to see who'd

40

called. Number withheld and no message. Probably a cold call. If she'd leaped from the bath only to be offered cavity wall insulation, she'd have been very cross indeed.

Invigorated again, and aware of the need to do something, she called Andy, the Big Earth travel guide commissioning editor who had sent her to Seville. He'd have had time to look at her updates now and she wanted his feedback. She'd done a good job, she thought. By the time her call was put through, though, only a few minutes later, she was beginning to feel less confident. This was the first book she'd done for Big Earth and, if it was good enough, it could lead to more. And getting paid to do the two things she loved most, writing and travelling, was perfect for Alice. She could feel the tension in her stomach as she spoke breezily. 'Hi, Andy! Alice Fenton. Just wanted to check that you've got the copy I sent through and that everything was all right?' Please let it be all right.

She could hear papers being shuffled. 'Alice— hello there. Thanks for calling, I was just about to call you, in fact. Yup—I've just had a quick look through, but it's looking fine. You've got the tone exactly right and you've come up with some good up-to-date stuff. It's just right, in fact.'

Alice could hear the smile in her voice as she replied, as evenly as she could, 'Great— well, I really enjoyed doing it. It was a fantastic experience. So, can I invoice you for that now?'

'Yes, absolutely. Send it in, along with your expenses and so on. Erm—are you busy now you're back? Much to catch up on?'

'Well, you know how it is. Just a few things to straighten out.' She laughed, willing him to go on.

41

'Riiiight. So are you available at the moment? It's just that we've had someone drop out.'

Play it cool, Alice, play it cool. 'Let me just check my diary. When were you thinking?'

Andy's voice was apologetic. 'Well, more or less straightaway, if possible.'

'Well, I could juggle things. It's all long-term stuff at the moment, you know,' she lied expertly. 'Is it for the same series?'

'It's New York. We need a quick update and some stuff for the website. You know how quickly things change over there. We particularly need a lot of work on the restaurants, clubs and bars section.'

Alice's mouth was wide open in a silent scream of delight and her fist pumped the air.

The call-waiting tone sounded and she ignored it happily, writing down the details as Andy spoke. 'I'll confirm it all by email, of course,' he ended and with a breezy goodbye, Alice hung up and danced around the room.

She was poring over the website that explained the US Visa Waiver Program when the phone rang again.

'Hello,' she muttered distractedly.

'Hello—I'm trying to get in touch with a Miss Alice Fenton,' a cool voice said.

'Speaking,' Alice replied unenthusiastically. It sounded official.

'Miss Fenton, my name is Jeremy Peake. I'm calling from Rogers Wakeman Solicitors in Oxford.'

'Right. . .' Alice carried on peering at the screen. This website was really very confusing.

'I'm ringing you about Mr and Mrs Piers Waverley.'

42

What was he talking about? 'Sorry, I don't understand.' Alice was paying attention now.

'Ah, as I suspected, you haven't heard.'

'Heard what?' She felt a bit uneasy at his dour tone.

'Miss Fenton, I'm afraid I have some bad news to tell you.'

Alice held her breath.

'I regret that I have to inform you of the death of Mr and Mrs Piers Waverley. They were killed in a car accident last Saturday.'

'What . . . ? What!' Alice stood up, breathing fast. 'Ginny? You don't mean Ginny and Piers? You can't—'

'I'm sorry to be the one who has to break the terrible news to you. I believe Mr Waverley's family have been trying to contact you.'

Alice felt as though a trap door had been opened under her and she slid down the wall onto the floor. 'But . . . when? I mean—are you sure? This isn't . . . Oh God—I can't believe it.' Her mouth was dry and her heart hammered in her chest as though she'd run uphill. 'There must be some mistake.'

'I'm afraid there's no mistake. I'm so sorry you've had to find out this way. We have been trying to get hold of you.'

'I've been away . . . I didn't know. There weren't any messages. How did it happen?' Her body had gone cold and she was struggling to breathe.

'I understand they were on their way to a barbecue with friends.'

Alice gasped, a sudden thought coming to her. 'Scarlett? Was she in the car?'

'Scarlett is fine,' the solicitor said quickly and calmly. 'She was staying at a friend's house for the

43

night. She is being cared for by her grandparents at the moment.'

Alice was silent, trying to assimilate it all, then remembered he was still on the line. 'Well, thank you for letting me know.' That seemed inappropriate. Then it struck her. 'When's the funeral? Oh God! I haven't missed it, have I?'

'No, no,' he reassured her. 'It's being arranged now. I'm not sure of the exact date and time but I'll find out for you.'

'What can I do? What should I do?' Alice was in turmoil.

'You've had a terrible shock, Miss Fenton. However, there is a pressing matter I need to discuss with you. I have Piers and Virginia's wills here. They were lodged with us, you see.'

Alice could hear the pounding in her ears. Was this relevant? What was he talking about?

He went on in measured tones. 'Scarlett's welfare is obviously our immediate concern and the reason I am calling is that you are, of course, her official guardian.'

Chapter 7

August 1997

Virginia tried to smother her disappointment and her feelings of guilt again for Piers' sake.

'It's OK,' she curled into the crook of his arm after coming back to bed from the bathroom. 'These things take time.' He didn't reply. She could only hear him breathing. 'I'm sorry,' she said eventually.

'Oh God, don't say that,' he rolled her over so he was looking down at her. 'It's not your fault. Perhaps we're not doing it right!'

'We're certainly doing it enough,' Virginia giggled. With Piers at home because of the school holidays, he was having trouble filling his days and had taken to texting her naughty messages during meetings about what he was going to do to her when she got home, timing them to be as inappropriate as possible so she'd have to suppress a giggle as Derek bored on about room revenues. It served its purpose and, by the time she got home, already aroused by his words, he'd be lying in wait, ready to drag her into the bedroom before she'd even put down her briefcase, ravishing her in her work clothes until they were both exhausted and sated.

But each time her period arrived, disquiet began to settle in her chest, as it was now. 'We'll have our brood eventually, I'm sure,' she said with more confidence than she felt, touching his face. 'Until then we ought to make the most of it. Let's do all the things we're never going to be able to do when we're parents, like eating breakfast in bed. Your turn to make tea, I think.'

He swung out of bed and Virginia admired the muscles on his back. Even though he didn't get out rowing on the river as often as he used to—just stood shouting on the towpath at his crews—he still looked toned and fit. She slumped back against the pillows and gazed into space as she heard the kettle go on and Piers clattering about emptying the dishwasher. They'd been to see *Men in Black* the night before, and Piers had nattered on about the plot so she hadn't told him about the appointment at the GP's. She liked Dr Adams, who hadn't said anything conclusive or glib, but simply looked at her intently over his glasses as she stumbled on about her cycle. But this time, instead of telling her to 'relax' and 'have more sex' as the previous doctor had, he studied her for a moment.

'Yes, perhaps things have gone on long enough.' He made a note on the pad in front of him. 'I'll refer you to the fertility clinic and they can look into things a bit further.'

She looked down at her body, in vest and stripy knickers, as her period pains began to start. It had never occurred to her that she wouldn't become pregnant again as soon as she chucked out her pills. Everyone else seemed to manage it, didn't they? Christ, most people managed it even when they didn't want to. Had she and Piers waited too long? Tried to time things too perfectly to suit them? Had she jinxed herself by being relieved that she'd miscarried that time? It was stupid, of course, but irrational thoughts were pushing themselves to the fore. They hadn't been ready for a baby then. Now they were so ready, and it just wasn't happening.

Chapter 8

May 2010

Alice was so determined not to be late, she was actually over an hour early, giving her plenty of time—too much time, in fact—to mull over the many occasions she had been late for the remorselessly punctual Ginny in the past. One time at Covent Garden tube, before either of them had a mobile phone—brick-sized and still an indicator of extreme importance or pretension at the time— she'd been almost forty minutes late and had seen Ginny standing there, pale and wide-eyed, looking so anxious that Alice had been engulfed in a wave of unfamiliar guilt. Why had she been late? Something stupid, probably. No reason at all. Why had she made Ginny worry?

In the few days since the lawyer had called her with the news of Ginny's death, Alice had veered between disbelief and fury. How could the world exist without Ginny in it? It didn't seem possible. And how could a car as carefully bought and well maintained as Piers' allow its precious cargo to be destroyed? It was like a horrible logic puzzle; a conundrum that wouldn't stop turning and turning in her head. And if only she could solve it, everything would be all right.

Except it wouldn't. And nothing ever would be all right again. The bubble that had surrounded Alice since she'd heard the news had kept her from engaging with anything and anyone else. Work emails from Andy at Big Earth went unanswered, she'd avoided people in the village, dodging into the car if she saw anyone she knew, and had even ignored calls from Vince and Krissy. The few phone calls she'd made to mutual friends or received from Piers' brother, Dominic, about the details of the accident and the funeral had been painful, stilted conversations that caused her a tight ache low down in her throat from swallowing back tears that was so intense she felt as if only shouting out her rage and grief would relieve it. She felt like a ghost.

Last time she'd been here, to this Oxford church, it had been for Scarlett's christening, and she hadn't even glanced at the churchyard, hurrying happily—and a bit late—in through the stone archway and studded wooden doors into the cool interior, scented with wax, damp and flowers. Today, she wished she could be anywhere else at all.

Parked here under overhanging trees, close to the church where she'd only known Ginny happy and radiant, Alice gave way to tears that came in gut-wrenching sobs, painful and ugly in the silence of her little car.

After a while other people started to arrive, so Alice took a deep breath, checked her puffy eyes in the rear-view mirror and slowly, stiffly got out of the car. This time, as she walked along the path to the entrance, all she seemed to notice were the memorials, some aged to the point of illegibility, others shiny new granite, and the flowers laid carefully in front of them. Her parents, sensibly cremated, had a little memorial in a soulless north London cemetery that she visited at increasing intervals. It had been awful, of course. You never really got over losing your parents, but at least that had been in the right order of things. Ginny and Piers dying was all wrong. What possible comfort could this neatly trimmed cemetery bring to such awful loss?

In the church, pungent with white lilies and sweetheart roses, the same flowers that had decked it for the christening, Alice slid into an empty pew on her own and closed her eyes. Maybe she should pray? She couldn't think of what else to do, but no words came to her. Then she opened the order of service, handed to her at the door

48

by one of Piers' cousins, and on the inside front cover was a photograph of Piers and Ginny taken on their honeymoon, both smiling fit to burst. Flooding into Alice's head came other images of Ginny, like snapshots over the years: nights spent drinking cheap wine in the student union bar; days out shopping; long evenings sharing pizza when they'd both been broke; noisy discos where they'd danced—in true traditional style—around their handbags; Ginny staying at Alice's parents' house during the vacs when she'd needed a quiet place to study, then Ginny and Piers' little flat—such a love nest it had sometimes been embarrassing to stay there!

Alice opened her eyes as she felt someone else coming into her pew. Since she'd come in the church had filled up, with people standing in the side aisles, and there must have been some signal she hadn't detected because the little pipe organ swooped into life with a Bach chorale that had everyone rising slowly, checking to see that it was the right thing to do. There was a sudden increase in the light level as the doors opened and a slow procession made its way to the altar, Piers' brothers shouldering his coffin alongside his friends from the rowing club. Ginny's coffin was smaller and in lighter coloured wood, borne by other young men; Waverley family members she vaguely recognised.

Walking in the wake of the two coffins were Piers' parents, who appeared to be holding each other up, their grief agonising to see, and between them was Scarlett. Alice was aware that everyone was staring at her, this pale, dark-haired young girl who was staring at nothing, carefully dressed in a pretty floral skirt but her thoughts clearly somewhere else

49

other than this terrible place. They moved on past her pew and behind them she recognised Ginny's sister, thin, and looking far older than her years, her head bowed and her fingers meshed tightly in front of her. With her were two teenagers—what *were* their names? Cameron and something?—who were looking around with naked and self-conscious curiosity. They'd dressed all in black, but in an odd assortment of separates that made Alice realise that life hadn't got any easier for them. Ginny had never gone into much detail about her family, but Alice knew that she and her sister hadn't always seen eye to eye. Alice pressed her lips together and felt her face contort with the effort of not crying again. And now there would be no time for the sisters to ever make up their differences—and that was so sad. She watched Rosie shuffle sideways into the front pew, glance over at the coffins, placed—heartbreakingly—side by side in front of the altar, lean across to say something to her children, and then bow her head. She looked devastated. Alice made a mental note to talk to her afterwards.

The funeral continued agonisingly, with each hymn more poignant than the last: *Dear Lord and Father of Mankind*; *The Lord's My Shepherd*; *The Day Thou Gavest*. Alice quavered and sobbed her way through, tears now spilling, unstoppable, from her burning eyes and her shoulders shaking. Vaguely, through the grief, she was aware of a clean, pressed cotton handkerchief being tapped against her bunched fists by someone standing in the pew behind her and the warm pressure of a hand squeezing her shoulder gently. She took the handkerchief gratefully—her tissues were shredded already—comforted by the thoughtful gesture.

Whoever it was, she'd thank them later.

As they all filed out afterwards, she turned, beyond any sense of embarrassment at her appearance, and smiled wanly at a group of people in the pew behind—two men, two women, about her age and presumably friends of Piers and Ginny's that she'd never met. They didn't have quite the public school look that most of Piers' mates had, though. One of the women—whom she vaguely recognised from the christening—was in a beige linen dress and jacket and had been crying as much as Alice. The other was more composed, putting an arm around her waist as they walked out into the sunshine; both the men had very short hair. Alice looked between them questioningly. The darker-haired one smiled briefly and sadly back, his face strong and kind and his eyes crinkled with concern. He fell into step beside her as they shuffled towards the door.

'You OK?'

She shrugged in reply, then offered the mangled handkerchief shyly. 'Is this yours? I can wash it and send it back to you, if you like,' she whispered.

'It's all right,' he replied. 'I've got plenty more just the same.' They moved to where the rest of his friends were standing and he breathed out in a long, deep sigh. 'That was hard. I hope I never have to go to a double funeral again.'

'Are you ... I mean, were you a friend of both of them?' Alice asked. 'I don't think we've met before.'

'No—I'm ...' He stopped and pressed his lips together impatiently. 'This is going to take some getting used to. I *was* a colleague of Virginia's.' He indicated the others with him. 'These are

51

her colleagues from the hotel in Oxford but I only worked with her on a few projects. Hotel developments. I was in the area yesterday on business and I wanted to be here. I didn't know her well, but she seemed brilliant at what she did.' He stopped and looked down. 'But what about you? You known her long?'

Alice nodded. 'Feels like forever.'

*　　　*　　　*

Alice had decided to stay overnight in Oxford and had arranged a meeting with the solicitors for the day after the funeral. She'd booked a room at the inn on the river where she'd spent long boozy hours with Ginny and Piers when they were first married. The wake—a word that sounded far too joyous for such an occasion—had gone on for some time. It had taken ages for the families to get back from the cemetery, and no one at the hotel—where Virginia had worked and where Piers and Ginny had celebrated their wedding—seemed to know whether they should start to eat or drink. All the staff had known Ginny, of course, and their normal professionalism must have been challenged by the tragedy of the situation. More than one of the waitresses looked as red-eyed as Alice.

Alice had brief conversations with the people she knew, embracing Piers' parents, Judy and Bill, utterly incapable of articulating her grief to them. Piers' brothers had been warm towards her, but all of them looked grey and drawn, and Rosie folded into sobs the moment Alice put her arms around her. Eventually a kindly soul put a cup of tea into her hand and she was taking a grateful sip when the man from the church came to stand beside her.

'You OK?' he asked gently.

'As well as I'll ever be now.'

She was quiet for a moment then, under his careful questions, she started to talk about Ginny and their shared past. They chatted for a while, or at least he listened then, as everyone started leaving, they awkwardly exchanged cards. It seemed like an oddly formal thing to do, but she wanted to cling onto any part of Ginny she could. 'Greg Mullin' she read, before tucking it into her bag.

The next morning, in her room with the sloping ceiling and the casement window that looked over the river, her head throbbed with tension and she showered briskly before her meeting with Jeremy Peake.

Sitting across from the tall, thin-faced solicitor, she frowned as he explained the situation. 'Even though she is currently living with her grandparents in Sussex—the school have been informed that she won't be going back under the circumstances— you have an important role as Scarlett's guardian. It's an awful lot more than just being a godmother. In fact, you assume all of the responsibilities of a parent, in both a legal and practical sense. Furthermore, you will be legally responsible for things like Scarlett's school attendance and her medical welfare. To all intents and purposes, you will have to take on the role of parent.'

Alice rubbed her face with her hands. She could understand the individual words he was saying, but somehow none of it was making sense. 'Don't be ridiculous,' she almost snorted. 'I can't do *that*. I haven't got a clue what to do!'

The solicitor looked back down at the papers

in front of him. 'I quite understand. One takes on these responsibilities never imagining that the worst will come to pass. She will be well provided for financially, once we get probate, because their estates have been left in trust to her, but there will be provision for her care and any expenses incurred by you. It is up to you to decide if you think she is better off with her grandparents, especially—as you so modestly say—you are inexperienced and it may be difficult for you, but ultimately it is your decision.'

Alice looked at him blankly. She was a woman who was used to making her own decisions, but this was one she wished she'd never been given.

*   *   *

It was while Alice was packing to go to New York a couple of days later that Judy called. She sounded stronger than she had at the funeral, and explained with her usual efficiency that she and Bill had had a cruise booked for months. That they both needed to get away, Bill especially, she explained and, despite their protestations, her 'boys' had insisted that they go. Would she be OK to have Scarlett for a 'week or so'?

She agreed readily, of course. It was the least she could do. But, as the conversation went on, it became apparent that Scarlett's stay was going to be nearer three weeks and, as she put the phone down, panic set in. What did she know about dealing with an eleven-year-old, let alone one who had just lost her parents? The last time she'd spent any time alone with Scarlett was to take her to Drusilla's Zoo when she was still in a pushchair. What did

Alice know about children? About dressing up, lip gloss and boy crushes? Babies were hard enough, but *tweenagers*? She thought for a moment, then realised she knew someone who could help. She picked up the phone.

'Hi, Vince. It's me. I need your skill and expertise.'

*   *   *

The terrifying prospect of being responsible for Scarlett faded as soon as she stepped onto the plane. But not the memory of the funeral, which she seemed to carry around with her like a filter that made everything she saw seem melancholy. To drive away the mood, she threw herself into a punishing itinerary each day, walking for hours, trying hard not to remember the long weekend she had spent there with Ginny, just before Ginny's longed-for pregnancy with Scarlett had pinned her friend to her home, like a butterfly to a card.

Fortunately, there was little, apart from a cursory visit to Brooklyn to try out a new and acclaimed deli, to remind Alice of that trip. And, of course, there had been plenty of visits on her own in the intervening years. This time she paused gratefully in restaurants and galleries, seeking out the new and original for the guide book, absorbing the atmosphere that never failed to energise her and, even now, lifted her mood, sometimes for hours on end. Until she remembered. There were people she could have spent the evenings with, friends who would have been delighted to see her but, uncharacteristically, Alice didn't bother to contact them, preferring her own company and thoughts.

On the flight back, she fell into a deep, restless sleep in which coffins creaked open to reveal piles of books and crumpled clothes and she jolted awake to find her face wet with tears. She arrived back home exhausted, and certainly not prepared in any way for Judy's efficient answer phone message inviting her for tea and to collect Scarlett from their house.

It was less an invitation than a three-line whip. Fortunately, Judy and Bill lived only fifty minutes' drive away from Ulvington, and Alice was there a mere ten minutes late. The phone call had reminded her what a powerhouse Judy was, but she had never been anything other than unfailingly charming to Alice. Although she had seen a few moments of tension between her and Ginny, and had listened to her friend's occasional gripes about her mother-in-law, she seemed to be a decent person, if a tad bossy.

Judy was on the doorstep waiting as Alice crunched to a halt. She was looking just a bit less soignée than was usual for her, her sleek bob looking very slightly windswept, although the day was as calm as could be. 'Ah, there you are, Alice. How lovely to see you. You look well rested from your holiday.'

Alice opened her mouth to contradict her, then decided to save her breath. In the house all was quiet, with no clue as to the whereabouts of Scarlett. Ginny and Piers' house, even before Scarlett was born, was always alive with music, from a radio or CD playing somewhere, or laughter or chat. The quiet atmosphere made Alice feel she should be on tiptoe.

'So, how *are* you?' Alice asked, in that pregnant

way reserved for enquiries of a delicate kind. 'I've thought about you and Bill so much while I've been away.'

For a moment, Judy seemed to sag and she immediately looked years older, then she visibly braced herself and turned to face Alice. 'It's the worst pain you could ever imagine,' she said quietly. 'It's all wrong, to see your child go before you. It's against everything you ever expect in life. Piers . . .' She stopped and took a deep breath. 'It's not that Piers was my favourite. It's not like that, really. Well, perhaps you wouldn't understand, as you've never had children. But he was so special to me. Always so thoughtful. Of all the boys, he was. . .' She stopped and shook her head, squeezing her eyes tightly closed. 'Having Scarlett here means I have to keep a brave face on things, and perhaps that's for the best. But it's terribly tiring. That's why it's so helpful having you step in like this. She's in the drawing room.' She turned away and Alice followed. Jeremy Peake had told her, in no uncertain terms, that as things currently stood, *she* was responsible for Scarlett from now on and the implications of this had terrified her. Yet Judy made it sound as though Alice was merely a stopgap. A guilty sense of relief swept over her.

The drawing room was shady, the blinds lowered against the bright sunlight. Alice glanced around. She'd only visited the house on a few occasions— the engagement party and then a couple of drinks parties when Piers and Ginny had come to stay. But she wasn't sure she'd been there at all since Scarlett was born.

Alice waited for her eyes to grow accustomed to the light, then saw Scarlett, curled up in a boudoir

57

chair, her feet pulled up underneath her. Judy's voice took on a timbre Alice hadn't heard from her before—the kind of coaxing tone you might use with a recalcitrant toddler. 'Now then, Scarlett— look who's here to see you. It's Alice! You remember Alice, don't you? Oh dear, you're not wearing that skirt again are you?'

Scarlett glanced up and looked intently at Alice, her eyes dark and wide against her pale skin. Her hair was loose today, and the way it fell, dark, straight and thick, to her shoulders was so like Ginny's that Alice had to restrain herself from gasping in sudden pain. She'd never realised how like her mother Scarlett looked but, as she was growing up, the resemblance was becoming stronger and stronger. Alice quickly composed her expression into what she hoped was a warm smile. 'Hello, Scarly. Lovely to see you. Are you all packed ready to come home with me while Granny and Grandpa go on hols?'

An expression that came close to a flinch crossed the girl's face and she looked down at her hands. 'Yes, thank you,' she said tonelessly. 'I've packed my bag. It's upstairs. Thank you very much for having me.'

'Tell you what, Scarlett,' Judy breezed. 'Why don't you go upstairs and fetch all your things and perhaps choose some books to take as well. You *love* reading, don't you, dear?' Scarlett unfolded herself silently—it looked as if she'd inherited her parents' height as well—and drifted from the room.

Judy watched her go, widening her eyes at Alice, then made some anodyne comments about the weather and the garden until they heard the light, slow footsteps fading on the stairs, then she sighed deeply. 'I *know* it takes time, but she's drifting around like a little ghost. I can hardly get a word out of her. I'm not complaining—far from it. She's my granddaughter and we're her closest remaining relatives so I know it's right for her to be here. It's very good of you to have her, though, just for this short spell. We've had this cruise booked for a while you see. Bill . . . well, he's taken all this very hard, of course, and he's struggling a little to come to terms . . . you know, and a holiday will do him good. The solicitor did mention the terms of the will but, obviously, you can't be expected to take over permanently.'

Alice found herself starting to nod in agreement then, feeling disloyal to Ginny, stopped abruptly.

'I mean, look at your lifestyle—darting off here and there. We do understand that you don't have— well—how shall I put it?—the most stable of existences so, as soon as we get back, we'll have her here again.'

'Look, it's really no trouble,' Alice said quickly, suddenly mindful that the quiet little girl might have found a place to listen in to their conversation. Being referred to as if she was some awkward package would not be helpful to anyone—and particularly not Scarlett at this time. 'I'm actually looking forward to spending time with her. I never felt I did enough as her godmother anyway. It's the very least I can do.' Feeling more magnanimous than she would have if the arrangement was permanent, Alice continued in a firmer voice. 'I've got lots of things planned to do with her over the next couple of weeks, so don't worry in the slightest. And when you get back, we'll see how things go. I'm sure we can come to some arrangement if Bill still isn't feeling too well.'

Judy seemed mollified. 'Well, getting away will do Bill the world of good, I'm sure. And perhaps it is good for you to get to know Scarlett better. I just wish the circumstances were different . . .'

She nodded slowly, and they were both silent for a minute.

'Perhaps,' Judy continued, 'you could have her while we go to sort the house out, once we return. I'm just not sure I can face it yet. All Piers' things . . .' She broke off and Alice wondered if Rosie would be able to come to Oxford and sort out Ginny's possessions. She might be glad of some of them, but Alice couldn't imagine her and Judy sifting through the kitchen implements together, divvying up spatulas and slotted spoons. She closed her eyes and was immensely relieved to hear Judy say, as though nothing at all was wrong, 'Well, let's go and have tea before you leave. I've set it out on the terrace—I thought it would be nice to sit in the sunshine.'

Chapter 9

Christmas 1997

Piers and Virginia set off for Sussex at midday on Christmas Eve, hoping they'd miss the early traffic. That was one of the joys of being at the marketing end of the hotel industry. While the general managers, waiters and chefs worked like Trojans over Christmas—usually, hopefully, the busiest time of year—the work of the marketing director was done. Christmas for Virginia had happened sometime in May, when she had worked on the brochures. So, as the sun had beaten down outside and the roses were scaling the terrace and showing off their blousy blooms, Virginia had been steeped in log fires and plum pudding, designers' proofs and package costing. And she must have made the descriptions of sprouts and chestnuts sound alluring enough and got the message out to the right places because all the hotels in the group were full and she could drive away now with the sense of self-satisfaction of a job well done.

They'd hoped to take some good news with them to Piers' parents, but the visit to the consultant two weeks ago hadn't delivered the news they wanted to hear.

'We've got a bit of a problem, I'm afraid,' said the surprisingly prim woman in her early fifties, 'in that we can't find a problem. Your hormones, Mrs Waverley, are showing slightly inconsistent levels which may not be helping, but there is nothing we can pinpoint.'

'Is that treatable?' Piers had leaned forward anxiously. Over the past few months he had become as involved in this as Virginia, reminding her when she needed to take her temperature, even coming home at lunchtime for a quickie if the ovulation test had dictated it.

'Possibly,' the consultant had continued gently, 'but Mr Waverley, unless we have real evidence as to why conception isn't happening, it makes it very hard to progress. Unfortunately you don't qualify for free IVF treatment, especially as you've managed to conceive before. So we will simply have to keep trying and hope for a miracle. And,' she

61

leaned forward, 'trust me. They do happen. Your wife may become pregnant when you least expect it. Let's just hope, shall we?'

Piers had sat back in his chair and run his fingers through his hair, and Virginia was aware what all this meant to him. For her burly rowing-jock husband, this was emasculation, especially when his brothers had provided a brood of grandchildren with no trouble at all. Now, as they turned off the M40 onto the M25, the prospect of the next two days with them raced towards them. Two days filled with children and new toys and over-attentive parents. And the necessity to keep a smile on their faces throughout.

Dominic and Barney would be there with their families. Theo was doing whatever screenwriters do in New York, having a Christmas up-state with his wife Christie's apple-pie family and their three-year-old prodigy, Stone, a name that had caused much mirth amongst the entire Waverley family.

The car was warm and they didn't talk. Virginia could feel her head beginning to nod uncomfortably and she surrendered to it, letting herself doze as they chewed up the miles. She hadn't slept well the last few nights, waking at around four, the darkness velvet black around her, and only Piers' heavy breathing breaking the silence. Worried it was because she wasn't tired enough, Virginia had put herself through a pounding workout at the gym each day, punishing her body for letting her down. When she came to, she looked at Piers' profile as he concentrated on the road. It had been a busy time for him, with end-of-term events and the prospect of mock GCSEs and A-levels looming in the New Year, and he looked pale with fatigue.

Piers fitted his job like a glove. He was the eternal schoolboy, able to talk to his pupils in a relaxed, teasing way—a bit too relaxed at times, Virginia thought—but they seemed to respect him. He was without guile, funny and easy to be with, which is why she'd fallen for him straightaway when they'd met. Aware they came from opposite sides of a social divide—state and private, tea and supper, lounge and sitting room—his ease and self-confidence had helped smooth the way, not to mention his lack of ambition beyond the passionate desire for the success for the school rowing eight. He preferred to concentrate on his writing (a much-researched and little-written book on Charlemagne) and inspiring his pupils to understand the Arab–Israeli conflict and the Cold War enough to get good grades.

But today he looked tense.

'Shall we go somewhere exciting at Easter?' Virginia asked eventually, into the silence. Perhaps they needed something to look forward to, to plan towards.

'I'll be doing crash revision days,' he replied, slowing down to a queue of traffic ahead.

'All holiday?' She tried to sound light.

Piers shrugged. 'Most of it.'

'Well I just thought it would be nice, that's all.' She felt a bit surprised by his lack of enthusiasm. She was trying, wasn't she?

'It doesn't change anything, sweetheart, does it?' Piers muttered and looked out of his window with his head turned away.

'Maybe not and I want a baby as much as you do—maybe even more—but for God's sake, we

63

can't put our lives on hold!'

'Maybe even more!' He turned to her abruptly. 'I didn't realise how much I wanted this . . . children, I mean, until we saw that doctor!'

'I know,' Virginia paused. 'She made it real, didn't she? It'll be OK, I'm sure. She said miracles can happen.' Neither spoke for a while.

'But I've let you down,' he said quietly into the silence.

'No you haven't!' Virginia turned quickly to reassure him. 'The problem's with me, darling, and you heard what she said. Sometimes pregnancies happen without any interference. Look at what happened to Nick and Jane.' Friends from the rowing club now had a beautiful baby girl after years of trying. 'Let's just see what happens, hey? We managed it once, didn't we?' She sounded more confident than she felt. Recently their lovemaking had become laced with purpose—a means to an end—lacking the naughtiness and passion they'd had together in the past. Spontaneous sex on a Sunday afternoon now happened because of her body temperature rather than because they couldn't keep their hands off each other.

They didn't talk again until they pulled into the gates of his parents' house in the leafy outskirts of Haywards Heath. The first time Piers had brought her to the house she had nearly thrown up with fear as they'd pulled in, and its imposing size still made her nervous. High Edwardian gables looked down imperiously on anything in the driveway, and the brick was dark and austere. Even the garden planting was regimented, the climbers that scaled the walls kept in neat check, as was anyone who dealt with Judy.

64

The black lab, Sylvester, Bill's closest friend, came up to greet them, his tail wagging frantically, and he pushed his muzzle into Virginia's hand. 'Hello, mate,' she greeted him, rubbing his head. 'How are you doing?'

The front door opened and Bill came out, his arms spread in greeting. He embraced his son warmly, then gathered Virginia into a hug. 'Lovely to see you both. A bit of sanity in the mêlée.' Virginia loved the way Bill talked—so refined and proper. She could imagine how he sounded to defendants in court as he sentenced them from his lofty judge's seat.

'Is there still time for us to run for the hills?' Piers asked, pulling a suitcase and a massive bag of presents, which Virginia had been wrapping until midnight, out of the boot.

'If you're quick I'll tell them I never saw you. Now, darling,' he turned to Virginia and put his arm around her. 'It's Christmas and it's time you had a drink. Judy has made something that frankly smells vile, but which she says is essential to the festive celebrations. That, or I could slip you a G&T. What's it to be?'

'Better not anger the hostess this early on in proceedings,' she giggled and they went inside.

*   *   *

'It's me,' Virginia hissed down the phone.

'Where are you?' Alice hissed back.

'*You* don't need to whisper. They can't hear you.'

'Oh yes!' Alice laughed. 'Are you at the Addams' Family mansion? How's Morticia?'

'Ghastly,' Virginia replied, feeling guilty for

having slipped upstairs after dinner had broken up. The grandchildren, overtired and overexcited now, were being bathed under the doting eye of their parents. Bill and Piers had retired with the papers and Judy was on the phone to a friend in the village about the time of the Christmas Day service. 'She can really hit my switches. She asked everyone what they'd been up to, then she turned to me and asked "what sort of thing" my sister did for Christmas, as if she had tinned turkey or went down the bingo.'

'Isn't she a piece of work!' Alice sounded a bit pissed.

'She's changed the lounge curtains. Again. The others seemed fine to me. I nearly asked if I could have them.'

'Well, she's nothing better to do, sweetie, and it's a drawing room by the way. A room that has a grand piano and a drinks cabinet is most emphatically *not* a lounge.'

Virginia, curled up on the spare room bed, looked around the exquisite room with its matching floral wallpaper and curtains and small walnut dressing table in front of the square bay window. 'Sorry. Where are you?'

'Most of the way through a second bottle of champagne actually,' Alice giggled. 'The villa is gorgeous and Pete's taking me to a midnight service at the village church in a bit. They might have to prop me up against a pillar though.'

Virginia had visions of where Alice was—a white-washed villa in southern Spain overlooking the twinkling Mediterranean. What a trial! How did Alice manage to net these men? Pete, a failed novelist and the latest beau on the scene, seemed to have friends everywhere—mainly because of his permanent supply of coke—and had been asked to house-sit the pad for one of his customers, and Alice, by all accounts, was loving it. It didn't sound ideal to Virginia, but then Alice would probably move on soon. She invariably did.

'How are the young prodigies?'

Virginia could hear Dominic telling his son to get into bed without much conviction. 'Picture perfect.' She wanted so much to share the pain with Alice. Would she be too drunk to understand? 'There's been lots of ... digs about us getting on with it too. Barney's Maggie kept asking when we'd be producing 'cause she has lots of clothes to hand down.' She stopped, worried she was going to cry.

There was quiet down the end of the phone. 'Nothing doing in that department?' Alice said eventually.

'Er ... nope. I don't even feel like having sex any more.'

'I gather it's quite an important part of the process.' Virginia could hear the smile in Alice's voice.

'So I'm told.'

They didn't say anything for a moment. 'It'll be fine, Ginny,' Alice whispered, using the nickname Virginia hated but had always let Alice get away with.

'Hope you're right.'

'Gotta go. Don't have too much fun at Morticia Towers.'

'It'll be tough, but I'll do my best,' Virginia laughed and, clicking her phone shut, summoned up the energy again to toe Judy's line.

Chapter 10

June 2010

Scarlett didn't turn to wave at her grandparents as they pulled out of the driveway. Alice studied Scarlett out of the corner of her eye. She was holding tightly, with both hands, onto the straps of the flower-patterned backpack she had kept with her after they had stowed her suitcase in the boot. She'd placed it on the floor, next to her feet, but she was hanging onto it, her knuckles pale with the effort.

Alice took a deep breath. 'Not far to go,' she said in a voice of forced cheer. 'We'll be there in no time!'

In the mirror she could see Bill and Judy standing together on the doorstep. Judy hadn't been exaggerating about Bill. When he eventually appeared, plodding slowly downstairs to join them for a cup of tea, it was all Alice could do to prevent herself from gasping. He looked appalling. He seemed to have shrunk even since the funeral, and he'd looked bad enough then. His neck, in his checked shirt collar looked stringy, and his normally perfectly shaved face was patchy with bristles he'd missed. He could only just have shaved, because he still sported a little patch of tissue stuck over a cut, starkly white against his yellowish cheek, the crimson centre still fresh. And when she'd embraced him, after an embarrassing little hesitation of feints and advances on both their parts, she realised he smelled old and stale, quite unlike his usual crisp scent of West Indian Limes. It was as if Piers had sucked out half his father's life force with him when he'd died. And it was just as well, under the circumstances, that they'd had the cruise booked and that it had been too late to cancel. Perhaps the break would help. Judy's air of tight self-control began to make more sense. She barely seemed to draw breath once Bill appeared, saying over and over again, in slightly differing ways, that everything would be absolutely fine once they'd had their little holiday. Alice wondered whom she was trying to convince.

As they drove through the gates, Alice wound down the window and waved goodbye with disproportionate enthusiasm, as if to make up for Scarlett's resolute forward stare and immobility. She felt a little bit guilty, she had to admit (if only to herself), that she'd been regarding having Scarlett so soon after the New York trip, as a bit of a trial. But seeing Bill so diminished and Judy so defiantly courageous made the next three weeks seem much less of a chore. And it was only three weeks—what was that compared to the lifetime of care Judy and Bill were so willing to shoulder? She shouldn't be so selfish.

Approaching the A-road that would take them back towards Lewes and, eventually, Ulvington, Alice cleared her throat. Scarlett's silence was a little bit unnerving and she glanced at her with what she hoped was a warm smile.

'We'll be home in no time.'

Scarlett didn't move. 'You said that already,' she said matter-of-factly. 'And it's not *home*. It might be yours but it's not mine. My home's in Oxford.'

Alice felt a rush of heat over her face. 'Of

course. I'm so sorry. That was a stupid thing to say. My house—that's what I meant.' There was a long silence in which Scarlett picked at the straps on her backpack. After a while Alice continued, slowly. 'My house, yes, you're right, of course. But . . . but I want you to think of it as yours. I mean—you're welcome to stay with me as long as you like, or any time you like. What I mean is . . .' she swallowed, suddenly emotional. 'I'll always be here for you, Scarly. I mean it. And I hope we'll get to know each other better and better.'

Then she took the opportunity, while pulling out onto the main road, to study Scarlett carefully as she checked the traffic coming from the left. She was still holding onto her pack, but with one hand now. The other elbow was resting on the ledge in front of the passenger window and her chin was resting in her hand while she looked out. Alice could see her blinking rather fast and her heart tightened with emotion. She didn't reply until they were some way along the main road.

'Your car's filthy,' she smiled slightly. 'Don't you ever clean it out?'

Chapter 11

February 1998

The hotel group CEO, Derek Rawlings, sat back in his chair, a position he liked to assume, Virginia suspected, because it made him look pensive and important.

70

'Good figures, Virginia. Good figures. And they were difficult months to get business, as always.'

'It helped that Valentine's Day fell on a Saturday.' Jeremy, the general manager, was doodling on his pad. Virginia knew how much he hated these meetings with Head Office, who swooped down every now and then and shook their feathers, making the hotel team jumpily justify their every move.

'Good. Good, let's keep it up. Now,' Derek leaned forward again to look at his notes. 'The Dales Hotel launch in Harrogate. We're still aiming at opening the doors just before Easter. The website is ready to go, I think, Virginia?'

She nodded. He knew it was because she'd had a long and detailed meeting with him the day before. Recently acquired and overhauled by the group to add to its bijou portfolio, The Dales Hotel was going to be its flagship, eclipsing the Oxford hotel with its luxury. Oxford was Virginia's base, of course—mainly because of Piers' job—but the decision to buy The Dales precipitated a question she had suspected was coming.

'Good, good,' Derek had tapped his pen as he wound up the work of the day. 'So, how do you fancy moving to Harrogate?'

Her heart sank. 'Oh?' she'd laughed lightly. 'Is that really necessary?'

'I think it makes sense,' he'd carried on, as if it were as simple as that. 'The Dales Hotel will be our lead hotel now, I think and, geographically, it makes sense for you to be more central.'

Virginia looked down at her hands. He had her cornered. If she said no, would it affect her job? There were precious few jobs like hers around

Oxford and she wasn't going to take a step back and work for a smaller operation. Not now she'd worked so hard. But how could she say yes?

'It's a lovely town,' he'd gone on. 'We'd help you relocate, of course, and I'm sure Piers could find a job in a school close by. Yorkshire schools are great, I'm told, which will be useful when you have a family.' He'd leaned forward. 'I won't ask you what your plans are in that department, Virginia but, suffice it to say, you're valuable to us. But I need you in the right place. I'm as broad-minded as the next man,' he'd leaned back again. 'But you women seem to find it hard to be as flexible as men. I had to move where the work took me, and Glenda came too.'

Virginia hadn't been able to bring herself to speak. Alice would love this. In one little speech he'd managed to set back women's liberation fifty years.

'I do believe,' she'd replied eventually, 'that I can be just as effective regardless of where I am based.' Derek had raised a sceptical eyebrow. 'I will have to talk to Piers, but moving is not that easy for him and it certainly wouldn't be possible before the beginning of the next school year.'

Derek had tidied his papers and stood up. 'Well, you know what's needed.'

His comments hung over her and, after the sales meeting ended, she left the hotel and walked into the crisp February sunshine. Early for her meeting with the brochure designers in the centre of town, she diverted and, picking up a cheese and pickle sandwich and a coffee, found herself walking down St Aldate's and turning into the gardens of Christ Church through the ornate Memorial Gardens

72

entrance. There were a few office workers who, like her, were braving the cold to soak up the rare sunshine and, as she turned down Long Walk towards the river, she could see a couple of women up ahead with well-wrapped babies in buggies. Her heart lurched and she looked away as she always did now when she saw prams and, for diversion, looked over the water meadow at the cattle with their silly long horns.

So many times over the years since she'd first met Piers, they'd walked along the river from here, looping round where the Cherwell meets the Isis, and she sat herself down now on a bench looking over the wide stretch of water onto the bank beyond and sipped her hot coffee. There were no leaves on the trees now, of course, but it was while they were in full leaf, with the sun warming the people who'd come to feed the ducks, that he'd proposed to her in characteristically over-the-top style in front of all the passers-by. And when she'd tearfully accepted and he'd handed her a bunch of hastily picked cow parsley, they'd received a round of applause from a group of Japanese tourists.

Virginia quickly sipped some coffee and opened up her sandwich to distract herself. They'd been so full of hope then. Piers had planned that they'd produce their own rowing eight, though Virginia had thought a coxless pair was more realistic. At this rate they wouldn't even manage a single scull. And now there was the pressure to move. If she wasn't going to be able to have a baby, a concept which left an ache of emptiness inside her, then why shouldn't she build the best career she could? And Derek was right, Piers could move schools if he had to. He was a good teacher. He'd find it easy to get another job. She'd only been to Harrogate to check over the new hotel, but it seemed a nice enough place and, she laughed wryly to herself, it was further away from Sussex and Judy, which had to be a plus point.

She threw the crust of her sandwich to the greedy ducks. She'd met Piers on this river too but again, it had been summer then. The end of August and the Royal Regatta. She'd been away for a couple of weeks before with Alice to Spain. It had had to be a cheap holiday as neither of them earned much in those days, so they'd stayed at a tiny little hotel which Alice had managed to negotiate a daylight robbery deal on, and they'd read trashy novels and indulged in nothing more active than rubbing sun cream on each other's backs. Alice had been smarting after another failed love affair—a Lithuanian poet who regaled her with verses she couldn't understand but suspected to be revoltingly smutty—and they'd spent hours slagging off the fickleness of men and the fact that Virginia couldn't find anyone to date who wasn't a waiter or an unhealthy-looking *chef de partie*.

The result was that she had an impressive tan when she came home and, after weeks of training too, she was looking what Alice would call 'hot and horny' by the time the regatta came around. Her four were, for once, on form and she had clambered out of the boat after a comprehensive win, tired but elated. She'd noticed his legs first of all—strong, tanned and athletic—and the rest of him had been just as tantalising.

'Virginia,' Rachel, one of her four, had panted, clambering out after her. 'Meet Piers. He works with me, but he's in the history department. Piers,

74

meet Virginia Russell.'

It had been a *coup de foudre*, to be honest. She'd liked him on sight. He was well-built, sporty and good-looking but, most of all, fun to be with. He made sure she was included in the club parties and after-training drinks and then, when he finally started to take her out, there were no 'will he phone' games. He managed to charm everyone from the receptionist at the hotel to Derek, and he had even managed to make Rosie smile. Alice was as circumspect as always but, as ever with the posh (Judy had famously announced one day that it wasn't a 'small world, just a thin upper crust'), there were fewer than six degrees of separation between them and inevitably they had friends in common. A fact that made Virginia feel a little *de trop* at times.

Virginia had never ceased to delight in the fact that Piers adored her, and she knew that she was irrefutably *his*. But what would he make of Derek's suggestion? Sensing she knew the answer already, she eased herself up off the bench, dropped her lunch in a litter bin, and followed the boundary of the water meadow back round to the gates beside the Botanical Gardens and out onto High Street.

*   *   *

'No way!' Piers barely missed a beat in reaction to her gentle suggestion, made later that evening after he'd finished two helpings of lasagne and the best part of a bottle of wine. The doctor had suggested they cut down on the alcohol but tonight she didn't want to raise the point.

'Is it totally out of the question?' she asked meekly.

'Gin, why should we go through an upheaval like that when ... well, when hopefully you'll get pregnant and here, well, here we're surrounded by friends.' He cast his arms out as if they were all in the kitchen with them. 'I've got a good job, and I think I might be offered head of department in the next year or two ...'

'But what if it *doesn't* happen?' Virginia asked in desperation. 'They want me to be more centrally based because they have plans to add to the hotels in the group, and I'd get a great pay rise. And Yorkshire *is* lovely. And there are rowing clubs. I Googled it.'

Piers poured himself another glass of Merlot. 'Harrogate is hardly Henley, darling. And Yorkshire schools don't really do rowing like they do down here. They're all into rugby and I'm not going to coach rugby. It's for boneheads.'

Virginia picked up the dirty plates and felt an overwhelming sense of despondency come over her as she filled the dishwasher. He was right, she supposed. For all her twenty-first century liberalism and awareness of a woman's place, shoulder-to-shoulder with her man, she knew that if—and God please grant it be so—she managed to become pregnant, she would need Piers to be the breadwinner for a while—and in a place he felt happy and could succeed.

Piers said no more about it as he helped her clear and took out the full bin bag to the bin outside for collection, sighing as usual that she'd filled it too full. He pushed a pile of marked essays into a folder and put them into his backpack and, after a few moments in front of the news, nodded off, his head lolling on his chest. Rousing him, as she did most nights now, they made their way to bed and, backs turned to each other, fell into a deep sleep.

Chapter 12

June 2010

As they arrived in Ulvington—not a moment too soon for Alice—she drove round, past the pub, so she could see whether Vince's car was still outside the cottage. If it was, they'd agreed she'd take Scarlett for a Coke and a bag of crisps to give him more time. It was too early to spring Vince on her goddaughter.

A quick glance revealed that he'd left already and Alice felt a pang of panic. It was good that he'd finished, of course, and she had absolute faith in his abilities, but the warmth and clatter of the pub might have been preferable to going back to the cottage alone with this silent little girl. Alice shook herself. She tried to inject as much enthusiasm and warmth as she could into the first comment she'd made for the last twenty minutes. 'Here we are. Let's go inside and get you sorted.'

She lifted the suitcase from the boot and waited for Scarlett to walk slowly up the path in front of her, watching the turn of her head as she looked around. She winced as she saw things through the girl's eyes—uneven bricks with weeds sprouting up between overgrown flower beds leading up to a front door painted, frankly, a rather garish purple. Compared with the clipped elegance of Judy and Bill's home, hers looked shabby and uncared for.

And, thought Alice, stooping quickly to pull the head off a dandelion before it seeded, it was. She sighed softly and reached over Scarlett's shoulder to unlock the door.

The smell of polish hit them. Well, that was a promising start. Vince must have gone through the house like a whirlwind after he'd waved her off. He had 'a firm plan' in his head to 'welcome Scarlett', he'd said just before Alice left to collect her earlier, and he hadn't been kidding. The sitting room was like a showroom, with cushions plumped up the way she had never been able to manage, and vases of sweet peas stood on every surface. Scarlett stepped into the centre of the room, her backpack clutched to her chest as she looked slowly around. Alice held her breath for a moment.

'Would you like a drink? Something to eat?' She hadn't had time to go shopping but Vince had said he'd stock up the fridge. She just hoped he'd remembered. 'That's the kitchen.' She gesticulated towards the open door. 'Er . . . but you know that. I'll just go and . . .'

Scarlett still hadn't spoken and Alice was beginning to feel slightly unnerved. Much more of this and she'd be talking away nineteen to the dozen, like Judy had earlier.

'Could I see my room, please? I'd like to put my things in there.'

'Of course! Sorry—I should have shown you straightaway. Just up the stairs.'

She seized the suitcase—which felt heavy enough for a term at university, never mind a three-week stay—and followed Scarlett up the staircase, the wooden tread painted to look as though there was a patterned runner up the middle. 'It's the door on

78

the left. The bathroom's on the right.'

Scarlett turned the door handle. 'Oh!' She stopped dead and Alice practically tripped over her.

'Oh!' Alice echoed, then quickly tried to cover up her surprise. 'Do you like it?'

Vince had been as good as his word. If anything, he'd been slightly better—or worse, depending on how you looked at it—and Alice winced a little as she saw the extent of his labours. Ahead of her, Scarlett stepped slowly in. What must she think?

Pink. Everything was pink. He'd spread a pink gingham cloth over the little pine table in front of the window and set out a row of jam jars along the back, crammed with pencils and crayons, with a neat pile of notebooks, the topmost of which was adorned with a photograph of a kitten. The lamp on the bedside table now sported a shocking-pink shade with a feather trim. Alice's old sleigh bed, its dark wood polished to a deep shine, had a new set of deep-pink bedlinen and a raspberry-coloured fleece blanket spread smoothly on top, a stack of fluffy pink towels at one corner.

Alice felt queasy. 'We can change it, if it's all too much?'

Scarlett was still looking around slowly. Outlining the fireplace he'd fixed—not with nails, she hoped—a string of pink fairy lights, slowly flashing in sequence, and in the hearth he'd arranged, artfully, Alice had to admit, a collection of feathery fans, in varying shades of pink and—in contrast— bright orange to look like a roaring fire. She strongly suspected he had only had to plunder his own extensive collection. The final touch, at which Scarlett was staring now, her mouth slightly open, was a white sheet, suspended from the wall opposite the window, glowing in the afternoon light that streamed in from over the Downs, decorated round the edges with clusters of buttons in every shade from palest rose to deepest magenta, a border of sequins enclosing the painted message:

WELCOME, SCARLETT

The moments seemed to drag, in silence, and Alice suddenly had to suppress the urge to giggle. Eventually, Scarlett turned to her, two spots of bright colour on her cheeks. 'Can I unpack? I'd like to be on my own for a bit, please.'

She hated it. Alice started to back apologetically toward the stairs. 'Of course, of course. The wardrobe should be empty and the chest of drawers.' She'd asked Vince to move her stuff out. She hoped he hadn't been diverted from that more mundane task, and quickly went to check, moving round Scarlett who was still planted in the doorway. In the emptied top drawer he'd tucked a little pink cat with a goofy smile and absurdly long stripy legs. The rest might have to go, but that was adorable. Alice smiled and closed the drawer for Scarlett to find it herself. She'd have to give Vince a particularly big hug for that when she next saw him.

'Right—I'll leave you to it. Supper in half an hour?'

Scarlett nodded without turning round and Alice walked slowly downstairs. It was going to be a long three weeks.

*   *   *

80

The following couple of days were challenging, to say the least. Alice felt as though she was walking on eggshells with Scarlett in the house, trying to second-guess what she might want to do, and it was knackering her out. What Alice found hardest was knowing what behaviour was normal, and what was a result of a bereavement that was too devastating to imagine. And Scarlett gave no clues whatsoever.

Alice had imagined a scenario of tears and hugs, with Alice able to share her grief with her. That would have been hard enough, but this silence—almost sullen in its impenetrability—was impossible to break through. Should she try and be cheerful or was that trite? Should she raise the topic, or was it too early? She just didn't know how to handle it, and simply suppressed her own grief, swallowing back tears, except for snatched moments in the bath when she couldn't hold back any longer.

By the end of the second day, after every single question she posed—would you like to eat? Drink? Have a bath? Go for a walk? Watch telly?—was answered with the same shrug and a muttered, 'Don't mind', Alice had guiltily started counting off the days until she could return Scarlett to her grandparents and get her life back again. Bit by bit, her image of herself as ministering angel, coaxing the grieving child back to something like happiness, was disappearing with every rebuff, and Scarlett's wan face and closed expression felt like a constant mild reproof. Alice was running out of ideas—and there were still nineteen days and at least five hours to go.

Watching from the kitchen while she cut up a pizza into slices, she studied the back of Scarlett's head as she watched the tiny television in the corner. A cartoon character—it looked like a slab of Swiss cheese, although it seemed to be wearing trousers and living underwater—was grinning inanely while singing a song to what looked like an overweight pink starfish. It was just another thing that Scarlett had immersed herself in totally since her arrival, though it was an improvement on the earphones or the constant messaging to friends on her laptop. Wireless broadband was the only thing Scarlett had shown any enthusiasm about, but it didn't exactly open up the channels for polite conversation.

Alice divided the pizza between two plates, added some salad and carried it through, handing Scarlett hers before sitting down nearby. Scarlett didn't move her eyes from the TV. 'Thanks, Mum.'

Alice froze. Then she decided to pretend she hadn't noticed. 'Like some orange juice?'

There was a long pause. 'Don't mind.'

This time it didn't irritate her. 'Well, I'll get some for you anyway. You might fancy it in a bit.'

Chapter 13

March 1998

There was no other noise around her except the distant hum of early traffic and water lapping against the edge of the boat. The morning was misty after the unexpectedly warm spring sunshine the day before, and it lifted off the river eerily. Virginia pulled the oars towards her in a familiar rhythm, stretching her arms and pulling herself just a little bit more than was comfortable. As the seat slid on the runners, she could see her thighs tensing. She was strong and athletic, her body toned and fit. She just wasn't functioning like a woman should.

Her body had become something of an obsession over the last few weeks and, only last night before they went out for dinner, she had stood in front of the mirror after her shower and looked at herself. By any standards, it was OK. Flat stomach, neat hips and bum, and small boobs. Her skin was smooth and elastic, but inside nothing was how it should be. Piers had given up asking about her period, and there was no reason for him to know when she was having one as days and days were going by without them having sex and, when they did, it was intermittent and passionless. The night before last they'd made love wordlessly, and he had thrust into her almost ruthlessly in the dark until he'd come, then flopped over and fallen asleep. What hurt Virginia most was how much this was a departure from the tender love-making of their early time together, when they'd clawed at each other, unable to resist the feeling of each other's skin. Sometimes it had been dirty, sometimes tender and sweet. Now it was just functional.

She knew she was being stubborn about Judy's recent offer, conveyed via Piers, of help paying for IVF. It made sense. They couldn't afford it. But her mother-in-law's largesse seemed to the beleaguered Virginia as if Judy was making some investment in a grandchild, like a venture capitalist and, if one ever came, she'd 'own' part of it like a shareholder. She knew Judy too well—this would not be an offer without strings attached and an 'open-ended loan', especially with so much of Virginia's money going

on her mother's care, was too much of a burden—
and not just a financial one. She had stalled and,
now she thought about it, Piers hadn't mentioned it
for a while. Perhaps he'd given up asking, knowing
Virginia wasn't going to back down on this one.

Virginia observed with interest the way in which
friends handled it. Some had the tact not to ask,
knowing that both of them wanted a family. Others
waded in with jocular references to 'getting on
with it'. Only last night, at Natasha and Sebastian's
dinner party, Sebastian had asked when Virginia
was planning to 'pop one out', as if she was laying
an egg. Dinner parties were becoming quite dull
as everyone obsessed over the one thing they had
in common—children of varying ages and stages of
development—and, at this point, Virginia would
sit back and zone out. Even Piers, surrounded by
them all day at school, could at least make some
contribution to the subject. She couldn't.

Alice was about the only person Virginia could
have a child-free conversation with. It suited them
both—Alice because she had no interest in them,
and Virginia because, just for a moment, she could
forget the nagging void and relax. Only last week
she'd met up with her—eventually, after a long wait
outside the tube—and over a large glass of wine and
a panini in Covent Garden, Alice had regaled her
with a long and far-too-detailed story about Clive,
the theatre director and latest man on the scene,
who had a penchant in bed for fantasies about
nurses.

'I can make up a story as well as the next girl,' Alice
had snorted, catching the attention of the couple
at the next table. 'I mean, Mills & Boon hospital
romances were my staple diet at school and you just

84

need to add the juicy bits, but I draw the bloody line at dressing up. Can you imagine me in a little dress and matron's hat?'

'Well, now I come to think about it . . .'

'Getaway. Vince tells me I'm being a prude but you know how he loves dressing up.'

Virginia laughed. The last time she'd seen Vince had been at the Go-Go Club in Brighton, where he had a regular slot on the bill, and he'd been wearing a pink catsuit and a blonde wig—not a look she could imagine floating anyone's boat. No one straight anyway.

Alice, being Alice, Virginia wasn't sure if she avoided the topic of *no baby* because she was being tactful or if, in her single-minded single life, she really hadn't given it any thought. Sometimes Virginia wanted to climb inside Alice's head to try and understand how it functioned. She suspected that all the glib joking was a cover for real concerns sometimes—though she'd never seen evidence of it—and she was envious of how matters like lost car keys, massive overdrafts, hopeless men and the scratching about for work didn't seem to faze Alice in the slightest. What would it be like living with her full-time, Virginia pondered now as she rowed on down the river. They'd lived together for the last year of university and had had holidays together, but that wasn't the same, was it? Virginia suspected she'd be ready to murder her after a while, but perhaps some of Alice's spontaneity and fun would rub off on her. And she could do with some fun right now.

Her brain ached with tiredness. The last few weeks had been so busy that some days she sat down at her desk in the morning and didn't know where to start. Derek was in full-on mode, with Project Harrogate

85

at the forefront of his mind. He'd even called her from the golf course to ask if the PR company were making the most of 'the bathroom story'. Virginia had reassured him that they were aware of all the hotel's selling points, but then annoyed herself by calling them and checking they had included the drench showers and spa baths in their literature. The pattern seemed to be that she'd either check things had been done two or three times, much to the irritation of the designers putting together the launch brochures, or she'd forget things entirely. In fact, she'd Blu-Tacked a notepad onto the car dashboard for notes, so many random thoughts were entering her head.

This sort of stress level probably wasn't helping anything, and at the last appointment with the consultant—another fairly pointless exercise where she'd gone over the same stuff—she'd advised her to 'take it easy' and to 'try and focus on other things'. Taking it easy she wasn't, but you couldn't argue with the 'other things'.

What worried her most was that they'd slipped from 'secondary infertility' into the category of 'unexplained infertility'. 'How long should we expect to wait?' she'd asked her again and, once again, the consultant had gone over the statistics: how most couples managed to conceive within three years but a minority didn't manage it but, of those, two thirds, when they had no major underlying problem, managed it if they continued trying. 'And you must keep trying,' she'd said, like a music teacher ticking her off for lack of practice. 'Every two or three days if you can. Of course conception can get more difficult as you get older, but I am confident that you will succeed in the end. Nature has a way of sorting things out,' she'd finished kindly.

Virginia had gone back to the car with a heavy weight inside her. Nothing had ever seemed impossible if she'd tried hard enough—exams, rowing, learning to drive, work—but this seemed beyond her control.

It was bliss to be back on the river. Weekends seemed to be spent on the M6 up to Stoke. Piers always used to accompany her if he could, especially if it was school holiday time, even if he didn't always come in and see her mother. He'd drop her off and go and find a café or take a walk. He'd tease her about how he was more familiar with the town now than she'd ever been—and he was probably right. But latterly he hadn't come with her, using regattas at school, marking or 'research on the book' as an excuse. She couldn't blame him—the visits were harrowing—but she suspected that it was more that he didn't want the hours in the car in a fog of tension, unspoken recriminations and soul-searching. They would both flinch if the DJ on the radio talked about her toddler or there was some news item involving children. It was unavoidable and ridiculous to expect it any other way. Children and babies were an occupational hazard of life.

So Virginia faced the hours with her mother alone, Rosie understandably having a reprieve from dropping in. She'd try to give her the full attention she deserved but it was difficult. Taking her for a walk was out of the question now, and she seemed more and more chair-bound. Virginia had taken her new clothes on the odd occasion, but when she next went to visit they always seemed to have been put away and she'd be in yet another shapeless dress Virginia didn't recognise. When she asked the staff, they told her that 'it was easier for her to use the toilet in a loose dress', and Virginia had felt stupid for not having thought of that.

Conversation became stilted and broken. She'd chat on to her mother about the hotel and the plans for Harrogate. She even brought pictures and brochures, but she wasn't sure any of it was registering, which was all the more depressing because her mother had always been so excited by Virginia's job. 'We were never lucky enough to stay in hotels, your dad and I,' she'd say and for their thirtieth wedding anniversary, their last as it happened, Virginia had arranged for them to stay at the hotel in Chester. Her mother had called her from the room and described it all to her in detail, as if Virginia had never been there. She'd smiled at her mother's enthusiasm, not realising at the time that it was the first signs of the confusion which would deteriorate to this. There had been a growing number of 'incidents' after that—getting lost in places she knew well, forgetting people's names and where she'd put her glasses—and, days before her father's death, he'd called Virginia with his misgivings.

'Look after her,' he'd said just before he put the phone down, as if he had a premonition that he wouldn't be there for long.

Her mother would look blankly at the pictures she brought now. 'Very nice, dear,' she'd say as she handed them back. 'Is it somewhere I know?'

'No, Mum,' Virginia replied patiently. 'I told you, it's the hotel we're opening in a few weeks.'

'We never stayed in hotels, your dad and I,' she said again.

'I know you didn't, Mum.' Virginia knew what was

88

coming next, she'd heard it so often now.

'Our wedding night was at a pub just outside Uttoxeter. A lovely place. Pink candlewick bedspread and a little bunch of daisies on the dressing table. Your father carried me over the threshold.' She'd chuckle at this point and shake her head.

'And you had steak and kidney pudding for your tea, and a glass of sherry which made you feel sick.' Virginia finished for her.

'And do you know, we had steak and kidney pudding for our tea downstairs, and a glass of sherry which made me feel sick. Last time I ever touched the stuff.'

Virginia found it hard not to feel envious of Rosie, who could visit more often but didn't need to sit for great lengths of time like this, going over the same old ground. All Virginia wanted to do was lay her head on her mother's lap and tell her how unfair it was that she couldn't conceive and how it was causing a rift in her relationship with Piers, and for her mother to stroke her hair and say 'there, there, it will all come out in the wash', but how could she do that now?

'Are you doing any knitting?' she'd asked instead.

'My fingers get all muddled,' her mother explained. 'I keep dropping stitches. It's so frustrating. And besides, these reading glasses are hopeless. Can't see a thing.'

'Let me get you some better ones,' Virginia had leaped up, glad to have something constructive to do and had walked down to the chemist to buy some stronger ones in a racy pink which had made her mother laugh when she brought them back. But on her next visit they were nowhere to be seen and her mother had no recollection of them whatsoever.

Pulling up to the boat house, Virginia clambered out of the boat and pulled it out of the water, glancing at her watch. Time for a quick shower, then into the office. Wasn't she due a reprieve?

Chapter 14

June 2010

It was when Alice came upon Scarlett a couple of days later, reading on her bed, the fleece wrapped round her and the toy cat on her chest, that she realised Vince had got it absolutely right. Alice marvelled at his insight—unless it had been pure luck. She would never have had the flair to transform the room like that and would never have been so confident of her ability to anticipate Scarlett's wants. But the girl had even refused to take down the welcome home banner and she spent more time up there than downstairs with Alice. Was that normal, she wondered? Did kids take to their rooms for hours on end these days? She couldn't remember with any accuracy what eleven felt like, but she didn't remember hours of solitude. Mind you, Alice hadn't lost both parents, been taken away from everything familiar and shunted from elderly grandparents to the care of a relative stranger. But nor, the cynical part of her chipped in, had Alice owned an iPod, a Nintendo DS, a mobile phone or a laptop. Did all children have those things now? Alice had asked her friends and, whatever the age of their children, they'd all shaken their heads in shame-faced resignation—

kids today! But that wasn't good enough for Alice. Her childhood memories might be vague, and her parents no longer around to check, but she could definitely remember afternoons spent baking and decorating cupcakes—or fairy cakes as they were known then. It couldn't have been sunny all through her childhood, but her memories were: holidays to the beach, stumbling awkwardly on the pebbles as she struggled to chuck a frisbee around in the teeth of the wind; walks on Hampstead Heath; trailing round Charleston while her mother—who adored Sussex—waxed lyrical about the Bloomsbury Group and she and her father waited patiently to be allowed an ice cream.

But that was exactly it. Most of Alice's childhood memories featured her parents or her friends. As an only child, like Scarlett, she'd relied on her network of girlfriends—and later boyfriends— to give her an identity as much as she had on her parents. And Scarlett had none of that now. There wasn't even a posse of local kids she could have gradually insinuated herself into. Ulvington wasn't that type of village, as far as Alice knew. It was all couples apart from her it seemed, and a few aged widows. It wasn't a thought she cared to dwell on so, as usual, she'd thrown herself into action instead.

She'd made the call a couple of days after Scarlett arrived, inspired—if that was the right word— by the sight of her own bike, rusting forlornly at the side of the house. She hadn't gone out on it in ages; it was so much easier to jump in the car, or simply to walk to the village shop if she needed anything. But her friends in Lewes with grown-up children and a tendency to hoard had come up

91

trumps. They'd dropped a bike off one morning on their way to the supermarket, stopping in for a quick coffee and to meet Scarlett, who had been polite but not enthusiastic, and now Alice's unused bike had a companion. Had she got it right? Would Scarlett take the bait?

After breakfast the next day—pancakes with maple syrup, and the last recipe in Alice's extremely limited repertoire—she put out of her head the pressing need to finish her chapter on the East Village, and rubbed her hands together in a show of enthusiasm. 'Right. It's a lovely day—far too nice to stay indoors, so I thought we could go for a picnic ... if you like.' Alice could feel herself trailing off apologetically and pasted a cheerful smile on her face.

Scarlett's gaze flicked up from her plate, then slid away. She really didn't do eye contact all that well. 'How far?'

'Not very,' Alice laughed. 'I haven't ridden my bike in literally years. I'll probably have to pump the tyres up and do whatever you have to do to the chain. Oil it? Not even sure I've got any oil.'

Scarlett took another neat bite of pancake and finished her juice before asking, 'Why don't you ask that man up the road? The man who wears the cap. His bike's really old so he must have loads of stuff for keeping it going. Tools and things. Oil probably.'

Alice hesitated. It really wasn't the moment to explain that Walter was the most miserable old git on God's green earth, and that he'd had it in for Alice since the first day she'd moved in and the removals van had driven up on the verge outside his house and flattened his plants. 'Well, we could, I suppose, but he's probably out somewhere. I could ask him later, of course, but I was thinking I've got to go shopping later anyway, so we could drop in at the bike shop at the same time.'

Scarlett wiped the last traces of syrup with her finger, concentrating hard on her plate. 'OK. Can I have a practice outside on the lane for a bit? You know, get used to the bike.'

'Of course. I'll clear up the breakfast things. Just be careful if you hear any cars coming. You know—stay into the side, and stay on the left, won't you? Er—that's the hand you don't write with.'

The withering look Scarlett gave her made Alice momentarily grateful that eye contact was so rare an occurrence. 'I did cycling proficiency at school,' she said quietly. 'And, as a matter of fact, I'm left-handed.'

'Oh—sorry,' Alice laughed uneasily. Why hadn't she noticed? What kind of a godmother stroke temporary guardian was she? 'Well, you'll probably have to teach me about road safety, then. I think I failed cycling proficiency.'

Scarlett turned on her heel and went out through the front door. Moments later, above the clatter of the plates in the sink, Alice could hear her experimenting with the bell. She could only hope Walter hadn't turned on his hearing aid today.

Within twenty minutes, Scarlett was back in the house, looking quietly pleased with herself. 'How did it go?' Alice asked, measuring orange squash into a couple of plastic bottles for the picnic and filling them carefully with water. 'Is it like riding a bike?'

'What?'

'Oh never mind. Is it OK, the bike? Is it the right

93

height and everything?'

'Yup—everything's just right. It's a corker.'

Alice turned to look at her. That was an oddly old-fashioned expression, but rather quaint. Probably picked up from Bill and Judy. 'Well, my bike is far from being a corker, I'm afraid, so you might need to wait for me to catch up. Salt and vinegar crisps all right?'

Scarlett wrinkled up her nose. 'Can I have cheese and onion?' she asked.

Alice rummaged in the bag. 'Sorry. I'll put them on the list. Plain?'

Scarlett conceded with a shrug. 'I haven't got a helmet. I always have to wear a helmet. Mum says.'

They both froze. Alice hoped the expression on her face didn't show.

'I don't have one, I'm afraid,' she replied as evenly as she could. How stupid! She should have thought of that.

'Oh. Can we still go?'

'Yes, just try not to fall off. No hang on. I'll make some sarnies first. Will you be warm enough?'

'I'll be outside.'

Alice smiled to herself as she finished wrapping the picnic in old carrier bags before fitting it into the day sack she always used when she was travelling. This was more enthusiasm than she'd observed in Scarlett since the day she'd arrived—and although that was less than a week ago, it felt an awful lot longer. Even sharing a bathroom was a shock. Was that what it was like, being a mother? Always putting yourself last? No wonder they always looked so harassed.

Realising with a jolt that she hadn't heard the persistent ring of the bicycle bell for a few minutes,

Alice dropped the bag and listened carefully. Silence. She went outside and down the path to the road—still only the sound of birds and a far off tractor. She felt an unfamiliar wave of disquiet. But that was ridiculous. This was the safest place on earth, wasn't it? But where had Scarlett gone? What if she couldn't find her? What if she had to call Judy to tell her she'd lost her? What if she had to call the police? How embarrassing would that be? Her first week with the child and she couldn't even keep track of her! 'Scarly!' she called sharply. 'Scarly! Where are you?'

On the lane all was quiet, and the bike was nowhere in view. Alice looked up and down and called again, trying to keep the tension out of her voice. The kid couldn't have gone far, after all. She remembered a Border terrier from her childhood— one of a series her parents had owned—that would never come when called if he thought he was going to be in trouble. Oddly enough, his name had been Charlie. Who'd have guessed that looking after a dog would be good practice for looking after a tweenager? 'Scaaaarly!' she called again in a tone of utmost nonchalance.

Then she heard it. The bell—tinging away irritatingly, but oh-so-reassuringly. Relief surged through her. Relief tempered with annoyance— Alice felt like giving Scarlett a piece of her mind but, as she appeared around the corner and came steadily closer, the sight of her face reminded her so much of Ginny. That look of concentration as she cycled determinedly along, trying not to look at the gears as she changed up, and the expression of surprise as the chain leaped on the cogs. Catching her breath, Alice had to look away, staring hard

95

at a squirrel dangling from the horse chestnut tree across the road to prevent the tears from coming.

'Well done,' she said a little gruffly. 'Looks like you've got the hang of it all right. I'll just get the food and we can go.'

Scarlett was looking at her carefully. 'You weren't worried about me, were you?'

Alice paused, then forced a laugh. 'Me? No—not at all. I mean, you're eleven—not a baby. You're hardly going to wander off on your own at your age, are you? And anyway, you'd struggle to get lost round here. Now, can we get going?' She turned and walked back up the path she'd so recently raced down, feeling the pounding of her heart gradually slow. Had she played that right? She didn't want Scarlett to think she was fussing—she must have had enough of that from her grandmother—and it wasn't like she was trying to be a mother to the kid. No one could replace Ginny—and Alice wouldn't even want to try. No—she'd be more like a cool aunt or an older cousin. That would be the best kind of relationship to build. Alice hauled her bike up. It didn't look great and she hadn't found the pump to top up the tyres. Compared with Scarlett's it looked even worse than she'd realised.

'Right then,' she said with more confidence than she felt. 'Let's go. This'll be fun.' Scarlett glanced over at her uncertainly and Alice nodded reassuringly. Though who needed more reassurance was, perhaps, debatable.

*   *   *

It wasn't as much of a struggle as Alice had thought, keeping up with Scarlett, as they pedalled down the lane towards the road. It was a beautiful day with cow parsley leaning in towards them from the verges. Wood pigeons were cooing in the trees above their heads and Alice commented on them, risking pointing at one whose clapping wings caught her attention. She wobbled, then recovered, laughing as they approached the junction.

Scarlett turned to her. 'I think it would be better if we went in single file on the road. It's safer if a car wants to overtake.'

'Oh. All right. Yes, you're probably right.' Alice felt rather deflated. 'Well, you'd better go in front so I can keep an eye on you. Although you don't know the way, of course. Erm . . .'

'You haven't got a bell.' Scarlett pinged hers a few times to demonstrate. 'So you won't be able to warn me if we need to turn off. Why don't you go in front and, if I need you, I'll ring mine?'

Alice couldn't argue with her logic so she set off ahead of Scarlett, keeping in to the side of the road as much as possible. But she kept looking back to check that Scarlett was behind her, so much so that she took to pulling irritated faces at her every time and shaking her head, even going so far as to let go of the handlebars to gesture, palms upwards, in a habit Alice recognised as pure Piers. She still kept checking, though, trying to keep her surveillance down to quick glances that didn't make her wobble too much. That was far too embarrassing and making herself feel stupid in front of an eleven-year-old was a whole new experience.

When they reached the meadow where Alice had planned they would eat their picnic, her legs were trembling and there was an ache in her thighs that really didn't feel good. She hadn't been able to drop into first gear and so had struggled, forcing the pedals slowly round and wobbling all over the road while Scarlett passed her easily, long legs pumping swiftly as she climbed away in front. Alice would definitely have to get some oil. If she'd been a bit less out of breath, she'd have been more appreciative of Scarlett's uncharacteristic exuberance. As it was, she struggled to join her on the crest of the hill, horribly aware of her red face and shortness of breath.

The view that dropped away in front of them, though, took her breath away even more. It was one of Alice's favourite vantage points and, she realised, one she hadn't visited in absolutely ages. They stood there in silence for a while, side by side, Scarlett seemingly as entranced as she was. And no wonder. The sea in the distance merged almost seamlessly with the sky with the bright sunlight reflecting off, what looked from their viewpoint, its mirrored surface. Perfect little sailing boats dotted around, the colours of the sails impossible to make out, and the odd power boat left in its wake ski-like tracks in fresh snow. As she gradually got her breath back, Alice had a sudden feeling of contentment and even the ache in her legs was starting to abate.

'We could go down to the sea tomorrow, if you like. Get an ice cream, maybe.' She placed her hand gently on Scarlett's shoulder, hoping to convey the warmth she was feeling at that moment. This was good. This was how it should be. But after a brief pause—presumably what she considered the bare minimum required by politeness—Scarlett slid away, leaving Alice's hand to drop to her side.

'Don't mind. Can we eat soon so I can get back in

time for *Tracy Beaker*?'

The sandwiches hadn't travelled particularly well but Scarlett ate the crisps and pulled slices of cucumber out from between the bread to eat with her fingers. In silence, Alice pointedly ate all hers up and folded the bags up efficiently, returning them to her backpack. 'Shall we go, then?' she asked politely. Scarlett rose to her feet in a fluid motion and Alice felt her watching as she struggled up, her knees protesting. By the time she had swung the pack onto her back, Scarlett was halfway to the gate.

Alice's legs were aching terribly by the time they got home and something didn't sound at all right on her bike, but she wasn't admitting it to Scarlett. Out of sheer bloody-mindedness, she put on a burst of speed so that she arrived back at the cottage only just behind her. As she bent for the key under the pot of geraniums by the door, she noticed a child-sized helmet on the doorstep.

'Oh look,' she exclaimed, forgetting that she was supposed to be offended. 'Jess and Simon must have left it. How nice of them! I expect they found it among the kids' stuff. I must ring and thank them.'

'Let's see.' Scarlett peeped around her. 'Ohhhh! It's brilliant. This is just like mine. I described it to . . .' She trailed off as Alice turned it over and looked at the inside.

'Look, it's brand new! That's so typical of Jess— what a darling! They must have got it in town and dropped it off on their way back. Tell you what,' she said quickly, hoping to take advantage of Scarlett's uncharacteristic enthusiasm. 'Do you think you could write them a thank-you note? You could do it

99

after—erm—*Tracy Beaker*. OK?'

Scarlett looked up at her. 'I think it's actually from that nice man who lives up the road.'

'Nice man?' Alice was flummoxed.

'The one with the old bike. He oiled my chain and adjusted the seat for me.'

'Walter!'

'Yes that's right. His wife's nice too. She gave me a biscuit.'

At that Scarlett steered her bike around the side of the house, leaving Alice speechless. Moments later, she could hear that ridiculous theme tune blaring out of the TV and, with an amazed shake of her head, Alice went inside.

On her desk the answerphone was blinking and she dialled in to pick up her messages, wandering out to the kitchen to dispose of the dregs of the picnic. There was just one. 'Hi, I'm trying to get in touch with Alice Fenton. This is Greg. Greg Mullin. We met a few weeks ago at . . . Er, in Oxford. Sorry not to have called sooner—I've been away. Work stuff—you know. Anyway, I was wondering if you felt like meeting up for a coffee? I'll give you my number.' His deep voice read out the digits and she scrambled for a pen. 'And . . . er . . . Well, give me a call if you're free. OK. Bye.' He rang off.

Alice smiled at hearing his friendly voice. She hadn't expected him to call, but now she was glad he had. He'd be a good link with the past to maintain, but maybe not until Scarlett had gone back to Haywards Heath. She didn't need any more reminders just yet.

Chapter 15

April 1998

Virginia knew she shouldn't have stormed out. It was immature behaviour, but they'd both been gritty with each other for a few days now and, when she'd had the temerity to criticise his mother, Piers had snapped and shouted at her. 'You just can't let it be, can you?' he'd boomed, and she'd quickly shut the window before the neighbours heard. They had probably witnessed everything over the last few weeks but at times she was past caring. 'She's just trying to help!'

'Help?' Virginia had snarled back, all the tension and frustration of the last few months swelling up inside her. 'She just wants to control everything. It doesn't help that she "knows a man in Harley Street". We both know that our chances of having a bloody baby are, at the best, remote and the people at the John Radcliffe are just as clever and skilled and . . .'

'But why won't you let her talk to him?' Piers had run his hands through his hair.

'Because he won't be any more help than they were at King's. We don't qualify for IVF on the NHS—you know what they say about secondary infertility—and we can't afford to pay. Simple as that.'

'We could try. You know Mum and Dad have even . . .'

Virginia put her hand up. 'No way. If they pay for us to get treatment and I get pregnant, she'll never let us forget it. It'll be *her* success and she'll take ownership, like she does with everything.'

'Oh for fuck's sake, don't be ridiculous.'

'Piers, she can't face the fact that we've failed in some way. Everything in her bloody life is perfect and, if it isn't, she'll find someone who'll make it perfect. Someone,' Virginia threw her arm out, casting for an example. 'Someone on the Bench, or at the cricket club. Some Old Wykehamist,' she spat out the words, 'who once met someone who knows about these things. She comments on my house, my clothes, my job—do you know she even rang that new hotel near Banbury the other day to see if they had any *part-time* marketing posts 'cause she thinks I should go part-time! I'm not having her rule every part of our lives!'

'It's only because she *cares*!' Piers smacked his hand on the top of the table. 'Why do you reject everything she does?'

'God, you're such a mummy's boy!' Virginia hurled back and that was when she slammed out of the flat.

She kicked the bin on the pavement which was waiting for tomorrow's collection and, drawing her thin cardigan around her at the cool April air, she stomped off down the road. Her immediate reaction was to call Alice to have a self-pitying rant, but she'd forgotten her phone, which annoyed her even more. She couldn't even recall what had started this fight, but all she knew was that it had become a familiar pattern. They'd even rowed recently about who'd spent what on the credit card, an area of life they'd never fallen out about before.

And it was all about the baby. The Baby with a capital B. The only thing their lives now focused on.

102

Virginia walked faster. There was sod all chance she'd get pregnant anyway. You had to have sex, didn't you? They couldn't have had any for at least a month. Instead, one of them would wait until the other went to bed and was safely asleep before following.

There had been an awkward moment a few nights earlier over post-supper coffee with friends. They'd all been, or still were, members of the rowing club, and had attended each other's weddings. Tom and Sue now had a two-year-old and were expecting their second and, as Sue had suppressed a yawn, talk had turned to kids and how exhausting they were.

'I've given up trying to get my leg over,' Tom had teased his wife, gently rubbing his hand on her knee.

'I'm permanently knackered,' Sue had replied. 'Carrying this monster and chasing after Josh.'

'What's your excuse?' Piers had said loudly to Virginia and, for a moment, there had been a painful silence around the table.

'It's hard bloody work doing what Virginia does, isn't it?' Robin had chipped in quickly. A bear of a man and a fellow teacher at Piers' school, with a petite wife and robust eight-month-old, Virginia had always liked him. 'And why the hell would she want an ape like you mauling her after a long day anyway?'

On another occasion Piers would have laughed at this but that night he simply emptied his glass and topped it up again with the last of the bottle, which he'd got through on his own. The conversation had moved away to something about the Northern Ireland talks, everyone trying to defuse the charged atmosphere, but Virginia had a strong sense, which had grown over recent months that lately, whenever they were with friends, people tried to avoid the subject of children out of sympathy. She'd find herself going over the top with questions about their offspring, though the pain of asking made her heart ache, and the discovery, after a slip from Robin's wife Jan, whom she'd met in the Covered Market a few weeks ago, that there had been a couple of dinner parties that she and Piers had been excluded from made her feel more inadequate and self-pitying than ever.

Alice tried to be sweet and understanding but how could she understand? She was the only woman Virginia had ever met who actively did not want children. It had brought a couple of her more hopeful-looking relationships to an end and one lovely man, an art restorer, would have been perfect for Alice—he even tolerated her unreliability— but had eventually left when he'd given up hoping Alice would cave in. Alice's technique for dealing with Virginia's pain was to divert her with spa days or silly gifts in the post—well-meant but a woefully inadequate bandage for the open wound Virginia was carrying everywhere with her.

She must have walked for an hour and had looped back to the shops in Summertown before she slowed her pace, and realised how dark and cold it was now, so she turned on her heel and, head down to avoid encountering anyone, she headed back to the flat, letting herself in quietly. The clock on the cooker told her it was after eleven and Piers had apparently gone to bed, leaving all the lights off and his tea cup on the side as usual. Irritated, she put it in the dishwasher and slammed

104

the door shut more violently than she intended, breaking a glass. By the time she was lying beside him, his breathing too deep for sleep so she knew he was pretending, it had gone midnight and it took her another half an hour to calm down.

Late nights were the last thing she needed too. The pace of work had been cranked up even more as the team prepared for the launch of The Dales in Harrogate. All the press releases had gone out, and Virginia was trying to pin down the printer to make sure the brochures were there by D-day. They weren't ideal—a last-minute job thrown together using a mixture of stock images—tasteful close-ups of lamps and crisp linen pillowcases—and the few pictures she'd managed to have taken of the hotel by creating little 'sets'. Beyond the edges of the picture there had been carpenters, electricians and plumbers falling over each other as they put in the final touches, fixing lights, and tiling shower cubicles. The furniture had arrived but was still wrapped tantalisingly in thick polythene until it was safe to unveil it, so she'd had to improvise spectacularly.

When she came back from a grabbed lunch in the kitchens, there were two messages from Head Office and she knew Derek would now be on the daily hassle as the launch approached. His ability to put on the pressure, whilst ignoring any constraints caused by others, made Virginia want to scream more than ever. There were even two emails from him, one asking when he'd have brochures 'in his hand' and the other confirming details of the soft launch staff stay-over at the weekend. Virginia's heart sank. It would be like the office party, only without the tinsel. She'd already had one hundred per cent take up from the invitation to key staff to be there—all keen to have an envious peek at the new flagship hotel which made their properties seem tired in comparison, not to mention a free night away from work with someone else doing the waiting and the worrying.

The design team would be there too, a prestigious London firm that Derek had hired on recommendation. According to their website, the company had handled projects from New York to Dubai, all cutting-edge glass and steel hotels from what Virginia could tell, and she felt nervous about what they'd do with Victorian splendour in Harrogate. As she ran through her copy and press packs again, she just hoped the polythene-wrapped furniture was as good as everyone anticipated.

'How was it?' she asked Piers when he got home. She'd got back late and was finishing off the last mouthful of a risotto from M&S. She hadn't even changed out of her work dress. The school holidays were in full flow and he'd been down to see his parents for the day. It was Bill's birthday and, though she'd like to have celebrated with him, she was grateful that she hadn't had to accompany Piers, using the impending launch as an excuse. She wasn't sure she could stomach the prospect of Judy right now.

'OK. He loved the shirt.'

'Good. Mum OK?'

'What do you care?' Piers had now pulled his rucksack out from the chaotic mess under the stairs and was starting to sort clothes for a school trip to the Somme.

She let it pass. 'When are you back?'

'Sunday, late,' he grunted back.

106

'OK. I'll be back Sunday morning.'

'Whatever.' He pulled some underpants from the towering pile of ironing. 'Any chance any of this could be ironed?'

'Iron it your fucking self!' she shouted. 'You're the one with the time at the moment. Why should I do it?'

''Cause it might be something about being a woman that you *can* manage,' he said quietly, and left the room.

Eyes stinging now with tears of outrage, fury and disbelief, Virginia's heart raced, then she went through to their bedroom. Ignoring Piers, she barged past him, threw some underclothes and her wash things into her bag and, grabbing her car keys, she slammed the door of the flat so hard she cracked the pane of glass in the fanlight.

Chapter 16

June 2010

In her room, Alice spoke quietly into the phone. This was ridiculous—Scarlett was so glued to the telly, she probably wouldn't hear an atomic bomb going off. 'Thing is, Vince, I could really do with reinforcements. I don't know what to do with her. I don't think she even likes me and I've got to get some work done.'

'Oh get real, Alice. Of course she likes you. What's not to like? You're adorable.'

Alice laughed grimly. 'Yeah, well, normally flattery would get you everywhere but this is something of an emergency. I mean, the only thing she seems to like is going out alone on her bike. Only round the village, of course, dropping in on geriatric neighbours and eating all their biscuits, but I can't really concentrate 'cause I'm kind of worrying about where she is.'

'Awww—that's so cute. My little Alice, all grown up and acting maternal.'

'Do you mind!' she retorted. 'What a repulsive idea! Anyway, I was thinking, could you come over and meet her, then maybe—I don't know—take her out for a walk or take her out to the cinema or something, just so I can get this last batch of stuff finished? I've been staying up late to do it, but she gets up so early and that means I have to as well.'

'Oh stop whining, you big baby. Uncle Vince will sort it out—as usual. Have you 'fessed up that it was me that did her room out? Or are you stealing my thunder?'

'Well ... Oh, come on, Vince. I need all the credit I can get with this one. And I'm the guardian, not you. So—could you come over later, before you go to work, or whatever you call shaking your tail-feathers in the spotlight? We could play scrabble? *Not* the rude version.'

Vince sighed theatrically. 'If you absolutely insist. And I'll bring Kriss, if you like. Camouflage— Scarly will never guess. And before you ask, I'll dress as straight as straight can be. I'm sure I've got some drab, ill-fitting trousers and a boooooring polo shirt.'

'Oh, Vince,' Alice giggled. 'I think it would take more than ill-fitting trousers to make you look straight!'

'You say the nicest things, honey. Tell you what,

108

just for that, I'll make supper. Pasta OK?'

'Lovely. I've got pesto but you'll need to bring everything else.'

'I'll bring pesto too, just to be on the safe side. Last time I looked in your fridge, everything had a little green beard. See you later then—around eight?'

Alice sighed. 'Could you make it earlier? You have to feed kids by seven, at the very latest, apparently.'

'Riiiight. This is going to take some getting used to. Does that mean they don't drink mojitos either?'

'Definitely not! Come on, Vince. Man up! I'm relying on you to be the sensible one.'

'Then, my dear, we are all completely fucked!'

'See you later,' Alice laughed and hung up the phone. Suddenly, things didn't seem so bad. She flopped back on her bed. If the choices had been *either* looking after Scarlett or working, she probably could have managed it. Just about. But doing both was totally messing with her head. She realised, with a sinking feeling, that what she needed was some kind of routine. How depressingly sensible that sounded. Was this what it had been like for Ginny? Alice tried to remember the things Ginny had said early on in motherhood, admitting guiltily that it wasn't all roses. That had seemed obvious to Alice but Ginny obviously felt that, after such a struggle to get pregnant in the first place, she wasn't allowed to complain or even admit how bloody knackering it all was. She had Piers to help, of course, and even Judy bustled in to hold the fort sometimes, though her methods were probably very old school.

And now Alice had to fit it all in too. What

troubled her more than this balancing act, though, was Scarlett's calmness. Alice didn't know her well enough to judge, but she seemed spookily buttoned down and detached for someone who'd lost her parents. What would a psychologist make of it? Would they encourage Alice to 'draw her out'? Or was Scarlett simply not trusting enough of Alice to show her feelings? There had been a moment the other morning when Scarlett had gone upstairs suddenly and had come down some time later, red-eyed, but hadn't responded when Alice gently rubbed her back, not daring to hug her, and asked if she was OK. She simply went rigid at her touch.

The thought of the child lying lonely and heart-broken in her bed was excruciating for Alice, but she couldn't see a way through. She sighed heavily and went downstairs to rejoin Scarlett who was flicking through a book, curled up on the sofa.

'Right,' Alice rubbed her hands together. She realised she had developed a habit of phoney enthusiasm whenever she spoke to Scarlett, rather like a hockey teacher trying to jolly-up her team. 'Some friends are coming over later. I thought you might like to meet them. We can have supper— pasta all right?—and maybe play Scrabble.' The look on Scarlett's face said it all. 'Or not. Anyhow . . . I need to get on with some work today so I was wondering what you felt like—'

Scarlett was up in a flash. 'I could go out on my bike for a bit and see Walter. He said I can help him with his veg patch and he'll show me how to tie up the runner beans.'

Alice tried to conceal her relief. 'Great idea. Can you make sure you're back in time for lunch? And keep your phone switched on this time—'

The door banged closed behind her. 'Please,' she finished, to an empty room.

The next few hours worked out better than Alice had hoped. She managed to finish the final edits and looked over the layouts the designer had sent over. She'd even been able to make some suggestions that had gone down really well—and all before lunch. Scarlett had been surprisingly sweet when she came in and had come over to look at the screen, asking questions about New York and Alice's trip there, although clearly dissatisfied that Alice didn't know how much Abercrombie joggers (whatever they were) cost.

In the afternoon Alice tidied up and did the laundry for both her and Scarlett, who seemed to get through clothes at an alarming rate. She'd asked Alice to launder the little floral skirt she'd worn to the funeral as quickly as possible. Alice didn't ask, but clearly this skirt was of some significance, like a wearable security blanket. Then they went to the supermarket together for groceries and Alice entrusted her with choosing two flavours of ice cream for dessert for that evening. From Scarlett's reaction, Alice had a sneaky feeling that this was a treat she hadn't often experienced, but the girl deserved it, didn't she?

The rest of the afternoon passed quietly but, thankfully, at six thirty on the dot, the doorbell rang and, on the doorstep, behind a huge bunch of larkspurs, stood Vince, in a tight striped cotton shirt and chinos. Kriss, in her usual mixture of drapey layers, her hair bright from a recent henna session, was standing next to him.

Feeling oddly formal, Alice made the introductions. 'Right, Scarly, meet Vince and Kriss. Krissy, Vince—this is Scarly.'

Vince extended his hand with military crispness. 'Delighted to meet you, Scarly,' he said gruffly, in what he clearly thought was an extremely heterosexual tone. Kriss, in her turn, enveloped her in a huge hug from which a furious little voice could be heard.

'Actually, my name's Scarlett. I absolutely *hate* being called Scarly.'

Kriss quickly released her and there was a stunned silence at her outburst. Scarlett stared from one to the other, then turned and ran upstairs.

'OK,' Vince said eventually. 'That went well.'

Chapter 17

April 1998

The aroma of fresh paint and new wood hit Virginia's nose even before she pushed through the rotating doors of the Harrogate hotel. The reception area was a buzz of activity like something from a Laurel and Hardy film, with workmen walking in all directions in hard hats and high-vis vests with lengths of skirting board over their shoulders, dodging the painters up ladders adding the finishing touches to the Victorian cornicing. The potential for slapstick-style disaster was tangible.

Virginia felt a flutter of excitement despite her mood as she took in the ebony black low tables and lime-green, oversized sofas with their sweeping backs, like something from Alice in Wonderland. The effect was achingly stylish and contemporary, yet relaxing and fresh. And not Virginia's taste at all.

'Wow!' Virginia gasped to Lorraine, the head receptionist, who'd been poached from their nearest competitor, a corporate four-star on the other side of town. Her credentials were faultless, but Virginia hoped she'd show more charm towards the guests than she did towards her colleagues.

'Oh that,' she batted her hand uninterestedly. 'It's been a bloody nightmare getting everything in, especially those ridiculous sofas. They had to come in through the ballroom, and even then the builders had to take the sodding doors off.' She rifled through her papers on the desk in the back office as Virginia put down her overnight bag. 'And now I can't find the bloody new key fobs, and that pillock they've taken on as a night porter is as good as ruddy useless.' The phone chirruped on the desk next to her and she snatched up the receiver. 'The Dales Hotel, this is Lorraine speaking,' she cooed softly. 'Can I help you? Yes, yes of course, no problem. I'll pass on the message.'

She dropped down the phone and reverted to normality. 'That was the idiot designers responsible for the sofas. They are in a meeting which has overrun and they'll be later than "anticipated",' she mimicked the voice of the PA on the other end of the line. 'Fuck me,' she blurted, looking at Virginia for the first time. 'You looked buggered.'

Virginia felt it but didn't want reminding of it. She had barely slept last night after her row with Piers, crawling into bed in a room at the hotel in Oxford, ignoring the suspicious expression of the night porter who had checked her in. The marketing manager turning up late with an overnight bag asking for a room, when she lived only a couple of miles away, was highly irregular, after all. By the time she dropped by home earlier in the day before leaving for Harrogate, Piers had left, leaving washing up and a mess of packing behind him, and she'd thrown her work clothes into a bag and left the flat as quickly as she could. Then she'd cried all the way to Harrogate, making her progress up the motorway treacherous at times. Clearly her repair job in the car park hadn't been good enough.

'Thanks for that. It's been a busy week. Look, any sign of the brochures?'

'Nope.'

'Shit.' Virginia glanced at her watch. They'd promised her they'd be there by lunchtime. 'Keep an eye out for them, will you? I'll go and check everything's in order for the party. Can I dump my bag in my room?'

Virginia barely had time to take in the decor of her bedroom, except to note that it was beautifully new and luxurious, before she was back downstairs. There was something quite appealing about being the first person to sleep in the bed. Though she was in the business, Virginia tried not to think too hard about the concept of sleeping in a room that had been occupied by hundreds before her. It sometimes struck her as odd that people paid money to use a loo or shower that so many others had used, let alone lay their head on a pillow that someone else had dribbled on. In fact, the idea was so bizarre that she tried not to dwell on it too much. What people tended to get up to in hotel rooms was almost too unbearable to contemplate.

The rest of the afternoon was spent frantically preparing for the party, which was due to start at six. The idea was that they would welcome the local press and dignitaries for a 'soft' opening and, once they'd dispatched them off into the night, the staff, the group general managers from the sister hotels, Derek, the chairman, and the designers associated with the refurbishment would enjoy dinner, putting the new chef through his paces, and have a moment's respite before the hotel officially re-opened for business in forty-eight hours.

Virginia was still adjusting her dress—a wrap-around, clingy number that she hoped didn't display too much cleavage—as she walked down the sweeping stairs, like a latter-day Scarlett O'Hara, trying not to turn her ankle on her ridiculously high shoes as she went. Her make-over had been reduced to a five-minute repair job; removing the mascara that had slid down her face and quickly re-applying the basics. All she'd wanted was a shower and the chance to blow-dry her hair into some kind of style, but instead it looked fluffy and chaotic. As she reached the bottom step, the first guests started to emerge through the revolving doors, and she had already greeted the mayor and the editor of the local newspaper before she had time to grab her name label and pin it on her dress.

Within fifteen minutes the reception and lounge were buzzing with local dignitaries and VIPs, including a few faces from Yorkshire TV and a locally filmed soap opera, all keen to have a nose at the new-look hotel, and be seen doing it. Cameras flashed as people grinned for the society page photographers, and the beautifully arranged canapés were disappearing fast. Whatever shenanigans had gone on all afternoon behind the scenes, the chef had managed to pull the proverbial culinary rabbit out of the hat. Virginia's face hurt from smiling after a while and as she introduced people, she started to feel exhausted by how often she'd repeat the company line about 'flagship properties', 'high-end product' etc. The brochures, hastily stuffed into goody bags and fanned out on the tables dotted about the room looked sensational, she was relieved to see, even if they had arrived a little late to the feast. She was trying to concentrate on a long, tedious story from a quietly spoken local gentleman about the history of the hotel when Derek arrived at her elbow.

'Sorry to drag away this lovely lady,' he said rather brusquely to the local historian, an intense little man in tweed who was just getting onto the bit about the discovery of the sulphur spas in Harrogate. 'Virginia, come and meet the design team who've just arrived.'

Virginia, unaware of how hard she'd been concentrating, swung round and nearly lost her balance. She looked down at the empty glass in her hand and couldn't recall how many times it had been topped up. She had eaten nothing all day, except a disgusting square of carrot cake grabbed at a motorway service station, and her head was swimming alarmingly.

'Get a grip,' she chided herself and started to follow Derek through the throng before being waylaid by a tall, imposing woman who grabbed her arm. She bore a remarkable resemblance to Princess Fiona in *Shrek*. After sundown.

'Virginia, isn't it? I'm from …' She mentioned

116

a design publication based in Leeds. 'Can we have a quick chat about the vision for the hotel? I'm thinking of doing a feature on Victoriana. A reaction to contemporary minimalism.'

Virginia arranged to send information to her, then had a cursory look for the design team before speaking to the mayor and going through to the kitchen to check that everything was ready for dinner. In the process, she must have downed another two glasses of champagne and was running on nervous energy and two smoked salmon canapés hastily grabbed from a passing tray. The early guests had completed their tours and had started to get the hint the party was over, and Virginia said goodbye to the last straggler before checking if there was any change to the text silence resolutely being maintained by Piers. Perhaps he'd fallen in a trench. Or was just being a bastard. Instead there was a text from Judy, perfectly spelt, asking if Piers was OK because he'd 'sounded upset earlier'. By then the restaurant manager had already announced dinner was served and the remaining party had made their way through to the restaurant, a magnificent room with a glass ceiling and stained-glass panels, ornate marquetry and stone pillars. It was alive with chatter as Virginia walked in and had been laid out with one vast table, Derek holding court with loud pomposity at the end. Virginia did a quick head-count to check the numbers were right, then, spotting the empty space for her, slipped onto the chair between the general manager of the group's Chester hotel, and a dark-haired man she didn't recognise.

'Hi, I'm Virginia,' she put her hand out. 'I'm in charge of marketing. I'm sorry, I don't know your

117

name.'

'I'm—' His reply disappeared beneath Derek who, at that moment, had stood up, a full glass of champagne in his hand, and launched into a five-minute self-congratulatory speech about the hotel, the company, and his role in its success. Virginia had demolished two bread rolls, hoping that they would stop her stomach rumbling by the time he wound up with 'a toast to the success of The Dales and if we don't make a profit in the first year, you're all fired,' to which everyone guffawed dutifully.

'Peckish?' the man beside her asked quietly, his eyes sparkling with amusement, and Virginia acknowledged somewhere in her addled brain how attractive he was. Dark wavy hair, dark eyebrows and blue eyes—that very appealing Irish colouring.

'Bloody famished,' she confided quietly. 'It's been a busy day. Everybody and everything has conspired against me—people being late, brochures being late, chefs bickering. Frankly, I can't wait till everyone buggers off!' She could feel her tongue loosening as she spoke, but she knew he wasn't Head Office, so what the hell? 'I ought to know, but what do you do?'

'I—'

'Virginia? Can I have a moment?' Lorraine was at her shoulder. 'There's a call from the local paper. Can they have a quote, 'cause they have space in tomorrow's edition to give the opening a mention?'

Virginia sighed, excused herself, and made her way through to reception. The starters were being cleared away by the time she had finished the mini-interview, emailed some images over, and gone for a much-needed pee.

'Oh damn,' she muttered as she sat down and took in her empty mat.

'Oh, you're back. I tried to save you some but they whisked it away.' Her neighbour smiled apologetically.

'I'm not moving again!' she laughed, almost ready to weep with hunger now. 'Perhaps I can have two puddings to make up for it!' She wasn't called again, and as she devoured the beef main course and the panna cotta and rhubarb dessert, she could feel herself beginning to unwind. The man beside her was good company and they talked about rowing—he knew nothing about it—holidays in the Algarve and favourite meals (his steak and chips, hers Italian). He asked her about her job and seemed genuinely interested in the answers. He also asked about her mother and growing up in Stoke, and, in an orgy of self-pity and exhaustion, she just wittered on; her job was done, she'd engineered a great launch party, Derek was happy, they'd be all over the press for the next few weeks, her husband was being a bastard and was sulking with a group of little boys somewhere on the Western Front, she had a nosey interfering mother-in-law and, frankly, she deserved this. A moment to be someone else.

And so it was that, at two in the morning, she found herself alone with this handsome stranger in the lounge, everyone else having weaved drunkenly to bed. She didn't feel drunk now, despite the glass of port she'd just finished, and he certainly didn't seem it. She felt mellow and she felt sexy, and she thought he was gorgeous and, for the first time in months, she sensed someone else thought she was too.

*   *   *

She was up and dressed too early for anyone other than the night porter to be around, and with no guests and no receptionist until eight thirty, she had the place to herself. Making her excuses on a hastily written note which she left on the GM's desk, she headed out to her car and drove blindly back down the motorway.

She worked frantically for the remainder of the day and the day after, and exhausted herself by rowing for an hour after work each day. Anything rather than think about Piers' imminent return. She was sleeping when he crept into their bedroom that night. She tensed as he woke her and listened, half-asleep, as he pottered around the room undressing, trying not to make too much noise and swearing under his breath.

His body was cold as he slipped under the sheets, and the familiar smell of him filled her nostrils. He hesitated for a moment, then slipped an arm across her body. She tensed involuntarily.

'Gin, I'm so sorry, darling,' he whispered. 'What I said was unforgivable.'

Unable to speak, she turned towards him and slipped her body around his, wrapping her warm legs around his cold ones and, in an attempt to turn back the clock, started to make love to him.

Chapter 18

The morning after Vince and Krissy's visit, Scarlett was downstairs earlier than usual. Alice could hear the stairs creak as she went down, not her usual two-at-at-time gallop, but quietly. Almost furtive. The plate of pasta that Vince had quietly left outside her bedroom door had disappeared by the time Alice had gone up to bed, still reeling after the outburst. That had to be a good sign, didn't it? But despite the reassurance of her friends during the rather subdued evening that she should just leave well alone, and let Scarlett calm down—that tantrums and tempers were usual at her age, especially in her circumstances—Alice hadn't slept well. Consequently, this morning she was shattered and drifted off into a doze, despite her best intentions.

When she finally woke, it was after nine and she sat up guiltily, an unpleasant thudding feeling in her chest. Downstairs, Scarlett was watching television and didn't acknowledge her presence so Alice slipped into the kitchen while she thought of what to say. She looked round, screwing up her eyes and trying to remember how she'd left things last night. She remembered waving away Vince's concerned offer of help. 'It's fine,' she'd said, over-enunciating the way she always did after a few drinks. 'You've done enough, Vinny. I'll do it in the morning—honest.' Krissy had looked relieved and the two of them had eventually left with hugs and reassurances, promises to call, kisses and confirmation that she *was* a good person, that she *was* doing fine and that everything *would* be OK. And the kitchen had been a mess, with the plates stacked by the sink and glasses jostling on the counter.

Now, everything was gone and the surfaces, although dripping with water and suds, were clear. Alice rubbed her face hard. This was the last thing she expected.

'Erm, Scarlett,' she called quietly.

'Uh-huh?'

'Did you come down and do all this clearing up?' Stupid question, she realised, but she couldn't think of what else to say.

'Uh-huh.' It was hard to tell from two syllables, but there seemed to be a conciliatory note in Scarlett's voice.

Alice leaned in the doorway and looked at the back of Scarlett's head. 'Wow!'

Silence.

'Just—wow! Thank you, Scarlett.'

A tiny dip of her head. 'I liked that pasta.'

'Vince is a great cook.'

A long pause.

'Is he married to Krissy?'

'Er—no.'

'Is he gay?'

'Er, yes he is, as a matter of fact.'

'Thought so.'

Another long pause.

'Have you had any breakfast, Scarlett?' Alice was aware that she was using her name far more than was necessary. 'Can I make you—I dunno—some pancakes? It's the least I can do, after you've done all this clearing up. It was so kind of you.' Stop gushing, Alice.

122

'Could I have some toast?'

'Coming right up.'

It was excruciating. They were pussyfooting round each other like a couple after their first fight. Alice made far more noise than she needed, clanking the knife onto the plate and closing the fridge door so hard it rattled all the jars. She put the toast and a glass of juice on a tray and took it through.

'Here you are. Scarlett, could you turn that off, just for a sec. Or down, anyway.'

She complied immediately, with no sigh or tut. This was serious.

'Look, I just wanted to say sorry about the Scar— about your name. I didn't realise . . .'

'No, I'm sorry. I should have said. I just—I don't know.'

'It's all right. I do understand. Well, I mean, I don't, but it must be so hard for you. You do know, don't you, that if you ever want to talk about it, about Mum and Dad . . . ?'

Scarlett swivelled quickly away from her and turned the television back on, pressing the switch to turn up the volume. But not before Alice had seen the look of sheer terror enter her eyes. She stayed on the chair next to her for a few moments while she started to eat her toast, then slowly got to her feet. It was still too soon. Still far too soon.

*　　　*　　　*

Alice was eyeing her laptop longingly when the phone rang the next day. Scarlett, cross-legged on the sofa, singing along tunelessly with her iPod, didn't even hear it and, eyes tightly closed, didn't seem to notice Alice reaching across her to lift the receiver.

'Yullo.'

'Hello, darling. May I speak to Scarlett, please?'

'Vince?'

'Yup—is she there?'

'Well, yes—but . . .'

'Then put her on—go on. I haven't got all day, y'know.'

'What *are* you up to?'

She could practically hear him smiling in that infuriatingly smug way he had. 'That's for me to know and you to drive yourself crazy trying to guess. Are you still behind with your work?'

'You know it!'

'Then put tiny on and let Uncle Vincey solve all your problems.'

''K,' Alice replied cautiously. 'Scarlett,' she said softly and, getting no response whatsoever, leaned over and tugged out one of the earplugs. 'It's for you.'

Scarlett hesitated and pulled the other earplug out before taking the handset from Alice's hand. 'Hullo? Oh—hello. Yes. Er, no. Er, I think so. I'll ask.' She turned, and covered the mouthpiece as she whispered (unnecessarily), 'It's your friend Vince from last night. He wants to know if I want to go shopping with him later on. What should I say?'

Good old Vince. 'Well, it is what he does best—after cooking. Do you *want* to go shopping?'

Scarlett shrugged, but was starting to smile. 'Dunno—it seems a bit weird. Do you mind?'

What was the best way to reply? 'No, I don't mind at all. I mean, provided you want to.'

Scarlett was thinking. 'I suppose I could. Would we just go to boring grown-up shops?'

124

Alice snorted. 'I doubt it very much. *You'll* probably end up being the sensible one. Just don't let him have too many sweets. It makes him terribly hyper.'

Scarlett widened her eyes and Alice wondered if she'd gone too far. 'Not really,' she hurried on. 'But he does have a taste for ice cream. Anyway, you haven't been into Brighton yet. It's a great place—there's really nowhere else like it. Go on—you deserve a treat.'

Scarlett turned away again and spoke quickly into the phone. 'Yes, she says that's fine. Can we go somewhere I can get a magazine?' She glanced at Alice. 'It's one I normally get.' There was a brief hesitation. 'I mean, I used to get.'

There was a silence as Scarlett listened intently and nodded several times. 'Yes please. What time, again? All right. Bye-bye. See you in a bit.'

She replaced the phone, then turned to Alice, her face slightly flushed. 'He says he wants me to help him choose some summer clothes for his holiday. He'll be here in half an hour. Am I all right like this?' She indicated the wholesome cotton shorts and T-shirt that had still been new when she arrived. Clearly supplied by Judy.

'Provided you've got comfortable shoes, you'll be fine. Vince is rather picky about what he wears and he'll have you tramping all over town before he makes his mind up.' Alice couldn't help wondering if asking an eleven-year-old for help selecting a wardrobe for his yearly trip to Mykonos was one of Vince's very best ideas.

'Alice, I'm eleven. I don't have anything *but* comfortable shoes,' Scarlett retorted irritably, sounding scarily like Judy. There was a moment's silence, during which Alice resisted the temptation

125

to laugh.

'Fair point,' she said, at last. 'But that's a good idea at your age. I mean, you don't want to be wearing stiletto heels, do you?'

Scarlett shrugged and pursed her lips, and Alice saw her glance down at the dusty espadrilles she'd brought back from Seville and had been wearing around the house ever since. Maybe she wasn't the best person to be giving out fashion advice. 'Here— let me give you some money. Erm—is twenty quid enough?' From Scarlett's wide-eyed reaction, she realised it was far too much, but she could hardly change her mind now and she handed the note over. With the prospect of a clear afternoon of work ahead, it was a very fair exchange.

Scarlett scampered off upstairs and by the time Vince arrived (still, Alice was amused to note, dressed as a raging heterosexual), Alice had arranged her notes into bundles and revved up her laptop, ready to go. Was it her imagination though, or did Scarlett seem rather pinker in the cheeks when she came down again? And she did seem to be keeping her face turned away as she went outside to wait while Vince and Alice exchanged hugs and made arrangements for getting her home. Looking over his shoulder as they hugged yet again, her suspicions were confirmed. Scarlett was wearing make-up and lots of it—foundation a couple of shades too dark, mascara definitely, doll-like splotches of blusher and some lip gloss that made it look as though she'd been eating strawberry jam with a ladle.

'Bloody hell, Vince. Don't let her out of your sight, will you?'

Vince glanced over at the girl, then suppressed a snort of laughter. 'She looks like she's been Tangoed!

She must have inherited her maquillage skills from her godmother.'

'Oi, cheeky! I know you're doing me a favour, but you can't get away with that kind of insult, y'know. I shall take my revenge and I'll refuse to wax your back next time you ask.'

Vince pulled a face, then strode out to where Scarlett was waiting, booming in his most manly tones. 'Right then—let's be off. Brighton, she awaits us and Brighton, she does not like to be kept waiting!'

Alice hovered at the door, waving goodbye, then let out a sigh of relief and turned back to her work.

* * *

Four hours later, Alice had finished it, sent it off, hung a load of washing on the line and put another load in, eaten some chocolate spread straight off the spoon, cut her toenails, made and drunk a pot of tea, emptied her handbag of receipts and even sorted out her recycling. If they didn't get back soon, there'd be a real danger of her doing some ironing. It was most peculiar—she'd never had any trouble amusing herself at home before and had relished the solitude and quiet once she closed the door of her cottage. Now she felt restless and kept checking through the front window if she saw any movement outside. When, at last, she heard the unmistakeable rumble of Vince's ancient Beetle—he really should get that exhaust looked at—she rushed to the door to greet the returning shoppers, relieved to see that they were chatting quite amiably as they came up the path and realising only now how anxious she'd been that they might not get on.

'Well—have you had fun?'

Scarlett glanced at Vince conspiratorially. 'Brilliant,' she sighed. 'But I'm shagged out now.'

'I *beg* your pardon?'

Vince shrugged helplessly. 'Sorry, petal. It must just have popped out.' Clearly he'd allowed the hetero act to slip, somewhat. 'But she's right—we've been *everywhere*! Any chance of a cuppa?'

Alice stood back to let them troop past and eyed their shopping bags with interest. 'OK, but only if you talk me through everything you've bought.'

They each flopped into an armchair and Alice bustled off into the kitchen, feeling oddly pleased. The murmur of conversation between Vince and Scarlett was indecipherable as the kettle started to boil, but it sounded contented enough. Alice tipped a few ginger nuts onto a plate and hurried out with a tray bearing two mugs of tea for herself and Vince and a glass of milk for Scarlett. 'So, where did you go? The Lanes?'

Scarlett tutted. 'No,' she said dismissively. 'That's only for tourists. Well, we walked through, obviously—'cause we had to see the front and the pier and everything. You have to, really, don't you?'

Alice tried to conceal a smile at Scarlett's blasé tone and her precise trotting out of what Vince had obviously told her. She was talking like a real Brighton girl! 'No, we started off in North Laine. That's Laine with an i. It was amazing. And we went to this brilliant place called Lick.'

Alice shot a startled look at Vince. There were some pretty explicit shops around there, but he smiled back sanctimoniously. 'Frozen yoghurt, as a matter of fact. To the pure, all things are pure. Haven't I ever taken you there? We must put that right, mustn't we, Scarlett? Too yummy!' The gruff

128

voice had gone and he was back in full-camp mode. 'I had banana and peanut butter flavour with white chocolate sprinkles. Madam here had honey flavour with honeycomb, mango and macaroons on top. Then she decided she hated macaroons and muggins had to scrape them all off and eat them! Honestly, the things I do for you.' He turned to Scarlett in mock annoyance and she giggled happily.

Scarlett continued. 'Then we went through the Lanes and it was really crowded. The shops are really expensive there and it was all antiques and boring stuff like that. It was all right, though. I got my magazine.' She indicated vaguely at the bags still clustered at their feet. 'Then we went to New Look. It's huuuuge. Much bigger than the one in Oxford.'

'Huge,' Vince agreed. 'We were there ages.'

'Did you have enough money? What did you get?'

Scarlett giggled again. '*I* hardly got anything—just some shorts and T-shirts in the sale and stuff. Look! They almost always have sales there—it's brilliant.'

'I *so* agree,' Vince explained. 'I bought stacks of stuff. So cheap! So catwalk!'

Alice sipped her tea. 'Right, so did you get what you needed for your holiday, then?'

'Mmmm—mostly. Flip-flops—can't go wrong with them. T-shirts, some baggy shorts—bit too baggy, to be honest, but they might come in handy for travelling—a hat, some sunglasses, a belt. The only thing left is some swimmers—but I'm holding out for Speedos. I hate those loose ones. So uncomfy! So dangly!'

'Vince!'

He covered his mouth in horror, but Scarlett was engrossed in her magazine. They exchanged glances over her head; Alice's outraged, Vince's apologetic, and lapsed into silence for a while. But not for long.

'And then we went to MAC.'

Scarlett looked up. 'Yes, it was brilliant! All those little eye shadows. It was like a paint box. And Vince and the lady worked out what mineral foundation I needed and the lady showed me how to put it on. And I've got a proper brush.'

'MAC! I haven't even got any of that—and I'm a real grown-up!'

Vince shrugged. 'Well, that's a matter of opinion, of course. You ought to go in there. Get yourself kitted out.'

Scarlett nodded earnestly. 'Yes, it's a false economy, isn't it, Vince?'

Alice looked from one to the other, bewildered. 'Buying cheap cosmetics, of course,' Vince explained. 'If she's going to wear make-up, she should have the best. And you should never skimp on foundation. Honestly, Alice—you get what you pay for. When did you last turn out your make-up bag, eh? Did you know it's dangerous to keep mascara longer than six months? It's heaving with bacteria after you've used it a while—honestly. I've seen photos and it's enough to make you sick!'

'So hang on ...' Alice tried to steer the conversation back to more familiar ground. 'MAC is really expensive. All right, Vince—I meant good quality. But it is pricey. Did you have enough money, Scarlett?'

Vince shrugged extravagantly. 'Oh, it was my treat. The least I could do after she spent so long choosing T-shirts with me. And call it an investment. It'll pay dividends in the long run. Don't you think she looks great?'

Alice squinted at Scarlett. Sure enough, the

orangey tint of earlier had been replaced by a soft, naturally dewy look. 'Yeah—you look fantastic. But you're not wearing any make-up now, are you? I mean, earlier you looked absolutely—ouch!'

'It's a question of working out your natural skin tone and working with it,' Vince said through his teeth, glaring at her. 'Molly said that you should choose a shade with cool undertones, didn't she, Scarlett? Anything too orangey is all wrong for you.'

Alice furtively rubbed the ankle Vince had kicked. 'Yes,' she went on a little waspishly. 'But Scarlett has perfect skin as it is. Why bother wearing make-up to look natural when you're naturally gorgeous anyway? And she is only *eleven*?' she added, as pointedly as she could.

'Oh she's hardly got any on. Most of us can do with a little bit of help. Even the best of us.' Vince smoothed an eyebrow and brushed his cheekbone gently with his index finger. Alice started to laugh, but noticed him scrutinising her own complexion with a slight frown.

Alice turned to Scarlett. 'Do girls your age wear make-up? God, I sound about a hundred. I don't know—what would your—' She stopped herself, but not soon enough. The relaxed moment was gone and the unfinished sentence hung in the silence. And now the only feeling was one of desolation. It felt as though the air had been sucked from the room. They would never know what Virginia would think. Not now, not ever. About anything.

Vince jumped to his feet, his distress almost palpable. 'Haven't you got anything better than ginger nuts?' he babbled. 'Honestly, Alice—this won't sustain exhausted shoppers. Let me go and forage in the kitchen.'

131

His words and flurry of activity filled the silence that had fallen, but Alice and Scarlett sat still, both staring ahead of them, looking at nothing.

Chapter 19

Summer 1998

It wasn't until late June, just days after they had booked a last-minute break to Italy, that it finally dawned on Virginia that she might be pregnant. Being a bit irregular, she wasn't alerted by the lack of periods, and had put the sore breasts down to the occasional wave of hormones which sometimes came over her then came to nothing. She put the tiredness down to the fact that she was up and down to see her mother, and to Harrogate once a week where the launch of a fabulous new spa was in the offing, and therefore rushed off her feet. Piers was steeped in school exams, report writing and end-of-year Duke of Edinburgh trips and they passed like ships in the night most of the time.

But when the ships passed, it was good. Since Easter they'd been much easier in each other's company, both of them trying hard to repair the damage and bitterness that had pervaded the winter, and they even escaped for a weekend to a small hotel in the Lake District just before the summer term started. They had barely got out of bed, screwing like rabbits: Piers out of relief that the worst period yet of their marriage was hopefully over and Virginia out of relief that by giving herself to him, body and soul, she would hopefully mend the cracks that had threatened to break them.

Perhaps the hunger for each other's bodies had finally done the trick. By the time she finally did a pregnancy test, she had no idea how many weeks gone she was, and was sent for a scan within days. They emerged from the hospital elated, Piers whooping with joy because he had seen their baby bobbing about like an alien in Virginia's womb and Virginia veering between terror and delight.

Throughout the trip to Italy Piers treated her like porcelain, even more so after they had spent a tense night in a hospital in Verona, struggling with the Italian emergency medical system and the language barrier, when she experienced some unexplained spotting. They even resorted to calling Alice, whose Italian was better than Virginia's even at two o'clock in the morning, and they had a weird conversation via their translator tucked under her duvet in England, with a well-meaning doctor who told Virginia to rest and to come back if it worsened. It didn't, but Piers still refused to let her spend hours on her feet looking at old churches, despite her protestations, and maybe the days spent sleeping at the hotel, their bodies tucked into each other like spoons, were a better holiday than any tour of ancient monuments. 'Seen one fresco, you've seen 'em all,' Piers had joked over spaghetti one night and she had to agree he had a point.

So they spent their days getting up late and having frothy cappuccinos out of enormous cups, then idly looking at shops before taking a siesta. Piers magnanimously did his bit exploring the produce of the local vineyards and, because she shouldn't, he went to bed each night and snored loudly, having drunk a whole bottle single-handed. Beside him, Virginia slept badly, avoiding his flailing arms, her skin sticky from the intense Italian heat and plagued by dreams about deformed babies.

By the time they returned, tanned and relaxed, she was unable to do up her buttons—and it wasn't just a result of good pasta—so she was holding up her gaping trousers with Piers' belt hidden under a baggy shirt, feeling soft, round and feminine (a new sensation for her) as they travelled down south to Bill's seventieth birthday party in the garden at The Gables.

The invitation, sent weeks before by Judy so no one had an excuse not to be able to attend, had sat on the mantelpiece in the kitchen and, by the time they set off, it had curled through age. The party marked Bill's retirement too and, even before they had reached the motorway, Virginia was rehearsing in her head the type of things she should say to the legal friends and colleagues who would undoubtedly be there. She'd done this every time—at Dom's wedding, Judy's sixtieth, their wedding—running through possible conversations in her head. Over time she'd created a bank of subjects she could discuss—the economy, the weather, where they'd been or were going on holiday—so that there wouldn't be any awful pauses.

'You're very quiet. Do you feel OK?' Piers asked, putting his hand on her stomach.

'Yeah,' she smiled reassuringly. 'Usual thing.'

He shook his head, not unkindly but with the lack of understanding of a man completely at ease in all social situations. 'I don't know why you get so worked up.'

'You know why.' She couldn't count the number of times she'd said this to him.

'Oh, they're just people, Gin, and most of them are pompous farts. Besides, you'll be the centre of attention.'

Virginia looked out the window, wondering how soon the next service station would hove into view because she needed a pee, and wondered if that was what was bothering her. That it had taken her pregnancy, such a long and painful time coming, to finally put her on the same level with these people. She didn't doubt that their enthusiasm was real. The night that Piers had called his mother with the news, Judy had sounded genuinely thrilled and had asked all the right questions, making it sound as though he'd been offered a good job, but there was a faint unease in the base of Virginia's stomach that this was the first time she'd got something *right* in Judy's eyes and, worse, that she'd been making a fuss, hadn't been trying hard enough even, and that, if she'd just applied herself (or not been too proud to refuse the offer of the cost of IVF), she would have become pregnant earlier. QED.

Alice had squealed with delight at the news, as Virginia knew she would, and Rosie's reaction was equally enthusiastic when Virginia had called her from work. 'Well, you took your time!' she laughed down the phone. 'I shan't be able to lend you any kit, I'm afraid. Not that you'd want any of my crap—it's completely wrecked. But that's what you get when you buy it from a catalogue.' She laughed wryly. 'I expect Waverley Jnr will get everything from Harrods.'

Virginia laughed. 'Very likely. Have you still got the cot blanket Mum knitted?' she asked.

Her mother had spent hours on a pretty Fair Isle pattern and had finished it in time for the birth of Rosie's first baby, hoping perhaps that the birth of her first grandchild would be a cause for celebration, despite it being the result of a coupling that should never have taken place at all.

'Somewhere,' Rosie said. 'I'll have a look in the loft. But you'll have to wait. I'll give it to you next time you're here. When will that be, by the way? She's asking after you.'

Rosie's question had made Virginia feel desperately guilty and she'd made a mental note to plan a visit the weekend after Bill's party.

'You OK if I go up and see Mum next Saturday?' she asked Piers now. 'I can't take any more days as holiday. Derek is already treating this pregnancy as a major hiccup in his empire-building ambitions.'

'Course,' he smiled at her. 'Do you think she'll understand when you tell her?'

Virginia fixed her eyes on the road ahead as the broken white lines splitting the motorway lanes shot by. 'I hope so.'

Because of an accident on the M23 just near Gatwick, they parked in the lane in front of Alice's cottage later than they had anticipated. Virginia had rationalised to Piers that it would make sense to stay with Alice rather than at The Gables, where the spare bedrooms would be full of Dom, Theo and Barney's families, and he had conceded. A concession to Virginia in the face of a family onslaught.

'Hello, Mummy-To-Be,' Alice tottered out of the house, dressed in a floaty floral-print dress and retro mule slippers with pink fur, her arms outstretched in welcome. 'Are you blooming?' She

136

wrapped Virginia in a fragrant hug, a mixture of perfume and toast.

'Not yet,' Virginia laughed. 'Just feeling fat.'

'Piers!' Alice hugged him too, then tucked her arm into Virginia's. 'Now, have you time for a quick glass of rosé before you go to the royal garden party?' She winked at Piers.

'I'm off the sauce.' Only Alice didn't know the rules of pregnancy. 'But a glass of water would be lovely. I'll drive, darling.'

'God, how dull babies make you—even before the little buggers are born!'

The day was warm and sultry and, as Virginia changed upstairs, she could hear Piers and Alice chatting on the terrace in the garden. She slipped off her T-shirt and shorts and let the faint breeze from the window cool her skin. She'd have liked a shower but there wasn't time now so she made do with a wash in the bathroom sink. She loved the view from the cottage across fields full of barley, still green and unripe, to the gentle South Downs rising in the distance. What a lovely place this would be to live and bring up children. There was a haze in the air and she hoped the weather held for Bill and the party. No doubt Judy had a wet-weather strategy in place, but she'd be bitterly disappointed if guests couldn't wander amongst the borders and admire the planting scheme. Virginia smiled to herself as she compared The Gables to the comfortable garden here at Alice's—which wasn't so much a scheme as a colourful riot: dense shrubs that needed pruning, leggy flowers peering desperately for light, and half-forgotten pots of various sizes that looked tired and beaten, having struggled through lack of water when Alice was

137

off on some trip. All this set around a scruffy little terrace made of uneven bricks, lifted by recalcitrant plants and weeds pushing their way where they shouldn't.

Alice was sitting on an uncomfortable-looking little metal chair, one bare foot tucked under her and a large glass of wine in her hand, her head thrown back laughing at something Piers had said. Piers looked huge perched on the other little chair, and she felt a wave of love for him. He was a far better person than her—tolerant of everyone without the social chip that weighed heavy on her shoulder. She put her hand on her bare, rounding belly. Pregnancy must be softening her. She resolved to be more tolerant too, and slipped the silk dress over her head.

*   *   *

It was not an easy resolution to keep. The Gables was a flurry of activity when they arrived and, in place of a welcome, Judy, her hair immaculate but her face a little flushed, launched out of the front door and snapped that they needed to 'move the car out of the way' and put it in the improvised car park—a field opposite, owned by their neighbour. As they turned out again into the lane, into the driveway pulled a large white van, 'Carrington's—Sussex's Finest Catering' logoed on the side.

'The caterers are leaving it a bit late to arrive, aren't they, Mum?' Piers asked when they found her again, this time directing green-aproned waiters in the marquee.

'Don't be ridiculous. They came ages ago. That van was the second wave, bringing the pudding.

138

Now, Piers, darling, can you check with your dad that he's happy with the champagne arrangements. Oh and Virginia—you look lovely, darling, that colour suits you—would you mind checking the name places are all straight? You're good at details like that.'

Judy then wafted off out of the marquee, leaving behind a fragrant breeze that hung in the air with her instructions.

Guests arrived in a steady stream, all much the same age except the odd cousin of Piers', and Virginia found herself on a table that included Piers' brother Barney and his wife Maggie, as well as a smattering of old friends of Bill and Judy's. The tables seated ten, and conversation across them was impossible thanks to the large table centrepiece, a cascade of peonies and other early summer flowers that Virginia couldn't name.

'I hear congratulations are in order.' A woman Virginia vaguely recognised leaned across her neighbour and tapped Virginia's leg. 'Another one for the Waverley brood. Let's hope it's another boy, then they'll have an entire football team.'

'Rugby, I'd have thought!' laughed Gerald, an old legal friend of Bill's seated next to her.

'I think there's enough boys in the family already,' Virginia smiled back. 'Don't you?'

'Going to carry on working when it's born?' the woman asked. 'Aren't you in catering of some kind?'

'Hotels. I'm a marketing director.'

'That's it. I remember Judy saying it was something like that.'

'No, no, I'll keep working.' She hoped she didn't sound too assertive. 'Got to keep food on the table.

Teachers are paid peanuts, you know.' She looked across at Piers who was deep in conversation with the pretty wife of his cousin Ben.

'You girls, I don't know how you do it,' the woman went on.

'I can't!' Maggie butted in. 'It's been au pairs all the way for us. I'm always trying to find an ugly one so Barney won't fall for her!'

There was general laughter. 'One does need help with the little blighters, doesn't one?' Gerald snorted.

'One'. Virginia pondered it as they chatted on. That little word was probably the biggest social divider of any. More than your lounges and serviettes and teas. She wasn't aware that she had ever used the term 'one' in conversation. 'One has looked at the sales figures and one is quite pleased.' Or: 'One really expects a holiday to be relaxing, doesn't one?' She smiled to herself and, hungry now, started to make headway into the roll on her side plate.

Later, after the delicate salmon and kirsch-laced strawberries had been eaten, the speeches made, the glasses chinked and the toasts drunk, Virginia perched herself on the long bench on the other side of the garden for a couple of moments. People were wandering about stretching after lunch—old friends of Bill's in linen suits and straw hats, too formal to loosen their ties in the heat. Immaculately dressed ladies in bright summer patterns and white shoes that must pinch by now. Across the lush grass, the marquee dominated, one side open, and Virginia could see people chatting and joining other tables, between which the grandchildren darted, released after hours of sitting still and behaving. Once she'd started to relax—a forbidden glass of wine helping things along—she'd quite enjoyed herself and had had a lively conversation with Gerald about rowing. It turned out he'd been a Cambridge Blue. How clever of Judy to have matched the two of them. But then that was typical of Judy. She had triumphed. Everything had gone beautifully and Virginia had to admire her skill. She'd been a loss to the events management business. If she'd had a career in it, she'd have been the best around.

'How's my precious daughter-in-law?' Bill was sitting beside her on the bench before Virginia noticed he was there.

'Hello, birthday boy. Have you had fun?' she asked warmly, tucking her arm into his. 'Shouldn't you be touring tables or something, and being fêted?'

He leaned against the back of the bench and sighed. 'Oh, I think at my great age I can take five minutes off. Besides, it can all get a little wearing, can't it?' His eyes twinkled with amusement and they both knew what he meant. Perhaps Bill understood how Virginia felt more than Piers did.

'She's done fantastically well, hasn't she? I was just thinking how good she'd be in my line of business. I could do with her working for me at the hotels!'

'Women of her generation didn't have the urge or the necessity to work like you girls, but someone like Judy feeds off a project. Sometimes I hardly dare mention an idea—even if it's moving a couple of plants in the garden—before she's organised it all like a military campaign!' He chuckled deeply and they sat in companionable silence for a while. 'You learn a lot as you get older,' he went on

141

eventually, 'and one thing I've learned is not to worry too much what other people think.'

Virginia jerked her head round to him. Had he read her mind? He was looking straight ahead pensively.

'I can't help noticing that sometimes you get a bit fazed by Judy and you seem to have some daft notion that you need to achieve what she expects, but it's not like that at all, you know.' Virginia didn't say a word. 'And besides, she's as guilty of doing the same thing.'

'What thing?'

'Doing things out of the need to *impress*. Worried about what other people think. This, for example.' He indicated the scene in front of them with a wave of his hand. 'Yes, it's for my birthday and all that, and I'm grateful for it, don't get me wrong, but it's also about Judy and what people will think of *her*. Of *us*. Of what we've achieved. And no one should care, really.'

He smiled and his shoulders shook with a laugh. 'I probably shouldn't tell you this, but she's not quite as top drawer as she'd have you believe.'

'Isn't she?' Virginia's eyes widened. 'I thought it was all finishing school and a secretarial course.'

'Yes it was, but that's because she's always had a sharp eye for doing the right thing. When I first met her, she was so worried about getting it right when we went to visit my parents—my father was a Law Lord as you know—that she went to a class in etiquette.' He looked at her sideways, one eyebrow raised. 'Daft woman, but I love her for it.'

Virginia didn't know what to say. Instead, Bill leaned over, kissed her briefly on the cheek, and with a 'hope my next little grandchild is cooking

142

nicely' patted her leg and wandered back across the garden on stiff legs.

Chapter 20

Early July 2010

There were times when Alice could have done without modern technology. The thing about emails and texts was that anybody could get hold of anybody at any time. And Judy was making her wishes known loud and clear from across the globe.

The email from Ginny's mother-in-law was crisp and very, very direct. Was Alice aware that Scarlett was due to start secondary school in September? Alice wasn't. And had Alice realised that, of course, she couldn't now go to the one Ginny and Piers had chosen in Oxford? Alice had, but then what did she know? She hadn't been at school for well over fifteen years. But never fear; Judy had sorted everything out and had been in contact with a private girls' school near their home. She had arranged for Alice to take Scarlett along for a visit before the end of term, which was imminent. The dates and times were all detailed and would she please email back afterwards to let her know Scarlett's thoughts and first impressions?

Not that Scarlett's opinions would count for much. At least, that was the impression Alice got from the email. And she had to admit to being slightly miffed by Judy's imperious attitude. She, Alice, was officially responsible for Scarlett's well-being and education and, although she hadn't given it much thought until Judy's email, it would have been nice to be asked, rather than told. But Judy was a blood relative and that, apparently, meant that her opinion counted for more than a mere guardian's—or at least that was what she managed to convey. And Alice couldn't really find any reason to disagree. After all, it made sense for Scarlett to be at school near her grandparents and Haywards Heath.

So it was that, on a Thursday morning ten days before Judy and Bill were due home, Scarlett and Alice, both neatly dressed and more than a little apprehensive, arrived at the gates of Fitzwilliam Lodge in Alice's clapped-out Renault. As she changed down into second, compliant with the speed limit signs, she felt the engine hesitate and shudder. She knew how it felt. And so, she thought, glancing sideways, did Scarlett. She gave a couple of little revs and they continued slowly in. 'Nice lawn,' Alice said, as much to break the silence as anything else.

Scarlett was staring out of the window, a pair of Alice's sunglasses—worn on condition that she took them off as soon as they got out of the car—hiding the expression in her eyes. 'Mmmm. Big gates.'

'Maybe they have trouble with break-outs,' Alice joked feebly as they approached the visitors' car park. 'They've probably locked the guard dogs up 'cause they don't want to frighten us.'

Another quick check once they'd parked, insignificant between Range Rovers and top-of-the-range Beamers, revealed that her efforts had failed miserably. Scarlett had her hands clenched in her lap and there was a distinct droop to her head. Alice sighed quietly. Perhaps Scarlett was worried she wouldn't get in—that she'd be judged and found wanting by this edifice of a place. She could relate to that feeling. This school was so much like her own—where she'd been a boarder from the age of thirteen—that she was instantly transported back to the time when *she'd* been the one anxiously waiting in the car park, ready to go and meet the white-haired and patrician head mistress. As if there'd been any likelihood of that school, or indeed any fee-paying school, turning down the daughter of a well-known advertising executive and his wafty, intellectual wife. If anything, having Alice there was a feather in the school's cap—something she didn't fully realise until years later, as a sixth former, when her repeated infractions of the rules were overlooked, while other girls (with less influential fathers) were politely asked to leave.

These days things were different, surely? Alice wouldn't wish her school days on her worst enemy—and Scarlett certainly didn't count as that. Prickly, resistant, stubborn and sometimes downright rude though she could be, Alice felt they were starting to rub along a little bit better since Scarly-gate. But it would still be a tremendous relief to hand her back.

And with that in mind, Alice was putting a far more positive spin on this school visit than was strictly sincere. She checked her watch in a slightly exaggerated way and declared, pointlessly, 'We've still got fifteen minutes before our appointment. We could go in, if you like. Although I guarantee it'll smell of cabbage throughout the whole school. Or we can stay here and spy. Look, I've got provisions.'

With a flourish, she produced a bag of Minstrels,

145

bought at a petrol station on the way. 'Want one?'

Scarlett took off the sunglasses and handed them back with a tight smile. 'Yes, please.'

Alice shook a few into her open hand. 'You didn't have much breakfast, did you?'

'Wasn't really hungry.' Scarlett tossed the Minstrels into her mouth and started chewing, then looked down and fiddled with the little silver ring Krissy had given her. Krissy had told her the stone was good for emotional healing and Alice hoped she was right. If it did have any magic powers, they'd certainly come in handy now. Alice pondered what to say.

'Are you feeling a bit nervous? I mean—about this. This whole school thing.'

Scarlett nodded silently and Alice, still fumbling for words, offered the bag of chocolates over again, having eaten a handful herself. 'Here—your need is greater than mine. And my backside is greater than yours, so you'd be doing me a favour.'

Another wan smile.

'Is this place . . . Is it anything like the school you were expecting to go on to? You know, near where you lived?'

Scarlett looked around warily. 'No—not at all. It's mixed. Like my primary school. And everyone in my year—well, just about everyone—goes there. And it's all modern. Not like *this*!'

Alice hid a smile at Scarlett's scornful tone. The faded stone walls and leaded windows were exactly what would appeal to most parents, anxious for a tone of respectability and tradition. But Scarlett was only just getting started. 'I'm not saying I like boys. They're mostly stupid and annoying, but I think it's really weird to have boys' schools

146

and girls' schools. And I bet they've got a stupid uniform here. I'd just be wearing black trousers and a white shirt, and different colour sweatshirts depending on what house you're in. My mum said ...' Scarlett stopped for a moment and Alice held her breath.

A shrill bell rang out and Alice cursed it silently. It was time for them to go in and she slowly opened the door. She didn't dare push the issue. If Scarlett was going to talk about Ginny and Piers, she'd have to do it on her own terms. 'Come on—we'd better go in. It wouldn't do to be late, would it? I don't expect your granny would be very pleased with me!'

Alice meant it as a joke, but she realised, as they followed the signs to the reception, just how true it was. Still, there was no reason Scarlett should have to see this visit as more of an ordeal than it really was. Ginny would have hated it though. 'Come on. Remember, we're the client here. Any school would be lucky to get a girl like you, so head up, shoulders back. Let's give 'em hell!'

Scarlett gave Alice the look she'd become used to in the past couple of weeks. A kind of look that said: 'I've no idea what you're on about, but you're embarrassing me anyway, so would you please shut up?' Alice suspected that parents everywhere would recognise that look. This time though, for some reason, it made her smile.

*   *   *

Alice was still shaking hands with the headteacher, but she could feel Scarlett willing her to leave. The last hour had felt like one of the longest she'd ever had to endure. From the very outset, it

147

was clear that Judy had gone into elaborate detail over Scarlett's tragedy and everyone they met had adopted a sickly, sympathetic expression as soon as they'd been introduced. Their over-solicitous and oh-so-sensitive questions grated on Alice and she could feel her hackles rising. A quick glance at Scarlett revealed that she was all too aware of the special treatment she was receiving, and she responded, Alice noticed, by adopting the same mutinous expression she'd had on her face at Judy's the day Alice had picked her up. Her eyes might be downcast, but that didn't conceal the furious resentment that was veering dangerously close to tears. For the first time, Alice realised this was Scarlett's way of coping with the unspeakable truth and, for the first time too, she actually felt on Scarlett's side. It was the two of them against the world or, in this case, the rather self-satisfied staff of Fitzwilliam Lodge.

She finally disentangled herself from the attentions of the head, a woman who couldn't be more than ten years older than Alice, yet seemed to belong to a whole other generation. Scarlett was lurking just far enough away—and in the direction of the car park—to make it clear that she couldn't wait to get out of there. 'Bye now,' Alice called again over her shoulder. 'And thanks for making us so welcome.' She grabbed hold of Scarlett's arm and bustled the surprised girl over to the defiantly scruffy little car. 'Phew. Let's get out of here,' she murmured, then paused. She shouldn't put ideas into Scarlett's head—although she was pretty sure they were there already. It might not be Alice's idea of a school that would suit Scarlett, but honestly, what business was it of hers? It looked as though Judy had already made up her mind about Scarlett's future and, although she might not share her vision, the very least Alice could do was refrain from making trouble. And really, what was the alternative? She was aware of Scarlett glancing over at her now—a reversal of their usual pattern—as she drove smartly down the drive, blatantly ignoring the 'Beware Children 5MPH' signs in her haste to get away. This time, Alice waited for Scarlett to speak. And it wasn't long before she let out a long and theatrical sigh. 'I hate that place. I'm not going.'

'Riiiiight,' Alice said slowly. 'Well, that sounds pretty decisive. Anything in particular you weren't happy about? I'm sure they'd be open to—you know—accommodating you if they can.'

She could feel Scarlett's glare, but kept her eyes firmly on the road, afraid she'd give her own feelings away if she turned to face her. Scarlett's reply, when it came, was low, determined and furious. 'Everything. I hate *everything* about it. The way they all talked to me, all fake and pretend-sympathetic. All sounding as though they care, but they don't. You can tell if someone cares, and they don't. They just want me to be grateful and convenient so they can feel better.'

Alice wondered if Scarlett included her in that sweeping statement and felt a wave of discomfort as she realised how much more perceptive Scarlett was than she'd even begun to imagine. There was something sanctimonious about the teachers they'd met today—the head, in particular—and she couldn't help feeling that Scarlett had got it exactly right. She had been labelled as a 'little project' by the school. And Judy had probably started the ball

149

rolling herself. It was unbearably patronising. But how to proceed? 'Well, look—I agree the place did seem a bit starchy, but don't write it off completely. When your granny and grandpa get back from their holiday, perhaps they'll go and have a look too, and if you explain how you feel—if you still feel that way, I mean—then you can discuss it with them. I mean, they do want you to be happy, you know. They're not going to send you somewhere where you'll be miserable. Just don't worry about it for now, eh?'

Scarlett sat back hard in her seat. 'It's all right for you to say that. You're not the one that might end up there.'

It was a fair point, and Alice didn't even attempt to argue it.

On the way home, Scarlett lapsed into silence and stared through the passenger window again, the sunglasses firmly back in place. Even without speaking, she could create quite an atmosphere. Her mother hadn't been like that at all. She didn't communicate her feelings very readily. Maybe this was another Piers characteristic, although if it was, Alice had never witnessed it. But there again, you never really know what goes on between couples.

As much to lighten the atmosphere as for real necessity, Alice diverted into Lewes to go to the supermarket. She'd probably remember something they needed as she scoured the shelves. 'Are you coming?' she asked as brightly as she could. Scarlett shrugged and got out, gazing around her. Then her eyes fell on a group of schoolchildren, slightly older than her by the look of them, walking through the car park. She watched them closely before pointedly turning away, but still watching them sideways from behind Alice's sunglasses.

'What school do they go to?' Scarlett asked quietly, nodding towards the group—four girls and three boys with backpacks and sports bags swinging loosely as they ambled along.

'Can't remember what it's called. Something Dene, I think. It's supposed to be quite good. Jess's kids all went there. Come on—do you fancy pizza tonight?'

'Could I go there?'

Alice stopped in her tracks. 'What? It's miles away from Haywards Heath. And anyway,' she chuckled at the thought, 'I can't see your granny going for it, can you?'

Scarlett's face fell. 'I could get a bus, couldn't I? I could get up early. I don't want to go to Fitzwilliam Lodge. I wouldn't mind getting up. And I could stay with you, couldn't I?'

There was a kind of desperation in Scarlett's voice that made Alice tense up. Had she really not understood what her life was going to be now? Had anyone explained it to her properly? It seemed not. And, Alice realised, she was as guilty as Judy of avoiding what could be an awkward and painful discussion with the child. Everyone had been skating over the surface, with the pretext of not upsetting Scarlett as the cover up for their own cowardice. She hesitated, then smiled in what she could tell was an unconvincing way as, once again, cowardice won the day. 'Let's go and get that pizza,' she said, 'and what about some choccie muffins for pudding, and we'll talk about it later.'

But Scarlett was made of sterner stuff than any of the adults in whose care she'd ended up. 'On the way home, I'd like to drive past that school. Just to have a look. It won't take long.'

151

'OK,' Alice nodded weakly, relieved that, for now at least, she could brush Scarlett's questions about her future aside once again.

Chapter 21

February 1999

Wrapping the blanket tightly around her, Virginia gently laid the baby in the Moses basket, confident she would sleep for a while now. It had been a fractured night; Virginia had struggled inexpertly to deal with her tiny daughter's demands and she wondered how Piers was going to get through the day on so little sleep. He'd soldiered on bravely in an attempt to support Virginia as she tried to settle Scarlett, but eventually she'd de-camped to the spare bed and they had both fallen asleep, Virginia propped up against the pillows with the baby against her chest. She was woken by a light kiss from Piers as he headed off to work but she'd fallen asleep again until Scarlett had woken her again, ready for another round of feeding.

It was now lunchtime, and she tucked the Moses basket carefully into the corner of the kitchen and, for the first time since yesterday evening, managed to take a deep breath and re-fuel with a cup of fresh tea and a sandwich made from the pickings off last night's roast chicken, with a squirt of mayonnaise and some limp lettuce she found in a bag at the back of the fridge. Domestic concerns had flown out of the window almost entirely, and Piers laughed that the moulding square of cheese in the fridge door was now a dear friend.

But none of this mattered because here was their beautiful baby daughter just four weeks old and, even though she tested their novice skills, she was so precious all had been forgiven. Virginia had even managed to hold off Judy, who seemed to take it as read that she would be maternity nurse, and was at Virginia's bedside almost before the umbilical cord had been cut. But Piers, for once, had taken control and sent her home again, declaring that there was no room for four in their tiny flat.

There was barely room for three. How could something so small take up so much room? Virginia wasn't entirely sure they needed all the equipment they had managed to amass, but Piers had gone a little wild in preparation for Scarlett's arrival and had followed the advice of the over-zealous sales woman in the nursery department to the nth degree. Virginia was quite sure they could bring up their baby without the need for a depth perception mobile, but she didn't want to rain on his fabulous and much-anticipated parade. Presents had poured in from friends too—even Piers' school had sent a basket of booties, rattles and soft toys, put together by Val, the head's secretary. The entire staff room had chipped in, and Virginia had burst into tears as she'd opened it, overwhelmed by their generosity. But then she wept at practically everything these days.

So, in addition to the boxes of playmats—three—and the drawers full of babygros that there would not be enough days for Scarlett to wear, there was also a pile of estate agents' details on the kitchen table. The choice of properties was pretty thin. The mortgage meeting with the bank had revealed that, if a bigger place were ever to be a possibility, there was no question that Virginia would have to go back to work and soon. Every shred of reason in her being agreed, but she'd cherished the vague possibility that they'd manage on Piers' salary alone. But, add to the mortgage the increase in the cost of care for her mother, and the life of a stay-at-home mum was not to be.

During the last couple of months of her pregnancy, Virginia had tried to see more of Elizabeth. Though the midwife had told her to curb the amount of travelling she was doing, Virginia had used the advance planning meetings at the hotel in Harrogate—hours and hours of scheduling for marketing campaigns while she was on maternity leave—as an excuse to detour home via Stoke. It made for long days—she tried to avoid staying over at the hotel which meant being on the M40 by six in the morning to fit it all into a day.

'You're just fitting visits in around your work, aren't you? Rosie had said in a sharp tone on one recent visit. 'It's obvious what your priorities are.' Virginia almost hadn't replied, feeling too tired to challenge her sister. She hadn't the energy for a scrap. Strictly speaking, Rosie was right, but what alternative did she have?

The baby had leaped in her stomach and Virginia had flinched. 'I know, Rosie. I just want to see her as much as I can, 'cause it won't be that easy once the baby arrives.'

'I managed,' Rosie sulked and Virginia let it drop. She wasn't going to win this round.

The reaction to her pregnancy from her mother after so long was interesting. Mostly she didn't seem aware of it—or Virginia when she visited, but on her last visit before Scarlett's birth, her mother had suddenly noticed the changes in her daughter's body. The visit had started as normal— her mother's concentration poorer than ever, so Virginia had fussed over a bunch of Sweet Williams she'd brought with her, trying to find a vase to put them in, when her mother had turned from the TV and said, 'How long?'

'How long what, Mum?'

'How long until the birth?'

Virginia had grasped onto her interest. 'Three weeks. I wish it was sooner. The baby keeps doing aerobics on my bladder.'

Her mother had chuckled at this. 'You used to do that. Never stopped moving. Rosie, on the other hand, was sluggish.' She paused. 'Nothing changed there then!' She roared with laughter. Virginia's heart gave a leap at this moment of clarity. Then her mother put her hand out. 'Let me touch.'

Virginia moved in front of her and, as she placed her bony hands on Virginia's belly, the baby moved, causing a wave across her skin. Her mother put a hand to her mouth and gasped in delight. 'You'll have a long labour, you know,' she said, matter-of-factly. 'I did.' And she'd been right.

The moment had evaporated as quickly as it had begun, as a familiar theme tune came on the TV and her mother's scant attention was distracted. After a while Virginia had heaved herself up to leave. She'd kissed her mother's unresponsive cheek and was almost at the door when her mother's voice had rung out.

'You didn't deserve this, having to see me falling apart,' she said, looking hard at her daughter. Virginia had been about to reply when she had put

155

up a finger, shakily. 'But then neither did I.'

Sitting now, watching Scarlett sleep, Virginia realised what she had missed about her past. It was all the details that had never been filled in, parts of the picture that hadn't been painted. When she was growing up there had never been time to chat about family stories. Every holiday, as soon as she was old enough—and even before she was strictly allowed to—she'd worked in restaurants and hotels for the money and the experience, too wrapped up in her own life to bother asking her mother and father about theirs. By the time she'd felt grown up enough to ask, her father was dead and her mother had begun her descent into dementia. She knew the basics—aunts and uncles, what had happened to relations who'd moved away. But what was missing were the *feelings*, the emotions behind these incidents. She couldn't recall having seen her mother cry, and her parents had rarely argued or showed anger.

Of her parents' meeting and courting she knew little. She knew they'd met at a dance and, whilst nosing in a drawer in the front room, she'd once found a small photo album containing a handful of faded photographs of her mother in a short white dress and a hat with a veil holding a small bouquet of roses, and her mother and father standing outside what looked like Stoke registry office, young and gauche and smiling broadly. But any more than that wasn't spoken of much.

In Piers' family it was quite different. Bill and Judy, right from her first awkward visit to the house in Sussex, had filled her in on their family background. Relatives and ancestors who were judges or army colonels had been recalled. One

156

who'd been in parliament, though in no great position of power, was mentioned often, and people were referred to by the school they went to. 'Wasn't he an old Carthusian?' Bill would ask, as if that somehow put them in context. Virginia had never dared ask what Carthusian or Salopian were, fearful of showing her ignorance and therefore her inferiority.

But, pompous as it might be, at least there was a context, a *history*, and not a void of fact and emotion. She wasn't going to let that happen to Scarlett.

Out of the carrier bag on the table she pulled the empty notebook. The cover was made of pink and purple fabric—she'd reverted, shamefully, to gender stereotyping!—and inside the pages were blank and waiting to be filled. She'd always loved stationery like this and had filled book after book with notes from lectures at university, religiously cataloguing them so that, when it came to revision, she could put her hand on a topic immediately.

On the opening page of the diary she wrote in large, fancy letters Scarlett's date of birth and her full name: Scarlett Elizabeth Waverley. Then she began:

To my darling daughter
I am not sure where to start, except to say that you are the most precious gift I could imagine. I am watching you now lying in your Moses basket—a gift from your grandparents (but more about them later) and I can't take my eyes off you. Your skin is white and perfect, and your hair as dark as your father's and mine. I can't make out which one of us you look most like yet, though when you are

157

cross you do have a tendency to look like your Aunt Rosie, so please grow out of that as fast as you can.

Today you are wearing a dark-pink outfit that my friend Alice gave you—amongst a mass of other presents that arrived in a huge box with a ribbon around it. It's typical of Alice to go over the top, but that's what makes her so lovable. The babygro looks as if it might be hideously expensive, and I know the cashmere cardigan that came with it must be, so please don't sick up on it, will you? Alice is one of my oldest mates and I hope you and she will become good friends—she drives you mad half the time, but she's the sort of person who makes a room light up when she walks in. She can make even the most boring stuff fun, and I hope she'll eventually have children so that then we can all have fun together.

What can I tell you about the world you've entered into? There are wars on, of course. When aren't there? I'm glad you are a girl, because I couldn't bear the idea of you going off to war. Sometimes when I pass one of those war memorials I wonder how the mothers coped with losing their sons on the Front. Sometimes two or even three sons. Oh, now that's set me off crying again. I never used to cry like this—that's your fault!

I'm not sure I am supposed to cry about something that has made me and Daddy so happy. You have made us complete, the family we always hoped for, and you're the missing piece in our jigsaw. The joy of you has spread to other people too: my mother, who finds nothing now to make her happy; Grandpa and Granny Waverley, who have so longed for a granddaughter, and even Alice

158

seems to change when she holds you. Maybe one day she will be lucky enough to have a daughter as beautiful as you are.

Chapter 22

July 2010

The rest of Judy and Bill's cruise passed far more quickly than Alice was expecting, punctuated by increasingly detailed emails from Judy about exactly when and where they would expect Scarlett to be delivered on their return. The last week positively flew by and the two of them fell into a curiously comfortable routine. Scarlett would make it her job to get the milk from the village shop of a morning and seemed happy for Alice to get on with work while she occupied herself pottering about in the garden. Alice could see her out of the window talking to herself, tidying up the beds, and nursing the little tomato plant that Walter had given her. They'd even had a fun trip to a bookshop in Brighton, after it occurred to Alice that Scarlett should perhaps be doing more with her brain than simply watching *The Jeremy Kyle Show*. Though, on reflection, that was quite an education in genetics and moral philosophy.

They'd returned with a pile of teen reads and some vampire titles and Scarlett had curled up in the sunshine in the garden, engrossed in the stories, until Alice brought out supper on a tray which they ate at the garden table. Scarlett wasn't exactly bubbly—though why would she be?—but the sullen moods had receded slightly and she would chat quite comfortably about this and that.

Until the day came to return to The Gables.

'It's boring at Granny and Grandpa's,' Scarlett had complained over breakfast, after Alice asked her what she needed to have washed ready for her return.

'What? More boring than it is here? That must be really boring.'

'I've got my bike here. I can go out when I like and there are people in the village like Walter and Betty.'

Boring? That seemed an odd choice of words. Her time with her grandparents before they left had been a cloud of grief. For boring did she actually mean stressful, a reminder of what had happened and the future ahead of her? Alice reached over and gently took hold of her wrist. 'But you'll be coming back here, you know. Promise. I am your legal guardian angel person, so I'm not going anywhere—apart from work and stuff. But when I'm here, you can come over any weekend you like.'

Scarlett looked down and finished her cereal without any further comment.

While she was upstairs, sorting out her washing and starting to pack her bag, or out exploring on her bike, Alice would log onto her computer to see who had been in touch—and particularly to scout for more work. But recently she'd also been checking to see if Greg had left a message. They'd been in touch by email since his initial answerphone message, and now they were moving towards an arrangement to meet up, maybe for coffee.

Though they'd only met once, at the funeral, it had been such an extraordinarily emotional day that Alice felt as though they'd bypassed the pleasantries. His emails were frank and funny and Alice felt as though she'd known him for ages. Maybe he was just that type of bloke. He'd been so kind and thoughtful to her that day. He seemed happy for her to talk about Ginny. With Judy, it would be wrong and cruel to talk about her. And Alice still hadn't worked out how to do it with Scarlett. University chums had only distant memories for the most part; Alice didn't know their Oxford friends and although Vince, Krissy and some of her other Brighton mates had met Ginny for the odd weekend, they barely knew her. Talking about her with Greg allowed Alice to pretend she still existed and might still come bounding through the door at any moment, full of life and smiling broadly. Alice was still not used to living in a world that didn't have Ginny in it. She wasn't sure she ever would be.

Sure enough, she had a message from him. He was going to be coming back from the Middle East before too long, he said. Certainly by the end of the month, and he would be around for at least three weeks. He hadn't been to Brighton for ages. Would she like to meet up for coffee or lunch, maybe?

She would. She certainly would. And when Scarlett was safely back with Bill and Judy, she would be freer to do so. She flexed her fingers and typed her reply.

*   *   *

As they drove closer to Haywards Heath, Alice felt her spirits sink a little. She had a feeling that Judy would quiz her about the improving activities she'd devised for Scarlett, about her diet, her habits and, most significantly, about their visit to Fitzwilliam Lodge. And that was something Alice was not looking forward to.

161

Since their cursory drive-by to the local high, Ashton Down, she now knew, Scarlett had been more and more adamant that she would not go to Judy's planned alternative. It had looked like a perfectly ordinary high school to Alice, perhaps a little scruffy, but Scarlett had gazed at it through the car windows as though at the Promised Land. All the pupils had left for the day by then and only a few teachers were in evidence, heading for the car park with stacks of papers under their arms.

In some obscure way, Alice knew that Scarlett's antipathy towards Fitzwilliam Lodge would become her fault, once Judy cottoned on. Maybe she should have been more enthusiastic while they were there, but she couldn't fake her approval, and it seemed that Judy was the only person who was actually keen on it. Alice needed Ginny to whisper advice into her ear; to tell her what she would have wanted. Then Alice would know what to do. She sighed deeply.

Maybe there was a compromise solution. There had to be a high school in Haywards Heath or the surrounding area. Even a mixed public school would be preferable to that draughty temple to lady-like learning and manners that smelled of damp wool. What was absolutely certain was that there was going to be a clash of wills between Judy and Scarlett. And Alice was equally absolutely certain that she didn't want to be around when it happened.

'Hello, darling! Oh goodness, Scarlett, your hair! You look as though you've been dragged through a hedge!'

It was almost the first thing Judy said to them, standing there on the doorstep, and Alice felt a fleeting moment of disappointment that Judy's opening gambit had been so negative. Something

Ginny had once said came into her head briefly, something about nothing ever being good enough, but Judy interrupted it with: 'Shot out of a cannon,' she added with a laugh, 'as your grandfather would say.'

Under her fierce scrutiny, Scarlett's face took on the closed, furious expression Alice had learned to dread, but she couldn't prevent her hand snaking up to push it back behind her ears.

In her annoyance at the implication that she'd been dragging Scarlett through hedges, Alice couldn't help being slightly pleased that Judy didn't look too great either. Her normally immaculate make-up was conspicuous by its absence and she looked drawn and tired, not in the slightest revived by her holiday. Probably the long flight, Alice thought, chiding herself for being so uncharitable.

'Well, come in both of you. Don't wait around on the doorstep.'

'I'd love to,' Alice lied. 'But I've got to get to the tip before it closes.'

'Don't be ridiculous, Alice. You need to fill me in on what's been happening. And Scarlett needs to get changed out of those old things, don't you, poppet?'

In a single sentence, all Scarlett's carefully chosen purchases from her shopping trips with Vince— and there had been several since the first, some even including Alice—were dismissed. Alice could practically feel her seething beside her.

The house had been aired and cared for by Bill and Judy's daily, a quiet, stooped little woman whose hands were never still. Alice had seen her a couple of times but had never been introduced. Today was no exception, but the kitchen was as immaculate as ever when Judy led them in. Over tea, and juice

163

for Scarlett, Judy related the holiday, with frequent references to people they'd met and places they'd visited, and Scarlett and Alice exchanged glances as the stories went on and on. Finally, Judy turned her attention to her granddaughter.

'And you, Scarlett. How have you managed at Alice's? Are you glad to be home?'

Alice watched Scarlett carefully. She was gradually reverting to the sullen, withdrawn child she'd picked up three weeks ago. It was as if they had never been in Ulvington. Suddenly, she realised the progress Scarlett had made in the time they'd spent together. It all seemed to be draining away—all that confidence and fun. Perhaps her intuition had been right—being with her grandparents reminded her of everything she'd lost. Alice reached under the table to find Scarlett's hand clenched in her lap. She tried to give it a reassuring squeeze, but she couldn't tell if the gesture was welcome or not.

'You're very quiet, darling? Perhaps you're overtired. I'm sure you have heaps to tell me about? I hope you've been helpful to Alice around the house. Remembered your pleases and thank-yous? Because it really has been very kind of you, Alice, to take her on like that. But Bill and I simply had to get away. I think it's done him *some* good. It's rather hard to tell at times.'

There was a definite edge to her voice, and Alice wondered just how much of a holiday it had been for Judy. 'Never mind all that now,' she said, smiling warmly at Scarlett. 'You're back with granny, and you're such a comfort to me, my darling. I've missed you tremendously, you know. Now, let me show you what I've brought back for you—another doll for your collection. What do you think about that?'

Alice couldn't stand it any longer. It was too painful to witness the gap between Judy and Scarlett and the loss that seemed to be all they had in common. She stood up, ashamed of her cowardice. 'I really must get going now. Shall I call later, Judy, and I can fill you in on what Scarlett and I have been up to? The tip closes at midday on a Saturday, you see, so I must dash.'

Scarlett's accusing stare was enough to make Alice wish she'd thought of a better alibi, but she hardened her heart and made her getaway. Judy proffered a cheek in farewell, and Alice turned to give Scarlett a hug, surprised at the intensity of the one she received in return.

'I'll call you later,' Alice whispered in her ear and, back in the car, she let out a long breath that she hadn't realised she'd been holding since they'd arrived at the house. But she couldn't help worrying about both Scarlett and Judy as she drove away.

Chapter 23

May 1999

Virginia glanced round the church, which was surprisingly full. The early summer sunshine was creating a pattern of jewel-like colour on the faces of the congregation as it sneaked through the stained-glass windows. She knew Judy would have preferred a private christening for Scarlett and had even had the temerity to suggest they have it in Sussex where they 'played bridge with the vicar'. It had taken all of Virginia's strength and powers of persuasion to make Piers stand up to her to make sure it happened at St Joseph's in Oxford.

Virginia's dress felt tight and uncomfortable. She was struggling to shift the weight she'd gained while she was pregnant and the linen pulled under her armpits. She willed Scarlett not to cry or she'd start leaking horribly, then checked again that she had her cardigan in her bag, put there in case of emergencies.

But her beautiful daughter lay quietly in Piers' arms, irresistible in the Waverley family gown, gazing around her with that all-knowing look she seemed to have. Virginia felt a wave of intense love for her. Disappointingly, her sister Rosie hadn't been able to make it—a litany of excuses including the cost of the petrol—but there was a good smattering of friends and Piers' brother Theo, who'd come all the way over from the States to be godfather. Next to him in the pew sat Judy and Bill. Judy's mouth was pinched in disapproval as if Scarlett would be nearer God were she not being baptised alongside another baby to be called Kylie.

But of Alice there was no sign. Virginia wasn't surprised. Alice was pathologically late for everything. It was a good thing she worked for herself because if Virginia were that unreliable she'd have had her P45 years ago. Alice had even managed to be late for a French final at university and had panted in just as the invigilator was about to start the clock. Of course she'd charmed him into letting her stay and sit the paper.

Virginia supposed it didn't matter if Alice missed saying the actual vows. They were only a formality, after all. But as the vicar, a hearty woman whose sensible sandals peeped out from under

166

her cassock, announced they had 'not one but two special babies today', Virginia suddenly realised it was actually very important that Alice was there and she felt her shoulders relax with relief as she heard the latch of the church door lift noisily and Alice appear.

'Sorry, sorry, sorry,' she mouthed as she tottered in pink suede high heels across the church. Virginia smiled back at her and at her wildly inappropriate clothes—a tight-fitting floral dress and what looked like a man's overcoat—but felt another wave of love for her friend too. The only person in the church who was totally on her side. She felt tears prickle behind her lids. Bloody hormones.

*   *   *

By the time they got back to the house, Scarlett had fallen asleep in her car seat.

'Can you put her somewhere quiet?' Virginia asked Piers as they pulled up in the short drive, mentally ticking off in her head what she needed to do before everyone else arrived, which could only be a matter of moments away. Thank goodness they weren't still living at the flat. There would never have been enough room for everyone. She glanced at the front of the house, modern, boxy and uninspiring, wondering what the others would make of it when they pulled up. Theo hadn't seen it at all, and neither had Alice, who'd only made it to the hospital to meet Scarlett. She knew Judy's opinion already. She'd come up from Sussex to look after Scarlett when they moved in, and had described the house, with its John Lewis curtains and furniture store discount settee, as 'cosy but functional';

for 'cosy' read 'poky' and for 'functional' read 'dull'. And Virginia had heard herself justifying it. 'It's closer to school for Piers so he can cycle, and that's great now that we're down to one car.' What she hadn't told Judy, out of some misplaced sense of pride, was that it was all they could afford, a concept Judy would struggle to get her head around. Even in the early days of her marriage to Bill, a thrusting young barrister then, he'd earned enough to keep her from having to work.

'Don't take her out of the seat, will you?' she called after Piers' back as he carried Scarlett in her chair carefully up the narrow stairs. 'She'll wake and then I'll never get the lunch ready. Why isn't Alice behind us?'

'She flashed her lights and pulled into a garage,' he whispered loudly over the banister. 'Probably stopping for petrol. She won't be long.'

But she was, and Piers had circulated champagne and Scarlett was awake and being passed from grandmother to uncles to small cousins by the time she bustled in through the door. By which point Virginia was red-faced and even more uncomfortable. She knew she'd been overambitious with the lunch and should have settled for cold meats or something, and she longed for them all to go away and to be able to slip into a T-shirt and jeans.

'Where have you been?' Virginia threw her arms around her friend, who embraced her warmly back, smelling deliciously familiar.

'Well.' Alice took a deep breath to launch into the explanation. 'I wanted to get you a bottle of fizz and it took me ages to find anywhere that sold it. Bloody Sundays. Why don't they sell booze earlier? Then I went back to your old flat—I wasn't thinking! Lovely couple live there now by the way.'

'Yes, I know!' Virginia laughed.

'Anyway, bloody good thing they were in 'cause they told me how to get here.' She shrugged off her coat and handed over a wrapped christening present that looked like a picture. Virginia helped her and noticed the label said Vivienne Westwood. Only Alice could make designer look like cheap high street.

'How are you, my darling?' Alice asked, turning back to Virginia. 'Tits sore?'

'Not sore. Just feel more like a cow really.'

'Yes, but look at the cleavage on you! Let me go and see the little one then.' Alice did look genuinely excited at the thought of seeing Scarlett, which pleased Virginia no end. She'd been wrapped in blankets so only her head was visible when Alice had come up to the John Radcliffe back in January, and she'd been more interested in the gory details about the birth. Virginia had loved her for trying at least to show an interest.

Checking that the salmon was nearly ready, and hoping that there were enough canapés to stave off everyone's hunger for a while, Virginia picked up her own glass and led Alice through to the garden where she was greeted with a hug from Piers who, ever the gent, introduced her to everyone else, including the group of friends—teachers from school and Virginia's mate Charlotte from the hotel—who were tight in the corner of the garden, intimidated perhaps by the dominance of the Waverley gang.

'There's my girl!' Alice put down her drink on the table and put her arms out to Scarlett, who was lying in Judy's arms. 'Can I have a cuddle?'

A flash of reticence passed across Judy's face. 'She's very peaceful at the moment. All this excitement must be exhausting for her.'

'Oh.' Alice let her arms drop to her sides and there was a painful moment as no one knew quite what to say. 'Perhaps later.'

Virginia caught Judy's eye and Judy looked away quickly. 'We'll be eating later,' she said and put her arms out to take her daughter. Judy handed her over and Virginia nuzzled her face into Scarlett's neck. 'Come on, Alice, come and sit in the lounge. You'll be more comfortable with her in there.' She turned on her heel and walked back into the house.

'Mother hen or what?' Alice whispered.

'Mmm. She-wolf, more like,' Virginia hissed back, and realised how desperate she was to blurt out all her frustrations. To share with Alice how many times Judy had said how relieved she and Bill were—she always spoke for Bill—that Piers finally had a family, as if Virginia had fallen short in her wifely duties through laziness or stubbornness in some way. But even more, Virginia wanted to admit how annoyed she was with herself for cooking two whole bloody salmons with new potatoes in their tiny kitchen in some pathetic desire—need—to earn her mother-in-law's approval.

An hour later than planned, she eventually carried the large salmon plate through to the dining table. Painstakingly, she had layered a line of cucumber along their pink flesh and the hollandaise sauce looked thick and enticing. Everything was laid out perfectly around the christening cake, a hideously expensive confection ordered from The Cake Shop in the Covered Market.

'Wow!' Barney's wife Maggie exclaimed as they swooped on the table, probably beside themselves with hunger by now. 'It looks very professional. Did you get caterers?' She gently slapped the hand of her small son as he stretched it out to steal another crisp.

'Caterers? Virginia?' Judy scoffed with a smile, making it sound like a criticism. 'She always does it herself. It's all that hotel training, isn't it?'

Whatever she said, Virginia knew she had done a good job and she hadn't let Piers down. An hour later, the empty salmon plate had been whisked away and the pavlova and trifle plates were scraped clean.

'That was delicious,' Bill came and stood beside her as she was talking to Charlotte, and kissed her on the top of her head.

'Thank you,' she smiled winningly at him, sensing that he at least realised what today had cost her in effort.

From outside Virginia could hear Scarlett beginning to cry so, taking her from Piers, she slipped away upstairs and, settling herself in the small chair in her daughter's bedroom, made herself comfortable and began to feed her. As Scarlett suckled, she rested her head back against the chair and closed her eyes, listening to the voices in the garden below.

'This the beginning of a brood?' She heard someone say. She wasn't sure how much Piers had shared with his friends about the trials of the last three years and waited for Piers' reply.

'Bit of a set-back having a girl,' Barney laughed, his voice deep and plummy. 'We nearly had a full rugby scrum.'

'Bully for you,' thought Virginia without opening her eyes as the door opened.

'Ah, thought you'd snuck away,' Alice said quietly. 'Can I come in and perch? Or will I be interrupting a mother/daughter bonding session?'

'So long as you don't make any reference to how late lunch was served or the fact that Scarlett is a girl,' Virginia opened one eye and smiled ruefully.

'Be a silly name for a boy,' Alice replied, sitting down on the floor using a giant teddy—a gift from work—as a backrest.

'I'm knackered. Remind me not to do this again.'

'You've done brilliantly,' Alice said warmly, holding up her tea cup in a toast. 'I shall have you cater all my parties.'

'I'll pass if you don't mind.' Virginia shifted the now sleeping baby up onto her shoulder and rubbed her back gently. 'Are they starting to leave?'

'Yup, Judy and Bill are heading the exodus.'

Virginia put her head back against the chair. 'Oh hell, I should go down I suppose.'

'Nah. Take your time. Scarlett's welfare is far more important.' They chatted for a while, Alice describing a recent job she'd done in Stockholm and Virginia trying hard not to bore on about breast-pads and nappy rash. 'How's the love life?' Virginia asked eventually.

'Been a bit slow lately but, as it happens, I've got a hot date tonight.'

'On the Sabbath?' Virginia smiled, content that she didn't have to play this game any more.

'This one is so hot I couldn't care what it was! He's an actor and very, very sexy indeed.'

'You should have brought him.'

'God no. I don't know him well enough yet—he

might be the type who licks his plate.'

'I can't tell you how lovely it's been to have you here.'

'As chief godmother, it was the least I could do. And I have to see that my godchild is being looked after properly.'

Virginia could hear the sound of people in the hall and Piers calling up to her, so she pushed herself up off the chair and laid Scarlett in her cot, the sheets cool against her warm face. 'Best go and see off the hordes. Can we make a date to do something soon? I can't get away for the day or anything yet, but maybe . . .'

'What about a spa day?' Alice asked impractically, following her downstairs.

'I don't think Scarlett is old enough to appreciate a hot stone massage just yet. Oh, I don't know. What can you do with babies?'

'They are quite nice fried,' said Barney, and embraced Virginia as she got to the bottom of the stairs. 'We've got to dash. School night and all that. Thanks for a lovely day and head-wetting. Bring her down to see us soon, won't you?'

'Of course,' Virginia replied, not sure she could cope with a whole weekend of Maggie's expert advice on child-rearing and suitable prep schools.

From then on, the flood gates opened and everyone began to prepare to leave. Charlotte's boyfriend, much the worse for champagne, wine and hot sunshine, waylaid Theo in the hallway to test out his knowledge of NFL since discovering that he lived in New York. Maggie was shouting at one of her sons to put his shoes back on and, in the mêlée, Alice squeezed Virginia in a hug.

'See ya, darling. I'll call when I have a moment's

break from the passion which is bound to ensue after tonight.'

Virginia laughed. 'Oh, and tell all!' She leaned forward in a whisper. 'I've forgotten what it's like!' Alice picked up her coat as Virginia remembered something else that she'd almost forgotten in the stress of the day. 'One thing—silly really, but you get all responsible when you're a parent and we've had to write wills and stuff. Can we put you down as Scarlett's legal guardian?'

Alice looked alarmed for a moment.

'It's only a formality,' Virginia offered.

'Does that mean I can lead her astray?'

Virginia laughed. 'Of course. It's the only thing you'll have to do!'

'Course, sweetie,' Alice kissed her cheek as she headed out of the door. 'Just don't go dying on me. I'll be useless.'

Chapter 24

July 2010

After a few answerphone messages, Alice and Greg had finally managed to speak to each other and had fixed a time and place to meet. She wasn't usually the indecisive type and she didn't think he was either—it didn't fit with the impression she'd formed of him over the last few weeks. Maybe he didn't know the area and was hoping she'd come up with a brilliant suggestion. Whatever the reason, they'd faffed about for some time before agreeing to meet for lunch at a pub in a village along the coast and maybe go for a walk if the weather was nice—which it was. This meant there was no real need to get gussied up, and for that Alice was very glad. Nonetheless, she chose a colourful pair of linen trousers, a vest top with a light fleece and a pair of sparkly Converse. In her backpack, she had a couple of bottles of water and some chocolate. Scarlett would have approved.

For no particular reason, she was slightly late leaving the house and, though she drove as fast as her little car would let her along the winding lanes, he was already in the car park, leaning against his car—something dark-blue, shiny and low-slung— with his face tilted up towards the sunshine. It gave her a moment to study him unobserved and, as they'd only met the one time and she'd been crying for much of that, she was relieved that she recognised him straightaway. He was much more tanned than he'd been—not surprising, since he'd been working in Dubai—and much more informally dressed, of course. He had on a pair of lightweight walking trousers with lots of zipped pockets and a green polo shirt. His jacket and a small pack were on the roof of his car and he had his arms folded across his chest. She parked nearby and walked towards him, noticing that his eyes were closed. She was quite close before he realised she was there—she'd kicked a pebble and the noise roused him.

As soon as he caught sight of her, his face broke into a slow smile and she felt her own reflect it back at him. They greeted each other warmly and there was an awkward moment when they went in for a cheek kiss and both went the same way, but he said, 'That was a near miss!' And he laughed, thank goodness. Alice felt herself relax as he stood back to let her go

175

into the pub first. The door was low and he had to duck—he seemed taller than she remembered, but she had been wearing heels when they'd last met.

The pub was one she'd been to several times before, but not for a while. Fortunately, nothing had changed much—still no juke box or games machines to disturb the peace. Only the seagulls outside, through the open windows, and Alice had long ago reached the point where she didn't notice them any more. The flagstone floor was as shiny and clean as she remembered and the room was cool. It was early enough for them to have their choice of tables and she chose an alcove by one of the small, leaded windows, near a large fireplace that, in cold weather, would contain a roaring fire.

'Let me get you a drink,' Greg offered, and she asked for a white wine spritzer. It seemed more ladylike than a pint of cider, and she didn't feel comfortable enough with him yet not to make a bit of effort. He came back with half of the local bitter for himself and two menus, which they studied in silence while sipping their drinks. Alice flicked a quick look at him while he concentrated She hoped this wasn't going to be awkward, that he wasn't going to regret the whole meeting since the only thing they really had in common was the very thing that would make her cry if they spoke about it too much. But he looked relaxed and, after a moment, spoke, 'I bet the scallops are good. I might have those as a starter. And I could definitely go for a steak. Do you fancy some chips?'

'Yes—I most certainly do.' Alice reached for her spritzer and took a hearty swig. He liked chips. It was going to be all right.

From then on, she couldn't believe she'd been

worried. They spoke about everything and anything. His work, her work, the places they'd visited, the pub, the area, Ginny—and she didn't start crying. He told her about growing up in Gillingham and art college, and about starting up his own design consultancy with a colleague who'd since moved to live in Provence. He was amazingly easy to talk to and so straightforward that Alice felt, before they'd even finished their starters, that she could probably tell him anything. And trust him with anything. The only thing she held back from mentioning, though she wasn't sure why, was Scarlett and the fact that Alice had been looking after her, nor that she was back with her grandparents and that she'd already texted Alice to say how bored she was and could she come back soon. That she didn't mention.

After lunch, they did go for a walk, though they both agreed it should be a shorter one than planned because they'd shared a sticky toffee pudding and weren't actually sure they could manage to go very far. And when they got back to the car park, it seemed the easiest thing in the world to arrange to meet again, later in the week, once Greg had settled in on the new project he was managing. When they kissed goodbye this time, there was no nose bumping. He went left, then right and it all came together beautifully. As Alice waved goodbye and pulled out onto the lane, she knew for certain that she'd made a good new friend, and thought she'd even introduce Greg to Krissy—he might be her type—and Vince—he was certainly his type—when he got back from Mykonos.

* * *

Alice had ignored some of Scarlett's texts, answering about one in three, but the sentiment was clear. She wanted to come back as soon as possible. At Vince's top-floor flat in Brighton a couple of days later, she discussed the matter with Krissy after supper while Vince finished his packing, or rather modelling a series of outfits, rushing back into his bedroom once they'd given their verdict on each one. They were lolling on the most comfortable sofa in the universe—although she hadn't thought that on the day Vince had dragooned her and about six other friends into manoeuvring it up the stairs while he directed operations from above.

'I'm happy for her to come and stay, of course, poor darling. But I can't help thinking she's not going to get settled at Bill and Judy's if she keeps bailing out. That works, Vinny. But I think the shirt would be better untucked.'

Vince tutted. 'I don't think you're quite getting this. If it's untucked, it hides my best assets. Maybe I'll try it with a T-shirt. Hang on—I'll be back.' And he darted off.

'But you can see why she'd prefer to be with you. What you've told me about Judy doesn't sound much fun,' Krissy went on. 'Would you have wanted to go and live with your grandparents when you were eleven? And she hasn't even hit the teenage years yet. What's it going to be like when she does?'

Alice rubbed her eyes. 'Yeah—I dread to think what's going to happen then. If it gets too difficult, they might end up sending her to boarding school. All their boys went. Ginny would have hated that! She'd never have agreed to it.'

'That looks better. Really shows your ... er ... six pack. And your southerly regions. Thing is, Al,'

Krissy turned back to the conversation as Vince returned to his bedroom. 'I don't think the poor kid knows where she belongs. And I don't think anyone's helping her to work it out either. She knows you're her mum's oldest friend, right?'

Alice nodded. 'Yes—she's in no doubt about that—although we still haven't really talked about Ginny. It's just too upsetting for her. And she knows I'm her godmother and everything.'

Krissy nodded. 'What about the guardian thing? Does she know Ginny chose to put you in charge if something like this ever happened?'

Alice hadn't thought about that. 'Well, yes, but I don't know that she really understands it, to be honest. I'm not sure. I mean, I didn't want to make too big of a deal of it because it undermines what Judy and Bill want. And they're blood relatives, aren't they? So that gives them first—er—first dibs, I suppose.'

Krissy shrugged. 'I'm not sure it does, actually. I think it's what's in the will that comes first, surely? I mean, if you choose to leave all your money to a cat's home, instead of your revolting relatives, then the moggies get it, don't they? It's the law.'

'It's not quite the same, though, is it? And you do hear about people contesting wills like that. I'm sure I saw a film about that once.'

'You know what, you should ask Vince.'

'Come again? The last advice he gave me about Scarlett ended up in a lecture on blackheads.'

'Oh, I know—I've had that one too. It's like a mission for him. I was thinking more about his mum—you know she left his dad, just upped and offed, when he was a bit younger than Scarlett.'

Alice thought for a moment. 'Yes, he did mention

179

that once but he didn't go into much detail. How did he cope with it?'

'Well, that's just the thing. At first, no one talked about it because his dad was so cut up, but then his granny—you know, the one from County Clare, his dad's mum—came to take care of them and she made Vince and his sisters the centre of her life. And she even got in touch with his mum and arranged for the kids to meet up with her. She didn't tell his dad— her own son. Not at first, at least. He wouldn't even mention his wife's name.'

Alice shook her head. 'I'm not really seeing the point. This situation with Scarlett is completely different.'

'I know that. But there are things you could learn from how Dolores—that's his granny—handled it. She put the children first. I remember Vince saying she wouldn't blame his mum—or his dad, for that matter. She said what grown-ups did was their own business and there was probably fault on both sides. But she said it wasn't fair for the children to suffer and that everyone should focus on trying to make it all right for them.'

They both turned as Vince reappeared. Alice shook her head. 'No, I don't like that top so much— it makes you look like you should be wearing a medallion.'

Vince pouted. 'You say that as though it's a bad thing!' and flounced out.

'I just wonder what Scarlett thinks about it all. Has anybody really *asked* her?' Krissy went on. She seemed remarkably insightful for a childless woman into chakras. Perhaps this alternative stuff she was into had some benefit after all.

Alice paused. 'Actually, no. Well, I haven't, because

180

I don't really think it's my place to. And I don't want to cause trouble with Judy, I suppose.'

'Yeees,' Krissy replied slowly. 'You seem to be doing a lot of that.'

'What?'

'Avoiding confrontation with Judy. Are you aware of that?'

Alice shifted on the sofa. Where was Vince? He seemed to be taking an awfully long time to change into his next outfit.

'Well?' Krissy persisted. 'Are you?'

'Yes, I suppose so. But I don't want to upset her. She's always so tightly wound and she's just lost her son, for God's sake.'

Krissy paused for a moment. There was a sound of tuneless singing from Vince's room. If he'd started practising his dance moves, he wouldn't be out for ages. 'Yes, she's lost a son—and that's terrible. But she's a grown-up, Al. She'll find a way of coping. You've lost your best friend, and that's terrible too, but you will cope—if you ever give yourself a moment to really think about what's happened, instead of distracting yourself with travelling and work. But Scarlett. She's lost her whole world. Her home, her parents, her friends, her school. Everything she knows and everything that's familiar to her. And she's only eleven. She's the one everyone should be thinking about. Her and what Ginny and Piers would have wanted for her. You see, it's not so different to Vince's story, in some ways.'

Alice fiddled with her nails. There was still a trace of the varnish Scarlett had carefully applied for her the day before she'd left and Alice had been picking it off ever since, Scarlett having taken her remover with her when she went; when Alice had driven her to Haywards Heath and delivered her back, like a parcel. Dumped her and run. Unexpectedly, tears came flooding to Alice's eyes and overflowed as she turned to Krissy who, quite unfazed, simply gathered her friend into her arms and held her as she sobbed and sobbed.

'All right! I'll leave it untucked. Jeez Louise, no need to overreact!' Vince had emerged at last, and Alice lifted her head to see him resplendent in lurid Hawaiian shorts and a neon string vest.

'Vince,' she sobbed. 'I'm so sorry about your mum leaving you.'

'You what?' he asked, shaking his head.

Krissy stepped in. 'I was just telling her about your granny and how she looked after you all, and I was thinking Scarlett could do with a bit of that kind of TLC.'

Vince put his head on one side. 'Awww—Dolores. My little Dolly. No one could stuff a cabbage like her. She was wonderful. Taught me everything I know— well, not quite everything. She used to tuck me in at night—every single night until I was seventeen. Used to tuck the blankets in so tightly, I could hardly move. And she always made sure my hands were on the outside. Bless her—she made me the man I am today.' He paused and his lower lip started to quiver. 'Oh don't. You'll start me off, too. Shift over, Kriss—I'm coming onboard.' And Vince squeezed in beside Alice on the sofa, sniffling in sympathy as Krissy gently rubbed both their backs.

Chapter 25

May 2001

'You're buying a house *where*?' Virginia asked, picking up bits of ricotta that had missed the pizza and popping them into her mouth. Alice had always rented—it suited her mercurial personality not to be tied anywhere—so her revelation that she was actually investing in property had taken her by surprise.

'Sussex.'

'What, Brighton? Near Vince?'

'I can't afford that,' Alice sighed, 'I'm not going to live in a shoebox like Vince's. It's no better than the student digs we had, and at least we didn't have to pay a mortgage on those.'

'Hove?'

'Nah—not in town.'

'Don't tell me you're going rural?' Virginia's eyes widened as she slipped the pizzas into the oven. Piers wouldn't be back until late—some regatta miles away—and she had Alice all to herself. She'd arrived just after lunch, the chug of her old Golf engine announcing her arrival, and after an exhausting afternoon they'd finally got Scarlett to bed and were making serious inroads into the Martinis.

'Don't think I've got much choice.' Alice pulled the olive off the cocktail stick and put it in her mouth. 'Mum and Dad are too far away from London for me to visit enough—though why the hell they had to decamp to the seaside I cannot imagine. I can't understand why Dad wants to end his days looking out over the Channel from the window of some grim geriatric flat, but I just need to be near enough to them so I can keep an eye.'

'That's the burden of the only child,' Virginia topped up her glass with the remains of the contents of the cocktail shaker. 'Rosie may be a miserable old cow at times, but it's a relief to share the burden of my mum with her.'

'Mmm.' Alice tucked her legs up under her on the kitchen stool as she watched Virginia open the fridge and take out the ingredients for a salad. 'They've coped pretty well so far, but neither of them is very well now. Dad's Parkinson's is getting worse and worse and Mum has heart trouble. It would be perfection if they both rolled into the sea, simultaneously, in matching wheelchairs.'

Virginia watched Alice's face. She was employing that technique again, the one of being glib and facetious about really quite serious subjects that Virginia recognised so well. The one she did when men dumped her or she lost a work contract. Virginia knew better than to ask soul-searching questions when she was like this. Alice's style was to pretend she didn't give a monkey's and move on. What hurts had she buried over the years beneath that nonchalant exterior? Virginia wondered as she chopped the tomatoes and dropped them into the rocket leaves in the wide green bowl.

'So you didn't opt for a sea-view apartment in Eastbourne then?' Virginia asked.

'What and lower the average age of the population to ninety-six? What would that do for my image? No, actually I've put in an offer on a cottage.'

'A cottage?' Virginia spluttered. She couldn't imagine anything more incongruous.

184

'Don't be like that! Who knows, it might be the making of me. I might end up gardening and keeping hens.'

Virginia raised her eyebrow sceptically.

'OK, OK—you're right.' Alice ran her finger around the top of her glass. 'I've probably made a stupid mistake, but it was cheap.'

Virginia peered into the oven to see if the pizzas were brown and bubbling. 'For cheap, do I read derelict?'

'Not *exactly*. Mum and Dad gave me some money from the sale of the house in Highgate—well, quite a bit actually—so I have managed to buy it outright.'

'You jammy bugger.'

'Yes, I know. I am, aren't I? Perhaps being an only child isn't such a burden!' Alice smiled her wickedly frank smile which popped Virginia's little bubble of envy.

'What's it like?'

'It's quite sweet, I suppose. Roses round the door and all that. Bit of a garden with a few trees—think they're apple—and a kitchen that is circa 1955 by the look of it. It's got a staircase and three bedrooms, which is quite grown up for me.'

'What's the village like? Anywhere near Bill and Morticia?'

''Bout fifty minutes, I suppose, so you can come and stay with me instead of them any time you like.'

That sounded like heaven to Virginia, though she wasn't sure it would wash with Piers. 'So are you going to make it sweet and cosy, then join the WI and be worthy?'

Alice flicked idly through a catalogue for children's clothes she'd found on the breakfast bar. 'Doubt it. Sounds ghastly. All that homemade jam and village fêtes. I shall have to buy some things for the place though. I've only got my old sleigh bed and a sofa and that won't fill it. Most of the stuff that was worth anything in Highgate has been squeezed into their little pad.'

*   *   *

Virginia could vividly recollect visits to Alice's parents in their house in Highgate, the sale of which must have more than covered their new flat, Alice's cottage and their care with plenty to spare, because she'd never been in a place like it in her life. Large, brick, detached and set in one of those leafy Highgate roads, the house was a mirror to her parents' personalities. Alice's mother was fragrant and distracted, always researching some book about Vanessa Bell or a poet no one had ever heard of, and though Alice's unworldliness—the crappy car, the lack of interest in the news or what was going on around her—was definitely her mother in her, Virginia always thought Alice was much more like her father. Or at least, her father's influence over her was huge. The creative director of a massively successful West End advertising agency, who had headed up some of the most famous campaigns of the last thirty years, he displayed all the characteristics that went with the job—larger-than-life confidence and astonishing single-mindedness, with a hard edge to him that could make him quite ruthless at times. What Virginia wasn't sure of was if Alice was the way she was *because* of him, or because she was like him.

The house had been full of fascinating *objets d'art* they'd collected on their travels around the world,

186

which sat alongside abstract paintings that Virginia suspected were hugely valuable, modern Corbusier-style chairs and heavy, ornate furniture big enough to fill the large Highgate rooms. And people, the house was always full of people, something Virginia was completely unused to. In Stoke, a visitor was planned and prepared for. In Highgate, they seemed to drop in and be welcomed willy-nilly. 'Who *are* these people?' Virginia would ask Alice, as they lay on her large double bed (bought when she was fifteen to accommodate boyfriends her parents had never had any problem with staying over). They'd be listening to music or painting their toenails as the doorbell would go again and someone else would be let in to talk over the kitchen table and a bottle of expensive red wine.

'Oh, he's a theatre director, I think,' Alice would reply uninterestedly, 'and that other bloke plays in a rock band or something.' They were just a part of her life which seemed as changeable as gossamer. No wonder she had never managed to hold down a relationship.

'Well, I hope our little trip today has got you in the mood,' Virginia said now. 'You certainly showed a skill for interior design I've never seen you display before!'

'That's 'cause everything my mother ever bought was vintage or antique. Scratch the surface and I'm as kitsch as they come.'

Alice had embraced the expedition to decorate and furnish Scarlett's bedroom with vigour. Virginia had—perhaps foolishly—promised Scarlett, just out of a cot, that she could be involved in choosing her new bedroom. But her daughter's excitement was nothing compared to Alice's as they entered the children's furniture department. She doubted Alice had ever been in such a place—why would she?—but she scooped up Scarlett with her enthusiasm.

'Oh bliss!' she'd squealed. 'What's our budget?'

'Peanuts, but the most important thing is that we have to see Judy off at the pass. She is desperate to supply everything—but, well . . .'

'What? And take away all the fun? No way! Come on, Scarlett, we've beds to jump on!'

Virginia was almost surplus to requirements as Alice sat down and bounced on half-sized beds with Scarlett beside her in her little pink cotton dress and her Start-rite sandals, giggling fit to burst. Everything in Virginia's being knew that a half-sized bed was a stupid idea—they'd be having to buy a full-sized one in no time—but by the time Alice had finished, including commandeering the assistant into finding all the accessories she felt Scarlett would need for a bedroom fit for her goddaughter, Virginia had been talked into it, much against her better judgement and up to the limit on her credit card. She suspected even Piers wouldn't take her side—he was game for anything Scarlett loved, no matter how impractical.

Then, after Alice had taken them for a milk shake, which Scarlett had sucked noisily through a straw, she had insisted they went into a shop in Little Clarendon Street and—at her insistence—paid for strings of lights shaped like butterflies, thin, pale-pink silk fabric to hang like a canopy and a pink lampshade shaped like a hat Audrey Hepburn might have worn, complete with ribbon, which made Scarlett's eyes widen with excitement.

The result, once the bed was delivered and Virginia had put it all together, would be delicious. It would be the bedroom Virginia had always wanted as a child, she would write in the diary later, and she loved her friend for her unexpected enthusiasm. She slipped the pizzas out of the oven and put them on the table with the salad.

Alice peered into the cocktail shaker. 'Oops, we seem to have seen that off. Time for a bottle of wine, I think. Then we can celebrate Scarlett's new bedroom and me dipping my toe into the property ladder.'

'I think you've mixed your metaphors there,' Virginia slurred, knowing that she had drunk enough already.

Alice filled their glasses with the new bottle of white from the fridge, and held hers up in a toast.

'Here's to little girls, cheap cottages and mexed mitaphors!' She paused then, realising her mistake, they both shrieked with laughter.

Chapter 26

July 2010

Alice waited to text Scarlett until she'd phoned Judy on Friday. With Krissy in the background as her own personal cheerleader and life coach combined, she started off assertively. 'Judy—hello! It's Alice. How are you?'

'Oh. Alice. How nice to hear from you. We're all fine here. Scarlett has been up to the stables this morning and she's having her first lesson this weekend.'

'Oh—right.' Alice began to falter and Krissy was on her feet at once, gesticulating at Alice to breathe deeply. 'What day is her lesson? There's a party in the village here on Sunday. I was wondering if Scarlett would like to come along.' Alice braced herself, expecting a fight.

'Erm, let me see. Well, it's rather short notice. But her lesson is on Saturday morning. I suppose . . . Yes, you could pick her up after that. Yes, that would do. What time should I expect you?'

'Midday? Would that be all right?' Alice tucked the phone under her chin and gave a double thumbs-up to Krissy.

But Judy wasn't going to give up that easily. 'Oh no, dear. I've planned lunch already. Bill and I went shopping on Wednesday—or was it yesterday? If you come perhaps at two- thirty? I'll make sure she's ready. Will you bring her back after this—event?'

'Well, I was wondering if she'd like to stay a little bit longer. Maybe until Wednesday?'

There was a long pause. 'That might be possible. Will you be taking her out shopping again?'

'I don't know. I hadn't really thought about it. Why? Does she need anything? We can easily pop into Brighton. She seemed to like it there.'

'No—no need. It's just that some of the clothes she's come home with—they're not terribly good quality, Alice. It's rather a waste of money. But you must keep the receipts, dear, so that Bill and I can pay you back. Until probate is granted and we can get rid of that little house, we'll be paying the bills. Not that I grudge a penny of it, you understand. I'd just prefer her to wear, well, more substantial clothing.'

'Riiiight. OK. So till Wednesday, then. Excellent. We can arrange what time on Saturday. Shall I tell Scarlett or will you?'

'Oh, I think I'd better. She's rather touchy just

now. I'll choose the right moment. Well, goodbye, Alice. Until Saturday.'

Alice switched off the phone and stared at Krissy in astonishment. 'That was far easier than I was expecting. Maybe we've misjudged her all along.'

Krissy compressed her lips and frowned as though thinking deeply. 'Maybe,' she said slowly. 'But I doubt it.'

*   *   *

Alice plumped up the pillows on Scarlett's bed and stepped back to admire the effect. It looked cosy and she nodded in satisfaction. Vince would be proud of her. She looked at her watch. Scarlett should be arriving any minute—Judy had rung back suggesting that she and Bill would bring her over, and since Alice had, so far, done all the driving and delivering, that seemed fair. Plus, it gave her a little extra time to tidy up. There was something about Judy's arrival, and her scrutiny, that was making Alice uncharacteristically nervous. Was this what Ginny was always referring to? Alice had a nasty feeling she'd dismissed Ginny's anxieties too lightly in the past.

But it was nearly three o'clock now and she'd run out of surfaces to polish. The sound of a car slowing down in the lane had her running downstairs. Sure enough, Bill's Volvo was drawing up in front of her gate, so she quickly ran her fingers through her short hair and went to greet them. Scarlett was the first out, tugging out her case and looking around. At least *she* looked happy. The same couldn't be said for Judy, sliding neatly out of the passenger seat in approved, knees-together fashion. The slight tension on her face had Alice on the alert straightaway. Thank goodness she'd put fresh flowers—only ones from the garden, but better than nothing—in vases on the mantelpiece, and bought a better class of biscuit than she would normally spring for. It looked as though Judy would need mollifying.

'Hello! Lovely to see you!' Alice called cheerily, hurrying to the gate. 'Everything all right? Did my directions make sense?'

Bill had now unfolded himself from the car and was turning slowly round. Alice's cheery greeting trailed away. He was easing his shoulders but there was a strain on his face she hadn't seen before. Then he turned to her and his usual warm smile lit up his face, crinkling his eyes in a way that was still attractive. Alice felt herself relax as he came over and embraced her warmly. Poor old Bill had probably had his ear bent all the way. 'Cup of tea?' she offered.

'Ooh, yes please. That would hit the spot perfectly. Lovely to see you, Alice. It's been ages.'

She didn't like to correct him. In fact, she'd seen him more in the last few weeks than she had for years. Perhaps, she thought, time with Judy passed very slowly and turning to her now, she could see why. Judy was looking at the rusty garden gate with distaste. 'Hello, Alice, dear,' she offered a cool, powdery cheek. 'Sorry we're a bit late. It's a very long time since we've been here and I'm afraid we took one or two wrong turnings.'

Alice was immediately consumed with guilt. 'Oh, I'm sorry,' she said. 'I should have texted you the postcode—that would probably have made it easier. Anyway, you're here now. Come in! Come in!'

As they made their way slowly towards the front door, she turned to Scarlett who, unexpectedly, responded to her hug with a quick one-armed clasp and didn't duck away when Alice ruffled her hair. 'How are you, mate? Had a good riding lesson? It's great that you're getting into that—you'll have to tell me about it later.'

Scarlett smiled a bit tightly. 'Yeah, later.' She looked around her, as though checking everything was as she'd left it. 'Have you been watering my tomato plant and when's the party?'

They followed Bill and Judy in and Alice did her best to corral them into the little sitting room. 'Of course I have. I wouldn't dare not. Go and have a peep at it. And the village thing—it's tomorrow.' She leaned in confidingly. 'You don't actually have to go, if you don't want to. We could go and see Krissy instead. Vince is still away, but he'll be back at the end of next week.' Scarlett frowned slightly and Alice hurried on. 'Want some juice? Come into the kitchen and give me a hand. You can put out the biccies. Oh—sorry, Judy. Let me move those.' She bustled forward. Why, oh why, when she'd cleared two armchairs and stacked up the magazines on a third, did Judy choose that very one to sit on?

'It's all right, dear. I can do it. I've no idea why you buy all these rags—they all say exactly the same thing. I read *Country Life* at the hairdresser, and that's my limit. I really don't have time to sit about reading.' She peered at them. 'Oh, is this something of yours, Scarlett?'

It was the slightly day-glo magazine she'd proudly brought home from her first shopping trip with Vince and it was looking a bit dog-eared now, the grinning teenage girl on the cover wrinkled prematurely.

'What on earth? "Fit Lads and How to Get Them to Notice You"? "Snogging Tips He'll Love!"? "Your

193

Flirty Holiday Romance Secrets"? Alice, I think we need to talk.'

Shamefully, Alice's first instinct was to lie and say it had been left by the daughter of a friend, but she didn't have any friends with teenage daughters and wasn't sure she could carry it off. Then she remembered what Krissy had said about everyone pandering to Judy and replied, as coolly as she could. 'Yes, if you like, Judy. But perhaps not now and certainly not here.' She was aware of Scarlett, over Judy's shoulder, hovering in the kitchen, but didn't dare to look at the expression on her face, in case Judy dragged her into the discussion. 'I can assure you,' she continued smoothly, hoping that Judy wouldn't open it and read any of the content, 'this magazine is squarely aimed at Scarlett's age group. I know it looks a bit lurid, but it's quite harmless,' she bluffed. 'And Scarlett reads plenty of other stuff—she was reading the *Sunday Times* the other day, in fact.' No need to mention that it was the Style section and a piece on fake tan.

Judy sniffed and dropped the magazine on top of the pile Alice was holding. 'Well, she won't be reading anything of that sort when she's with us, will she, Bill?'

'What? What's that, my dear?' Bill seemed to snap out of a reverie and Alice felt herself relax as Judy's radar turned away from her.

'You're off again, aren't you? Will you please remember to wear your hearing aid next time we go out? Honestly, it's too tiresome . . .'

Alice took the opportunity to nip to the kitchen and bring in the tray she'd set earlier. Under the soothing influence of Earl Grey, the rest of the visit passed uneventfully apart from a couple of rather loaded comments from Judy and, eventually, they left. And the moment they did, Scarlett disappeared upstairs to her room without another word.

Alice slowly cleared away the tea things. She was trying as hard as she could to keep things friendly with Judy but she was beginning to feel there was a difference in their approach to Scarlett that could never be reconciled. It was more than just the choice of school. That was merely a symptom. It went far deeper and it was something she could no longer ignore.

*   *   *

It wasn't until later on that Alice remembered that she and Greg had discussed spending the day together on Sunday—something she'd forgotten when she'd agreed Scarlett should stay for the weekend. Now it looked as though she'd have to call it off, and although it was a shame because he'd offered to take her over to look at the new hotel refurbishment he was working on, she thought it was probably for the best because Scarlett was adamant about attending the village party and had even gone out, after Bill and Judy's departure, to watch the preparations on the village green and in the nearby hall. Alice, slightly baffled, had let her go, noticing with amazement that her legs seemed to have grown too long for her bike even in the few short days she'd been with her grandparents. That couldn't be, surely? Maybe the saddle had slipped down a bit. Did children grow that quickly? Watching her pedal determinedly along the lane, changing gear with confidence and checking over her shoulder every so often, Alice felt an odd little

195

surge of pride, then smiled to herself and went in. It was turning chilly, and she popped upstairs to get a cardigan and put her head around the door of Scarlett's room. Apart from a Scarlett-shaped dip in the quilt, it was unusually tidy; well, that wouldn't last once she unpacked. Then she stopped short. Her suitcase lay open and empty in the corner. Alice checked the drawers and then the wardrobe. She'd put away everything she'd brought with her, and her pink toy cat—Vince's early purchase—was sitting proudly on the windowsill, surveying the room.

Alice smiled again, and went downstairs to start making supper—pasta à la Vince.

Chapter 27

September 2003

Virginia closed the front door before crumpling. The sight of her daughter disappearing into the classroom with an anxious backward glance, her pump bag in one small hand and her other hand holding that of the teaching assistant, had been almost too much to bear, and Virginia had had to make a speedy exit. It had been a wise move to take the morning off work because she'd suspected she'd react like this. She'd postponed a meeting with the chef because arriving with piggy eyes from tears just because your daughter had started school was probably highly unprofessional.

Nursery, something Scarlett had experienced since she was six months old when Virginia had dragged herself back to work kicking and screaming, was somehow different. It was a—expensive—necessity, but they had fallen upon a small and very caring nursery close to the house and the staff had almost become friends. School, with its named pegs, kit-list and 'head teacher' sign on a closed door off the reception, was a far more serious progression and one which made it seem as if Scarlett had been wrenched away and handed over to someone else to raise.

Feeling as if a part of her was missing, Virginia turned on the radio to fill the void and listened to the news as she sipped her coffee. Tony Blair was making thin promises about the economy and then followed a more and more harrowing report about a famine somewhere. Guiltily, Virginia switched it off. She couldn't cope with anyone else's grief and, picking up her trowel, she did the most unlikely activity for her to be doing on an unusually warm Monday morning in September. She went out to weed the garden.

Though only a postage stamp in comparison to most, their little garden was now the centre of Virginia's small universe. It was March when they had moved in, and it had been full of uninspiring and regimented shrubs, with the odd clump of daffs, so she'd let it be, too wrapped up in Scarlett to have time for such things. But as their first summer at the house had begun to unfurl, something had awakened in Virginia. As she'd pushed Scarlett in her pram to the shops or to the park, she'd started to notice what other people had in their gardens and to bury her nose in roses or lilac that overhung the pavement. She'd even bored Natasha senseless last time they'd gone round for dinner about what she planted in her borders. This was a whole new world to Virginia. Her parents' garden in Stoke had been a square with a couple of feet of flowerbed around three sides, filled with urban shrubs and evergreens, in front of a high fence. In one corner, at a rakish angle, was an old metal swing, the ground beneath rubbed bare from sandals as Rosie and she used their feet as brakes before daringly jumping off. National Trust gardens held no appeal for Virginia and Alice's garden in Sussex was, like Alice's house, a chaotic mess. Bill and Judy's garden, Virginia's only other point of horticultural reference, was so manicured and tended by Graham (a gardener who'd been with the family so long, he had taught Piers to ride a bike without stabilisers) that it seemed a world apart. Every foxglove stood to rigid attention and the croquet lawn bounced beneath one's feet as if it were sponge cake.

Virginia stood for a moment by the French door and observed her little Eden. The cherry tree, the shade of which had protected Scarlett's pram as she'd slept, had grown quite tall now and she hoped it wasn't too much shade for the brassy dahlias whose brown leaves and dark flowers gave such a delicious contrast to the soft greens around them. There were still the vestiges of summer in the borders, with delphiniums and pink penstemons making a last, brave showing, and she'd spent the weekend dividing some of the perennials that had begun to dominate the tiny plot. Piers had teased her that they'd have to buy next-door's garden if she carried on packing so much into the borders.

'Look away, there's nothing for you there,' he'd goad every time they passed a nursery and he was

198

right to distract her. She couldn't be trusted. She hadn't bought herself any new clothes for months, and the last time she'd dragged herself to the shops, she'd come back with a bag of narcissus bulbs.

Crouching down, she tidied the bits she hadn't had time to do yesterday, distracted by Scarlett, who'd wanted to cut the lettuces in the little plot Virginia had set aside for her by the garden shed. She'd then wanted to pack her bag ready for tomorrow and lay out her new school sweatshirt and little grey pleated skirt. The sight of them on the chair ready for the morning, when Virginia had gone to check on her before she and Piers went to bed, nearly poleaxed her and she'd hurried out.

As she tidied, the phone shrilled in the lounge and Virginia, easing herself up, stretched and picked it up.

'So? How did it go? Did you cry?'

'Buckets.'

'Oh, Ginny,'

Virginia smiled at Alice's sigh and perched herself on the step outside the French window. 'I know. Pathetic, isn't it? It's only school and she'll be back by half past three. She just looked so adorable. Little red sweatshirt, shiny new shoes and a matching ribbon in her plaits.'

Alice laughed. 'She'll be dropping spiders down the teachers' necks and smoking behind the bike sheds before you can say national curriculum, I'll bet.'

'Oh God, don't. This step is big enough, thanks. Whatcha doing? How's Oscar?'

'It's Octavian, actually, and he's fine.' Alice paused for a moment and sighed dramatically. 'Well, he's not actually. I thought there was

199

something not quite right about him—he was a bit too fascinated by my clothes and seemed to prefer shopping to watching the footie so I should have seen the signs. Anyway, on Friday—or it might have been Saturday—anyway, the one before the one just gone, Vince came out with us and, when Octavian went for a pee, Vince put his fingers up like antenna and whispered "Gay alert, girlfriend". He says he could spot it before he even sat down to join us.'

'And, let's face it,' Virginia tried to sound sympathetic, 'Vince is the expert on the subject.' Noticing a browning rose in the bush she'd omitted to deadhead, Virginia had a mental image of Vince, possibly the campest man in Brighton, and certainly the one with the best shaved legs. He may have an encyclopaedic knowledge of nail varnish, but a nicer, more gentle man Virginia couldn't imagine, and she felt almost jealous of Alice's easy relationship with him, even though it was based on a mutual love of shoes.

'He was fine in the sack,' Alice conceded. 'Quite considerate, actually, which makes a pleasant change, but a bit particular about bodily hygiene, if you know what I mean?'

'Oh dear. Hours in the bathroom before and after and no damp patches allowed on the sheets?'

Alice giggled. 'Something like that. Anyway, he's history and another Alice Fenton romance bites the dust.'

'There'll be others.'

'Oh I don't know,' Alice sighed again, and Virginia smiled at how easily Alice had managed to divert the conversation entirely to herself. 'I'm seriously thinking of internet dating now.

Desperate woman seeks love interest. Arseholes and gays need not apply.'

'Unfortunate juxtaposition of words?' Virginia snorted and they both screamed with laughter. Virginia felt better already. 'Can't you try and find a bloke who's a bit more—I don't know—*straightforward. Uncomplicated*?'

'Where do you start?'Alice cried desperately. 'I thought I'd found one and he turns out to prefer men. How insulting is that?'

Virginia couldn't really answer. Compared to Alice, she was pitifully naive when it came to relationships. Alice was in a different league, and Virginia's experience was pretty much just Piers. Pretty much.

Once they'd said goodbyes and arranged a date for Alice to come up for the night, Virginia rang off. Feeling a bit guilty and pathetic that she wasn't in work and shouldn't really be gardening, Virginia pulled out Scarlett's diary, which was tucked away with her cookbooks. She'd managed to convince herself that she kept it hidden so that Scarlett wouldn't find it and use it as another colouring book, but something else kept her from showing it to Piers. She didn't suppose that he'd find the idea of a diary to Scarlett odd at all. In fact, he'd probably approve, so fanatical was he at cataloguing her development with photographs and the camcorder. Only this morning he'd taken a mass of pictures as she stood on the doorstep ready to walk to school for the first time. But writing down her thoughts seemed more personal than snaps they'd put in a frame of pictures on the landing, alongside shots of Scarlett at the beach or in the garden, and Virginia wanted to keep them to herself.

Making a fresh cup of coffee and curling her feet under her on an armchair by the open French window, she began.

Darling Scarlett,
What an important day for you! I'm sitting here
watching a blackbird hopping all over your little
vegetable garden looking for bugs and and thinking
about what you must be doing now. I'll never forget
my first day at school. We had to wear light-blue
aprons and bring in a bag to hang over the back
of our chairs for our exercise books. Mine was
made out of the old curtains Rosie and I had in
our bedroom and I felt so ashamed, as if everyone
would know.

I hope you love this school as much as I loved
mine. Sometimes your teachers can almost be the
most important people in your lives—not more than
Dad and I, I hope!—and Mrs Blackman and Mrs
Tait seem like they'll be pretty special to me.

Alice has just called to ask how you are getting
on. I hope she'll come and see us soon. We've
made a plan but one thing you'll learn about Alice
is that she makes plans and then changes them at
the last minute. She's always been like that, even
at university, and it makes me want to scream, but
you'll find as you grow up that there is something
rather exciting about unreliable people, especially
to reliable people like me. On the whole they are
disorganised and what Grandpa Sussex calls
'flighty', but when you are with them, it's a gas.
There have been a couple of times when she's kept
me waiting or been coming to stay and the plans
have moved at the last minute when I've wanted to
get quite cross with her, but I'm not good at getting

202

cross and I wouldn't want to do anything that would harm our friendship. It's far too special for that.

She's your godmother—well, you know that—and probably the only godmother anyone has ever had that sent a two-year-old a pair of pink heart-shaped sunglasses and drop earrings. So, hopefully, some of her wonderful spontaneity will rub off on you. One thing though—if you ever go out with her for the day, check she has fuel in her car. I once spent three hours on the M25 near Watford with her, because she was convinced she could get to Brentwood on fresh air.

Virginia took a sip of her coffee. The journal and her reasons for writing it seemed to have changed over the years. It had started off as a letter to her daughter, but now the reasons behind it were blurred. Even though she still addressed it to Scarlett, and had filled it with milestones and observations, sitting down in a quiet moment to write things down had become a curiously cathartic part of Virginia's life. A secret place that was all her own. Flicking back through the pages and reading some of her comments made her wonder if some bits shouldn't be edited out in case Scarlett—or anyone else for that matter—ever got her hands on it. Plenty of time for that though.

She picked up her pen again.

I have always wanted to apologise that you don't have any little brothers or sisters. It can be lonely being an only child, but I'm afraid it's unlikely that Dad and I will be lucky a second time. We're neither of us very good at baby-making. It's something that has caused us a huge amount of grief and is why you are such a very, very special girl. But trust me, sometimes being an only one can be an advantage.

The upside is that you have our entire attention. (I used to be very jealous of Alice not having brothers or sisters.) It's probably not good for you though, being the centre of our world, and the tantrum you threw about clearing your dinner plate yesterday lunchtime is a case in point. Dad shouldn't have caved in.

The downside is that sometimes you have to share in grown-up activities—activities which you shouldn't have to witness. For example, I'm sorry you were upset by seeing Granny Stoke last week. I wanted to take you to see her so, when you are older, you will have had at least some memory of another grandmother other than Granny Sussex (who may well be around forever), but what I hadn't realised is how poorly Granny Stoke has become. I have tried to see her as often as I could around you and work, but in the last few weeks she seems to have deteriorated.

It seems entirely unnatural—evil even—to wish your mother dead. Mothers should be with you forever, shouldn't they? Or at least until you are a grandmother yourself, but I cannot bear to see this woman as she is now. She bears no relation to my mother as I knew her. My mother was full of life, funny and exciting to be with. She was pretty too— though you probably can't imagine that—and you look like her sometimes, especially when you laugh. All she is now is a shell, dried up and empty, with nothing inside until she suddenly flares up as she did last week. She doesn't really hate me, Scarlett. When people have dementia, they say things they don't mean. Though, on reflection, she has every reason to hate me. I don't suppose I've been a very good daughter. Or so Rosie tells me.

Virginia stopped and, blinking back tears, she looked at her watch. She was straying into dangerous ground and, making herself close the book, she slipped it back between Nigel Slater and Jamie Oliver, and got herself ready for work.

Chapter 28

July 2010

'Actually, I think that'd be fun,' Greg said. 'I'd love to come.'

Alice took the phone from her ear and stared at it accusingly. 'Are you sure?' she replied after a moment. 'I mean, it's not going to be all that much fun. Honestly. Just stalls selling everyone's unwanted presents and bottles of revolting liqueur.'

Greg laughed. 'OK, confession time. I love that kind of thing. I know it may sound terribly glam, flying around the world and staying in five-star hotels, but, I promise, the appeal wears off after a while. A local village party is just what I fancy. And it's a lovely day. What could be nicer?'

Alice shrugged in resignation. 'Well, don't say I didn't warn you. And, please—if you value your life—don't ever tell me again that first-class travel is a bore. I just refuse to believe it. Even though there is going to be food here—a barbecue—you might want to eat first. Seriously.'

'Oh calm down. It'll be fine. Should I bring a

contribution for the bottle stall? Raffle? What do you think?'

'You do know your village parties, don't you? I should think if you bring a bottle, you'll be welcomed with open arms.'

She could hear him smiling as he replied. 'Yes, I'm quite the fête-alist. What time does it kick off? You've got to get in early at the cake stall, y'know, if you want to bag anything decent.'

'Two o'clock. Be there *and* be square.'

'Good. I'll look forward to it. And to meeting Scarlett.'

*   *   *

At quarter to two precisely, Greg drew up outside the cottage. Scarlett had already gone to the village green because, she'd proudly informed Alice, she was helping on the hook-a-duck stall. She didn't hear the car arrive until the last minute, its low purring engine not audible until it was under her window. Alice had expected no less. He was the punctual type and she'd have to raise her game.

He looked relaxed and content and, after a brief hug and a kiss on each cheek—they'd got it down perfectly by now—the two of them ambled together along the lane towards the centre of the village, chatting about work and what they'd been up to, and Alice recounted the story of Judy and the teenage magazine.

'Honestly, Greg. I hadn't even looked at it. It didn't occur to me that it would be like that. But when I read it, it was mad! Completely boy-obsessed, all about snogging techniques and really quite explicit in places. It's *way* too old for her. At her age, I was reading Princess Tina and had posters of ponies on my wall.'

'Very pleased to hear it. My sister used to read *Jackie*. There was a lot about snogging in that too.'

Alice looked at him with exaggerated suspicion. 'How do you know that? Did you sneak in and read it?'

'Yep—it was how I learned about girls, mostly, reading the Cathy and Claire problem page. And,' he cleared his throat modestly, 'it's why I'm such a good kisser now.'

Alice stopped and gasped in mock horror and he turned to face her, the sun behind him shining in her eyes and making her squint. Then a sensation of warmth in the pit of her stomach took her by surprise. Suddenly, the ideas of Greg and of kissing collided in her mind and she stepped back, shocked at her reaction. There was a pause that felt awkward to her, but he seemed unaffected, still smiling at her in that slightly wry way he had. 'Come on,' she said quickly, her voice sounding tight. 'We'd better hurry up or there won't be anything left at the cake stall but crumbs.' And she walked on along the lane.

Fortunately the sight of the street party, as they rounded the corner, saved Alice from having to think of something to say and distracted Greg from her now-burning-hot cheeks. She discreetly fanned herself with her hand. It was either menopause starting early, or—she dismissed the thought before it had even formed. He was so not her type that any inappropriate thoughts were just perverse.

'Wow! I had no idea . . .' Alice had always avoided village functions in the past. Altogether too hearty, she thought, and there was always the possibility of getting roped into something. Far better, surely, never to get too involved in the first place. But this looked surprisingly like fun. Bunting, an implausible mix of plastic Union Jacks and faded floral cotton, was draped between lampposts and the sound of an accordion floated over the voices of an already considerable crowd. It looked as though people must have brought along their own gazebo tent things because a string of them, in different colours and shapes, bordered the road on either side, each one housing a different stall. Presumably this was a precaution against rain. If so, it wasn't needed. The sky was cloudless and, although a light breeze kept her skin mercifully cool, Alice could feel the strength of the sun.

Beside her, Greg was taking in the scene. 'Speaking as a fête expert, this is a class operation. Let's dump this cherry vodka—vile stuff—at the bottle stall and find the cakes. And hook-a-duck, of course.'

Alice was peering around, looking for Scarlett. She really hadn't expected this much activity, and she could feel herself becoming slightly anxious as she scanned the crowd for the polka-dot T-shirt and head of sleek, dark hair. A light tap on her arm made her jump. It was Wendy, in another of her timeless hand-knits, despite the heat, her eyes bright with enthusiasm.

'Well, well—fancy seeing you here. And with a stranger. Hello—I'm Wendy Harcombe, pleased to meet you.'

Greg took her eagerly extended hand. 'Greg Mullin. This looks wonderful—are you responsible for organising? If so, well done with the weather.'

Wendy needed no encouragement and started to describe the structure of the village entertainments committee in minute detail. But Greg actually seemed to be listening and commenting intelligently—or at least enough to keep Wendy talking. Alice edged away. 'I'd just better find Scarlett. I'll see you at the cakes, Greg.'

As she made her way through the semi-familiar faces, nodding politely and moving on before she could get ensnared, Alice smiled to herself. So far, this day was turning out to be a surprise. She made a mental note of the location of the second-hand book stall and the plant stall—those she'd look at once she'd tracked down Scarlett. Finally, when she was quite close to the green itself where the barbecue was as obvious from the snaking queue as from the scent of frying onions, she heard a shrill voice.

'One go for ten pee. Three for twenty! Try your luck. Everyone's a winner!'

It was Scarlett. Standing next to an inflated paddling pool in which a flotilla of small yellow plastic ducks bobbed and dipped, handing out shrimp nets to children, toddlers mostly, who approached her, coins held out in their chubby hands. Scarlett was managing with aplomb, dropping the coins into one of those waist pouches market stallholders use—where had she got that? Handing out tiny packets of sweets to the winners was another girl—shorter than Scarlett but about the same age—and they were laughing together until the girl was called away. Scarlett was doing a roaring trade and Alice watched her for a while, amazed by her self-possession and confidence and by the slight frown of concentration that looked so familiar. During a brief lull, she glanced up and caught sight of Alice, and gestured her over. 'Here— you can hand out the nets. You sometimes have to help the little ones and make sure they're careful. They keep poking each other by mistake.'

Alice glanced round to see if Greg was in sight then, slightly reluctantly, edged her way round to where Scarlett was standing. 'Are you in charge?'

Scarlett rolled her eyes. 'I'm *supposed* to have a grown-up helping me, but she went off to the Pimm's tent as soon as it opened and I haven't seen her since. And she said she'd bring me some squash and she hasn't!' Her indignation was clear. 'If it wasn't for Immy, I'd have been stuffed.'

'Immy?' Alice questioned.

'Yeah. She lives at Holly House. She helped for a bit but her mother needed her.' She sighed. 'You can't rely on anyone!'

Resisting the urge to laugh, Alice rolled up the sleeves of her cotton blouse and took charge of the shrimp nets, handing them out to the children as Scarlett took their money. 'I said I'd meet Greg at the cake stall, but I'm sure he'll find us.'

'Oh yes—Greg. Is he your boyfriend, then?'

'Nothing like getting straight to the point. Nope. We're just friends.'

'Well, you talk about him as if he was.'

'Do I? No I don't. I hardly talk about him at all.'

'Don't you have a boyfriend then?' Scarlett pressed.

'Well, no. It's not compulsory to have one, you know. Why? Have you?'

Scarlett snorted. 'No, of course not. All the boys in my school were bo-o-o-ring. They were only interested in football and wrestling and stuff. I had a boyfriend in Year Four, but he was a show-off so I dumped him.'

'Year Four—what's that mean again? I mean, how old were you?'

'Eight. We used to hold hands at break.' She shrugged and then her face hardened. 'But if I have to go to that stupid school, I'll never get a boyfriend, will I? And when I'm not at school, I'll just be with granny and grandpa and I'll never meet any boys. I'll just have to go stupid *riding* all the time.'

Alice paused as she concentrated on collecting in a few nets, stooping to pick up the ones dropped on the ground. 'I thought you liked riding.'

'No, I hate it. Ponies are more trouble than they are worth. They make people upset and argue.'

'What do you mean?' Alice enquired gently, not sure what she was getting at.

Scarlett paused for a moment as if about to say something, then she went on, 'Ponies are smelly and so is the lady who teaches me. Grace, she's called. Huh—that's a laugh.'

'Have you told Granny you don't like it?'

'Duh—of course I have. But you know what she's like. She's all, "You have to give it time, Scarlett. Anything worth doing is worth doing properly, Scarlett. You'll meet a nicer sort of girl, Scarlett." Well, they're not very nice, actually! They've all been doing it for ages and they make fun of me when they think I'm not looking.'

'Right—well, would you like me to have a word?'

Scarlett shrugged gloomily. 'It won't do any good. You know what she's like. I told her I wanted to go rowing but she said "that'll give you shoulders like an ox".' She paused. 'Mum didn't have shoulders like an ox,' she added quietly.

Alice smiled with quiet pride as Scarlett doled out sweets and encouragement, speaking confidently to adults, standing her ground with some slightly older boys who were trying to cheat, and helping a toddler barely able to keep his balance to swipe a duck out of the water. She was such a funny mixture—sometimes endearingly innocent, at other times alarmingly cynical. All in all, she was quite a little character.

'Can I have a go?'

Alice was jolted from her contemplation by a familiar voice. Greg, several plastic bags by his feet, held out his twenty pence to Scarlett, who was looking at him with interest. 'Is it for you, or do you have any children?'

He shook his head. 'It's for me. Am I allowed?'

Scarlett contemplated him for a moment, then looked at Alice and back at him. 'You're Greg, aren't you?'

'Yes, I am. And you must be Scarlett.' He held out his hand. Scarlett hesitated for a moment, then wiped hers on her shorts and shook his briefly. She dropped the money into her pouch and nodded at Alice. 'Well, give him a net. You do know what to do, don't you?'

Greg shrugged. 'I'm guessing I have to catch a duck. What are the prizes?'

'Only Haribos. But they're good ones. There are some Tangfastics at the bottom of the box. You can have those if you want.'

Greg was concentrating hard on his task and didn't answer for a while. When he eventually, and triumphantly, presented Scarlett with a duck, he replied. 'Sure. I've no idea what those are, but I'm happy to take your recommendation.'

Scarlett turned to Alice and gave her a meaningful look which Alice, as surprised as she was amused, took to be one of approval.

*   *   *

Later on, back at the cottage, they sampled Greg's

cake purchases, which amounted to far more, Scarlett had pointed out, than one man living on his own could eat. He obligingly took the hint and divided up his haul, carefully leaving the ones Scarlett had said were her favourites. Alice was curled up on the sofa, flicking through her haul of paperbacks, listening to them talk. Scarlett had bought a pack of Uno cards at the toy stall and Greg was trying to explain why it was important to check if it was a full deck before buying it. Scarlett didn't see it, and they were arguing the point in an entirely good natured way, their voices blending as they interrupted each other, both bursting into laughter at the same time. Alice peeped over the top of her book thinking, in spite of herself, about the idea Scarlett had planted in her head about Greg.

Later on, when Greg had gone and Scarlett was in her bath, Alice thought about the day. It had been far more fun than she'd been expecting. Although, considering that she'd been expecting it to be about as enjoyable as root canal work, that wasn't difficult. What had surprised her though, was just how comfortable Scarlett had seemed and how many people Alice barely knew had come up to her and said how helpful she'd been, and how pleasant she was. It seemed that those bike rides had made her some friends. Scarlett had bedded herself down in the village in a few short weeks more completely, in many ways, than Alice, who had lived there for years. But was this a good thing? Given that she'd soon be based at Judy and Bill's house, albeit reluctantly, maybe it wasn't healthy for Scarlett to get too comfortable in Ulvington. More disturbing, though, was the fact that a number of people who spoke to Alice about Scarlett asked when she'd be going back home to Oxford. Alice had been shocked. So Scarlett hadn't told anyone the circumstances of her being in Ulvington and in Alice's care at all. And if she wasn't talking about it to Alice, or Judy, or any of her new acquaintances, maybe that meant she wasn't coming to terms with it herself. Alice rubbed her eyes. This was all getting more complicated than she'd ever expected. 'Oh, Ginny,' she sighed. 'Why the hell did you have to go and die? And what on earth made you think I could cope with all this?'

Chapter 29

January 2004

'I'll take her up,' whispered Piers, lifting Scarlett from Virginia's arms. He laid the sleeping child over his shoulder and walked out of the door. Virginia watched their progress, two dark heads close together.

'Look at the little thing. It's hard work being five,' Judy laughed from the other chair, sipping her cup of tea.

'Not as much hard work as it is organising the celebrations for being five,' Virginia sighed, resting her head against the back of the armchair. She was tired and happy to let Piers take over. She tried to ignore the debris left after the last small guest had gone—burst balloons, cake crumbs, wrapping paper from the pass the parcel and streamers—but it would have to be tackled sooner or later.

'You try too hard,' Judy put down her cup and saucer, a delicate flowered porcelain one that

Virginia had bought just for her mother-in-law, after she had made it plain that mugs were 'ghastly' and that tea tasted far better from porcelain. It sat on the shelf in splendour—Scarlett called it 'Gamma's cup'—and it was wheeled out at each visit.

'It is her birthday!' Virginia snorted.

'No, I mean your whole generation. You are always trying to *outdo* each other. Your children will all grow up expecting the earth because their parents do everything they can to deliver it.'

Virginia pinched the top of her own hand painfully to stop herself rising to the bait. 'I just wanted her to have a lovely time, that's all.'

Bill laughed deeply from the sofa where he had spent the best part of the party, playing the benign grandfather. 'Do you remember Piers' party—or was it Dominic's?—when that Murphy boy flooded the downstairs loo and then fell out of a tree!'

'Oh goodness, yes!' Judy gasped. 'You had to rush him to A&E and I had to field his mother when she came to collect him.'

'He went on to be a hedge fund manager, didn't he?' Bill frowned. He would have, wouldn't he, being a friend of theirs, thought Virginia, but grateful to Bill for changing the direction of the conversation. 'Lord knows how we'd have coped with a daughter! Look at all this.' His gesture took in the room, strewn with discarded gifts and glitter. 'Who exactly is Kitty and why do we have to say Hello to her anyway?'

Virginia smiled for the first time since the doorbell had been rung by the earliest arrival in a party dress, clutching a carefully wrapped gift.

The prospect of the party—the first proper one she'd ever done for Scarlett that involved real schoolfriends—had kept her awake at night, and the expectation was so high that, for once, she had caved into Judy's suggestion that *she* handle the cake. The resulting masterpiece, a pink confection with icing ribbons and flowers, had been given pride of place on the tea table and suitably admired by everyone, eclipsing Virginia's shaped sandwiches and pizza faces that had taken her the whole day to prepare. As Piers handled grandmother's footsteps in their tiny lounge, Virginia had cut it up, wrapped it in napkins and stuffed it into party bags with unnecessary venom.

'Your mistake, my girl, was having her in January,' Judy continued, looking over her reading glasses. 'A summer baby is always best because then the parties can be in the garden. We managed it, didn't we, Bill darling? May, July, August and early September.'

Bully for you, Virginia growled in her head. Even your bloody eggs popped on demand.

'It wasn't exactly a *mistake*,' Virginia replied wearily. 'She sort of happened that way.'

'And aren't we lucky to have her,' Bill smiled warmly at Virginia from across the room, and winked supportively.

'Anyone want a chocolate crispy cake? There are hundreds left.' Alice, Virginia's pink apron around her middle, came into the room from the kitchen, a plate of dark chocolate cornflake cakes in pink paper cases arranged on a pink spotted plate. 'I've had three but I can't manage any more or I'll be sick. Were you expecting an army, Ginny darling?'

Virginia laughed, still grateful to Alice for having

216

arrived unannounced on the doorstep an hour before proceedings began, bustling in and taking up precious space, but it didn't matter. She'd made the effort. 'I think they were all too full of fairy cakes.'

'Well, I thought some fairy cakes might go down well,' Judy smiled coyly, 'and I do make a mean fairy cake, though I say so myself.'

'Are they the opposite of Good Fairy cakes then?' Alice asked, her voice devoid of any irony, but Judy wasn't listening.

'I'll just go and powder my nose, then, Bill, I think we ought to head off to Angela and David's.'

Angela and David were friends who lived near Aylesbury and on whom they tended to descend rather than camp in Piers' and Virginia's tiny spare room. They were old friends from when Bill was a barrister and their boys were small, and where once they shared family holidays, the four of them now shared cruises and pride in their grandchildren. Virginia didn't like them. Angela was even more of a social snob than Judy, and at their wedding had been overheard laughing at Virginia's aunt's hat, describing it as 'looking as if it had come from a charity shop'. What annoyed Virginia most was that it probably had.

Once they had gathered their things, including the cake plate and biscuit tin for the fairy cakes, Piers had come back downstairs, and they did the thank-yous and fond farewells. With Alice's help, and fortified by a large glass of wine, they then cleared the detritus before Piers went upstairs for a shower. Virginia collapsed on the sofa, Alice beside her, too exhausted even to look at the Sunday papers which Alice had fished out from under a pile of stuff in the hall.

'How does Judy manage to make everything so toxic,' Virginia said after a while, watching Alice through half closed lids as she polished off a bowl of leftover Hula Hoops and turned the pages of the paper with greasy fingers.

'Oh, she's not so bad. The cake was yummy. You've got to hand it to the woman; she can work wonders with a bit of sponge. God, I hate these articles.' She held up the supplement she was reading. '"Twenty of the world's best lakeside hotels". According to whom? Some twelve-year-old researcher who's never been beyond the M25, I'll bet, and who thinks Wandsworth Common is rural. These articles—they just fill you with a feeling of inadequacy because you can't possibly afford where they're telling you to go. If it's not that, it's the best chalets, or the best place to watch the rare wara wara bird doing its mating dance.'

Virginia laughed, amazed she still had the energy to. 'Oh one can dream! The articles I hate are the chummy family ones. How to cook the best gingerbread or chocolate brownies and the pictures are of food wrapped in gingham cloths and there are families cycling off together to be hearty and ... well, *together*. It just cranks up the guilt. It's as if you have to live some dream and anything less is abject failure.'

'Crikey, Gin,' Alice looked up, picking Hula Hoops out of her teeth. 'The guilt thing really gets to you, doesn't it?'

Virginia felt a flutter of anxiety. 'All parenting is guilt, isn't it?' she laughed.

'How would I know?' Alice went back to turning the pages. 'I've never had the dubious pleasure.'

'And the mother-in-law doesn't help. She

218

manages to make me feel like a failure at every turn.'

'Why are you trying so hard to please her? She's a different generation and a different class—women who aren't like you and didn't have to work. Besides, she'll make you think her kids had the perfect *Swallows and Amazons* upbringing but I bet they didn't. I bet they were little buggers, just like we were.'

'That's not how Piers remembers it. Oh, I don't know. I can't help thinking she'd rather he'd married someone like Natasha, with her dinner parties, Tod's and social ease.'

'Well, he didn't. He chose you, and he's over the age of consent, so be happy with it.'

The man in question came back into the room, his hair wet from the shower. 'She's out for the count, still dressed. I didn't dare wake her. I bet she'll go right through until morning now.' He leaned over and gave Virginia a kiss. 'Well done, Mum. You gave her a great time.'

Virginia smiled back as warmly as she could, and swallowed hard. Piers poured Alice a drink and the two of them chatted but Virginia didn't listen, overwhelmed again, as she was every time Scarlett had a birthday, with the awful feeling she might be in possession of information that no one else had.

Darling Scarlett,
It's a red letter day! Today is your birthday and you
are five. In fact, the celebrations were so exciting
that you fell asleep in my arms and Daddy put
you to bed. You are still asleep now, curled up in
your party dress, but I bet you'll be awake at some
ungodly hour, jumping into our bed and expecting

219

entertainment. Alice has just left—she arrived without warning, so typical of Alice—and brought you the most beautiful doll which you might still have when you read this. It has long blond hair and a dress almost as pretty as yours, and I have put it beside your bed so you will see it when you wake. Who knows? It might stop you disturbing us too early. Tomorrow is a school day after all.

Alice has trundled off home in her decrepit old Golf. It is a miracle that she's allowed on the road at all, let alone in a car like that. That it ever passes its MOT is a disgrace to health and safety standards. She didn't learn to drive until she was about twenty-five—which thankfully kept the public safe for eight years longer than they could have expected—and she once asked me to take her out for a driving lesson. Once. After we almost knocked the cyclist off his bike and then mounted the kerb, I had to ask her to stop because my heart was about to burst out of my chest with fright. She drives in bare feet with the steering wheel practically under her chin, texting as she goes. I don't mind her being your godmother and guiding your moral welfare, but I'm not too chuffed about her driving you anywhere!

You seemed to get along well with your new friends today—that Lottie seems nice—though there was that small fall-out with Sally-Ann just before tea. Mind you, I know we've always taught you to share, but that Barbie doll was a present and she really shouldn't have commandeered it. You'd better watch that one. I've noticed, in my massive experience of four months as a school mother, that the mothers at the school gate can be a grown-up version of their children in the classroom (though if I'm a grown-up version of you, then that makes me

220

very happy indeed!).

The wonderful thing about childhood is how uncomplicated people can be, but as you get older they become more confusing and you don't always know where you are. That's why I love Alice so much. She's just herself and refuses to be false and divisive. She's kind and clever too, and we could all learn a lot from her. If Alice doesn't like someone, she doesn't let them get to her.

I used to go to school with a girl called Hilary Shields. She was a right gang-leader, only comfortable when she was surrounded by her coterie, which gave her the ammunition and the confidence to bully anyone who showed the slightest sign of weakness. My school wasn't like yours, which is modern and full of teachers who care. It was a massive school full of teachers who were ticking off the days until retirement when they wouldn't have to put up with fifteen-year-olds who didn't want to learn and were ticking off the days until they could leave. So someone as horrible as Hilary Shields—especially as she didn't actually resort to physical violence, just mental cruelty which is worse in my opinion—barely bothered the staff and I certainly wasn't going to dob her in.

It used to upset me terribly and I'd try to hide it, but I do remember my mum coming to say goodnight to me one particular night—not something she usually did once I was a teenager— and, without asking, she simply stroked my hair and said something like, 'Unpleasant people rarely have a happy life, you know. It's much better in the long run to be a nice person.' I know that doesn't sound like the granny you've seen, the granny whose brain is jumbled and strange. But she knew exactly what

221

was going on, and how to reassure me. I miss her, which is an odd thing to say when she is still alive.

And do you know, she was right. I've found out since that Hilary Shields has had a miserable life and I really do feel very sorry for her. Perhaps you reap what you sow in life.

I hope I can be as astute and supportive a mother to you as Granny was to me then. Perhaps that's why we have to look after her now, because of all she gave us. She didn't ask to be the way she is. It's hard on Rosie to have to visit her more than I can but, ironically, I do remember Mum—or was it Dad—once saying that if you give, you should give unconditionally and not resentfully. Otherwise, what's the point of giving?

What else did they teach me? Never to eat off your knife (I think you know not to do that!). Always to say thank you (which sometimes you forget in your excitement. Granny Sussex pulled you up on that today, didn't she?), and to look after the pennies and the pounds will look after themselves. We didn't have much money when I was small and no treats like you have now, but we'd make every penny count and Dad knew exactly what we could afford and what we'd get with the change. We took a day trip to Rhyl once and had chips on the front and, just before we left to come home, he rustled up enough for an ice cream for Rosie and me. I had strawberry and was so excited as we made our way back to the car. But do you know what happened? A boy passed me, barging into my arm, and the soft pink ball of ice cream fell out of the cone and onto the ground, hitting the toe of my sandals. I cried all the way back to the M6.

Virginia leaned back in her chair and bit the end of her pen. The house was deadly quiet, Piers having gone up to bed a while ago, and everything was in shadow except for the light over the table. What else had her parents taught her?

Not to tell lies and not to keep secrets.

Closing the diary, she switched off the light and made her way upstairs.

Chapter 30

August 2010

Scarlett was back with her grandparents the next time Alice and Greg met up. It was at Greg's instigation. Alice had been so unnerved by the subtle shift in the way she viewed him that she didn't trust herself to behave normally when speaking to him and hadn't dared to call. They'd gradually developed a habit of ringing each other in the evening while watching *CSI*, a guilty pleasure they shared, and discussing the plot as it unfurled. But the first two times after the fête, when she'd seen his name on caller ID, she simply hadn't answered and had watched the show solo. She hadn't enjoyed it at all, and had barely followed the plot.

Lying in bed each night, she asked herself why she was so nervous around him. In all her relationships, she kept control, responding to a man's advances when she was good and ready. There had been the odd heartbreak and, at times, she had been in love—though never enough to want to settle down and do the family thing—but as she watched the shadows on the bedroom wall, she realised that what was different with Greg was that it was a friendship. She loved chatting to him, and he got on with Scarlett. It was simple and uncomplicated, but she knew she was kidding herself that her pleasure at the sound of his voice was just some platonic response. Friendship and passion had always been kept well apart, but they were beginning to come dangerously close.

And this was where it had ended up—a trip to the cinema to see an over hyped re-make of an old thriller. So far, it wasn't measuring up to its press. With so little to distract her, Alice was painfully aware of Greg's shoulder close to hers and his elbow on the armrest. As aware as she'd been in the car on the way there, when he'd picked her up in his sleek car. She couldn't think of many men she knew who owned a car, let alone could afford one like this.

Afterwards, they walked through the evening streets of Brighton, gaudy with clubbers and hen parties, until they reached a wine bar in a quiet side street and were shown to a small corner table.

'So,' Greg began. 'That was a bit of a disappointment.'

'Same. Nostalgia ain't what it used to be.' Alice found herself watching his fingers as he fiddled with his cutlery. He seemed nervous too. Maybe it was contagious.

'So—Scarlett back with Granny and Grandpa? How long is she going to stick it out for this time?'

Alice sighed. Of the two subjects she didn't want to think about, this was probably the least worst. 'I don't know. But I can't help thinking that she really ought to stay put and get used to the idea. When she comes to me, she complains non-stop about Bill and Judy. But then maybe she complains about me when

224

she's there. I really don't know, but I don't feel as if I can have a proper discussion with Judy about it. I feel like she's always having a little dig, whatever she says. I'm beginning to see Ginny's point.'

She broke off as the waiter came to bring the menus and she took a piece of the sliced baguette from the basket he placed on the table, nibbling at the crust. Greg sat back in his chair. 'Didn't Ginny get on with her mother-in-law, then?'

Alice raised her eyebrows. 'You really *didn't* know her that well, did you?'

'Like I said, we were colleagues. All business and meetings. We never really spoke much at all about personal stuff. And I knew her before she had Scarlett, anyway.'

'She didn't get on with her even before Scarlett was born, but afterwards it was worse. Which is a bit strange really, because I always thought it was not producing another little Waverley that made things difficult between her and Judy.'

'I'm not following.'

Alice stopped short. She'd allowed her thoughts to run away with her again. Ginny had been discreet to the point of secretive about her infertility investigations and here she was, about to blurt the whole story out to someone who had known Ginny on an altogether less intimate level. 'Nothing—just me rambling on. Anyway, the point is Scarlett—I just think it would be better if she was more settled now. And with secondary school looming—and, believe me, it is looming—she has to get into some kind of routine, not to mention getting all the uniform and books. And she has to do that from Bill and Judy's house.'

Greg nodded slowly. 'And does that mean you're

going to be a bit freer? You know, in the evenings?'

'I guess so. It's funny, but I miss her when she's not around. She can drive me mad at times, but when she's in Haywards Heath I keep looking up expecting to see her. And I keep buying all this stuff that only she eats and then it sits in my fridge, just looking at me.'

There was a silence and she looked up. Greg was looking at her, the expression in his eyes quite unmistakeable and the wave of heat she'd felt that day at the fête swept over her again. 'That's not quite what I meant.' He leaned forward, his eyes never leaving hers. She felt acutely aware of her breathing. 'Alice.'

He stopped. She felt her fists clench and she closed her eyes. She knew what was going to happen and she knew he wanted it as much as she did. Had maybe wanted it for longer. She'd thought it was only her, and knowing that made her feel uncertain and out of control. 'Alice.' It was like a whisper and she opened her eyes slowly. He took one of her hands in his, gently spreading her fingers and massaging the palm slowly with his thumb. A tremor went through her whole body and her mouth felt dry. The waiter came back. 'Have you decided yet?'

Alice nodded, her eyes locked into Greg's. 'Yes. We've changed our minds. We won't be ordering after all.' They stood up, still holding hands. Greg reached into his pocket and, without looking down, threw a couple of notes onto the table. They almost ran to his car and, before he opened her door, he pulled her to him and kissed her hard, then released her, leaving her feeling limp and breathless. He drove back to the village faster than was really sensible, but it still felt like an age to Alice. As they drew near,

226

she gently placed her hand on his leg and smiled when she heard him hiss with pleasure. At the door she nearly dropped her key, her hand was trembling so much, and they fell through the doorway, limbs tangling and pulling at each other's clothes, not even making it upstairs before they found each other in the dark, quiet, empty cottage.

*   *   *

Judy was obviously an early riser, but her call a week later before seven thirty on Saturday morning was really too much. Alice disentangled herself from Greg's naked body and cleared her throat before answering. 'Hello? Is that you, Judy?'

'Yes—how did you know? Anyway, the thing is, we need to speak about Scarlett. She's being extremely naughty.'

Naughty? That didn't sound the way to describe an eleven-year-old—especially not one who'd just lost her parents, and she'd sounded fine when Alice had spoken to her during the week. 'Really? What's up?'

'She absolutely refuses to go to her riding lesson this morning. She's been most stubborn about it. She says she promised to come and see you! Is that right, Alice? Because if so, I wish you'd give me a bit more notice.'

Alice thought as quickly as she could, given the hour. 'Well, there is something we'd arranged but I just need to check on the time.' Although she was sympathetic to Scarlett's dislike of her stable companions, she did have a lovely weekend with Greg all planned out. Besides, it was a bit of a cheek of Scarlett to pull a stroke like this without warning her.

227

Judy's indignant voice interrupted Alice's train of thought. 'All of my boys loved riding. And the grandchildren too—well, the ones who are old enough. It's virtually a family tradition, but of course her mother never saw the point. She refused point-blank to even let Scarlett try. And if she'd started young, like all the others, we wouldn't be having this trouble now, so I'm very reluctant to let her miss any of her lessons.'

Alice was catching up now, and could feel herself beginning to come down on Scarlett's—and Ginny's—side. At that moment her mobile buzzed on the bedside table. It was a text from Scarlett. 'Save me' was all it said.

'Actually, I've just checked my diary,' she lied, leaning back against the headboard. 'And there is something—some friends Scarlett has made down here. They're having a barbecue on the beach and Scarlett said she'd help set up.'

'A barbecue? But that's hardly any reason . . .'

'It's for charity,' Alice improvised. 'A local charity started up by some friends of mine. Very worthy cause. It's for . . . conservation. I think it's something to do with the Prince of Wales, actually. You know, organic thingummy. Butterflies or meadows or something like that.' Yes—stroke of genius. She could almost hear the cogs turning at the other end of the phone, and she had to wriggle away as Greg poked her accusingly in the thigh before she started laughing.

'Oh well, perhaps this once,' Judy said slowly. 'Would you like me to bring her myself? I'd be very interested to meet these friends of yours.'

'No—don't worry. I'll be there to get her myself within the hour. It's all my fault, Judy. I'd written it

228

down in one place and not transferred it to my diary.'

'Oh well, easily done, I suppose. I must say, I'm glad to hear she's made some nice friends. There doesn't seem to be anyone her age in the immediate vicinity here. That's why I thought the stables ...' She tailed off. 'Perhaps I'll enquire at the tennis club as well. Anyway, we'll see you soon. And will you be keeping her for the rest of the weekend?'

Alice shook her head slowly, imagining Scarlett with a tennis racket—a dangerous prospect—then, looking again at the plaintive text and regretfully at Greg, his hair dark against her pillow as he pretended to doze, she replied, 'Yes, yes—I'll keep her for the weekend. It'll be fine.'

Chapter 31

July 2004

Darling Scarlett,
Brittany
You are fast asleep in bed and it's only seven o'clock, but you've had such an exhausting day that I'm surprised you stayed awake this long. I think the sea air has exhausted us all and my skin is glowing since my shower. We've only been here for three days but already I feel deliciously relaxed and rested. When you are a working mum, parenthood is full of guilt—I don't get home until you're back from school and your holidays are sometimes a juggle of childcare between Karen and friends if Dad's busy, so when we have whole days with you like this, it does assuage the guilt a little.

The cottage is sweet, a converted barn, and if it wasn't for the smell of damp it would be practically perfect. There have been a few yucky slugs about too. You trod on one earlier today and screamed as if you'd been murdered! I don't know what the neighbours will think! Dad has been trying hard all day to point out the plus points to the place—the fields around us, the pool (OK, so it's not heated!), our proximity to Concarneau—and it's made me smile. Last year we took a caravan in North Devon and he has made me promise that we will never do that again. Holidays for him as a child were in a cottage in Cornwall and a villa in Tuscany so a mobile home near Appledore wasn't really going to cut the mustard!

So, France it is, and I'm so glad we came. It's been expensive, and everything I earn seems to go on my mum's care home fees now. I don't resent it in the slightest—I want her to be in the best place possible, where she can be comfortable and cared for—but it does clip our wings somewhat. Teachers don't earn a great deal either, though Dad reckons he should be paid shed-loads for tolerating bolshy fifteen-year-olds and teaching the Cold War . . . again. He has promised me that this summer he will concentrate on his book so we can start to look for a publisher, but I can see it now. I'll come back from work and you and Dad will have spent the day playing or building an extension to the doll's house or taking a boat out on the river and not a word will have been written. Already you are a determined little rower, and tomorrow we thought we might take you in a canoe to see what you make of that.

Virginia took another sip of her cold wine and

looked across the small garden of the cottage. Her face felt tight from too long in the sun despite all the moisturiser she had applied, and it felt good. They had had such fun, walking on the beach and swinging Scarlett between them until their arms ached. Then she'd pottered about picking up shells and filling her bucket with sand as Virginia lay on a towel, her head resting on Piers' stomach.

You have been on a voyage of discovery today, and I can hear Dad in the kitchen making supper from the ingredients we found at the market. You, however, are full of galettes, which you seem to think are the greatest thing ever invented and I can see will be your staple diet for the next two weeks. That should put some meat on your skinny bones. We are going to determinedly eat Breton and we've bought a cookbook which I've just about managed to translate in my rusty French, which is why Dad is slaving over mussels and garlic and other delicious things. I'll go and help him in a minute, but just for now I'm going to lounge in the evening sunshine with my glass of Sancerre. Maybe next year we'll do the Loire if funds permit.

Holidays give Dad and me a chance to relax and re-boot and I've been longing for this one for weeks and weeks. Term-time is so busy and, even though people think teachers have an easy time of it with their long holidays, they more than make up for it during school. He's rarely home until late and then he's out so early, and our time together is snatched and fractured. I've been busy working on the re-launch of the Oxford hotel with its lovely new spa, which has been a massive project and has absorbed everyone's time and energy. The result has been stunning and I'll take you for a swim in the pool soon. You can splash around the Japanese ladies who swim like frogs up and down the pool in their sensible swimming caps, not getting their faces wet.

It took us a long drive to get here and all our ingenuity to keep you entertained in the car. I don't know how many games of I Spy we managed (Dad was cruel expecting me to do it in French), and I don't think I can bear any more Just William Stories on CD. Luckily we listened to the radio too and you have been singing along to all the hits, getting the words all wrong—and making Dad and me laugh until the tears rolled down our faces.

Behind her she heard Piers' footsteps come across the floor and out onto the terrace.

'Ready for a top-up?' he asked and, without waiting for an answer, poured some fresh wine into her glass. 'What you doing? Not working, I hope.'

Virginia closed the journal and picked up the postcards from the table. 'Oh you know, just enjoying the sunshine. Thought I might send Rosie and the children a postcard and one to your mum and dad.'

'Good.' He kissed the top of her head. 'Lovely to see you looking so relaxed. Your face is all freckled.' He smelled of garlic and his face was warm from the cooking.

'Well, why wouldn't I be with a top chef about to produce my dinner?'

'Don't get too complacent. I won't be doing this when we get back home. It'll be back to your pitiful offerings,' and he dodged quickly as she lunged to playfully slap his leg.

Chapter 32

August 2010

The elephant in the room for everyone was the house in Oxford. Every so often, Judy would mention it, obliquely and *sotto voce* in a way she probably thought subtle and sensitive, but that actually gave it a looming significance. Alice's recollection of it was as a happy, if rather unattractive, home full of laughter and Ginny's sometimes over-enthusiastic efforts at home-making for her family. The way Judy portrayed it now, the little new-build box, with its carefully tended garden and neat dolls' house windows, was as an albatross around her neck and somewhere she could barely bring herself to go.

But to Scarlett it had been home and Alice could almost see her flinch every time the word 'Oxford' was mentioned by Judy.

Finally, in mid-August, when Scarlett was spending another few days with Alice, it had been decided in some family conference to which Alice was not a party, that the place should be cleared—tackled, as Judy put it—with a view to renting or even selling it, once probate was granted. Alice, having received her last-minute instructions, raised the subject as sensitively as she could bear to with Scarlett.

'Thing is, Granny and Grandpa need to go there first because there's a lot to sort out. I know your Uncle Dom has been in to collect letters and to check up on the place—I think Judy said he'd mowed the lawn—but there's lots of stuff there that needs to be sorted out . . .' She trailed off, watching the colour slowly drain from Scarlett's face.

'Is anyone looking after Rodney and the hens?' she asked quietly, her voice small and her expression confused.

'I'm sure they are,' Alice reassured, hoping she was right. Once again, Alice felt herself so unequal to the task of interpreting real life for the girl that she was tempted to give up and suggest they put on the TV or that Scarlett go out for a bike ride. But remembering Vince's words about his upbringing, she stumbled on. 'I know it's going to be, erm, strange going back after all this time but we're going to meet up with the others there tomorrow, about lunchtime, once they've had a chance to tidy things up a bit, and then I'll be there with you the whole time.'

Scarlett was looking down now, picking at her toenails. A couple of weeks ago, Alice would have taken her apparent indifference at face value, but she could see the little fingers twisting the toes and the effort the rapt concentration was costing her. Tentatively she stretched out her hand and laid it gently on Scarlett's skinny shoulder. 'And we can bring back some of your stuff. I'll go to the supermarket later and get boxes—they've always got some—so we can pack it up properly.'

Scarlett nodded without looking up, and Alice stayed beside her until the toast had popped and the kettle boiled—normally her cues to jump up and change the subject. Today she didn't bother. After a while, Scarlett spoke without looking up. 'Can we go there earlier than them?' she asked quietly.

'What's that?'

Scarlett took a deep breath. 'I don't want to get there and see them there already, changing things and taking things away. It's our house, not theirs.

They shouldn't open the door to me as if I'm a visitor. It should be me there and them ringing on the doorbell and asking to come in. And me making them tea. That's what Mum would have wanted to do.'

Alice was silent. She hadn't thought about that. But she should have. Of course Scarlett would feel supplanted if she arrived at her own house for the first time since being plucked away from it to find it already taken over, buzzing with activity and herself sidelined—as she undoubtedly would be—by Judy's well-meaning efficiency. Judy had made her wishes quite clear—she wanted to get there first to clear things away so it wouldn't be too difficult for Scarlett. But say she was wrong? Say Scarlett needed the experience of revisiting her house quietly, alone, and seeing it the way she'd left it all those weeks ago. She replied slowly, 'Let me have a quick think. I'm not sure what time Judy and Bill are planning to get there. Leave it with me, would you? I'll make a couple of calls.'

Scarlett looked up, at last, and nodded. 'Shall I make the tea while you do it?'

Alice smiled and nodded. She was thinking hard. 'I'll just be upstairs.'

The first person she called was Vince, to run her hunch past him. He answered after a couple of rings, 'Hello?'

'Vince, it's me.'

'Oh hello, darling. How are you? And to what do I owe this pleasure?'

'It's about Scarlett.'

'Then fire away, I'm all ears.'

Alice explained the situation and waited for Vince to form an opinion. It didn't take long. 'You're absolutely right. Poor kid's got all sorts of memories of that house. She should have a chance to visit it quietly, just the way she left it. You may have to barricade the door though, or barge the old bag out into the garden.'

'No,' Alice smiled. 'I've got a better plan.'

At six the next morning, Alice and Scarlett left the cottage and set off for Oxford. The sky was grey and flat, with none of the heat and promise of sunshine that August deserved. They had a packed lunch, a car full of flattened boxes and enough parcel tape to wrap up the Bodleian Library. Piers' family planned to converge on the house at about ten. Alice had been instructed not to turn up until midday. Allowing for Judy's freakish punctuality and her assumption that Alice would always be late, those times could be revised to nine-thirty and one. But Alice, for once, would be early. She glanced at her watch. Provided there was no snarl-up on the M25—and that was the big if—she and Scarlett would be there at around eight. Scarlett had spoken to the babysitter, Karen, and Pat, her mum, the previous evening, passing the phone to Alice once she'd explained what she wanted.

'Hello? Pat? I'm Alice Fenton. I've been looking after Scarlett for the last few weeks.'

The voice that replied was decidedly tearful. 'Yes, I remember you. We met a couple of times when you came to visit poor Virginia and Piers. How is little Scarlett? She sounds so grown up, bless her.'

Alice felt guilty. She barely remembered the woman—just as the babysitter's mother, glimpsed briefly before she and Virginia headed out for an evening in Oxford, trying out a new wine bar Alice had read about, or going to the theatre together.

236

They'd almost never done anything that involved Scarlett. And now Alice wondered if Ginny had really wanted to go out on the town, or if she'd been falling in with what her friend wanted to do. Some godmother! Alice had considered her role then as the bringer of gifts—nothing more. She stifled this new and unwelcome feeling and replied, 'Yes, she is very grown up. She's tremendous, actually. And I know she's looking forward to seeing you. Now—did she explain everything?'

As they approached Oxford, Alice could see Scarlett's apprehension growing. She'd talked a little but lapsed into silence as they turned off the M40 and the surroundings began to look familiar to her, Alice guessed, and memories started to re-assert themselves. It went just as planned. Karen and Pat were both waiting outside on the pavement and flung themselves at Scarlett as she got out of the car. Alice stood back and watched the unrestrained affection with pleasure and—yes—just a little envy. She wished she could feel that spontaneous with Scarlett. Maybe she would, one day. Pat handed Scarlett her door key and then stood back to let her go ahead. She was looking carefully at everything, her face impossible to read. Alice followed behind. She'd get the camera out of her car later and take photographs of everything she could—the gate, the flowerbeds in front of the house, the front door, the door mat. Scarlett needed these memories to be recorded.

Scarlett paused on the doorstep, glanced once at Alice over her shoulder, then turned the key and went in. It was just as if the whole awful business had never happened. Although Pat had been dropping in, and despite it being aired regularly, the house had a

237

slightly stale smell, though it was absolutely the home Alice remembered. Ginny was here in every detail—the striped rugs, the naive paintings she'd picked up in Norfolk, the collection of shells in a glass bowl on the windowsill. Alice felt a wave of loss so strong she almost gasped. Ahead of her, Scarlett was moving slowly from room to room, touching things gently. Picking up cushions and rubbing her face against the velvety curtains. Quietly and privately, she was storing up her memories. Alice hung back, careful not to disturb Scarlett's private journey. She was aware of Pat hovering in the doorway, and went to speak to her.

'Is she all right?'

Alice shrugged helplessly. 'I really don't know. I mean—I don't expect she is, but how could she be after a thing like this?'

'I know what you mean. I didn't really mean "all right". I know she can't be—poor mite. But at least she's got you looking out for her. Virginia . . .' Pat swallowed hard and dashed a tear from her cheek. 'She was such a loving mother, you know. Busy, of course, like you girls are these days, trying to fit it all in, but it was always family first with her. Little Scarlett was everything to her—and that time she was so ill! Dear Lord, I shall never forget it.'

Alice nodded. She remembered Virginia looking wrung out after all that. When was it again? A thought occurred to her. 'I must make sure I get her registered at a doctor somewhere. I'll need her NHS number or something. I bet Ginny has it all filed away somewhere. Listen—thanks for everything. I'll pop round later, but I want to keep an eye on her for now.'

Pat squeezed her arm. 'You're thinking like a

mum. Welcome to the club! Never a moment's rest, is there? We've got Rodney, the cat, with us at home but the hens are out in the garden. I expect Scarlett will go out to check on them herself soon. I haven't fed them this morning. I thought she'd like to do it before you take them back.'

'Oh yes, the hens,' Alice repeated slowly.

'Good layers, they are. I think the carrying boxes are in the shed somewhere. I'll help you look if you can't find them. I'll leave you to it, bless you. Virginia would be so proud if she could see the two of you.' This time, the tears overwhelmed her and she hurried back to her house.

Alice turned back in, her thoughts darting between what Pat had said, her own emotions and her concern for what Scarlett might be going through. Plus the knowledge that Judy would probably be arriving in just over an hour. She saw Scarlett in the back garden, cuddling a black chicken, and sighed. That was one little detail that had totally escaped her. Of course she'd known they were keeping chickens—hens, she'd been smartly told was the proper term—but she hadn't factored them into the move. Would Scarlett insist on keeping them? The sight of her talking animatedly to the slightly sinister-looking ball of feathers was all the answer she needed. Who would end up having them? Her or Judy? And if it was her, how on earth was she going to fit them in the car?

With Scarlett occupied outside, Alice had a quick look in the other rooms. The kitchen, with its wooden cabinets and warm yellow walls, the colour of omelette, was neater than she remembered it ever being while Ginny was alive. It was always the centre of activity and, in her mind's eye, Alice saw herself, shoes kicked off and feet up on a stool, drinking wine and chatting while Ginny stirred something on the hob and Scarlett sat at the table, gluing paper shapes into a book. And now she was all on her own with Scarlett. If only Ginny had left her some kind of handbook to follow. *Instructions for Bringing up Scarlett.*

Alice was lost in her memories, drinking a coffee—black, since she hadn't thought to bring any milk with her—when Scarlett came back in, her eyes bright with tears and holding up two eggs. She put them carefully into a cast-iron egg stand in the shape of a hen that she clearly remembered buying years ago.

'I want to take this,' Scarlett said firmly. 'I want to take it with me.'

'OK, that's fine. Shall I get the boxes to pack things into from the car or would you like to have it at Granny's?'

Scarlett looked at Alice very intently without speaking for a moment, then turned away and, to judge from her footsteps, charged upstairs. Moments later, the sound of a door—presumably her bedroom door—being slammed made Alice jump and she could have sworn the paintings on the wall shook. 'Oh dear,' sighed Alice. 'What do I do now, Ginny? Can't you give me any clues?'

Slowly she finished her coffee, looking around the house left, like a museum, frozen in time. Through the window she could see a bag of compost and a row of little plant pots, each containing a dead and unrecognisable plant. Beside them lay a trowel, just as Ginny must have left it before they left the house that day. Taking a deep breath, she followed Scarlett upstairs.

The sound of furious muttering was clear even

over the music from the other side of the door and Alice had to knock twice before she got a grunted reply that might have been, 'Come in'. Of course, it might also have been, 'Go away.' But Alice was beginning to learn something, and gently opened the door. 'Wow!'

The choice of decor for Scarlett's room in Ulvington had been a lucky, but inspired, guess on Vince's part. If anything, this room was even pinker than that. It had evolved since Alice had last seen it and every available surface was now covered with soft toys, ranging from pocket-sized kittens to the large and luridly striped tiger on the single bed. Scarlett sat in the middle of it all, her face a picture of utter desolation.

'I don't want to live at Granny Sussex's house,' she gasped. 'I *don't want* to. She's always going on about how I have to be like the other grandchildren and be a Waverley and make her proud. She's not interested in what I think. She just wants me to be the way *she* thinks I should. Mum and Dad,' she took a long shuddering breath and Alice could see she was on the verge of tears. 'They always asked me what I thought about things. They listened and we used to talk about things. They would never make me do anything I didn't want to. They would never make me go to a school I hated. They wouldn't throw out my clothes without even asking me and make me wear horrible dorky things I didn't even choose. They wouldn't force me to go riding with girls I hate.'

Alice sighed. 'I know it's hard, honey, but Granny and Grandpa are proper relatives and they do want what's best for you.'

'They don't really want me.' Scarlett's voice was low with fury and husky with unshed tears. 'Granny

241

just wants to have Dad back. I heard her say so to Grandpa. She said having me with her is the next best thing. But I don't want to be the next best thing. Mummy and Daddy thought I was the very best. They always said so. They didn't want anyone else but me. And now I'm nobody's best girl. Nobody loves me the way they did. Nobody really wants me.'

And Scarlett flung herself full-length on the bed and cried and cried, the sobs shaking her body and leaving her gasping for breath, at last opening the floodgates that she had kept so tightly locked. On instinct, Alice rushed over and sat beside her, perched on the edge of the bed, at a loss what to do. And that, of course, was when Judy and Bill arrived. Alice heard their car pull up as she stroked Scarlett's hair away from her tear-stained face, making the kind of soothing noises she'd heard Ginny make to her as a baby. 'Oh great!' she muttered quietly to herself. Well, she wasn't going to leave Scarlett now. She imagined them getting out and stretching, Bill taking far longer than Judy, who would be looking around impatiently before her eyes lighted on Alice's car, distinctive with its stickers and ironic furry dice. Judy would just have to wait.

But waiting wasn't really in Judy's nature. She could just hear over Scarlett's shuddering sobs the exclamations over the front door being unlocked, then footsteps on the stairs as Judy followed the source of the noise. Alice felt a little like Goldilocks waiting for the bear. And she didn't have long to wait.

'Alice? What on earth is going on? Scarlett, what is it, my darling? Don't cry—Granny's here now. Alice, I think you'd better leave and let me take care of things.'

Help me, Ginny. Help me to do the right thing. 'Actually, Judy, Scarlett and I are in the middle of something right now. If you'd like to make yourself a cup of tea downstairs, I'll be with you.'

'I don't think so, Alice. I'd like to be with my granddaughter, if you don't mind. I think you've done enough harm, by the look of things. I don't even know what you're doing here. I made it quite clear that you were *not* to bring Scarlett until I had cleared things up. And now look what's happened!'

'I'm not going to discuss this now,' Alice said through clenched teeth. 'I think it was important for Scarlett to be here on her own and to see the house as she remembers it. And I'm not leaving her now.'

'You think? *You* think? Alice, it's not your place to think. I'm doing the thinking—for everyone as usual. And thank goodness I am! You are not a blood relative. You're merely Scarlett's mother's friend. You're not even a mother yourself and I don't think you're in any way qualified to make decisions concerning Scarlett's life.'

Alice had stopped stroking Scarlett's shoulder now, and was holding her hand. She wasn't quite sure how this transition had taken place—if it was her or Scarlett who was gripping harder—but as she felt the pressure of the warm, thin, little hand in hers, she knew what she had to do.

'Judy,' she said quietly. 'I know I'm not a mother, but I do know that Scarlett is a person with her own wishes and views and I know her opinions have to be listened to. And I don't think it's very productive to discuss this here, when she's clearly upset.'

'Clearly. But whose fault is that, Alice? If you'd done as I suggested, she wouldn't be in this state. The poor child has been through quite enough—

and, frankly, you're not helping.'

Alice stood up, still holding firmly onto Scarlett's hand. 'Judy, I'm not going to discuss this any further now. Please go downstairs. When Scarlett feels ready, we'll talk about it all together, calmly.'

'You're missing the point,' Judy hissed. 'Scarlett is too young to know her own mind. That's why the law protects people of her age from making stupid mistakes by giving the authority to make decisions to adults.'

Alice paused. She was beginning to realise what had motivated Ginny all those years ago to name *her* Scarlett's guardian. It hadn't been a sentimental gesture. It hadn't been meaningless. Ginny had seen something in Judy that she hadn't liked and hadn't wanted too close to Scarlett. At last, Alice understood what her friend wanted and what she had to do and was just opening her mouth to say so, when a voice called up from downstairs.

'Mum? Are you up there?'

It was Dominic. He must have arrived soon after Judy and Bill.

'Mum—come here, please. Quickly. It's Dad. He doesn't look well at all.'

Chapter 33

March 2005

'How is she?' Rosie swept up to the bed and stood the other side, looking down at her mother lying motionless under the sheets, an oxygen mask over her thin face.

244

'No change really.' Virginia rubbed her eyes and stretched her arms above her head. She felt lethargic after so long sitting without moving. She'd barely slept all night, the noise from the ward corridor and the constant hum and beeps of machines interrupting her dozes, and when she jumped awake she'd watch her mother carefully to check if she was still breathing. At times she'd tried to claw at the mask, and Virginia had gently taken her hand away, stroking it between hers in some pathetic gesture of reassurance, but since about four she had lain quietly. Feeling nauseous with tiredness, Virginia hoped that now Rosie had arrived she could stretch her legs and get a coffee from the canteen.

'Have they given you any idea about ... you know?' Her tone was brisk and businesslike.

'No. She seems to be stable at the moment.' Virginia silently indicated to Rosie to come away from the bed and, at first, Rosie's face showed incomprehension.

'Come over here for a minute, can you?' Virginia asked more urgently and eventually Rosie followed her outside the room into the corridor. 'The nurse said to be careful what we say in front of her. Being able to hear is the last thing that goes and she could hear us.' Rosie looked unsure. 'Think about it, Rosie,' Virginia could hear her voice rise a little. 'Imagine how you'd want it to be?'

'What to be?'

'The end.'

'You can fucking shoot me,' she said as Virginia saw tears well up in her eyes before she turned back into the room. 'I'm not ending up like this.'

They sat in an uncomfortable silence for a while

after that, one on either side of the bed, Virginia sipping the thin coffee and picking at the muffin she'd bought in the hospital shop. Their vigil was punctuated every now and then by the arrival of the nurse, who came to check her mother, lifting her wrist, the skin papery and thin. Of doctors there was no sign, but why did they need to come? They were simply playing a waiting game.

'Kids OK?' Virginia asked to break the silence.

Rosie shrugged. 'Getting them off to school is always a bloody nightmare.'

'Scarlett quite likes it,' Virginia replied, then realised that sounded smug and self-congratulatory.

Rosie didn't take her eyes off her mother. 'She probably goes to a school that gives a shit.'

Fifteen–love to Rosie. Virginia leaned back in her chair, defeated. The atmosphere was brittle and tense. She glanced at her watch. 'I'm going to have to go in a bit. If I can get this meeting over quickly I should be back about six. Can someone watch the kids after school? I'll get back as soon as I can. Just get a change of clothes and I'll head back up the motorway.'

'They can sort themselves out. Kerry does it all the time when I'm at work. She hasn't got much choice. We managed it and it never did us any harm, did it?'

Virginia tried to think. There must have been times that they had let themselves in after school if Mum had been held up, but by the time they were at secondary school she was usually home before them, and tea would be underway, ready for when their dad came in. He'd drop his overalls in the laundry basket, have a quick wash then, as a rule, they'd all sit down to eat together. Then it

246

was time for homework, though, now she thought about it, Virginia could remember fearful rows as Rosie slipped out to meet friends in the park and to knock about until dark. She'd come back to face their parents who'd ground her in a show of unified admonition, but Rosie would usually have ignored them by the next day.

They always say that one child gives you more grief than the others, and Virginia was hard-pressed to think of anything *she* had done which had precipitated being grounded. How square she must have been! She'd come home late from a party once when she was fifteen, and her father had been sitting on the stairs in his pyjamas, more fearful than angry and, instead of bawling her out, he had simply put his arms around her and said 'thank god'. Rosie's mistake was never to apologise. She'd scream back, then stomp upstairs noisily enough to rattle the lamp that hung over the landing and slam her door, leaving a silence that hung in the air and no one wanted to fill. Had Rosie ended up the better daughter though? The one always on hand to check up on her mother? Virginia rubbed her eyes, torn between a wave of guilt and a small voice that told her she had a right to a life too.

After another half an hour, she got to her feet, stiff from sitting. Her mother looked peaceful enough, her eyelids fluttering occasionally. Her skin looked bruised and sallow. 'OK. I'll get back as soon as I can—traffic permitting. Call me if there's any change, won't you?' She leaned down and put her lips to her mother's forehead and, as she stood back up again, her mother's eyes flicked open briefly.

'Bye, Mum, see you later,' she whispered.

The pressure from the vigil lifted slightly as she went out into the car park, bustling now with people who'd arrived to visit family or to attend appointments. It was as though life had been suspended and Virginia was surprised that people were still behaving normally. She fished her phone out of her bag and dialled home.

Judy picked up at the fourth ring. 'Hello, dear. How is she?'

'No change really,' Virginia tried not to sound as tired as she felt. 'Fairly stable, but ... well, the pneumonia is very advanced. They're not saying. How's my little girl?'

'Fine, fine. They both got off to school OK this morning, and I'm just sorting out the washing.' Virginia smiled to herself. Judy had nobly stepped in when Virginia had called to say she had to go up to Stoke and, even though she'd done a quick supermarket shop, she'd had to leave the house as it was, but she knew that Judy would be loving her role of despatching her son and granddaughter off to school in a way that was far more organised than Virginia would have managed.

'Thanks so much for this, Judy. I'm just leaving for Oxford now. I'll have to go straight to my meeting, then I'll fly by, grab some clean clothes and head back here. If I time it right, I might be able to pick Scarlett up from school. I'll let you know.'

After assurances that all was well, she clicked off the phone and texted Piers, who'd be teaching period two, then, starting the engine, pulled out of the parking space and left the car park through the barrier.

The motorway was busy with lorries thundering

248

around her, and she had to keep straightening herself in her seat to stay awake. Switching over from a soporific discussion programme on Radio 4, she selected a pop station and turned up the volume, opening the window slightly. By the M6 Toll services she needed a shot of caffeine and, checking she had enough time, pulled in gratefully. She left her phone in the car and as she slipped back into her seat and put the hot cappuccino into the cup slot, she noticed the flashing light of a missed call.

It was Rosie. She dialled the number quickly.

'She's gone.'

'What do you mean?' Virginia felt a curious perplexity, as if there must be some mistake.

'About twenty minutes ago. She just stopped breathing.' Her voice sounded flat and unemotional. 'Can you get back?'

Virginia was on high alert now, and forty-five minutes later, pulled back into the car park of the hospital. She'd driven too fast, as if getting to her mother's bedside now would make any difference, and her bustled arrival back on the ward was at odds with the atmosphere of calm, it's-too-late-now that greeted her.

The mask was no longer on her mother's face, which was calm and peaceful. Someone had brushed her hair off her forehead, the wires and drips had been removed and the machines pushed out of the way. Rosie was sitting a little away from the bed, and for a fleeting moment Virginia wondered if she was too frightened to move in closer. Virginia picked up her mother's hand, which was cold to the touch already.

'Was it peaceful?'

Rosie shrugged and, seeing that she had been crying, Virginia went over to her and awkwardly put her arm around the shoulder of her seated sister.

'You all right, mate?'

She shrugged again, perhaps not trusting herself to speak. 'You should have been here,' she said eventually, and Virginia was shocked by the harshness of her tone.

'I had to go. I had a meeting. She seemed OK when I left. It was just bad timing, that's all.'

'There's always some meeting, isn't there?' Rosie's mouth made an ugly shape as she talked, and Virginia moved away as if she'd been slapped. 'Leave it to poor old Rosie to hold the fort, why don't you? You just write the cheques and carry on with your la-la Oxford life, and I'll clean up her mess and wash her underwear and deal with Social Services. Oh, I've got nothing else to do. No important meetings for Rosie, don't worry.' Her voice had risen and echoed round the room. 'You did the bare minimum, didn't you? Just came here when it suited you, when you could fit it in to your Filofax or whatever it is you people have.'

Virginia watched in astonishment as Rosie went on, barely listening now to her diatribe, but then surprise at the onslaught gave way to sudden understanding. As her sister's face contorted with anger at Virginia, it occurred to her that this was guilt and grief talking. In her own extraordinary way, she had found her absolution for her behaviour as a teenager, the trouble she had given her parents, for her selfishness, and it was fitting that she, who'd had to give so much more care than Virginia could, had been there at the moment of her mother's death. Not Virginia. Rosie could now

250

carry that knowledge—that she'd cared until the bitter end—as vindication.

Virginia looked at the body of the woman on the bed. She'd gone, and with her had gone the stress of the last few years. But with her had gone the past and her childhood as well. Suddenly she was nobody's daughter any more. Had she been good enough to her? *I'm going to have to dig deep to find the right memories for me*, she warned herself, turned away from Rosie and left the room.

*   *   *

By the time she had sorted the arrangements with the hospital and the funeral directors—the same company who had buried her father and grandparents—it was mid-afternoon. Rosie made no move to be involved in the arrangements, except to interrupt when Virginia told the funeral directors they'd call tomorrow about the details, to say, 'It'll be a cremation,' with a finality that no one dared argue with.

They parted in the car park opposite the funeral directors' offices. No offer of coffee or any suggestion of going over memories was proposed by either of them. That was left to Virginia to do alone, and her return journey down the motorway again was filled with a mixture of recollections, combined with vivid images from the last twenty-four hours. Holidays on the beach, a new guinea pig, Aunty Sandra's wedding, where Virginia and Rosie had been bridesmaids, were interspersed with memories of her mother's growing confusion and illness. As each mile of the motorway shot past, Virginia ran through it all like a film. How they'd

251

had to rescue their mother from shops where her behaviour had caused problems. The night Virginia had stayed over and her mother had let herself out of the house in her nightie and was found at the bus stop. The meeting with the care home and the tragic weekend they'd cleaned out the house after it was sold. And what kept coming back to her was that, even though she was in her thirties, it didn't seem right to Virginia that she was an orphan now. The landscape had shifted and she felt a tsunami of loneliness.

By the time she pulled off the M40 for Oxford there was a bundle of wet tissues in her lap and her eyes ached with crying. She stopped at a garage and splashed water on her face in the ladies'. She didn't want Scarlett to see her like this.

'Mummy!' the little girl threw herself into Virginia's arms. 'You've been crying.' She touched her mother's eyes. 'What was it like, Granny dying? Did you see her?'

Virginia smiled at her daughter's questions which she knew she was going to have to answer at some point. Just not right now. 'Where's Granny Sussex?'

'She had to go.' Karen, their young babysitter, came out of the kitchen. 'She only left a little while ago, and Piers has called to say he'll be back in about half an hour. Come on, young lady, you've got your tea to finish.'

'Supper.' Scarlett followed her back into the kitchen, and Virginia brought up the rear, noticing how tidy everywhere was. Even the pile of papers and letters on the side in the lounge seemed smaller. 'Granny Sussex says it's common to say tea.' Virginia caught Karen's eye over her daughter's head and they both smiled.

'What's that you're eating? It looks delicious.' Virginia dropped her bag on the worktop.

'Cottage pie. Granny made it. She's says there's one for you and Daddy too.'

Virginia opened the door of the fridge. On each shelf was a pie or crumble, and the door and vegetable drawers were full of juice and fresh veg. 'Oh isn't that kind,' she said.

'She says she's done the ironing and it's in the airing cupboard,' Scarlett said, her mouth full of broccoli. 'And there's some stuff on my bed.'

'Right. Now I'm going to jump in the shower while you finish that. No talking with your mouth full, young lady. You OK to hang on a moment, Karen?'

Karen nodded quickly. 'Of course. You go and change. You must be wrung out.'

'I am a bit.' Virginia smiled at the young girl's understanding. Picking up her small holdall, she made her way upstairs. The house smelled of cleaning fluid, and Virginia wondered just how much cleaning Judy had done. Had the house needed to be cleaned? When Virginia had left it, it had seemed pretty spotless to her. Opening her bag, she pulled out yesterday's knickers and T-shirt and dropped them into the now-empty laundry basket, then dumped it on the floor in their bedroom. The duvet was smooth and unwrinkled—Piers would never have left it like that—and one of her silk work shirts hung on a hanger on the front of the wardrobe. Judy had certainly been busy. Slipping off her clothes, grateful to be home and aching for a hot shower, she slipped on her towelling bathrobe and padded across the landing to the bathroom. She could hear Scarlett chatting nineteen to the dozen downstairs, and glanced into her bedroom as she passed. The bed was as neat as her own, the toys laid out in regimented lines on the low toy box, and on the bed was a pile of clothes. Virginia went in to put them away but, as she picked them up, she didn't recognise them. Tartan trousers. A jumper that buttoned up at the neck. Two shirts with embroidery on the front and a thick cotton skirt in mustard yellow. All best quality and all with the shop labels removed.

Virginia sighed and closed her eyes to hold back the tears pricking there again. Dropping the items back on the bed, she headed for the bathroom, hopeful that she'd still find her own things there.

Chapter 34

August 2010

'But what do you want me to do with Ginny's things?' Alice had asked as Judy bustled out to the car. 'I mean, do you want me to clear it all out?'

Judy, distracted, and all animosity swept away by the turn of events, had looked over her shoulder as she followed Bill out to the car, her hand protectively on his back. 'Yes, yes—I think that would be best. Dominic and I will come back another day and take Piers' clothes and—I don't know—his books and trophies and ...' She'd faltered. 'There's no question of Bill coming again. I shouldn't have ...' She'd sighed deeply and allowed Dominic to lead him gently to the pavement, shuffling his way there like a man twenty years older. 'I knew it would be hard—for all of us.' She'd glanced over Alice's shoulder to where Scarlett stood, frozen-faced, on the stairs. 'But I didn't realise ... He's not sleeping, that's part of the problem. Every night he gets up and goes downstairs. I used to go and sit with him at first. But he doesn't want me there. It's not *me* he wants. And I can't comfort him—do you see?' She'd shaken her head and turned away.

A moment later, Dominic had returned from the car, shrugging helplessly. 'I'm going to take them to the local A&E, just to get Dad checked over. I don't think it's anything—well, nothing they can do anything about. Just exhaustion, probably.' He glanced over his shoulder to where Bill and Judy sat now, in his car. 'I'll drive them home, then we'll come back to pick up their car. And we'll take Piers' stuff then. Better take it home with us for the time being.' Dominic was thinking aloud now, his eyes unfocused. 'This is the hardest bit so far. Makes it seem so—I don't know—final. Anyway, if you could just deal with Virginia's stuff, it would make things a lot easier for Mum. And me, come to that. Could you get in touch with her people— see if they want anything? Actually, it's only her sister now, isn't it? Well, could you deal with that? Just take all the clothes and stuff. Kitchen things too, probably. I don't think old Piers was ever that much of a domestic god.' He sighed, then lowered his voice. 'And if you can have Scarlett until things calm down a bit. She does seem settled with you and she needs to be with someone who understands her.'

'Of course I will, though I'm not sure if I'm any good at it.'

'Well, you've got to be better than Mum and Dad.' He smiled tiredly. 'They're fabulous as grandparents, of course, but I wouldn't trust them with our lot. And vice versa. Theo feels the same—why do you think he emigrated? Look, sorry to dump all this on you, Alice, but you're the closest thing to family that Virginia had, from what I understand.' He checked the car once more, and Alice could see Judy gesturing impatiently to him. 'I'd better get going. Just do what you can here and give me a call if you need any help. Thanks.' He'd leaned forward and given her a quick kiss on the cheek, then walked into the house to give Scarlett a warm hug and was gone.

Alice had thought fast. There was a limit to how much she could fit into those boxes but she'd give it her best shot. 'Come on, Scarlett,' she said, more brightly than she felt. 'Let's get those toys of yours packed and then we'll sort out your clothes. You've grown so much in the past few weeks, I bet half of them don't fit.'

At that moment, Scarlett's composure had broken down again and she'd sunk down on the stairs, sobbing. Without hesitation this time, Alice had gone to her side and gathered her into her arms and held her, and rocked her, and tried, as best she could, to soothe her. And sitting there, side by side on the stairs, they'd cried together for a good long time.

And that was how she came to be sitting at home much later on the same day, long after Scarlett had gone up to bed, exhausted by the physical effort as much as the emotional one. Having carefully placed every single soft toy in its rightful place in Scarlett's room with her, she was now sipping a glass of the

256

red wine left over from when Greg had been for a takeaway a couple of days earlier, and was sifting through Ginny's recipe books. She'd scooped them briskly from the kitchen shelves and packed them into carrier bags to fit into the spaces around the boxes that nearly obscured the rear view from the car. Sitting alone in the quiet cottage, she wished, and not for the first time, that she'd accepted Greg's offer to drive them up and help. As she thought about him, a smile crossed her face for almost the first time that day as she wondered how he'd feel about packing two cross hens and a cat into that gorgeous car of his. She'd soon find out.

They'd managed all of Scarlett's stuff, apart from winter coats and boots that were stored downstairs in the hall, but she'd barely started on Ginny's clothes, and had no idea what she should do with them anyway. They were nowhere near the same size, Ginny being a good six inches taller, and their taste was miles apart. Alice smiled ruefully. Ginny always looked so pulled together and had once confessed to Alice that she never wore more than two colours at one time. Anyway, wearing Ginny's clothes would just feel weird. The only thing of Ginny's that would suit her even slightly was the Jo Gordon skinny scarf Alice had given her for Christmas a few years ago, and that she was sure Ginny had hated. She'd certainly never seen her wear it. Which brought Alice to the challenge she was currently facing. Judy's troubles had unexpectedly made Alice custodian of all Ginny's possessions for the time being and she felt the responsibility weighing heavy upon her.

Rosie was smaller than Ginny, and though she had the same colouring, it was the differences that

257

were more striking. It was hard to imagine Rosie carrying off Ginny's well-chosen separates, but she had to ask before even thinking of donating anything to the charity shop.

Finding the number in Ginny's phone book, Alice checked her watch before she lifted the phone. Not too late. Rosie answered after just two rings. 'Hello?'

'Oh hi, Rosie? It's Alice Fenton here. Ginny's friend. I was just wondering how you're doing? Are you OK?'

'I'm doing fine. Just fine.'

'Right, good. Erm—the thing is, Rosie, I was at the house today. Ginny and Piers' place, you know. And Judy and Bill were clearing Piers' things and I was wondering if you wanted any of Ginny's clothes, or anything?'

There was a pause. 'Yes, yes I would. It would be nice to have some of her things around me, to remind me of her I mean. Let Scarlett have any of our mother's jewellery, won't you? I don't think she left much, but . . . you know.'

'Of course,' Alice paused for a moment. Ginny had always said how hard up Rosie was and it suddenly struck her that perhaps she could do some good here. 'There's some very good furniture—a lovely sofa, for example—which I couldn't bear to see go to a house clearance. I'll have to check with Judy, of course, but I can't see that she'd need it.' They both laughed a little in unspoken understanding and Alice felt a bit of ice begin to melt.

'Yes, that would be great. Mine is wrecked. And . . .'

'Yes?' Alice asked gently.

'If there are any photographs. You know, nothing important that Scarlett wants, but I've sort of realised that I don't have any recent pictures of Virginia.'

'Of course!' Alice replied. 'I'll go through them. There's a lovely one of the three of them you might like.'

'That would be nice.' Rosie's voice sounded quiet and there was a long pause. 'I don't know what Virginia might have told you about me but . . . well, it was difficult with Mum being so ill. When she died . . . well, I said some things I shouldn't have.'

'We all say things we shouldn't have. But Ginny did tell me that you took very good care of your mum,' she lied.

'Did she? I realise now how much she sacrificed to pay for Mum's care and having to drive up here all the time. I wish I could tell her that now.' Alice could hear her sniff down the phone. 'I did love her.'

'We all did,' Alice said, not sure what else to say.

There was another pause. 'How's Scarlett? Poor little thing.'

'She's doing OK, thank you. Visiting the house in Oxford was very hard for her but it was another step.'

'What will become of her?' Rosie asked. 'Who will look after her?'

'She's with me at the moment, but really Piers' parents have been doing most of the caring. It's a strain for them though.' She suddenly felt the urge to share her fears with this woman who she hardly knew but was probably the strongest link to her dead friend. 'And I'm not sure Scarlett is happy there.'

259

Rosie didn't say anything for a while and Alice was wondering if she'd gone when she said quietly, 'I gave my parents hell, but imagine how much worse it would have been if they had been my grandparents. Would you like to have been brought up by your grandparents?'

Alice hadn't really ever thought about it but, on reflection now, the idea seemed absurd.

'Besides,' Rosie went on. 'It's not what Virginia would have wanted.'

When she'd put down the phone, Alice slumped back in her chair. How Ginny's death had changed her relationships and showed her the side of people she'd never known. She poured herself another glass of wine and arranged the books into piles: those she'd definitely read, those she might and those she'd never open, that could go straight to the charity shop. She assigned a Jamie Oliver to the 'might' pile and stopped. The next little book looked much more personal. It was one of those journals you buy in posh stationery shops and covered in a pink and purple fabric. Maybe Ginny had collected her own recipes. That would be something to keep and maybe Scarlett could have it when she was older. She opened it at random and frowned. It seemed to be a diary, dated from 1999. And each entry was addressed to Scarlett.

A rush of emotion made Alice feel faint and she was glad she was sitting down. The loopy, regular hand was so familiar from days when they'd sat side by side in lecture theatres, taking notes on Baudelaire and Racine—or more often writing each other notes on a piece of scrap paper. Alice was transported back to those days and the easy closeness that had developed between her and

Ginny. They'd seen each other every day for weeks at a time, and she'd taken it totally for granted. She closed the cover as if she could shut off the rush of pain and loss that swept over her. She might look at the journal—eventually, though she wasn't sure she had a right to. But not now. She stood up and, still holding the book, looked around for a place to store it. Somewhere Scarlett wouldn't find it. If it was too painful for Alice to tackle, what would it feel like to her daughter?

Chapter 35

May 2005

Darling Scarlett,
Two new members of the family today! They may only be hens, but already they feel like part of the family. I hope Rodney calms down a bit—he's got some attitude that kitten and, if he doesn't stop hassling them from outside the coop, they'll never lay. I think you are right—we shouldn't eat their first egg. We shall decorate it as a celebration of how clever they are!
I happen to think Precious and Charmaine are fine names for hens, whatever Daddy says. Besides, he chose Rodney, which is a ridiculous name for a cat (he only did it 'cause I wouldn't let him have Del Boy), and as the hens are ladies, we girls should have the privilege of naming them.
I shall make sure they go into the nesting box and shut them up in a while—it's not quite dusk yet— like the man at the hen place told us. We don't want

261

any foxes getting at them.

Virginia stopped writing and, taking a sip from her glass of wine, looked across the small garden at the smart new coop, occupied by two black Rhode Rock hens, strutting and pecking at the novelty of grass. The hen man had assured her that they didn't need much space but it seemed small for two fat ladies with large, feathery bottoms. 'They look like big mamas,' Piers had laughed as they were bundled into the box to go into the car earlier, and all the way back from the chicken place at Honeybourne they had tried to think of names. Precious came from Virginia, after the *No. 1 Ladies' Detective Agency* and it was Scarlett who came up with Charmaine—after the dinner lady. Virginia hoped to goodness Scarlett wouldn't tell her at school tomorrow they'd named a hen after her, but she wouldn't put it past her. Scarlett was never backward in coming forward.

The day had been long and hot—a surprise burst of early summer sunshine and, even though the visit to the chicken farm had been fun, watching and laughing at the rare breeds with their feathery bell bottoms, they were all a bit fractious by the time they got home through the late Sunday traffic. Piers kept asking how the hens were doing and Scarlett had become incensed by his teasing names.

'She's not called Char, Daddy, she's called *Charmaine*.' She stamped her foot as he put the chickens into their new home. 'I hate the way you do that.'

'Sorry, *Scarly*.' He'd nudged her and chuckled.

Scarlett had put her hands on her hips, a deep frown on her forehead. 'Do not call me Scarly!'

she shouted so loud that the neighbours three or four houses down must have heard. 'My name is Scarlett.'

'Well, pardon me,' Piers looked back at her in fake admonishment. 'I won't make that mistake again, young lady.'

Piers had grabbed a quick cup of tea and had gone back into school to take a late-afternoon training session with the first rowing eight and Virginia had bundled her very tired daughter into bed as early as was reasonable. She'd knock up some pasta for supper later, but for now she was enjoying the peace. She picked up her pen again.

I started writing this journal for you but, over the years it has turned into something a bit different. I wonder how old you'll be when you read it. Perhaps you never will—I'll just hide it away at the back of my knicker drawer, read it again when I am old and laugh at the silly things that have happened. I wonder if you will remember everything that has happened over the last few weeks? You have been so full of questions that you have worn me out, but I don't suppose you'll remember the answers when you are older. Besides, explaining death to a six-year-old is a completely different thing to facing it as an adult.

As you know, Granny Stoke has been ill for a while. I am struggling to remember her now as she was before—funny, energetic, pretty—and my head is full of her vacant stare and stooped body. I hope that by the time I am old they will have found a cure for this horrible disease, because the last thing I want to do is to put you through the hell that the last few years have been for Rosie and me. Sometimes

I have flashbacks to the times when I was small—you probably will too when you grow up. It's odd—I expect you to remember everything that is in the here and now, but this house, your bedroom, holidays we've had, will probably just be fleeting recollections. But if I really try, I can remember the clothes Mum used to wear and the way she had her hair done. She was very particular about her hair, and I hope she never realised how scruffy it had become. She was a proud woman, but not in a bad way. It mattered to her that she gave the right impression and that she never looked a fool.

I remember her being so nervous the first time she met your dad. I didn't tell her exactly, but she must have guessed that he was quite a bit posher than us. There aren't many people in Stoke called Piers! But your dad has an ease about him that I envy terribly. He simply is himself, whoever he is with, and when he saw that Mum had baked three—three—different types of cake for us when we arrived, and laid newspapers out on the coffee table—newspapers we'd never normally buy—just so he'd think well of us, he rose to the occasion.

'Mrs Russell, you have baked my three favourite cakes,' he announced, managing to consume about a third of each one. Then he picked up The Times *and announced that there was something in it he'd wanted to read that morning but hadn't had time to. She wasn't stupid my mother—far from it. Some of my friends tell me she was the best teacher they ever had. But her face lit up and I knew that she approved and that he'd accepted her. From then on, they were the best of friends.*

I've never quite had that ease with Granny Sussex. Luckily, your dad takes after Grandpa, whom

*I've always adored. Granny Sussex does manage
to make me feel as though her way is the right
one, and mine is somehow wrong. It's not a very
appealing trait and not one that anyone would want
to inherit. And I don't suppose you will.*

*Thinking about it now, I'm still not sure you
should have come to Granny Stoke's funeral. My
mother used to believe that funerals weren't for
women—which is a very Victorian attitude. I think
we're made of sterner stuff than that. If you can
go through childbirth, you can probably manage
a funeral. It wasn't as I'd have liked it though. We
weren't—aren't—religious people, but I know Mum
would have liked a church service and a few stirring
hymns, but Rosie thought the crematorium would
be adequate and, because she's been the one in the
frontline of Mum's care, I felt I couldn't really wade
in and argue. Could I?*

*It was no surprise to be told she had died. For
two weeks she had lain in the hospital, her body
growing thinner and more wracked, and the last
time I saw her, her skin was the same shade as the
sheets. I never believed in what they call the 'death
rattle', but now I do. I sat by her bed for hours,
feeling useless. Full of deep regret and sadness for
all the things I should have done and the daughter
I should have been. You must never think like
that. I just hope that when I fall off the perch—an
apt metaphor in view of the hens—it's quick and
painless.*

*So whether you should have been there or not,
you were and I expect you'll remember that day for
ever. You were certainly curious enough to lodge
it in your memory. You wouldn't believe me when
I told you that the bodies were burned and I don't*

265

suppose the crematorium staff have ever been approached by a little girl asking where the coffin had gone behind the curtain, and insisting she be shown, please? Bless you, Scarlett, you had us all in tears of laughter. Better than tears of sadness.

I'm sorry though that you witnessed the row with Rosie. I had a sense that it was brewing. She was so brittle before the funeral started, and I could recognise the signs, so by the time we got back to that awful hotel for the sandwiches and tea, I was on my guard. She still shouldn't have shouted across the car park though.

Let me tell you a bit about Rosie. I don't think you will be lucky enough to have a younger sister, and I'm sorry for that, but if you do, I hope you'll have a better relationship than I have had with Rosie, especially recently.

It didn't help, I suppose, that I managed to swan through school except for physics, on which I never quite got a handle; most other subjects I could manage. I was a bit like you—what they used to call a 'good all-rounder'. I wonder if your dad was the same? But Rosie really struggled. She wasn't bright, but then she never tried, and she'd walk beside me to school, her pace growing slower and slower, until I used to have to push her through the gates.

'It's all right for you,' she used to say, and that became the refrain for our relationship. It was 'all right for me' that I managed to get exams and go to sixth-form college and go to university, as if she hadn't had the same opportunities.

Our relationship really suffered when I met Piers. Have I ever told you about that? It came from a shared passion for rowing. I've always loved sport, and was captain of netball at school. So once I

*was at university, I threw myself into everything.
University was like opening a box of chocolates for
me, and I was greedy.*

*I met Alice virtually straightaway. In fact, I heard
about her before I actually met her.*

*'Have you seen that girl on M corridor?' the girl
in the next room asked me. I hadn't, but then I'd
kept myself to my room for the first few weeks,
overwhelmed by all the people milling around.
Don't forget it was the first time I'd been away
from home. Turning up for netball practice was
manageable—we were all a bit hearty and keen—
but socialising in the student bar? I was terrified.
Everyone else seemed so noisy and confident.*

*I eventually met 'that girl on M corridor' in the
foyer of the French faculty later that week when
Alice, the girl from M corridor, burst through
the door of our tutorial room. Most of her books
preceded her, splaying across the floor, with sheets
of A4 slipping under chairs and tables.*

*I think the first words I heard her say were
'buggery buggery bugger', which, as you will learn, is
not unusual for Alice. Interestingly unimaginative
words for a woman who's so good at languages! But
'seeing' was the vital part of experiencing Alice and,
as I helped her pick up her papers, I couldn't believe
that anyone could dress like that and get away with
it. Even now, she makes me gasp sometimes with
the combinations she puts together—but throughout
the years I've known her, I have managed to escape
every one of her make-overs, no matter how hard
she's tried to impose them on me.*

*'I am so glad you're my friend,' she said to me a
week later, slipping her arm into mine as we escaped
for yet another coffee when we should have been*

at a lecture. We'd spent most of each day after that tutorial together. She must have meant it, because we are still friends now. We are utterly incompatible on the face of it—but she makes me laugh, she knows me well, and I can rely on her totally. Except to be anywhere on time.

Besides the clothes, the only other area I don't agree with her on is men. Throughout university Alice had her fair share of relationships. No, let's be honest here, she had more than her fair share. But I can safely say that I didn't fancy a single one of her conquests. She went for the rangy, poetic type. If they had an issue, then so much the better!

I had no idea about relationships. I'd got as far as losing my virginity (that confirms it. You're not seeing this diary until you are a very old lady!). I gave it away to a boy from college, actually, just before A-levels, and it was the greatest gift I ever gave away to the undeserving. I hope you are wiser. I'm very cautious about myself—I don't share the body confidence that Alice has. She knows the power of the way she looks, her hair, her face. Her boobs were the hot topic of conversation in our year!

There was no one else of any real significance— just the odd boyfriend, including one called David who I travelled round Europe with one vacation. Sorry to report, my darling, but your mother was a sad rowing type and that was my university 'love'.

Sorry—I've got sidetracked. Rosie and Dad.

Rosie met him the first time I took him home— on the famous three-cakes occasion. It was both excruciating and sad, and I felt so awful for her. She came downstairs shortly after we arrived and I had never seen her like that. In fact, when she walked *into the room we were all struck dumb in a painful silence, unable to think of anything to say. She had put on a tight lycra dress in bright floral colours, and totteringly high heels. Her hair was pinned up on her head, platinum blonde and ringletted, and her eyes were black with mascara. It was the oddest moment, and has never been mentioned since (except between Dad and me, of course. He still can't believe he didn't spit cake across the room in amazement). But I fear that much of her resentment and hostility since then stems from her embarrassment and misjudgement that day.*

Chapter 36

August 2010

Scarlett received the news that she'd be staying with Alice for the next couple of weeks before school started with equanimity. In fact, Alice thought she was pleased about it, despite the fact that half of her possessions were still at Judy and Bill's. She'd stopped nagging about Ashton Down, which was a mercy. Perhaps she was finally resigned to going to Fitzwilliam Lodge, with the prospect of spending every weekend at Alice's. What she was agitating for now, though, was going to collect the hens. Judy had ruled out any question of having them, and Alice was slowly coming round to the idea, after a lot of hard sell from Scarlett about the wonders of fresh eggs for breakfast. The Rodney issue had been mercifully solved by Pat and Karen's offer to keep him, especially as they had more or less adopted him anyway, and Scarlett seemed pacified by promises that she could go and visit him.

'Cats are fickle creatures anyway. Cupboard love. Hens are another matter and I know nothing about them at all. You'll have to show me what to do.'

'Yes, yes, I can do that. I know all about it. It was my job looking after them.'

Across the table, Vince and Greg exchanged glances. Krissy was squarely on Scarlett's side. 'At least you could be sure they're free range,' she pointed out. 'I never really trust the supermarkets.'

'You'll have to get a van big enough for their coop,' Scarlett turned to Greg. 'It's about this big.' She stretched her arms wide. 'But the hens go in little boxes of their own. You have to make sure they don't get shaken up or it frightens them and they won't lay.'

'Right,' Greg replied slowly. He'd come up with the idea of a van for the next day—far more practical, Alice had to admit, than multiple journeys in either of their cars. He was going to use one of the ones his company ran and, since it wouldn't be in use at the weekend, he and Alice would do a round trip, or two if necessary, leaving Scarlett at the cottage in Krissy and Vince's capable care for the day.

Alice felt completely different about this trip. Of course, she knew what to expect this time, and wouldn't have the added complication of Scarlett being there. She'd have a clear run, with Greg, solid and capable, at her side. He'd added in the promise of lunch somewhere nice and the whole day was taking on the feeling of an outing, rather than an ordeal. For the first time in ages, Alice felt relatively carefree. Knowing that Scarlett would be

having the time of her life helped considerably—
Vince and Krissy were always fun and, whatever
they got up to, she knew she'd come back to find
her well-fed and watered, probably slightly spoiled
but, basically, well looked after. Was this why Ginny
only ever relaxed when she knew Scarlett was safe
and happy?

The sight of Greg the next day, dressed in
his scruffiest clothes and handling the van with
surprising aplomb, was curiously erotic and
she watched him furtively as he drove. The
relationship—for, amazingly, that's what it seemed
to be turning into—was unlike any relationship
she'd had before. Greg wasn't needy, broke,
self-absorbed or exploitative, yet she found him
fantastically attractive. He didn't even have the
urge to write poetry. Ginny would have approved—
at long last—of this one, she felt sure. And the
fact that she'd known him already, although only
as a colleague, made it even better. What a shame
Ginny hadn't got round to introducing them earlier.
Maybe she'd thought he was too grown-up for
Alice.

'What?'

Alice started. 'Sorry?'

'You were staring. Have I got something on my
face? Shaving foam or something?'

Alice reached over and stroked his cheek. 'Nope,
you just look lovely, that's all.'

A smile crinkled his profile but he kept his eyes
on the road. 'Thank goodness you left your specs
at home. Well, feast your eyes. I'm not going
anywhere—not in this traffic.' He slowed to a stop
behind a queue on the M40 and turned to face
her. 'You don't look too bad, yourself. Feeling OK

about this?'

'Yes—I feel a lot braver with you here.'

'Couldn't let you tackle it on your own again, could I? Besides, you might not be up to hen-wrangling. I suspect that's a two-person job—at the very least.'

Alice rolled her eyes. 'Those sodding hens! I can't help feeling I've been well and truly taken in. I bet you anything I'm going to end up taking care of them. Even at weekends when Scarlett's with me.'

He laughed. 'Very possibly. But I'll do them during the week, if you like.'

Alice bit her lip. What was he getting at? 'They need letting out pretty early, I think.'

'I know—but I'm prepared to make the ultimate sacrifice. That way I can bring you tea in bed while I'm at it.'

'But what am I going to do when you finish this Sussex project? The next one might be in Brazil or somewhere.'

He turned to look at her again, this time his expression far more serious. 'Well, I'll still be travelling, that's for sure. But I've been meaning to talk to you about things, anyway. And since we're stuck here . . . I was hoping that the new project—the main one, anyway—might be—erm—us.'

'Oh!' Alice could feel her face colouring. 'That sounds—that sounds pretty good to me.'

He let out a sigh. 'Thank goodness. If you'd said no, it would have ended up a pretty awkward day, wouldn't it?'

Alice laughed, suddenly feeling light-headed. 'Yeah, with only the chickens to talk to on the way back—that would have been tricky.'

After that, the day passed in a bubble of

sheer pleasure for Alice. Lunch in Oxford was wonderful—a new place in Jericho that Greg had heard about on the grapevine, with a young chef from a Michelin-starred hotel starting up on his own. And with Greg to help, everything at the house seemed easier. She put her head down and between them they cleared almost everything, efficiently, barely speaking but his mere presence was comforting, and they even found time for the odd break under the cherry tree in the sunshine.

'Nice here, isn't it?' Alice said sipping her tea. 'Though the garden isn't as spick and span as Ginny liked it. Look at those weeds in the veg patch. She'd have hated that.'

'Did you know that cherry trees symbolise mortality?' Greg looked up at the branches. 'The Japanese think they represent the ephemeral nature of life.'

Alice shivered. 'How symbolic is that.' She paused. 'Did you ever come here?'

He leaned forward, resting his hands on his knees. 'God no. We didn't know each other like that. Not socially. I only worked on a couple of projects with her and we only ever met when they were close to completion.'

'Oh, so you never met Piers then?'

He shook his head. 'No, no. Nothing like that.'

Alice put her head to one side. 'So why were you at the funeral then?'

He scuffed his shoe on the grass. 'I read about the crash in the paper and colleagues confirmed it was Virginia. I was in the area that day and it just seemed the right thing to do. It was such a tragedy and I always liked her. It was the least I could do.'

Alice nodded. 'That's kind of you. I've always

273

worried that no one would come to my funeral.'

Greg smiled. 'If you put Vince in charge, you won't have to worry. It'll be like the Mardi Gras.'

They worked on until the job was done and even the hens behaved themselves, going easily into their boxes. They were on the way back at about six when Alice's mobile rang. It was Krissy.

'Alice, brace yourself.'

Alice felt her stomach clench. 'What?' she snapped. 'Is Scarlett OK?'

'Yes, yes—she's absolutely fine. It's just, Judy paid an unexpected visit.'

'Right—is she there now? Do I need to speak to her?'

'No—no, she left pretty quickly.'

'Was there a problem? Did she have a row with Scarlett?'

'No—they hardly spoke. It was us, really.'

Alice was baffled. 'What do you mean? You and Vince?'

'Yeah—well, more Vince really.'

Alice groaned. 'Don't tell me . . .'

Krissy sounded guilty as hell. 'Well, he's working up his new act and he was just running through a few numbers.'

'Please tell me he wasn't in full drag. I don't really want Scarlett seeing that, let alone Judy. God knows, I find it scary enough.'

'No, thank goodness. He just had a feather boa and a fan, but he was lip-synching to Madonna and it was quite loud so she just walked into the cottage and none of us noticed her for a while.'

Alice groaned. 'Right—I'll wait for a call. Thanks for letting me know.'

Greg looked puzzled. 'Trouble?'

Alice closed her eyes and let her head fall back against the seat. 'Just Judy discovering I've left Scarlett in the care of a professional drag queen. She'll be demanding I return her to the moral safety of Haywards Heath after this.'

He paused. 'I thought that was what you were planning? What you wanted?'

Alice opened her eyes and took a deep breath. 'Yes, so did I. But now I'm not so sure. I'm getting rather attached to her, in spite of myself—and the blasted hens.'

*   *   *

Alice took Greg as reinforcements when she delivered Scarlett back to her grandparents' house, as planned, a few days later. In fact, to lend an extra air of responsibility, they went in Greg's car and he wore his most conservative suit.

'I can't believe you're using me as granny bait,' he grumbled as they approached the house. 'I don't really see myself in that role, to be honest.'

Scarlett was sitting arms folded and looking sullen in the back of his Aston Martin. Alice smiled over at Greg. 'Don't worry—you're not terminally respectable, Mr Mullin,' she whispered. 'It's just that compared to Vince, you are. And that's what we need here, a drag queen antidote, so butch up and talk posh.'

He laughed quietly and shook his head as they drew up outside the house. Alice swallowed. As she looked up at the austere gables, she suddenly realised how badly she wanted Judy and Bill to judge her as being suitable to take care of Scarlett, even if it was just for the weekends. Had she

275

blown it?

Also parked outside was Dom's jag. It looked as though there was going to be a family conference. Suddenly Alice felt nervous and Greg, perceptive as usual, reached over and squeezed her hand. Dom met them warmly at the door, and led them into the kitchen where Judy and Bill were both seated, Judy with a face like thunder. Alice began to fear the worst. But it was Dom who spoke first. 'Alice, Scarlett—it's good to see you again.' He stepped to one side to allow Alice to introduce Greg.

'This isn't the fellow, is it?' Bill asked, squinting at Greg.

'No, no,' Judy snapped. 'Quite a different type, I can assure you. I'd recognise that other one anywhere. The image is seared into my memory.'

'That'll do, Mum,' Dom soothed. 'The thing is, Alice . . .' he paused and looked at his parents. 'This is very difficult. For everyone.'

Alice's mouth was dry. Were they going to demand she return Scarlett to their care, just because Judy had witnessed Vince's performance and assumed the worst? Was she going to have to explain how wonderful Vince was? How kind and thoughtful? And would all that be brushed aside just because of Judy's prejudice?

Dom cleared his throat. 'Mum was fairly upset when she came to Ulvington the other day, I think it's fair to say.' Judy snorted, and glared—not at Alice now but, surprisingly, at her son. 'Nonetheless,' he continued, 'we've had a talk about what she saw and I have explained that that sort of thing is quite accepted these days. Especially in Brighton.'

Alice leaned forward in her seat. This wasn't

276

going the way she had feared. Dom glanced now at his father and continued. 'The thing is, Dad is a bit tired at the moment. I'm sure it's only temporary but it's quite understandable. So I think—and Theo and Barney agree, because we spoke about this only yesterday—that it would be best if Scarlett stays with you now, Alice.'

Next to her, Alice heard Scarlett gasp and take her hand. Alice frowned. Had she misunderstood? It seemed the whole landscape had changed. 'Do you mean permanently?'

'Yes, we think so,' Dom went on. 'Unless Scarlett objects to that? You know you can come and live with us, or Theo or Barney, don't you?' Scarlett simply nodded. 'And that would mean going to school somewhere local to you as well of course.'

Bill spoke now, in measured tones, sounding very much like the judge that he had been: 'We love you very much, Scarlett. You must never be in any doubt about that. You're our only granddaughter, after all. And you are very, very precious. But you need to be with someone with a bit of go. Someone young, like Alice. Not two old fogeys like me and your granny.'

Judy sniffed loudly. 'Scarlett, darling, you know we would keep you here if we could. I am sure we could manage, but I have been overruled. Of course we love you. You know that without being told. And I can't say I've managed to find any schools in your area, Alice, that quite match up to the Lodge. But it seems that matters are being decided for me.'

'Right,' Alice said slowly. 'So you're happy for me to look for a local school for Scarlett, is that right?' She felt Greg's hand slip supportively into hers.

Judy shrugged eloquently. 'I think that's the only

277

possible solution, since it's too far for Scarlett to travel to the Lodge every day.'

Beside her, Alice was aware of Scarlett wriggling in her seat, and hoped she'd have the tact not to look too pleased. Judy continued, 'I'd like her to spend this weekend with us, as planned, and I'll take the opportunity to take her shopping, get her suitable clothes for the autumn. A good warm coat and some sturdy shoes. What do you think, Scarlett?'

'Thank you, Granny. That would be lovely.'

Alice smiled as she heard the happiness bubbling in Scarlett's voice. Oh, Ginny, she thought, you'd be so proud of your girl. And somewhere inside it all felt completely right. She just hoped she could live up to Ginny expectations and care for her little girl as well as she deserved.

Chapter 37

October 2005

'Always nice to see such enthusiasm,' Scarlett's teacher said at the door as Scarlett quickly kissed her mother and darted into the cloakroom.

'She doesn't take much persuading,' Virginia laughed, watching her daughter hang up her pump bag and run through to the classroom beyond. 'I could almost be offended!'

'Oh you don't want a clingy one,' the pretty young woman in the beige skirt and bright jumper replied. 'They're a nightmare. No, Scarlett is a joy to teach. She's so chatty and bubbly and I'm so thrilled with her reading. Way ahead of her age, you know.'

Virginia felt a lump of pride in her throat. 'Is she? She seems to read voraciously at home—and not always the right stuff. She was reading the paper last night and Piers ended up having to explain share prices because she wanted to know what the FTSE was!'

'I'm not surprised. Sometimes she floors me with her questions. You should be very proud of her.'

'Oh we are. Better dash. I have the meeting from hell this morning.' Several other small children darted past them, squealing and giggling, and the teacher looked wry.

'I'll swap with you, if you like,' she laughed, her eyes twinkling.

'No way!' Virginia replied and headed out of the playground to her car, pulling her coat around her against the chill early autumn wind. The trees were beginning to turn and the pavement was scattered with curled brown leaves blown around like litter.

Derek was due to arrive at the hotel at eleven, so she had a clear couple of hours—interruptions aside—to finish her marketing report and collate the figures. She felt buoyed up this morning that she had something good to report to Derek, who had a knack of homing in on the lowest figure on a spreadsheet and demanding explanations. They had the weekend to look forward to with the prospect of lunch with friends too. But by twelve fifteen she had a headache, exhausted by having to be one step ahead of Derek at every turn. Why wasn't the website performing as well as the month before? Why had print costs gone up? Were Christmas bookings ahead of last year? Paper was spread all over the conference room table and she was desperate for a sandwich, her stomach rumbling ominously. There was a tap on the door and Erica, the reservations manager, popped her head around it.

'Sorry to interrupt, Derek, but there's been a call from school for Virginia. They tried your mobile but I said you were in a meeting.'

Virginia excused herself for a moment and went out to reception. 'Hello?'

'Hello, Mrs Waverley. Sorry to bother you but Scarlett has been sick in the queue for lunch. She seems OK otherwise, but I think she ought to go home.'

Shit. Virginia's mind raced. She couldn't possibly get away and Piers had taken a Year Eight group to the British Museum.

'OK. I'll have to arrange for someone to collect her. Tell her someone will be there soon, can you?'

'Certainly. As I say, she seems fine, so nothing to worry about probably. There are lots of bugs around.'

Virginia put the phone down then, rubbing her eyes, did a mental scan of the people she could turn to for help. Karen the babysitter might be free. She worked in a local supermarket but her hours were erratic. It was worth a go.

The phone rang for ages before Pat, her mother, picked up. 'Hi, Virginia. Sorry, Karen's at work until five today. Can I help?'

Virginia sighed, aware she had to get back into the meeting. Derek would not be impressed by childcare issues interrupting his flow.

'Oh, Scarlett's been sick at school, and they think she ought to come home. Trouble is, I'm right in the middle of an important meeting. I might be able to persuade them to keep her.' She rubbed her forehead.

'I'll collect her if you like. I don't have to be in work till seven.'

'Oh, Pat, could you?' Virginia felt a wave of relief mixed with immense guilt. 'I'll get away as soon as I can.'

'Don't worry, dear, I'll give her some lunch and you just let school know that I'm collecting her.'

'I certainly will, Pat, and thank you so much.' Putting down the phone, she quickly called school again, and, relieved, went back into the meeting.

By one o'clock the rumblings from Virginia's stomach must have been audible, and by the time Derek said, 'Well, I think that just about wraps things up,' she had made a mental note to make sure she had a couple of biscuits in her bag next time. 'We've a busy few weeks ahead, haven't we?' He tidied up his papers and started to stand up. 'Remind me to show you the plans for the refurb at Cotswold Manor. It'd better bloody work. It's costing us an arm and a leg.'

'Are you . . . we . . . using the same designers as we used in Harrogate?' Virginia asked without looking up from tidying her own strewn pile of papers.

'Yes, but this will be the last time. They're getting way too grand and expensive for us now. Off building dream resorts in Qatar and places like that. We'll be far too small fry for them next time round.'

'Oh right. Good. Yes.' A few sheets of paper fell to the floor and she scrabbled to pick them up. 'Right, I'll see you in a couple of weeks and I'll send you the minutes of this as soon as I can.'

281

It wasn't going to be today, she thought, as she grabbed a bowl of staff lunch from the kitchen en route to the back office, where she sank into a spare chair and began to shovel the hot tomatoey pasta into her mouth.

'Sorry, sorry, sorry. You know how he goes on,' she gasped to Erica, who'd been waiting patiently for an hour for her. 'You OK if we go through stuff while I eat? I promise not to talk with my mouth full.'

Erica laughed. 'Course not. Just don't get tomato sauce on my keyboard.' The phone started to ring. 'Oh bum, let me just get this. Hello, Reception, this is Erica. How can I help you? Yes of course, she's right here.' Erica pulled off her earpiece. 'Call on line one for you.'

Virginia frowned, swallowed quickly, and picked up the phone on the desk. 'Hello?'

'Virginia, it's Pat. Sorry to bother you but I tried your mobile and it went to answerphone.'

Virginia pulled her phone out of her pocket and quickly took it off silent.

'Is everything OK?'

'Yes, fine. Scarlett's had a good lunch and she's just watching telly but she says she has a headache and I wondered if I could give her some Calpol? I keep some here for the grandchildren.'

Virginia felt torn. Should she go and collect Scarlett now? It sounded as though she was going down with something. School had indicated there was a bug going round and Virginia knew that Scarlett's friend Lottie was off. But Pat was an experienced mother—she had five children of her own and Virginia had forgotten how many grandchildren—she'd be able to cope. She'd just

282

get through the afternoon's work as quickly as she could. 'That would be great, Pat, thank you. Let me know how she is, will you, and I promise I'll be with you as soon as I can.'

The pasta was finished and they had got as far as Christmas Party planning, when Virginia's mobile rang again beside her.

'Hi, Pat again. Sorry to bother you, but Scarlett says the Calpol hasn't worked. I know you can give Ibuprofen in between doses. You OK if I do that?'

'That's fine, Pat. I shouldn't be too much longer.'

It was quarter to five by the time she pulled up outside Pat's small house and tapped on the door. Pat, a squat and softly rounded woman, smiled as she opened it, but then furrowed her brow. 'She's taken herself off to Karen's bed,' she said. 'She doesn't have a temperature, I've checked a couple of times, but she said she had a bad headache and wanted to sleep.'

That sounded typical of Scarlett. Always forthright when she knew what she wanted. 'Thanks, Pat. You've been such a star to have her.' She handed over the little bunch of flowers she'd picked up from the florist in Summertown. 'Bit pathetic, I'm afraid, but it's all they had left.'

'You shouldn't have,' Pat took them from her, but her face was flushed with pleasure.

'I'll get her home now. She probably just needs a good night's sleep. School really takes it out of them, doesn't it?'

Karen's room was small enough, filled with posters and soft toys, but Scarlett looked like a tiny lump under the bright-blue duvet. She was almost completely hidden and Virginia carefully peeled back the duvet. 'Hi, darling girl,' she whispered.

283

Her skin looked pale against the sheet and her dark hair was spread over the pillow. Sleepy and disorientated, her arms went up to her face. Virginia gently pulled them away so she could feel her daughter's forehead.

'No, don't,' Scarlett said abruptly. 'My eyes hurt.'

Virginia felt a fleeting moment of disquiet. 'It's probably 'cause you've been asleep, sweetheart.'

'I haven't been asleep. I couldn't.' Her little arms stayed crossed over her eyes. 'My neck hurts when I put it against the pillow.'

It was then that Virginia noticed a patch of small marks on the underside of her arm as if she'd lain on Velcro. She pulled at the duvet again, trying to see if one of Karen's soft toys was in the bed and Scarlett had lain against it but there was nothing there.

Pat came into the room quietly behind her. 'How's my little patient?' she asked gently.

Virginia could feel her heart beating a bit faster in her chest. 'Pat, I think I might just call the doctor. Could you stay with her for a moment?' She slipped out onto the landing.

It was five o'clock by now and as the phone rang unanswered down the line she was worried she'd missed the end of surgery. She was just about to give up when the receptionist picked up. 'Surgery, can I help you?'

'Yes please. Sorry. I mean, you are probably about to close but it's Virginia Waverley here. I just want to check something.' She ran through Scarlett's symptoms to the receptionist. 'Could you possibly ask one of the doctors what they think?' She stopped.

'Can you hold for a moment please?' The

receptionist clicked off, and Virginia held on, looking at but not seeing the small, fading prints of fishing ports that were hung at perfect, regular intervals up Pat's staircases.

'Hello, Mrs Waverley?' Virginia recognised the voice of Dr Marchant, a fairly new doctor whom she'd seen a couple of times with Scarlett for ear infections. 'Can you get your daughter to us as soon as possible?' His voice was calm, but Virginia didn't like the sound of 'as soon as possible'.

'Yup, I'll be right there.' She hung up and went back into Karen's room. 'Pat, they say to bring her down. They're about to close so they want her now.' Leaning down, she carefully picked Scarlett up from the bed, and she curled in towards her mother, protecting her eyes with her hands and Virginia's coat.

In the car Scarlett answered a few of Virginia's inane questions about school, but didn't seem very interested in talking. Virginia glanced at her daughter in the rear-view mirror. Her head was resting back against the seat and she was watching the cars go by out of the windows, screwing up her eyes each time they went past a street light in the encroaching autumn dusk. Virginia turned the heat up, then turned it down again, not sure which was the right thing to do, then had to brake suddenly to narrowly avoid hitting the back of a bus that had stopped in front of her.

Gingerly they walked from the almost empty little car park into the surgery and Virginia hadn't even said her name before the receptionist said, 'Dr Marchant is waiting for you in room four.'

The young doctor stood up as they walked in and barely looked at Virginia. He crouched down in front of Scarlett. 'Can you tell me how you feel?'

'A bit sore and my eyes hurt,' she replied sullenly, as if it was his fault. 'Please can I sit down?'

'Of course,' he said kindly and, as he talked, he carefully pulled up her sleeves and looked at her arms. The Velcro mark was still there and he pushed his finger against it. 'Scarlett, do you remember having a little jab in your arm before you started school?' She nodded, interested by the question. 'I'm going to give you another little jab in your arm now if that's OK.' He moved over to a table across the small room. 'It might hurt a bit but I know you are a very brave girl, because your mum has told me so.' Virginia liked him for his little lie, but she couldn't take her eyes off Scarlett, whose head was now leaning limply against the back of the chair. She crouched down beside her, and gently brushed the hair off her face.

'She's not allergic to penicillin, is she?' he asked Virginia as he prepared a syringe.

'No. I mean, not as far as I'm aware, but she's not had antibiotics much really.' She was gabbling. An injection seemed quite radical for a school bug and she tried to read the doctor's face. Scarlett barely winced as the doctor pushed up her sleeve again and injected her.

'What do we . . . ?' Virginia started to ask and for the first time he looked at her.

'Mrs Waverley. I'm going to call an ambulance. We need to get Scarlett to hospital as soon as possible.'

Chapter 38

October 2005

Virginia watched as if from behind glass, aware that now everything was outside of her control. Her presence wasn't even being acknowledged. She realised that she had her hands cupped over her mouth as she watched, but she felt more helpless if she dropped them to her sides.

There must have been eight medics around Scarlett's bed, including the kind-faced Australian paediatrician who had greeted them and introduced herself as Dr Calvert when they'd arrived at A&E. In usual style, Scarlett had been adamant that she wasn't going to hospital, and they'd had a small row with Virginia being firm about 'how the doctors wanted to check you're OK' not sure herself what was going on. She wanted to ask, to catch the doctor's eye, but she couldn't in front of Scarlett and there was no way she was leaving her alone to leave the room to ask.

At the surgery, Dr Marchant had gone out to reception and, for what felt like ages, she sat beside Scarlett, saying nothing and stroking her head until Scarlett asked her to stop.

'The ambulance is here.' Dr Marchant had come back to his room. 'Can you walk with me, Scarlett?' The little girl had slid off the chair and carefully put her feet down on the floor.

'Mum, I can't walk.' She had looked up beseechingly at Virginia, and Dr Marchant had bent down and scooped her up into his arms,

287

and had deposited her in the ambulance that had backed up to the surgery door.

'This isn't funny.' The words kept wheeling through Virginia's head, and holding Scarlett's hand with one hand, she tried to call Piers. He must have left London by now—she couldn't remember what time he said he'd be back—but he wasn't answering his phone. She sent him a text asking him to call. She hoped it wouldn't frighten him.

Fear. The feeling had seeped into every cell of her body as she stood here in the emergency room. The doctors were talking quietly, a little coterie around the bed in those scrubs like an American hospital drama, set apart from her because they knew what she didn't. 'I'm her mother,' she wanted to scream. 'I demand to know.'

Scarlett was crying, her sobbing audible over the bleeps of the machines, and at one point she screamed 'Mummy' as the doctors turned her over on her side to do something to her back. It was all Virginia could do not to rush over to her.

A large nurse slipped through the doors and Virginia put her hand on her arm as she passed. 'Please. Can someone tell me what's going on?' She tried not to cry.

'I'll see if someone can come and talk to you,' the woman said kindly.

She looked around the room and, finding a chair, perched on the front of it, then stood up again. If she sat down, something would happen to Scarlett, she was sure. She couldn't even see her daughter who was screened behind a curtain of people, and her stomach cramped with tension.

After a few minutes, Dr Calvert peeled away and came towards Virginia and pulled her mask off her

288

small, freckled face. She wasn't smiling.

'Mrs Waverley, I'm sorry we haven't been able to talk to you but we needed to attend to Scarlett as quickly as we could.' She put her hand on Virginia's arm and guided her through the doors into the quiet corridor. 'As you may well have guessed, Scarlett has meningitis.'

Virginia almost smiled. How ridiculous.

'I'm sure you know, but meningitis is an inflammation of the meninges, the linings that surround and protect the brain. Lots of things can cause it—including bacteria or viruses—but your GP spotted it very quickly and acted fast by giving Scarlett a shot of antibiotics.'

Virginia felt a wave of relief. 'Does that mean she'll be OK?'

'Bacterial meningitis can be very serious and that is why we have to keep a close eye on her because we don't want it to develop. There can be neurological problems or trouble with her breathing, or sometimes it can develop into cardiovascular problems.'

'Meaning?' Virginia didn't take her eyes off her face.

'In very serious cases, it can cause multi-organ failure,' she said gently.

Virginia gasped and the doctor put her hand on her arm again. 'We have taken a lumbar puncture, which means we've taken a sample of cerebrospinal fluid so that we can see how things are progressing. You acted very quickly though, and that is so important with meningitis.'

'What now?' Virginia held her breath.

'We need to wait for about twenty minutes to see how she responds to the antibiotics and to see which way it goes.'

'What if she doesn't?'

Dr Calvert smiled gently. 'Let's take one step at a time, hey? Your daughter is a real fighter though, that's for sure.' She opened the door again and held it for Virginia to pass through back into the intensive care room, following behind her. A gap had appeared around Scarlett as the nurses worked, and she could see her small white form on the huge bed, with wires and drips coming from her tiny body.

Her phone vibrated in her pocket. It was a text from Piers. 'Am on coach. You OK?'

She glanced up at the bed. She knew she shouldn't use her phone but she couldn't bear to leave the room. 'Scarlett poorly and in John Rad Hosp. Come here ASAP?' she texted back, then looked at the words. She couldn't tell him like this. Deleting the text, she slipped out of the room again and walked over to a woman sitting at a desk in the little foyer. 'I'm so sorry but my daughter is in there and I need to tell my husband. I'm just going to call him quickly outside but please can you tell them where I am and to come and get me if they. . .' She gulped, swallowing a sob.

'Of course,' the woman answered and got up from her seat as Virginia bolted outside. The evening was cold after the warmth of the hospital and she'd left her coat in the emergency room. She hugged herself, her jaw shivering uncontrollably as the wind whipped through her thin silk shirt.

'Pick up, Piers. Please God, pick up.'

He did after the fourth or fifth ring.

'Darling,' she didn't even say hello. 'It's Scarlett. We're at the John Radcliffe and they say she's got meningitis.'

'Fuck.'

She told him everything Dr Calvert had said. 'How soon can you get here?'

'We're about junction four of the M40. I'll have to go back to school with the bus to get my car.' Virginia could hear someone muttering and Piers replying. 'I'll be there as soon as I can.'

*　　　*　　　*

The woman who had been at the reception desk smiled at her as she came back. 'Would you like a cup of tea?' she asked.

'I suppose. I don't know really!' Tea seemed so trite. So clichéd.

'You go back in and I'll get you a cup.' She patted Virginia's arm and her concern made everything seem more serious. A question shot through her mind: are they trying to prepare me for the worst? Random and terrifying thoughts ran around her head. Trivial details—who'd shut the chickens in?—combined with the unthinkable. What if? Oh God, please no. Every sound and movement made her jump. She couldn't take her eyes off the team as they worked around Scarlett, more quietly now and she could hear her daughter's small, high-pitched voice every now and then.

Virginia put down the cold cup of tea, barely touched, as Dr Calvert came back out to her, pulling the mask from her face again.

'Scarlett seems to be showing a bit of an improvement,' she said gently. 'She is lucid and stable, which is a good sign, and there's been no deterioration in the last few minutes. That means that she is holding up well.'

'Can I see her?' Virginia wiped away a tear roughly. She didn't want Scarlett to see her crying and frighten her.

'Of course. Come with me.'

Scarlett gripped her hand weakly as Virginia got to the bed. Her eyes were hollow and Virginia couldn't bear to look at the drips going into her arm. 'Hello, Mummy.'

'Are you feeling better, sweetpea?' She tried to sound light-hearted.

'A bit. Is Daddy coming to see me?'

'Any minute. He's been to the museum in London so he's coming back as soon as he can to see you.'

By the time Piers came into the room, bringing the scent of the cold night air with him, Scarlett's colour had begun to return and she had picked up. Virginia turned to see him, relief flooding through her. 'That was quick,' she said.

'Jeff made the coach divert and they dropped me here. How is she?'

Virginia released the tears that she'd held back for the last hour and let them fill her eyes.

'They think she's going to be OK,' she whispered to him, before he even had to ask. 'She's responded to the injection and . . . Oh God.' She put her hands up to her face and Piers put his arms around her.

'Thank God,' was all he said as he held her.

Chapter 39

End of August 2010

This was new territory for Alice. And not one she'd ever expected to explore, but here she was with a list of printed-out sheets to sign and a whole raft of decisions to be made. She rubbed her eyes and moved the papers around on the table in front of her, as though that made a difference. The Home/ School Agreement—that she could understand, more or less, and both she and Scarlett had signed it—but since when did going to school involve contracts? School lunches versus packed— fortunately, that was something they could decide as they went. School uniform—well, that, as Mr Williams, the head, had explained, was fairly minimal. It was just a question of a black skirt or trousers, white shirt and bottle-green sweatshirt. How sensible! Coming at this with no preparation at all, Alice was amazed at how much things had moved on since her own school days.

She was afraid she'd rather embarrassed Scarlett at the meeting, swiftly scheduled the day before with the head of Ashton Down, in the hope of finding a place in Year Seven. Term was due to start alarmingly soon. Armed with reports and assessments hastily emailed by Scarlett's old primary in Oxford, they'd arrived at the school, which smelled of fresh paint, absolutely on time. Scarlett had been most insistent.

'You're late for everything,' she tutted, sitting on the stairs tapping her feet, 'but you can't be today or they won't offer me a place, and then you'll have to home-educate me.'

'Christ!' Alice laughed. 'We'd better get a move on then for both our sakes!'

The corridors echoed emptily, and they were greeted by a tall, thin-faced man in a polo shirt and jeans with a crease ironed down the front. He'd smiled at Scarlett warmly and, after reading her assessments, reassured them within minutes that he'd be able to offer her a place—no problem— and proceeded to go over the admin with them. He addressed most of his comments to Scarlett, Alice noticed, drawing her out gradually and listening to her answers with full attention. He seemed nice— aware of Scarlett's situation as Alice had explained it over the phone—showing none of the mawkish sympathy the head at Fitzwilliam Lodge had shown. Watching Scarlett converse so confidently with this virtual stranger, pleasant but still slightly intimidating in the way teachers can be, she felt a wholly unearned sense of pride.

Finally, he turned to Alice and went through the final details with her. She was trying hard not to sound so out of touch, but she soon realised that she was speaking a different language with a vocabulary that dated from her boarding school days—distant in both time and ethos—and was subjected to a slightly terrifying teacher stare. What she knew as 'prep' was now 'homework', 'tuck' would apparently be taken care of by a vending machine, 'domestic science' was 'food tech', French had given way to Spanish, and she couldn't for the life of her work out what PSHE was. After asking twice, she just pretended to understand and simply nodded sagely. Mr Williams seemed to be looking

294

rather pityingly at her by that stage and she felt like a throwback to an Enid Blyton world which, now she came to think about it, she probably was.

Back in the safety of the cottage, she picked up yet another form requiring details of special needs and dietary requirements, and sighed deeply. There was so much she didn't know about this parenting lark but, with any luck, Scarlett would help her with it when she came in from her cycle ride. Ever since the fête, she had made a point of visiting various people in the village, including Immy who'd become a friend and, only the day before, had come back with a bag full of plums from Walter's orchard, sweet and succulent, that they'd shared sitting at the garden table in the late August sunshine. Despite the occasional wobbly moment, she seemed to be taking the sudden changes in her life and this deluge of new information in her stride—thank goodness. Alice envied her. But such was the resilience of youth and even Alice's concerns about a two-night stay at Lottie's back in Oxford the week before were unfounded. Scarlett seemed to revel in some level of normality and was returning to something close to the child Alice remembered.

She picked up yet another print-out. Homework diaries, if lost or defaced, would have to be replaced, price two pounds. Right—that was straightforward enough. PE kit—that was something she hadn't even looked at yet—seemed to consist of a plain white T-shirt and black shorts or cycle shorts. Clearly things had moved on since her days of pleated skirts for lacrosse, divided skirts for hockey (why?), a gymslip with a coloured sash for country dancing, for God's sake, and capacious navy gym knickers for gymnastics. She was glad, on balance, that she'd resisted explaining all that to Mr Williams.

Finally Alice wrangled the various lists into one of items that they could get on a single outing into town and, after lunch, they set off. Funny, she thought, as they drove towards Brighton, she couldn't remember seeing a single school outfitters in town—but then, she'd really never bothered to look before now. She glanced at Scarlett, who was looking surprisingly excited considering they were only getting school stuff. Alice had always hated getting uniform—scratchy wool jumpers and awful shoes, money belts and name tags and stripy ties from poky shops. And her mother had always bought everything with 'room for growth'. Alice shuddered at the memory. They'd get the buying done as quickly as possible and maybe go for a frozen yoghurt at Lick, which had now become one of Alice's favourite places. Maybe she could call Greg and see if he was free to meet them there. That would be fun.

About an hour later, in a shoe shop, Alice was wondering what had gone wrong. They'd trailed all over town without finding anything remotely like the school outfitters she remembered from her school days. Where did people get uniforms from then? In the shoe shop they'd had to take a numbered ticket, for goodness sake, like at the deli counter of the supermarket, and had been waiting for almost forty minutes already. Scarlett was slumped dejectedly on a bench by the window, eyeing up the other children waiting. Alice eventually exchanged eye-rolls with a mother about her age with a little girl, and they fell into

296

conversation.

'Every year, I promise myself I'll get this sorted earlier,' the woman sighed. 'There's hardly any stock left now. You'd think they could match supply to demand, wouldn't you? I mean, it's hardly rocket science!'

Alice smiled in what she hoped was a knowing way. 'I know! It's terrible having to queue as well.'

'God, yes! Lucy—get down from there, would you?'

Alice looked over and saw a small red-haired girl in wellies and shorts crawling over the benches close to where Scarlett was sitting. 'Be easier to do it at the start of the holidays, probably.'

The woman laughed shortly. 'Except they'd have grown out of them by the start of term.'

'Oh yes. Of course. Gosh—they grow so fast, don't they?'

'Tell me about it! How old's your daughter?'

'Oh, she's not . . . I mean, she's eleven.'

'Right—I've got a boy of twelve, too, but I'd sooner pull my fingernails out than bring him and Lucy shoe shopping together. I'll get my old man to bring him—and he can get the football boots at the same time. Where's your daughter at school?'

'Um—well, she was at school out of the area until recently. She's starting at Ashton Down though. Year Seven.' Alice thought she'd handled that one rather well. 'How about yours?'

'My son's going into Year Eight there. We're pleased with it so far. Do you have others?'

'Others?'

'Other kids, I mean.'

Alice laughed embarrassedly. 'Sorry—bit tired at the moment. Keep up, Alice! No, I don't. Scarlett's

297

the only one.'

The woman looked over at the girls. Lucy, obviously slightly in awe of the big girl, was edging closer. 'Scarlett. What a pretty name! Alice is nice too. It was going to be Lucy's middle name, but my mother-in-law ruined it for me. "What if she has a lisp?" she said! I'm Jackie, by the way.'

'Oh—hi.' Gosh—this was easy. Alice didn't think she'd ever fallen into conversation with another woman in a shoe shop before. Having children seemed to be a bit like having a dog—it provided an instant topic of conversation. 'Have you got all the uniform yet? Only I've been looking round and I haven't seen any shops.'

Jackie looked at her strangely. 'Have you looked in Tesco? Or M&S? All the supermarkets have the basics. Or did you mean those sports shirts with the crest on? They're optional, you know. I just get plain ones. Much cheaper.'

'Oh yes, of course.' Alice quickly recovered. Now she remembered seeing those 'Back To School' posters up when she was getting her groceries. She'd never even bothered straying into those aisles before. 'That's what I meant, of course. Right, I'll just get plain. That's good to know. Thanks.'

They chatted on for a while, Alice surprised at how much she was enjoying the chance to play at being a regular mother—and she was strangely pleased to be taken for Scarlett's. At least she must look the part, even if she didn't feel it!

At last the queue dwindled, and soon Lucy was being coaxed into new trainers with flashing lights on the soles. Alice was so astounded by this phenomenon that she wasn't really giving Scarlett and her choice of shoes her full attention.

Jackie jerked her head in Scarlett's direction. 'Careful,' she mouthed. 'Looks like she's trying it on!'

'What—the shoe?'

Jackie shook her head pityingly. 'Look what she's chosen! Get in there quick.'

Alice scooted over to where Scarlett was talking to the sales assistant. She was holding up a brown loafer with a chunky heel and a small platform, with little metal hearts in place of a buckle. They looked quite funky. The assistant turned to her. 'What size are your daughter's feet?'

Alice frowned. 'I'm not sure. Scarlett, do you know?'

'Would you like me to measure them for you?'

'Oh yes,' Alice agreed gratefully. 'It's for school, you see.'

'Oh right—so maybe something a bit more practical? And black?'

She turned back to where Jackie was feeling for Lucy's toes and raised her eyebrows. Jackie nodded firmly. 'Yes, black. And practical. Definitely.'

Scarlett put the shoe down and sat back down heavily on the bench, her arms folded across her chest. Looking back at Jackie, Alice was relieved to see a little grin of complicity. This looked like it might take some time.

*   *   *

By the time they'd bought as much as they could, Alice was exhausted and Scarlett mutinous. Since the shoe revelation, Alice was being a bit more cynical about Scarlett's requests and sticking more closely to the scant guidance provided by the school.

299

They'd had a sticky moment over school bags. Alice couldn't see the point of a backpack and they spent a fruitless forty minutes looking for a leather satchel, despite Scarlett saying she'd never, *ever* use it. The decider was finding one, and only one, in a horribly trendy vintage clothes shop, priced at over seventy pounds. Even the overpriced surf-brand bag Scarlett craved seemed a bargain compared to that. There was no time for frozen yoghurt, even if they'd felt like it, so Alice called Greg to update him on their progress and to see if he was free later on. His suggestion of a takeaway for the three of them struck her as a brilliant idea, though it took a while to work out what Scarlett's favourite dishes might be—just one more detail from her former life that Alice was struggling to reconstruct. And there were so many. Scarlett had come up in itchy bumps with Alice's usual washing powder, so she'd changed at once to a non-bio, but Scarlett had said it didn't smell like the one her Mum had used. There were too many pieces missing from the jigsaw and, with Scarlett upstairs trying on her new uniform and Greg probably still at the Chinese restaurant in town, Alice gave in to the temptation that had been gnawing at her since their return from Oxford that first time.

'Come on, Ginny. If I'm in charge of Scarlett now, I need some clues. It may be your private, secret diary, but you wouldn't have minded—I know you wouldn't.' And she parted the books on the kitchen shelf until she found what she was looking for—Ginny's notebook. She sat down in an armchair and started to read.

Chapter 40

October 2005

The next two days were surreal. Long hours sitting beside Scarlett who'd been moved into a private room off the Children's Ward—standard procedure apparently until they knew she wasn't contagious— hardly daring to wash and change into the clothes Piers had brought with him from home. But as each hour passed, Scarlett became more alert, struggling to sit up and asking for Ribena because she was thirsty. She veered between being her normal talkative self and curiously irritable, her little brow creased.

'It's common,' a nurse reassured Virginia. 'She's worn out and her head probably still hurts.'

Calls from work had poured in on Virginia's phone and she'd ignored them until she grabbed the chance to call in and explain what had happened, Piers taking up the bedside vigil.

Dr Calvert came in to see Scarlett every now and then. Still attached to the drip, she was soon sitting up in bed, and around her she had little gifts dropped off at the hospital by Karen and Pat, and a card from school that the entire class had signed. Alice had sent some fancy slippers 'for those corridors' and Judy and Bill had sent a small doll that Scarlett had sat on the edge of the bedside cabinet.

By Thursday—was it Thursday? Virginia had lost track—Scarlett was becoming cheeky. 'That's the best sign of recovery,' Dr Calvert laughed as she picked up the chart at the bottom of her bed. 'Sick children don't usually answer you back. For once we encourage it! Now, young lady, how are you today? I see things are looking very much better.'

'I feel fine thank you,' Scarlett replied in her best voice. 'Can I go home soon?'

'I expect so,' the young doctor lifted the sheets on the chart. 'Your test results seem good.'

'Like school tests?'

'Not quite,' she laughed. 'We took a bit of liquid from your spine which tells us lots about what's happening in your head—and if other people might catch what you had, which luckily they can't. And we took some blood too, in case we had to borrow someone else's blood and give it to you.'

'Yuck, no thanks.'

'Well,' the doctor put her head to one side. 'We might have needed to give you someone else's if you had become poorlier.'

'Would it have been the same blood as mine? Is blood different?'

'Oh there are lots of different types and you have to get the right one,' Dr Calvert went on patiently. 'We match it.'

'How do you know?'

The doctor smiled at her questions and sat down on the side of the bed. 'Because we're clever and we can see that you are an. . .' She looked at the chart, 'An A blood group. So we find other people who are an A. People like Mummy probably.'

'I'm not sure what I am,' Virginia replied.

'Then Daddy maybe,' Scarlett replied. She wrinkled her nose at the thought. 'Yuck. That would be weird. Having your blood inside me! How did I get poorly?' she went on.

'You know sometimes in school you all catch the same cold?' the doctor explained. 'Well, this is like that. You pass on bugs when you sneeze or cough at school, but in very rare cases those bugs are a bit too strong for some little people like you to fight and that's what happened, so we're giving you medicine to fight those bugs. Luckily for you, you have a very clever GP and he did the right thing. And because you're a skinny little thing,' she gently tickled Scarlett's stomach, 'the medicine went round your body very quickly.'

For the first time since they arrived at the surgery three days ago, Virginia began to relax. She liked this small, competent Australian woman. Her lilting voice and gentle manner were reassuring, a reassurance that had propped her up. She pushed away the 'what if's—what if she hadn't called the surgery? What if Dr Marchant had thought it was just flu?—and tried to make herself think positively.

Scarlett was discharged on Saturday morning. Virginia wiped out the whole of the next week, and got in to work a bit the week after to pick up post and have quick chats with people as Piers was on half-term, but each day was punctuated with a visit to the hospital with Scarlett for intravenous antibiotics. As they'd bundled her up to take her home from the hospital, Dr Calvert had mentioned a slight deafness she'd noticed in Scarlett's left ear and that it would need to be checked out as it could be permanent damage, but she had smiled at Virginia. 'You're a very lucky mum, you know? She was a poorly girl.'

The rest of term was a juggle. Scarlett was weak and listless, only able to watch TV and read for short periods. Her appetite was feeble, and they decided to keep her away from school until January, balancing the childcare between Virginia working from home, Pat, Karen, Judy when she could, and even Natasha came by when they were desperate. Virginia and Piers over-compensated appallingly, spoiling their daughter with anything she wanted.

'You'll regret it,' Judy had admonished. 'She'll have you over a barrel.'

'She already does,' Virginia replied. But who cares? They'd nearly lost her so what did a Gameboy or a dolls' house matter?

The days were sometimes dotted with tantrums and outbursts of anger from Scarlett though, her little face growing red with rage and frustration over the smallest thing. The nights too, were broken with Scarlett's cries from nightmares that woke her in the winter darkness. Virginia, desperately tired now, would simply slip in with her and hold her until she calmed down, and in the morning Scarlett would remember fragments and talk of being put in the back of vans and hospitals.

'Is this normal?' Virginia asked one of the nurses when they went back for a check-up weeks later.

'Yes, it can be,' she replied unhelpfully.

Scarlett's behaviour grew worse, combined with an uncharacteristic clinginess. As Virginia left for work, she'd hold onto her mother's leg.

'Don't go, Mummy, please don't go,' she'd cry, her face wet with tears, and it would take all Virginia's will and all Piers' or Pat's or Karen's gentle persuasion to get her to let go. At work Virginia was distracted. Brochure proofs went to press with typing mistakes and the wrong prices or timings on. She forgot meetings or to return

304

people's phone calls, and everything in her being wanted to be at home with her little girl.

It was late one evening as she was ordering Christmas presents over the Internet—a shopping trip was out of the question and, besides, she'd lost interest—that she Googled post-meningitis symptoms and was reassured to see that all the behaviour Scarlett was displaying was typical. She'd tell Piers later, when he woke from his snooze on the sofa in front of the TV on the other side of the room. He looked as exhausted as she felt. She'd tried to protect him from the broken nights, but school life was frantic as term drew to a close and that, combined with Scarlett's demands and behaviour, was evident in the dark shadows under his eyes.

She looked at him lying there for a long time then, unable to stop herself, typed in 'blood groups', scrolling through the pages of charts and blood group combinations for parents and children which filled the screen. She didn't want to look, but she couldn't look away. She found Scarlett's blood group, then her own which she'd found on a card in the filing cabinet, tucked along with her precious antenatal notes.

Piers stirred. 'Wha . . .? He rubbed the back of his neck as he struggled to sit up. 'What time is it?'

She clicked off the page and closed down the computer quickly. 'Gone ten thirty. Time for bed.'

'What you doing, you crazy woman. Not working, are you?' He stood up and stretched.

'No. I'm doing my entire Christmas list online. I hope your mum and dad don't mind something from iTunes!'

Piers laughed. 'That'll be fine, I'm sure.'

She told him about Scarlett's symptoms too, and as he cleared his mug off the coffee table and went through to the kitchen, he laughed and yawned. 'Thank God for that. I thought she'd become a teenager prematurely.'

As they climbed into bed, he buried down into the pillows and she knew within minutes he'd be snoring deeply.

'Piers?'

'Mmm?' He didn't open his eyes.

'What blood group are you?'

'Odd question for this time of night.'

'Oh I was just thinking about Scarlett and the hospital stuff.'

'Oh.'

'Oh or O?'

'O.'

'How do you know?'

His voice was slurred as he fell into sleep. 'I found out years ago when I cut myself badly on a nail in the boathouse. Bled like a stuck pig and I had to have a tetanus jab too.' Within seconds his mouth had fallen slackly and he was asleep.

Virginia lay wide awake beside him.

Chapter 41

September 2010

It was hard to tell who was more nervous on Scarlett's first day at Ashton Down. Uncharacteristically, Alice had rehearsed the school run and timed herself, completely forgetting that the traffic would more than double once term started. Fortunately, she'd left so much time to get there that they'd still been embarrassingly early and had sat together in the car until the first buses started arriving. Compared to the older pupils, Scarlett looked incredibly well-groomed, her hair in sleek plaits, of which Alice was particularly proud, not having plaited anyone's hair since she was about Scarlett's age. In the relative quiet of the car, Alice squeezed Scarlett's hand. 'You look great, you know. Really confident and grown up. I bet it'll go brilliantly today. And I'll try to get here early so I can park right in this spot. That way, you won't even have to look around for me.' Alice had already been warned off waiting at the school gate—according to Scarlett, that didn't happen beyond infants.

And who was Alice to question her? In all too many areas, already, Scarlett had proved the more knowledgeable, rolling her eyes indulgently when Alice got it wrong. 'Just you wait, though,' Alice had warned, a few days earlier. 'If we go to Paris or New York on holiday, I'm in charge.' And Scarlett had, for a moment at least, looked impressed, her eyes widening and her mouth open just a little bit, making her look far younger than her years.

'Would Greg come too? That would be great.'

Alice paused. It was all very well Scarlett running on ahead like that and making happy plans for the future; of course Alice had done the same, in her imagination at least. The grown-up equivalent of writing your first name with your crush's last name on your school exercise books, she supposed. But there was no way she was going to let her fantasies run away with her—at least, not out loud. On the trip to Oxford, Greg had shown all the signs of

307

wanting their relationship to move on, and since then he had been very attentive and loving. The prospect of Greg being part of their lives excited her more than she dared admit, so she risked it. 'Maybe,' she said reasonably. 'It might be fun going all together. We should look at your holiday dates and work something out.'

'Could I bring a friend too, if we went away somewhere?'

'What? To New York? Erm—maybe. Who were you thinking of?'

'Lottie. She's going to the school I would have done at home. I mean Oxford. They go back tomorrow.' She paused, and Alice held her breath, then she seemed to rally. 'We went on Brownie camp together once. It was such a laugh.'

'What, camping? I've never been camping. Well, Glastonbury once. But that was enough to put me off, I can tell you! Those loos!' She shuddered eloquently.

'It wouldn't be like that,' Scarlett countered. 'The place we went with Brownies was great, although the showers weren't very warm. We cooked sausages on the fire. They were yummy! I never went with Mum and Dad. We always said we would, one day, but we stayed in a caravan once and that was great. We were going to Turkey this summer, but then that never happened.' She trailed off. 'It would be fun to camp—probably more fun than New York, anyway!'

Alice marvelled at the way Scarlett dealt with this panoply of emotions. But then she was such a mass of contradictions. Sometimes she was so worldly-wise, sometimes she seemed far younger than her years. And the same was true of her appearance. All dolled up and sucking her cheeks in, the way girls did in magazines, she could pass for almost sixteen—a skinny sixteen, fair enough—but close enough to be worrying. At other times, when she relaxed and had fun—out on her bike or when they'd all gone swimming at one of the hotels Greg had designed, in Surrey, she had the most infectious giggle and a completely daft sense of humour that had both her and Greg in stitches. With some more local friends like Immy, who was her own age, Alice hoped that side of her would come out more.

And later that first day, when Alice sat obediently in the car, horribly early and unbelievably anxious, Scarlett emerged from the school gates with not one, but three girls, all laughing and nudging each other as they went, looking relaxed and happy and confident. And Alice felt tears start to cloud her eyes, though they didn't prevent her noticing that the mothers of two of the other girls were standing right outside the gate!

And in the days since then, when Scarlett disappeared upstairs to do her homework, sometimes pieces of writing on her laptop which would come churning out of Alice's printer downstairs, making her jump, she would carry on reading Ginny's journal.

Its discovery had been a turning-point, and Alice gobbled up the information. It had almost become an addiction, feeding Alice's need to know more about Scarlett and filling in the yawning gaps in her understanding of her little ward. Had she found it earlier, she might have avoided the incident with the cauliflower at lunch a few weeks before. It wasn't until Scarlett had burst into tears at the sight of it that Alice had read the entry about a

309

showdown at Judy's. Apparently, Scarlett had been refused the ice cream that the other, more compliant, cousins had earned by clearing their plates, and Ginny had vented in the diary all the anger she'd felt and couldn't show. If Alice had known that first, she'd have banned the stupid vegetable altogether—it was only anaemic broccoli anyway.

She checked on the fish lasagne, opened the page where she'd left off, and continued reading, immersing herself again in the details of Ginny's life. Sometimes acerbic, sometimes funny, and sometimes horribly frank and accurate about life, including her thoughts about Alice, Ginny had clearly started it as a letter to her daughter but, as time had gone on, it had become something more. A place for Ginny to voice her thoughts and share her anxieties. It was a learning curve all right.

Chapter 42

Christmas 2009

'Can I wake up yet?' Scarlett's voice whispered loudly into Virginia's ear and she put her arm out to gather her into bed beside her. Piers groaned slightly and turned away, taking the duvet with him and Virginia tugged it back to cover them both without even opening her eyes.

'What time is it?' she mumbled into Scarlett's hair.

Scarlett lifted her head to look at the clock. 'It says five fifty-five.'

'Oh, God.' Virginia's heart sank. There was no way her daughter was going to go back to sleep now, not with the prospect of a sackful of presents to unwrap. 'Half an hour. Let's just lie here for half an hour before we wake up properly.'

Scarlett lay still for a while then started to fidget, playing with Virginia's hair and kissing her, little gestures she knew her mother wouldn't be able to get cross about. 'OK, I submit, you win. Let's go and make some tea and then battle can commence.'

Wrapped in their dressing gowns they padded downstairs, Virginia hushing Scarlett who, even at only ten, was heavy on her feet with excitement. The kitchen was warm from the Aga, and Sylvester, the black lab, old and stiff now, gingerly clambered out of his basket and came towards them.

'Hello, old mate.' Scarlett crouched down and put her arms around his greying head. 'Happy Christmas.'

Virginia let him out into the garden for his morning wee, and put the kettle on. She still couldn't see the point of an Aga—it was just an expensive radiator as far as she was concerned—but this morning, and at such an ungodly hour, it was a welcome place to stand close to and warm your bones. The large table in the centre of the kitchen was laid for breakfast, something Judy must have done late last night before she went to bed. They'd had a long dinner which Scarlett had been allowed to stay up for, surrounded by older cousins, and Piers had had to get quite firm to persuade her to go to bed at all. Stone, Theo's teenage son, was the main attraction. Scarlett hadn't seen him for years and when they'd arrived yesterday and he'd lolloped downstairs to meet them, Scarlett had

311

been smitten and Virginia had her first inkling that her daughter was growing up.

She wasn't surprised her daughter was enamoured with him though. He had the arrogance of youth, combined with all-American good looks and a languid Californian drawl. Theo and Christie had moved to LA when he was five, and Theo was now making a fortune writing a massively successful hospital series for TV that was even showing on Channel Four. Over a dinner of rich venison casserole followed by boozy caramelised oranges, Scarlett was star-struck by the whole package.

Bill, too, had been in his element, surrounded by his sons and his grandchildren. He'd been seated at the end of the table, opposite Judy and, full of good red wine, had laughed and joked with them all, gently teasing Scarlett and talking to the teenagers about school and sport. He'd had a long discussion with Piers about the eight—rowing being a shared passion—and gave him some tips. He looked well and robust, and Virginia felt immense warmth towards him. Over dessert, Judy had given them a rundown of how tomorrow would be. Barney, Maggie and their boys had left after dinner, it being their turn to spend the day with her parents in St Albans, but Dom and Theo and their brood were, like Piers, Virginia and Scarlett, there for the duration and Judy informed them that they'd all be expected for church at ten thirty, then it would be lunch and tree presents. The goose was already dressed and standing to attention in the spare fridge in the larder.

Virginia let Sylvester back in, closing out the cold morning air as quickly as she could, and he hobbled over to his warm basket again. Scarlett sat in beside him and stroked his head as Virginia poured water into a pot for her and Piers. Scarlett's excitement at the feast of riches in the stocking at the end of her bed couldn't be contained much longer and by six thirty the bedroom was strewn with wrapping paper, the offering augmented by Judy, who had insisted she add to the haul, against Virginia's wishes.

'I do like to make a contribution to my grandchildren's Christmas,' she'd whispered the night before as she pressed some small parcels into Virginia's hand, and Virginia tried to see it as a charitable gesture she hoped it was meant to be.

'How very bright,' Judy commented on the new pink T-shirt Scarlett had insisted on wearing to church, a phrase loaded with disapproval.

Scarlett spent the service whispering to Stone, and to keep her quiet Piers had to swap places with her so she could sit beside him. Stone had an expression of nonchalance that transmitted loud and clear what he thought of the archaic carols and hearty sermon, and when he announced outside that 'religion was for idiots', Virginia whispered in his ear that 'perhaps you don't want to let Granny and Grandpa hear you say that. To some people it's important.'

The vicar duly congratulated, and 'Happy Christmas' greetings exchanged, they made their way back to the house where the goose was now cooking fragrantly and was waiting for another basting, and the potatoes were ready to be par-boiled and put in to roast. Virginia knew well the areas in which her mother-in-law would accept help and those that were hers alone to handle, so she simply said, 'Shall I start laying the dining room

313

table?' and commandeered Scarlett into helping her make it look lovely with Judy's fantastic table centrepiece of trailing ivy and amaryllis and the best silver and crystal wine glasses. Christmas in Stoke had never been on this scale (and latterly it had been a pathetic delivery of a scarf or box of toiletries), so Virginia quite enjoyed Judy's concept of a 'proper Christmas'. Everywhere was truly decked and the tree was smothered in a mixture of decorations carefully put away and preserved year after year, then gently unwrapped from their tissue paper and hung with solemnity. The tree lights sparkled and the highly polished silver candlesticks and small bon-bon dishes reflected them over and over again. Judy was in her element. Everything would be just perfect, Virginia could be sure of that and, though it might be the effect of Bill's good champagne flowing through her veins, she felt quite an affection for her perfectionist of a mother-in-law who was so keen to get everything just right. She might be an over-bearing old bag but, yet again, she'd pulled the proverbial Christmas elf out of the hat.

Judy fluttered about as they all sat down to eat, even managing to answer the phone which rang very inconveniently just as Bill slid the carving knife into the goose's perfectly browned breast. Judy snatched it up, and disappeared into the kitchen talking quietly.

'Everything all right, Mum?' Dom asked when she returned.

'Yes, yes dear. Just a neighbour checking something.'

Piers raised his eyebrows at Virginia across the table. Usually his mother would have gone ballistic

314

at someone calling at lunchtime on Christmas Day.

The meal was as delicious as anticipated, and after Christmas pudding and trifle, the family group picked up their glasses of wine and made its way back to the drawing-room to open presents. The stack was huge and Judy distributed them out to calls of 'thank-you, just what I wanted' as paper was ripped open. It was an orgy that Virginia had got used to over the years, though she guessed that most of the novelty soaps would end up left in bathroom cabinets and the thick celebrity auto-biographies would be neglected on bedside tables unread.

For her, Judy had bought a light-blue rollneck jumper in the softest cashmere. It was more than she'd ever have bought herself and she gushed suitable thanks.

'I thought it would suit your colouring,' Judy smiled.

For Piers there was a new golf club for his burgeoning hobby which Bill must have chosen. The grandchildren feasted on a pile of goodies, and within half an hour the carpet had disappeared under wrapping paper and ribbon.

'Too much, as always,' Bill laughed, leaning back in his armchair, a glass of port in his hand. 'I'm quite sure we don't need any of it. Put on the TV, Dom old chap, and we'll watch what the Queen has to say for herself.'

Virginia pulled her feet up under her on the sofa to survey the scene and noticed Scarlett on the other side of the room, a frown on her face.

'Granny,' Virginia heard her voice above the roll of the National Anthem and winced at her daughter's timing. 'Where's my present from you?'

'Well, my darling girl,' Judy clambered to her feet from her position by the tree. 'Your present is outside. Shall we go and find it?'

Virginia shot Piers a look, a feeling of disquiet growing in her stomach, and stood up, jerking her head to show she wanted him to come with her. He got the message and followed her out of the room. Judy had slipped on her ankle wellies at the front door, and Scarlett and she were making their way across the front drive in the direction of the road.

'Where the hell are they off to?' Piers asked, amusement in his voice.

'God knows.' Virginia pulled her cardigan further round her against the chill as they followed across the gravel.

As they turned the corner around the high hedge which abutted the gateposts, they could see that Judy had crossed the narrow lane in front of thc house, and she and Scarlett were standing at the fence of the paddock opposite, stroking the nose of a small pony.

*   *   *

The journey back to Oxford from Alice's on Boxing Day afternoon took place in virtual silence. They had been due to stay on at The Gables for lunch, but after a hasty phone call to Alice and a hurried breakfast, they'd packed up their bags and said their goodbyes. But Virginia's hope that she'd find succour and understanding in Ulvington had fallen short of the mark.

'Why can't I stay with Minty? He's so beautiful and he *is* mine,' Scarlett moaned from the back, and Virginia explained that Alice hadn't been able

316

to see them at teatime after all, so they'd changed plans and were going there for lunch.

'What a lovely early surprise!' A dishevelled Alice threw out her arms at the door and embraced Virginia. 'Anger on a scale of one to ten?' she whispered as she hugged her.

'Fucking twelve,' Virginia replied.

'Scarlett, you look lovely in your pink butterfly top. That Father C has really good taste,' she said as she led them all into the cottage. The place was in chaos. Through the kitchen door, Virginia could see the washing up piled up, and there were still glasses on the table with the sediment of red wine in the bottom of them. Virginia suspected that Alice had only just got out of bed.

'Sorry, sorry, sorry,' she said, frantically picking up plates with grape stalks and cheese crumbs. 'Had Vince et al over yesterday. Don't think we finished playing Twister 'til four this morning. Coffee? I'm not sure what I've got for lunch but I'm sure there's some stilton left over. Scarlett, do you like stilton?'

'What is it?' Scarlett asked, slightly ill-at-ease and hanging close to Virginia, confused by what had taken place over the last twenty-four hours.

'Smelly cheese,' Piers explained. 'That might not go down too well!'

Alice flicked on the kettle and brought down some cups from the cupboard. 'Just give me a sec and I'll be all organised.' She opened the fridge as they looked on. 'Buggeration. No milk. Piers, would you and Scarlett be a love and go down to the pub and ask them for a bit of milk? God knows, we spent enough in there on Christmas Eve. They owe me about six pints.'

Shutting the door behind Piers and Scarlett

she leaned back against it. 'So, what the hell's happened? You sounded terrible on the phone.'

Virginia slumped down on the sofa. 'Judy has given Scarlett a pony for Christmas.'

'Oh I thought it was something awful. How lovely!' Alice gushed, pulling her hair up onto her head and securing it with a clip. 'What a kind gesture.'

Virginia's mouth dropped open. 'Christ, Alice, don't you get it?'

'Get what? Surely they're just being generous? Scarlett can come down and stay with them more often—give you and Piers a break—and she'll have a pony to ride. What's the problem?'

Alice's words simply opened up the cavernous gap between them both, and the way they looked at the world, and Virginia felt a wave of disappointment.

'First off, I don't want to "have a break" from my daughter and, secondly, a pony is a huge present, the kind of thing *we* should have given her if we could have afforded it, and Judy just goes ahead and does it without even telling us. Just does it so that we'll all think how marvellous she is.' Virginia could feel the tears of frustration and anger pricking behind her eyes.

'Ah come on, Gin.' Alice sat down opposite her and slipped off her embroidered slippers. It was then Virginia realised the Chinese wrap she was wearing was actually her dressing gown. 'The worst crime she's committed is wanting the plaudits, but she probably did it because she knew you didn't have the space and because you can't afford it, let's be honest, so she's sort of done it to help.'

Virginia shook her head. 'No. That's very

318

charitable of you to say that, but you don't know the way she thinks.'

For a moment Alice had an expression of annoyance. 'No, clearly I don't.'

They managed to salvage the mood over the leftovers of last night's dinner party, and they even let Scarlett tell Alice about Minty and how she was going to come down after New Year, maybe even before, and ride her. Piers then deflected the conversation to talk about other things, and Alice made them laugh when she cranked up some story about a research trip she'd done to Brussels and a man she'd met there. It was clear that she'd slept with him, but a look from Virginia stopped her from going into all the gory details in front of Scarlett. Sometimes she had no idea about what was appropriate with children at all.

'Let's just go home,' Piers said as they pulled away from the cottage. Alice had put on a brave face but clearly would rather have been in bed than entertaining, and all Virginia wanted to do was to be in her own little house in Summertown. As they bombed up the motorway, Scarlett dozed and Piers put his hand on Virginia's thigh and squeezed it supportively. Virginia ran through the scene last night in her head. She didn't think she'd ever seen Piers so angry and the relief that he *understood*, at last, was immense, like a burden lifted.

'What the hell have you done?' he'd shouted, as he left Scarlett with the pony and her cousin James and virtually dragged Judy back across to the house.

'I've bought your daughter a pony, that's what I've done.' Judy's eyes were round with outrage at her son's response.

'What the bloody hell did you do that for?'

'So she has something to ride when she comes to stay.'

'And what are we supposed to tell her when she realises that she can't take it home? And are we supposed to drive down here every weekend when she nags to come and see "her pony"? We don't have time, Mum.' He raked his hands through his hair. 'You should have spoken to us first about this. This is bang out of order.'

She'd huffed, and looked wounded. 'I thought you'd be delighted. Minty's a lovely little pony. Just right for her to learn on.'

The rest of the afternoon had been spent in a toxic atmosphere that pervaded the whole house. Virginia couldn't bring herself to speak to Judy at all, so she pretended she had a headache and, after putting a very over-excited Scarlett to bed, spent the evening in her room watching the Christmas-night film. She didn't feel churlish; she felt incandescent with rage at her mother-in-law, and when Piers came up at about ten he reported that Bill had taken her side, and had told Piers to apologise to his mother for being so harsh.

'No fucking way am I apologising,' he said, and had slumped down on the bed beside her before they noticed Scarlett standing in the doorway in her nightie.

It was dark by the time they pulled into the driveway and it was beginning to rain, but the house felt warm as they let themselves in and dumped their bags in the hallway. Virginia quickly turned on the Christmas tree lights and Scarlett ran upstairs with her bag of presents to look them over once again. Virginia put the kettle on for a cup of tea, then went out to check the chickens had put themselves to bed, before calling Karen to tell her they were back sooner than they'd thought they'd be, and she needn't come over after all to shut the coop.

Then she turned back to the cupboard and took down their favourite mugs, dropping in a couple of tea bags for her and Piers. Just the way they liked it. As she looked up, she caught herself reflected in the darkened kitchen window. They were home. It was safe and it was theirs.

Chapter 43

October 2010

As the warm summer days gave way to the windier, more unsettled ones of October, Alice, Greg and Scarlett found themselves falling into a comfortable routine. Alice would leave her warm bed first and, wrapping her dressing gown around her, would put on the kettle before padding out to the coop to release the chickens, scattering a handful of corn which they fell on like refugees. If there were eggs, she'd bring them in and mark them with the date, immensely proud of how clever they had been and feeling a curious sense of achievement she'd never felt before.

On the days that Greg was there—which was as often as possible if he wasn't travelling—she'd put his cup of tea on the bedside table beside him for when he woke. She'd look at his dark head against the pillow, his hair ruffled and his stubble dark around his chin, and she'd marvel at her luck.

'Alice Fenton, you've landed yourself a good 'un here. How did you manage it?' she'd smile to herself as she gently opened Scarlett's bedroom door. It must have gone back to years of having been rudely awakened at boarding school, but she'd try and wake Scarlett as gently as possible, sometimes even with a kiss on the forehead if her head was above the voluminous pink duvet. Sometimes it was hard to find her in there at all beneath the sparkly cushions. Vince had fallen into a habit of buying her a cushion whenever he saw one that made him laugh. The latest, a sequinned affair with roses and cornflowers he'd found on a recent weekend trip to Amsterdam, was so over-the-top that they had all gasped when he'd pulled it out of the carrier bag with a flourish, but Scarlett had been enchanted and it now had pride of place at the head of the bed.

Alice would then use the bathroom first. One sacrifice she'd had to make for her ward was to forgo her long morning soak, but when she could, and once Greg and Scarlett had left, sometimes together if his schedule permitted him to drop her at school, she'd indulge in her guilty pleasure, slipping under the hot bubbles and lying there sipping a fresh cup of tea and thinking about the day ahead. And the days were busy. She had plans underway to re-fit the old-fashioned kitchen which was impractical for the three of them and the Big Earth travel guides had led to other offers of work so, by the time Scarlett came in through the front door from the bus at around four o'clock, Alice's neck would be aching and it was a welcome relief to lift her head from hours of writing about travel tips for visitors to Paris. She was aware that she was opting for work that wouldn't involve jumping on a plane to Turkey or Poland at short notice, but how could she now? And, more importantly, she admitted to herself, she didn't want to.

They'd come to a moderately happy arrangement about visits to Judy and Bill too. Usually it was Sundays, and Alice would drop off Scarlett so Judy could do a 'proper Sunday lunch', as if Alice starved her during the week, and they could spend some time with their granddaughter. When Alice went back to collect her, she'd often find Scarlett playing backgammon with Bill, who looked grey and old, his dog asleep at his feet, but had a look of immense pleasure on his face. Without being told to, Scarlett was even careful to dress right for the visits, leaving her garish clothes in the wardrobe and putting on what she knew her grandmother would think of as 'sensible'.

Some days—and it was usually Thursdays—she'd pick Scarlett up from school and they'd go somewhere for fun. Perhaps into a café in Lewes for hot chocolate, then they'd buy something delicious for supper. Scarlett was more adventurous than Alice had imagined a child of her age would be and she'd find herself buying things like squid and strange pasta sauces to 'experiment with', as Scarlett put it.

'It's like living with Gordon Ramsay!' Alice would laugh. 'Only prettier.'

'Mum and Dad would always make me try new stuff,' Scarlett explained, her face suddenly serious in that characteristic way Alice was growing used to. 'When we went on holiday, I'd never order off the children's menu, and I'd have to at least give something grown up a go. It was usually OK, but I did try eel once and that was cack.'

'Nicely put.' Alice relished the growing ease with which Scarlett would talk about her parents now. Once Scarlett started, Alice would hold her breath for fear of butting in and stopping her speaking about them. Often it worked, but sometimes it didn't. There were still times—sometimes a whole day—when Scarlett would disappear into herself. It wasn't a sulk. Alice could have coped with a sulk. It was as if she were a tortoise who had pulled in its head, and Greg and Alice were learning to leave her be.

'Kids are amazingly resilient, aren't they?' he said after lunch one Saturday as they washed up the dishes. Scarlett hadn't spoken much during the meal and had gone up to her bedroom, turning down Alice's idea of a bike ride in the autumn sunshine. It had taken some time to realise it was Piers' birthday.

'She's like a wounded animal sometimes, that takes itself off to recover.'

'Then we have to let her do that,' he replied, and Alice loved the 'we' in that sentence. It comforted her that she wasn't facing this alone.

'I know, and I know there are things I can't help her with, and memories I'll never be able to share, but what I don't want is her worrying about things I *could* help her with.'

Alice loved the Thursday forays because they had time in the car on the way home to talk about the day. Her little Golf was, like Bill's old dog, on its last legs. She knew she'd have to hand it in for scrap before too long and find something else, but she had a stupid sentimentality about it. Greg refused to go in it, and even Scarlett looked a bit alarmed at the rattles and squeaks.

'You are a terrible driver!' she'd laugh as Alice narrowly missed an oncoming van as she checked a mark on her face in the rear-view mirror. Alice had to admit Ginny had been spot-on in the journal, and it sounded as though she'd even shared her opinions with her daughter.

'I haven't had an accident yet!' Alice replied without thinking and almost gasped at her stupidity, shooting a side-long glance at Scarlett, but the girl was simply looking ahead, her hands tucked under her thighs.

'I feel much safer in Greg's car, and besides it smells nicer.'

'Pah! Just boys' toys,' Alice laughed back, breathing out. 'OK, OK, let's start to look for another car. You can help me choose. But it has to have *personality*. I don't want some boring estate.'

And once their supper was stashed in the fridge, Scarlett would take herself off up to her room to do her homework. If it was Spanish, Alice could help, and if it was maths and Scarlett was stumped, they'd have to wait for Greg to come through the door. Even though he'd schlepped from London in the dark and was tired, he'd never show it and would be ready to peer over her shoulder and help her work out fractions or equations. Alice would look at their two dark heads close together and muse that, for a couple of amateurs, they weren't doing too badly as 'parents'.

But Alice's complacency was given a sharp tug one evening just before half-term. Scarlett had popped into the loo during her homework, and Alice had gone into her room to put some clean clothes on her bed. She glanced over at the laptop on the small desk in the corner, expecting to see a page of homework. It still amazed Alice that homework could be emailed to teachers. How radical was that? But instead of the short paragraphs and pictures stolen off the Internet which seemed to pass for work these days, the screen was on Facebook.

Knowing she shouldn't really, but unable to resist, Alice went over to read the screen. She was a bit of a novice but wasn't there some kind of age limit before you could go on these things? Checking that Scarlett was still in the bathroom, her eyes skimmed the page. The way it all worked wasn't really obvious to Alice, and she didn't recognise any of the names of the people featured on the page as friends Scarlett had mentioned, but she was certainly familiar with the language. Here were girls, their profile pictures lascivious and pouting, talking about parents, boys and sex, each posting smattered with swear words. 'Top news is my mother is a f***ing cow' said one girl called Fay. Nice. Alice's eyes flicked down further. There was more about vile teachers and dads who were bastards. Then there was worse. Mentions of blow jobs and sluts.

Alice froze, horrified, as she heard the loo flush and the bolt being released on the bathroom door, then she hastily pretended to tidy the ornaments on the windowsill as Scarlett came back in. She was startled to see Alice across the room.

'Hello,' she said and, slipping into her desk chair, clicked out of Facebook quickly and focused intently on her homework page. Alice played for time, picking up the T-shirts off the bed and putting them in the drawer. Then she put Scarlett's knickers in her drawer next to the little bra that Krissy had bought her. For the first time, Alice had the overwhelming realisation that this wasn't a little girl she had taken on, but an adolescent. Ginny might have seen the beginnings of this— she'd mentioned in the journal her observations about Scarlett and her cousin Stone—but it would be left to Alice to steer this particular ship through the icebergs in the dark. And she was completely unprepared. Should she have talked to Scarlett earlier? And what was she supposed to say? Did she know about sex and all that? And periods! Had anyone told her about them? They could start anytime.

'Scarlett,' she asked, sitting on the edge of her bed and picking up a small purple rabbit as a distraction, playing with its ears. 'Now you're at big school and all that,' she began falteringly. Help me, Ginny. 'Erm, it's quite a grown-up world out there and you'll discover things that you might not understand.'

Scarlett didn't turn around, but Alice could sense the tension in her back as she waited for what was coming next. 'And?'

'I'm not really very well qualified at all this, but I do think there are some things you should know about.'

'Such as?' Scarlett turned around now and leaned her arm on the back of the chair. Her expression was unreadable.

'Well, has anyone talked to you about ...' Alice wasn't sure which mountain to try and scale first. 'About boys and sex and things?' she finished weakly. 'I mean, not that these things are necessarily an issue,' she hurried on, 'but they will be soon enough.' Christ! She was making it sound as though Scarlett should be off buying condoms as soon as possible. 'I don't mean soon, obviously. You're far too young. But you'll find people will talk about sex. You have been ... I mean, you do know about where babies come from and all that, don't you?' Alice crossed her fingers. Please say you do, 'cause I'm not sure I know how to tell you. 'And periods. Have they all been explained to you? I know these days schools are better at talking about these things—heavens, in my school our biology teacher told us in about three minutes and advised us "not to sleep around" before moving on to reproduction in geraniums and growing cress on blotting paper or something—but I think you ought to know about periods, because they can start at about your age and, well ...'

Scarlett looked long and hard at Alice, then she nodded with a very serious face. 'It's OK, Alice, Mum told me all about it and I'm prepared.'

Good old Ginny. 'Well, that's great.'

'And about the sex thing. I know all about that too—we do it in PHSE—and everyone talks about it, so it's OK.'

'Riiight.' Alice stood up and put the rabbit back on the bed. 'I'll go and put the supper on then,' she said leaving the room, not sure it was 'OK' at all.

*   *   *

With Scarlett in bed later and Greg staying over at his much-neglected flat in London before an early meeting in the morning, Alice had the evening to herself. Pouring a glass of wine from the fridge, she tidied up the kitchen, a chore that was new to her

328

but one that she now felt compelled to do. Greg—
and Scarlett for that matter—were much tidier
and more ordered than she was and, though Greg
had teased her about the mess at first, she knew he
didn't like it and so she took some pride in making
it nice for them now.

'My, Alice Fenton, how you've changed,' she
said, addressing herself in the mirror in the small
hallway. 'You're quite the family woman. That's
a first—changing things in your life for a man.
Anyone would think you cared.' She threw another
log onto the fire from the tidy pile—a sight which
genuinely gave her immense pleasure, chopping
and carrying logs being one of the major downsides
of being a single woman and a job she'd happily
given over to Greg—and curled up on the sofa to
dip into Ginny's diary again. She had to snatch
opportunities to read it these days with people
around her much of the time, but she had made
one important decision. She didn't want Scarlett
to read it. The content wasn't for her just yet and,
Alice had concluded that, at times, Ginny had been
writing to herself, not her daughter. But to Alice, it
was a window into her friend's life, the part she had
never revealed.

April 2004
Darling Scarlett,
You have been the perfect child today, doing things
just the way they say in the manuals, and you are
now sleeping in your bed, all clean and delicious
from your bath as you should be. Dad is at school
doing his tutoring duties with the boarders, and
the peace is wonderful. I had the day off to spend
with you but, do you know, sometimes I think it's

less tiring at work. I don't think you have drawn breath all day with your questions about everything you see and you've made me laugh with your funny faces and your profound comments about things around you. I am not sure if the man on that bench in St Giles was a tramp, but everyone within fifty metres will now be wondering if he is, thanks to you pointing it out!

We had a lovely walk by the river and fed the ducks, who must be the fattest, most over-indulged ducks anywhere, and we even took a punt, though next time we'll take Dad with us. It was too traumatic trying to punt and stop you from leaning too far over the side, but somehow you talked me into the idea, and you can be one persuasive lady, Scarlett Elizabeth Waverley.

I didn't realise for ages that your initials would be SEW. People can be so stupid about initials so I hope you don't get teased about that later. I knew a girl at school whose initials were VAG and she used to be ribbed unmercifully by the boys. But I do love it that you are Elizabeth because it has given my mother such pleasure to have a granddaughter named after her. When everything else around her seems to confuse her, you only have to wander into her room and her face lights up and she sighs 'Scarlett Elizabeth' and lifts you onto her knee. Singlehandedly, since you were born, you have managed to defuse the tension of Mum's illness, a wonderful little distraction to us all with your endless questions about the photographs around her room. It doesn't even matter if the answers she gives you are wrong, because you don't listen to them anyway before you are onto the next thing. You have even made her laugh, which is something I haven't heard for ages.

The picture above your bed with 'Scarlett Elizabeth' embroidered on it is from Alice, though you know that. It was a stunning surprise when she brought it for your christening gift. It's so delicate and old fashioned—quite out of character for Alice. Dad and I were sure she'd bring you something hilarious and quite unsuitable, and we had a competition as to who could guess what it would be, but I clearly did her an injustice. It looks like she'll turn out to be as good a godmother as I hoped she would. I hope so, because it's a responsibility I want her to take seriously.

Alice looked up from the diary, feeling a sense of pleasure and achievement. She supposed she *was* guilty of making life difficult for herself trying to find presents as alternative as possible—Vince had accused her of being 'contrary' at times—but she had been so excited by the embroidered picture that it had been all she could do not to blurt out her discovery to Ginny before the christening. She'd seen the embroiderer's work at a shop in Notting Hill and knew right away it was perfect—traditional and correct for a godchild, yet different enough to set it apart. It thrilled her that Ginny had liked it too and now it took pride of place above Scarlett's bed upstairs. She flicked back to the beginning of the journal and re-read an early entry:

March 1999
I'm not sure how your name came into my head. Piers and I had talked about names of course, and we had a long list of boys' names to choose from. He was keen on the traditional ones—he likes

tradition—and you might have been a Victoria or a Jane (or named after some queen from history like Matilda or Wulfrida). But, luckily for you, I won the day.

Mind you, his pleasure at your eventual arrival has been so immense I think he would have settled for you being called Ermintrude Beansprout. And it was 'eventual' because you kept us waiting for days. By the time I was woken at three in the morning with the first contractions, you were over a week late and I was beginning to think you'd changed your mind. I was frightened that something would go terribly wrong. As they attached monitors to me to trace your heartbeat in case you became distressed, as babies can, I realised just how essential you are to my life. It may sound odd that, after the difficulties I—we—had to have you, and after all the months of carrying you—that it should only hit me at that moment, but I was so close to holding you in my arms that the fear that I might not was too dreadful to imagine.

And then, after a struggle, there you were. You didn't cry, but looked around you as newborn babies do, not really seeing, but appearing wise and watchful. Your hair is dark, and as I held you for the first time wrapped in your blanket, it was as if you were assessing me, right there at our first meeting. 'So that's who you are,' you seemed to say. 'Are you up to the job?'

The entry finished there and Alice closed the diary and let it lie in her lap. She gazed into the flames, dying down now as they turned the log to ash. Scarlett still had that look of assessment at times. She'd looked at Alice that way many times as

332

she fumbled to do the right thing. Was *she* up to the job? She hoped to God she was, for Scarlett's sake.

Chapter 44

January 2010

'Now, don't get too excited,' Piers held up his hand in mock modesty as he came into the room. Virginia looked up from the *Sunday Times Magazine* article she was reading about Botox. Rodney, the cat, was tucked in next to her, sleeping.

'OK, I'll try and contain myself.' She sighed dramatically. 'Do I need to hold onto something?'

'Possibly.' Piers imitated a drum roll. 'I have now, just this minute, completed my synopsis on the Charlemagne book, tidied up the first four chapters and emailed it to that agent who expressed an interest.'

Virginia put her fingers under her chin and looked into space. 'Ah, would that be the literary agent who "expressed an interest" about three years ago?'

'OK, OK,' Piers slumped down beside her on the sofa and Rodney jumped off irritatedly. 'Don't make it worse. I did include a grovelling apology and I don't suppose there have been historians banging down the doors of every publisher in London wanting to drop off their synopses on the life of Charlemagne in a race to be the first to publish the definitive guide. He's hardly sexy reading, is he?'

'Indeed not,' Virginia laughed dryly and leaned

over to kiss Piers. 'Well done, sweetheart. Let's hope they like it, they publish squillions and every library in the world wants at least ten copies each.'

'Do you think it's very dull?' Piers looked despondent now. 'I mean, people seem to have exciting jobs and earn loads—look at Sebastian, for example. He just bought another company to add to his empire—and all I do is teach over-privileged children and write a boring book about a man who lived over a thousand years ago.'

'History *is* important. Someone's got to write it or else how would we understand the world we live in?'

Piers laughed. 'I think I said that to you on our first date!'

'Well, you were right and I haven't forgotten it. Besides, there have to be teachers and not everyone can be rolling in it. Having too much money can blur your judgement. As we know,' she added with emphasis.

'Mmm. Too right.'

'Have you spoken to her?'

'Yup. She wasn't happy. Not happy at all. I think it was the first time I've really put my foot down with her.'

'No shit, Sherlock.'

'OK, OK. You've made your point. I don't think Mum means to be undermining though, despite what you may think. I think she genuinely wants to make things good for people.'

Virginia sighed. 'Maybe, but you have to think about the implications of what you do, because things can be taken the wrong way.'

Piers grunted in agreement. 'I was watching Theo's Christie over Christmas. She's so like my mum in many ways. Quite dominating, but in a subtle way so that you don't realise it until you think about it. And then you realise that you've just been manipulated royally.'

'Perhaps Theo's married his mother.'

'Don't they say all men do that?' He put his hand on her leg.

'Oh please God, no. I know she's your mother and all that, but please don't tell me I'm like her.'

He sat up and leaned over her. 'No, you are not. And that's why I love you.' He kissed her warmly on the lips. 'And besides, she bakes better cakes.'

Virginia smacked him on the shoulder. 'Bloody mummy's boy!' she laughed. 'Now, go and collect Scarlett. First day of term tomorrow and you both need to sharpen your shoes and polish your pencils.'

'Yes, Mum,' he said, heaving himself up. 'Where is she again?'

'Lottie's house. Where else? She's bound to ask if she can do a sleepover, but placate her by asking if Lottie wants to come over next weekend instead, will you?'

Piers shrugged on his coat. It was getting dark outside and the January wind that had bitten since New Year was still mean and chilling. 'What is this sleepover nonsense? I'm sure my friends just "came for the night".'

'American import. Like everything.'

'Bloody Yanks. See you in a bit.' He picked up the car keys and left the house.

Virginia abandoned the article. It was boring anyway, and she wanted a cup of tea. As she passed the French windows she glanced out into the bare garden. This time of year was so frustrating with nothing to do outside and she couldn't wait for spring. There was a small clump of snowdrops pushing through under the cherry tree, and she had noticed the first shoots of daffs in the beds, but she was itching to get her hands into the soil. An idea had been growing in her head. She hadn't mentioned it to Piers yet. Money was tight enough as it was, but since the neighbours had sold their house for more than they'd expected, a germ of an idea had been developing in Virginia's mind that, now she wasn't having to pay for her mother's care and if they sold this, and moved a bit further out of Oxford—Abingdon, maybe—they might be able to afford a house with a bigger garden. It wouldn't be far for her (she'd finally persuaded Derek that Oxford was as good a base for her as anywhere), Piers could easily get into work and, depending on where Scarlett went to secondary school, she could get a bus or Virginia could drop her off.

She shook her head, unable to believe that it wasn't that long before Scarlett would be moving on; taking that quantum leap out of childhood and into adolescence, with all that came with it. Virginia clicked on the kettle. She hoped to goodness that she took after her parents on the teenage front and not her Aunt Rosie, or her cousin Kerry for that matter. Virginia had called Rosie the other night— sadly a less and less frequent occurrence now that they didn't need to discuss their mother and it was always Virginia who called—and Rosie had spent ten minutes ranting about her daughter who had dropped out of school and had moved in with her boyfriend.

'She'll be up the duff in no time,' Rosie was certain of it, 'just so they can get a council house.

Stupid, stupid girl.'

Virginia carefully said nothing.

Taking her tea now and slipping the diary out from between the cook books, she went to the table and picked up a pen.

Darling girl,

I've been a bit remiss in writing this for a few weeks, so I thought that I'd catch up now. Dad has gone to collect you from Lottie's house so there's a bit of peace before I put the tea—oops, supper!—on. I was going to make that lemon sponge pudding but we're a bit low on eggs. It must be this vile weather because the hens aren't laying so well at the moment. I just want some sunshine on my skin. I feel quite jealous of Granny and Grandpa's plans for a cruise this summer. Granny was full of it over Christmas, wasn't she? Maybe on my way home from work tomorrow I'll pop into the travel agent and pick up some brochures for a holiday for us. Somewhere warm and exciting. Italy maybe, where Dad and I went when I first discovered I was expecting you.

What news for you? You had a final hearing test last week at the hospital and they gave you a clean bill of health at last. I didn't tell you, but we were all worried that the trouble you have had hearing in your left ear was permanent damage. We have been watching it carefully because the hospital had warned us that this can happen, and I am so pleased that it has righted itself. Sometimes though, I think you choose to be a bit deaf, especially when I ask you to tidy your room!

Some people do have a knack of choosing not to listen, and it can be dangerous. It wasn't a very good Christmas at The Gables, was it? It must have been very confusing for you, and I am sorry you heard all that shouting between Granny and Daddy. I don't expect you to understand at your age what happened. Even Alice didn't get it, but then Alice has no experience of these things. I don't mean that in a patronising way. It's just a fact. She has no children, has never been married, and so there are experiences she has simply never had.

I need to explain to you about Minty and why she won't be a present after all. We will tell you tonight that she was borrowed and had to go back, and I expect you will be very angry and upset, but that's not entirely the truth. A pony is a lovely thing to own—I wish I'd had one as a child, but then I was always a bit scared of horses, to be honest. But they are a big responsibility and need a lot of care. Obviously we can't have Minty here—the garden would be terribly crowded with her, the cat and the hens! Can you imagine? But nor can she stay at Granny's.

There are two reasons for this. One is that, with school, Dad's work and my job, we wouldn't be able to get down to Sussex as often as we should, and Granny and Grandpa would be left with an unridden pony to care for. The other is that a pony is the kind of gift a parent should give a child. Granny trumped our ace by giving you Minty and she was especially wrong to do it without asking us first. Much as I would like to think she wanted to make it a thrilling surprise for you, I think there was an ulterior motive for it that you may not understand until you have a mother-in-law yourself. Women can be very divisive like that, couching their actions in a way that makes them beyond reproach,

338

and it's a trait that doesn't make me very proud to be female.

If you want to learn to ride, Scarlett—though I have to admit you have never shown any interest—then we will do all we can to give you lessons, but that is for us to provide, not Granny.

Virginia was worried that she had been too honest but she heard the car pull up on the drive and quickly had to shut the diary, slipping it back onto the shelf. Then, putting on an apron, she opened the fridge and pulled out the mince for cottage pie. With the news about the pony about to overshadow the evening, it was going to have to be the best cottage pie she had ever created.

Chapter 45

October 2010

Greg brought the letters up with a cup of tea for them both. He was fully dressed and poised to leave for the long journey to Stevenage where an ongoing development needed his immediate attention. From there he was back to Heathrow and onto Dubai again, where the project that had kept him busy for most of the last two years was coming to a close. 'I just checked my emails,' he said, placing the cup on her bedside table and, kissing her forehead, sat on the edge of the bed. 'We've had the confirmation for the booking. I hope she won't be disappointed it's not camping, but I think we could arrange a couple of nights in a tent in the Sahara. I did it once, years ago. You wouldn't believe how clear the sky is, and how many stars you can see.'

'Mmmm—I can't wait,' Alice smiled sleepily. 'I love Marrakesh. It's such an exciting city. And I wouldn't have fancied camping in the Brecon Beacons during the Christmas holidays. I really don't think she's going to be disappointed.'

'Hope not. It's a bit significant, isn't it? Our first holiday together. I'll be on my best behaviour, promise.'

Alice reached up from the bed and ran her hand up his back, under his jacket. 'Oh—shame. I was hoping for some really disgraceful behaviour from you, to be honest.'

'Mmmm! I'll see what I can do. Listen, I'll call you from the airport. And I'll see you in about a week. But we can Skype in between, and I'll be thinking about you all the time, anyway. Even in meetings. You're a terrible distraction, Ms Fenton!'

'Likewise, Mr Mullin, likewise!' Alice blew him a kiss and sipped her tea while she listened to the sound of his car purring away into the distance, then she opened the official-looking letter in the thick cream envelope, postmarked Stoke. It was from a firm of solicitors. But not the one she'd visited in Oxford, who had dealt with the will and the guardianship. The covering letter didn't really make sense. It said they'd been informed of Virginia Waverley's death by the firm in Oxford and were following instructions to forward a letter to her. Alice threw it aside, confused, and stared at the enclosed envelope. The writing was Ginny's and it was addressed to her. She felt a deep sense of unease and her hand trembled as she opened it.

10 December 2005
Dear Alice,
I hope that this is a letter that you will never have
to read, but you and I both know that shit happens
and it's best to be prepared.

But if you are holding this letter in your hand,
it is because something has happened to me and,
because you are Scarlett's legal guardian (a mantle
I don't suppose you really imagined you'd ever have
to wear), I need to give you some information which
is very important indeed. In fact, it is so important
that you are the only person I am going to tell. What
you do with the information is up to you—you may
never need to do anything—but please know that
I am trusting you with something that transcends
everything else—secrets about boyfriends, gripes
about work, rows with loved ones. Whatever you
think of me when (and after) you read this, please
consider the bigger picture and never, ever use the
information just because, oh, I don't know, we
might not have been on the best of terms when I
died. God, that's a weird thing to write.

This is why I have lodged this letter with my
parents' solicitor in Stoke, with private instructions
in my will that they be contacted in the event of my
death and this letter be sent to you. I hope they don't
have trouble finding you.

As you know only too well, Piers and I had
trouble conceiving. I never really told you how
stressful it all was, and how our marriage was put to
the test in a big way. In the spring of 1998 we were
barely speaking, I was snowed under with work and
things were very bad. There's no excuse, but I did a
very stupid thing and had a one-night fling with a

man at a work event. He was lovely, but it shouldn't have happened and emotionally it meant nothing. I was lonely, stupid, a bit drunk, and full of self-pity, almost the most unforgivable of emotions.

Piers and I made things up and, soon after, I discovered I was pregnant. Scarlett is so like Piers that I assumed, and I admit I was massively relieved, that she was Piers' daughter. However, when she had meningitis, I found out what her blood group was and, according to science, there is no way that she can be Piers'.

Piers, of course, does not know this—I could never do that to him. He is a brilliant father and adores her. But there might be a reason one day—I can't think what, right now—that she needs to know who her father is. This has been like a time bomb in my life and, as I write this, I don't know what to do, should the truth ever come out. I have had to make myself think of the consequences of what I might leave behind but then, anyone who says they don't worry about the impact of their own death is either a fool or a liar.

About Scarlett's father. I haven't kept in touch with him, though we worked together again briefly and at arms' length, and I never mentioned that night in Harrogate, so I don't know where he is. But he is a designer, his company is called MTG International and his name is Greg Mullin.

Very much love, my greatest friend,
Virginia

Alice had no idea how she held it together to get Scarlett to school that morning. Frighteningly, she had no recollection of the drive. Her mind was so full of what she'd read, in Ginny's own hand,

342

that even walking seemed an effort. She was on autopilot.

It couldn't be true. It couldn't. And yet how could Ginny be mistaken? But could she be sure? Worst of all, did Greg know?

Back at the cottage, the facts and her suspicions were clunking into place with sickening thuds, and she felt herself grow cold and rigid with the realisation. Did that explain why Greg, who claimed barely to know Ginny, had been at the funeral in the first place? Then the appalling thought, that maybe Ginny wasn't telling the truth in her letter and that they'd had a love affair, began to seep its way into her imagination. And that's when things really took a turn for the worse.

Say Greg knew. Say they had been lovers. Say he knew about Scarlett. Had he targeted her, Alice, from the outset, as a way of getting access to his daughter? *His* daughter. Alice felt as if the world had lurched suddenly and violently beneath her. She'd been in a earthquake once, in Italy, and the sensation reminded her of that. And the aftershocks kept coming.

Maybe he didn't care for her at all. Once, last week—in another lifetime—she'd said to him that she couldn't believe he wanted to be with her. He'd laughed it off and silenced her doubts with kisses. But maybe she'd been right, after all. What did he really want, then? Would he suddenly want custody of Scarlett? Alice felt as though she'd been punched in the guts. He couldn't take Scarlett away from her. She was too precious to her and, besides, they'd both lost Ginny—they needed each other.

She was trying to be logical, but her brain didn't seem to be working right. Questions kept popping into her head and her usual ability to bat away calamities by turning them into a joke had abandoned her. She climbed straight back into the bed she'd left to wake Scarlett just over an hour earlier and tried to read the letter again. It was only when she struggled to make out the blurred words that she realised tears were pouring down her face. He'd lied to her. She'd trusted him, and he'd lied to her. The whole thing was a sham, right from the start, from the day of the funeral when he'd given her his handkerchief. And she—who prided herself on being smart and cynical, and her head ruling her heart—had fallen for it like an idiot. And she'd fallen for Greg too. Because now she knew for sure what she'd been wondering about for the last few weeks. She loved him. It wouldn't hurt this badly if she didn't love him, would it?

She stumbled through the day, unable even to distract herself with work. She didn't even turn on her laptop, but sat staring into space for hours, until it became perfectly clear what the only possible solution could be: she couldn't see him again, certainly not now. She had to end things to protect herself. To protect Scarlett. Because he'd lied to her. There was so much he hadn't told her—about sleeping with Ginny, about Scarlett, about his feelings for her, about his reason for coming on so strong. And she'd told him everything.

But she wasn't going to tell him about this. And she wasn't going to play into his hands. Had his plan been to take them all on holiday, play happy families with Scarlett, biding his time until he claimed her as his own daughter? And he'd be able to prove it beyond doubt with a DNA test. Alice clenched her fists, resisting the temptation to tear

344

the letter into a thousand tiny pieces and just ignore it.

That was it. She had to break up with him, but without letting him know why, and she'd fight him off if the time came. Alice sobbed her betrayal out as she roamed around the house unable to sit still, her mind working frenziedly. She couldn't do it while he was still in the UK, because then he'd come back and the battle for Scarlett would begin straightaway. She had to wait until she knew he'd left for Dubai. Then she'd text him. She couldn't possibly talk to him. A nice, careful text would do it. And, in the meantime, she'd ignore his calls. For Scarlett, she'd have to stay strong. Ginny had given her the information to do what she felt was right.

By three o'clock, there had been a few calls, and then a couple of texts asking if she was OK and why hadn't she replied. He even asked, jokingly, 'Are you ignoring me?' She ignored every one, and she stared at the phone accusingly, as though it was in league with him. The more she thought about the past few months, and the way their 'relationship' had developed, the more she wondered why she hadn't suspected him before. But he'd seemed so sincere. She shuddered as the phone rang once again, tears of grief pouring down her face. She should have known that a man as together, as rich as he was, wouldn't really be into a ditzy mess of a woman who drove a shit car and lived in chaos. She should have known.

Worst of all, she was starting to feel angry with Ginny. She'd lied as well. And not just to Alice. She'd lied to Piers, her loving, faithful husband— OK, so the diary had revealed that there had been some friction between the two of them, but that was no excuse. Apart from anything else, it was so unlike Ginny to do anything so mad and ill-considered. The friend she thought she knew so well had been an illusion. And she wasn't even there for Alice to shout at.

The phone rang once more. Then, a few minutes later there was a text from Vince. Greg had obviously been onto him, saying he couldn't get hold of Alice. She ignored that too. She had never felt so alone.

It was Thursday, and when she picked Scarlett up from school, she could feel the phoniness of her smile and the way the girl wriggled uneasily from her rather desperate hug. Alice never normally hugged her at the school gate. She made some excuse about why they wouldn't be going into Lewes today—she really couldn't face that—and, once they were home, she was aware she was making an excessive effort. She'd forced herself to make cupcakes and had bought food colouring and chocolate sprinkles so they could decorate them together. Scarlett complied, but without enthusiasm and she could feel her looking at her strangely. Alice, too, was analysing Scarlett's face as covertly as she could, scanning her features for similarities to Greg. And they were there, no doubt about it. The mouth, the straight nose, the dark brows. Why hadn't anyone noticed before?

'What's wrong?' Scarlett asked eventually. 'Have you got your period, or something? I hope I don't go like this when I get mine. You look really weird.'

Alice laughed harshly. 'No, no—I haven't. I don't know what you're talking about. Weird how?'

Scarlett rolled her eyes. 'You keep staring. Take

a picture, it'll last longer.' Then a slow smile crept across her face. 'It's Greg, isn't it?'

'What?'

'Well, he's gone away for a bit, hasn't he? You're missing him. That's what it is. You luuuurve him.'

Alice focused all her attention on the cupcakes. 'I certainly do not. He's OK, I suppose. I'm not sure we're going anywhere, though.'

'What?' Scarlett sounded shocked.

Alice carefully licked some icing from her fingers, keeping her eyes fixed on the table, still avoiding Scarlett's glare. 'Well, it's not as though it was anything serious. It's probably just as well he's gone away for a bit. It was getting a bit boring, to tell you the truth.'

She jerked her head up as the plate Scarlett had been holding smashed to the floor and she ran upstairs and slammed her bedroom door. Alice sank into a chair. 'You bastard, Greg. You bastard!' and she dissolved into tears once more.

*   *   *

It was a carefully thought-out text, timed for when she was sure he'd be somewhere over the Channel. She despised people who ended relationships like this, but she was being the coward she felt. For something so short, it had taken a lot of planning. It went like this:

Been thinking, we shld really cool things off a bit while I concentrate on Scarlett. Not sure hol is such a gd idea. Pls cancel. C u round. A

347

Alice stared at the screen for a long time before she pressed Send, then she turned the phone off before going to bed.

*   *   *

The next morning, Scarlett was icily polite. The shadows under her eyes made it clear she'd slept as little as Alice. The egg she'd boiled to Scarlett's usual exact specification was coldly refused. 'Come on, Scarlett. You've got to eat.' Alice attempted a smile. 'After all, you've got a terrific amount of brainal activity to get on with today. And that comment by your Spanish teacher might be worth giving some thought to. I know it's complicated at first but, believe me, languages just click after a while. I promise.'

Scarlett shrugged. 'I don't know why you're giving me a hard time all of a sudden. It's not like you really care anyway, is it?'

'What do you mean? Of course I do. I want you to do well at school. And if that means sometimes having to work a bit harder and spend less time chatting with your friends on Facebook, then that's what it takes.' Alice knew she sounded harsh, but she felt too bitter to pretend. 'Maybe you should do your homework down here in the future. We could work together.'

'What? No. No way. Why should I? I can't work down here. I can't concentrate.'

Alice frowned. She really didn't feel up to this.

'Look, I don't want to argue about it, but if your Spanish teacher says you need to learn your vocabulary, then it's a no-brainer. You work down here and, when you've finished, you can go back

348

upstairs if that's what you want.'

Scarlett screwed up her face into a horrific scowl. 'You can't make me.'

'As a matter of fact, I think you'll find I can,' Alice sighed, pouring herself another cup of tea.

Scarlett's voice was tight with fury. 'You're not my mother. You never will be. You can't boss me around like this.'

Alice slammed her mug down on the work surface, sending a tiny tidal wave of tea slopping over a book beside it. 'Oh bloody hell! For the purposes of your schoolwork, I am your mother, and you'll comply with this or . . . or I'll have to take your laptop away.'

'I *hate* you! Greg would never do a thing like that. Greg listens to what I say.'

'That's enough, young lady. Greg has nothing to do with this.' Alice turned to glare back at Scarlett. 'We'll discuss this later when you've had a chance to think, but I am *not* giving way. We're going to be late unless we leave in the next two minutes, so do whatever else you have to do, and then we're out of here.'

Scarlett slunk upstairs and returned in under a minute with her sports bag over her shoulder. They were both struck silent by their first proper row and not another word was said until she got out of the car and went through the school gates. Alice sank her head into her hands.

Chapter 46

By the early afternoon, Alice was feeling worse if anything. Added to her misery about Greg, and the uncomfortable feeling that she hadn't known Ginny nearly as well as she'd thought, was guilt over the way she'd broken the news of the break-up to Scarlett. That was selfish. The poor kid had enough to contend with, for goodness sake, without problems that were entirely of other people's making. As if it understood exactly how she was feeling, the weather had taken a turn for the worse too, and she watched the rain trickle down the windows of the cottage and shivered in the grey, fading light.

Her initial anger towards Ginny had softened. Far from blaming her for this bombshell, she realised now she ought to be grateful to her. If it wasn't for the letter, she would never have discovered the truth about Greg—maybe until it was too late and he'd made some claim over Scarlett. As her only genuine blood relative, besides Rosie and her children, he could probably make a very convincing claim for custody—and what that would do to Judy and Bill didn't bear thinking about. And if the 'relationship' had gone on any further, she might have fallen for him too far to get free. She was way too old to be nursing a broken heart—though this felt painfully like one. So maybe it was a good thing, overall, that she knew the truth, though how anything so painful could be classed as 'good' escaped her.

But the knowledge brought another unwelcome

realisation in its wake. Ginny's diary had revealed a network of tensions and ambiguities that Alice simply hadn't been aware of. And she hadn't even thought to ask her friend how things were really going. She had simply, lazily, taken everything in Ginny's life at face value, even though she knew perfectly well that her friend was a stoic, uncomplaining about problems that Alice would have dramatised and turned into a performance, and shared with everyone in her circle of acquaintance in excruciating detail to get a laugh. Ginny had never complained and Alice had never bothered to ask.

The bottom line was that Alice had believed herself to be Ginny's best friend, but now realised that she had let her down in the worst possible way—she simply hadn't been there for her when she'd been needed. Alice had been too quick to assume that, once Ginny had got her man, everything in life was perfect for her. And because she had never had that hunger to have her own child, she'd assumed that Ginny was the same and that the years of waiting before she had become pregnant had been carefree and fun. She'd even been a crap friend over the issue of Judy. She'd dismissed her reservations about Ginny's mother-in-law—and now, thanks to the journal and being on the receiving end of the woman's little digs and implicit criticisms, Alice could see exactly what Ginny had complained about. How must Ginny have felt when her best friend had told her she was simply being 'over-sensitive' about issues like the pony? Alice sniffed morosely, overwhelmed with self-pity. She'd been a terrible friend. And now it was too late to make up for it.

Too late for Ginny. But not for Scarlett. This thought was a tipping point in the day for Alice. Scarlett would be arriving home soon. The very least she could do was make up to her for being so moody. And over what? A man! This was not Alice's way. It was time to pull herself together—for Scarlett's sake, even if not for herself. She and Scarlett had a life together. Alice might not be family, but she'd do her best to be all the family Scarlett would need. She stood up from her slumped position on the sofa and unfurled like an old crone in the darkening room. She turned the light on. She checked her watch. Scarlett was due home from school any minute. She'd go and meet her off the school bus.

Alice opened the front door and shivered, then went back in and pulled on her duffle coat and walked off down the lane. The fresh air and activity made her feel better at once. It wasn't so much cold, but wet and windy, and she took a slightly masochistic pleasure in the sensation of the raindrops stinging her face. Her thoughts felt clearer now, and she planned the evening, thinking what she could do to make Scarlett feel happy and secure. Maybe they could watch a DVD together after supper—one of the teen flicks they both enjoyed and that made Greg roll his eyes in mock long-suffering. Alice stamped her feet on the uneven pavement—not because she was cold, but to snap herself out of thinking about Greg that way any more. He was history, she lied to herself.

At the bus stop, she bobbed up on her toes and stretched to look round the corner. She couldn't hear the bus, but the wind was making quite a noise, bringing down the remaining leaves on the trees in flurries that danced along the ground. She checked her watch and, sure enough, just as she was about to start fretting, it came swinging round the corner, its headlights blinding her for a moment. Alice smiled in anticipation as it slowed to a stop and the doors opened. But of Scarlett there was no sign.

The bus driver looked at her questioningly, expecting her to get on and she stepped up onto the platform, looking along the aisle, hoping to see Scarlett struggling with her bags. Nothing. Had she missed it? Was she waiting at school? With a jolt, Alice realised that she'd turned her mobile off to avoid any calls from Greg. Had she missed a call from Scarlett too?

Instead Immy was clattering down the aisle, a school bag and violin in her overloaded arms. 'Immy, have you seen Scarlett?' Alice stepped off the platform. 'She didn't miss the bus, did she? Did it leave early?'

Immy dropped her bags on the ground and wiped the hair from her face. 'I thought you must be collecting her. She hasn't got any afterschool stuff today, has she?'

'I didn't leave early,' the bus driver sounded defensive. 'Sometimes they're messing about and they don't see the bus. I waited until the teacher sent me off. The school should call you if a pupil misses the bus. Have you been out? They might have called you at home.'

Alice stepped further back on the pavement as the bus pulled away and Immy set off in the other direction home. The best thing would be to go home and turn on her phone, tell Scarlett to hang on, and drive to school as quickly as she reasonably could. Things like this must happen from time to time. There'd be a teacher on hand to keep an eye on her, surely. She'd probably be inside, safe and warm, and getting increasingly irritated. It might take a big mug of hot chocolate to coax her into a good mood, but Alice would manage it. She'd manage it all, somehow. She let herself into the cottage and picked up her landline phone, in case there had been a call since she left. Nothing. Her mobile showed nothing either. Alice stared at the screen uneasily. What was she supposed to do now?

Chapter 47

May 2010

'Can you both come to dinner on Saturday? Terribly last minute, I know, but the forecast is good and we thought we'd risk an informal barbecue. You have to grab the best days when you can, don't you?'

Virginia knew that Natasha's version of an 'informal barbecue' would be like a photograph from one of those country-style magazines with gazebo, matching table linen and Moroccan lights to twinkle as the sun went down. The food would be executed to perfection by the aproned Sebastian, who'd fuss over a huge barbecue on wheels, with a lid, that looked like some kind of crash machine you'd find in intensive care. She smiled. 'That sounds perfect.'

'See you about eight then.' It had been a long week and the thought of being entertained on a warm late May evening was irresistible. She had learned long ago to put to rest her feelings of anxiety about Natasha and Sebastian. They might be posh but they were good friends and kind people. Virginia shrugged off her linen jacket. It really was unusually warm and she threw open her office window to let in some breeze, anchoring down her papers before they blew away. In front of her was a to-do list, much of which she could hand over to her new assistant Dawn. Though she was only young and had little or no experience of the world of hospitality, except the odd holiday-work stint at a Travelodge, she was friendly and keen to learn and, best of all, took some of the pressure off Virginia.

It was a call from the MD of a rival company in March that had precipitated Dawn. It became clear that Virginia was being headhunted, with promises of salary increases, perks and a pension and, joy of joys, an assistant to help her.

She'd talked it over with Piers in bed that night. 'With Scarlett about to go to secondary school, I really don't want to be travelling to this lot's head office in High Wycombe every day. Besides, their properties are all over the place. I'll be away all the time.' She weighed up the options. 'But it is a great offer—especially the promise of an assistant. I am *desperate* for one, but Derek keeps telling me the company can't afford it.'

'We could move? I could look for another job,' Piers offered unconvincingly, and she'd lain against his chest.

'Kind offer, but you've a book to write remember? The publisher ain't going to wait for ever and now you've had an offer, you don't want to blow it. They might even commission another one.'

'Charlemagne, the Sequel?' she could hear the laughter rumbling in his chest.

'I'm liking it.'

'Come on, Gin, use the offer as a bit of leverage with Derek. "Better my package or I'm off" kind of thing.'

'I'm crap at that.'

'I know you are. You need to learn to be more forthright. Let's start right away.' He gave her a look she knew well.

'Right then, Mr Waverley,' she said, slipping her hand down into his boxer shorts. 'Ravish me now.'

'That's more like it,' he replied, rolling her over onto her back. 'I do love it when you get all dominating.'

And so it was that she'd told Derek about the offer the following day, fingers and toes crossed that he would take the bait and, miraculously, he had. His management skills when it came to employee praise might be lacking, but she took his agreement to a pay rise and an assistant as some validation that she was more valuable to the company than chopped liver.

Meanwhile, they had the holiday to look forward to. Two weeks in Turkey, just the three of them, reading books, lying in the sun and swimming in the warm sea. She was counting the days. As soon as Scarlett finished school, they'd pack their bags and head off.

'Natasha and Sebastian have asked us for a barbie on Saturday,' she said as they ate at the little garden table. 'That OK? I checked your fixtures and it's an early one on Saturday. You should be back from Radley College by then.'

'Yeah, that would be nice,' Piers replied. He was

in the middle of exams, with a packed schedule to juggle, and he looked tired. But his publisher had agreed that they didn't need to see anything until after the summer holidays, which was a blessing. Virginia wanted him to relax and recover from the term.

'What about me?' Scarlett asked. 'I don't have to come, do I? Natasha's kids are way older than me. It'll be so boring.'

'I thought you could go and stay with Lottie? I've spoken to her mum and they're cool about that.'

'OK.' Scarlett put a new potato into her mouth. 'But don't say "cool", Mum, it's incredibly embarrassing.'

'Beg pardon,' Virginia replied, trying not to laugh and be told off even more. She shot a glance at Piers, who raised his eyebrows in a way that said 'that's you told, mate', then he winked. Virginia finished her last mouthful of salmon and leaned back in her chair with her glass of wine, watching the two of them as Piers asked Scarlett about her school tests. Her husband and daughter were physically so alike. Same dark wavy hair, same stature—tall and lean—though Virginia also had that athletic build. Even their eyes were dark. They were good together, Scarlett still not always able to cope with Piers' teasing but getting better as she grew up. Despite her high spirits, Virginia suspected that she would always take herself a bit too seriously at times, which was a characteristic that reminded Virginia of Rosie in many ways, but she hoped that some of Piers' *laissez faire* attitude would rub off on her.

But what if she'd been different in some way? Virginia felt a flash of something like relief run through her, as if she'd dodged a bullet.

*　　　*　　　*

As predicted, Saturday dawned warm and sunny with a clear blue sky and the promise of a fine day ahead. Piers left soon after breakfast to go to the school boathouse and prepare the boats to take to Radley. Virginia envied the kids who'd be rowing. The water would be perfect today and she craved a day on the river. Maybe tomorrow she'd take Scarlett out.

'Let's go shopping,' she suggested to her daughter as she drank her tea and watched Scarlett's head, bent over her bowl of Crunchy Nut Cornflakes.

'Oooh, yeah!' she looked up, her eyes excited. 'Can we go to Bicester Village?'

And so they spent the morning wandering through the outlet village that always reminded Virginia of a film set for a Western—temporary-looking buildings incongruously set in the middle of a parking lot. They laughed over the racks of ugly dresses, usually in yellow, that had clearly not been a hit last season and tried on strange and ridiculously high shoes to the annoyance of the shop assistants, but Virginia had to talk Scarlett out of a silk halter-neck that was way too old for her and they settled on a pretty floral skirt and top from Jigsaw. Virginia, who hadn't intended to buy anything, ended up paying for a floaty dress that she thought would be perfect for the barbecue and some shoes that, for once, didn't look silly on her large feet and would be great for work.

'That was fun,' she said, as they packed their goodies into the boot. 'Now, let's go and cool down at home.'

The remainder of the afternoon passed quickly. Scarlett cycled, helmet on and pavements only, up the road to buy an ice lolly—a sliver of independence that still made Virginia anxious—and she tidied the flower beds and started to prepare tubs for tomato plants that would ripen, juicy and red, by the end of the summer. She wouldn't have time to finish them today, but she put the compost and trowel out ready for tomorrow.

Piers came in at around four, his expression wreathed with success. 'Almost a full house,' he smiled. 'The girls' coxless four didn't do too well but the eight were unstoppable.' He gave Virginia a kiss and swung Scarlett around. 'I think that warrants a cuppa, don't you?'

They sat in the shade of the cherry tree, its branches heavy with blossom that would soon be gone, and sipped their tea. 'Had a good day?' he asked, as Scarlett ran upstairs to her room.

'It was fun. She's growing up, you know. She was looking at clothes that wouldn't have interested her at all a year ago.'

Piers winced. 'Eeek, I hope we're not heading for a tricky teenager. I've got enough of those to contend with at school.'

'Then you'll be well qualified to cope!' Virginia laughed, but she too wondered if their good luck was running out and they had a few years of slammed doors and sulks ahead of them. 'Oh I hope not. We've been so blessed so far.'

Piers rested his cup in his large hands between his thighs. 'Perhaps because we only had to cope with one. One should be a doddle. God knows how my parents managed four without one of us going off the rails spectacularly.'

'Yeah, you have to hand it to them.' She imagined Judy regimenting her brood on beach holidays. Perhaps that explained her military organisation. 'Perhaps we got off lightly managing it only once. Well, twice but . . . You know.'

'No, once.' Piers' expression didn't change. Perhaps her miscarriage, so early in her pregnancy, though a disappointment, had affected him less than she'd given him credit for.

'It *was* an early miscarriage but it was still a pregnancy,' she replied quietly.

'That's not what I meant,' he turned to look at her.

She felt a shiver of fear. 'I don't know what you mean.'

'Darling Virginia,' he said quietly, almost whispering. 'I know she's not mine.'

Virginia looked at his eyes, expecting anger and hurt, but they looked back at her almost kindly. 'She is yours, she's—'

He put his hand on her thigh. 'She's my daughter because I raise her—we raise her—and I love her as much as I love you. But I know she's not my daughter.'

Virginia swallowed, unnerved by his calm. 'How . . . I mean, she . . .'

'Darling, there is something I never told you. When I was at university we were all trying to make a bit of money and I donated to a sperm bank. Or at least I tried to, but I was rejected after the first . . . sample . . . because my sperm count was too low. Stupidly low, actually.' He looked down at the empty mug in his hands. 'I suppose I went into denial. I felt as if I wasn't a real man, and it got

360

worse as my brothers started popping out kids like peas. I wasn't functioning like I should, and that really hurt on some caveman level.' He shrugged.

'But you said that the tests at your GP . . .'

'I never had any. I knew what they would say, so I lied that they'd come back OK and amazingly no one questioned it.' He looked up at her again; this time his expression was almost begging, seeking forgiveness. 'I just hoped, Gin, that there would be a miracle. Well, there was, because you did get pregnant early on, so one of the little buggers must have got through, and I just clung to the hope that it would happen again. And then it did, and I was over the moon. She was so beautiful. Do you remember?'

'How could I forget?' Virginia answered barely audibly, her mouth dry.

'But as she started to grow, I could just feel that there was nothing of me in her. Her hair, maybe, but there was nothing about her face that was Waverley, and there were elements that weren't from you either, so something was missing. Then, after the meningitis, Scarlett and I were in the car going somewhere and she was rabbiting on about the doctor and what she'd said and she told me what her blood group was. That confirmed it really. I looked at your old antenatal notes in the filing cabinet and saw what group you were and did the research.'

They both sat in silence for a while, punctuated by the distant screams of children playing a few gardens away and the hum of a lawn mower somewhere. The hens pecked the grass around their feet, oblivious to this seismic turn of events. Virginia held her breath, dreading what the next

361

question was bound to be.

'The odd thing is, Gin,' he went on eventually, 'I don't want to know whose she is.' Virginia shot a glance at him but he was looking across the garden at the house. 'I don't blame you, because it was awful around that time between us and I said some terrible things.'

'It doesn't make up for it,' was all she could manage.

'All I need to know,' he turned in his seat earnestly towards her, 'is did you love him? Was it a love affair?'

'Oh no.' She rushed to reassure him, turning to face him head-on. How could she tell him she barely knew the man? 'No, it wasn't anything like that. It only happened once. I was angry with you. It was stupid. Unforgivable.'

'Thank God, I couldn't have borne that. But it brought us Scarlett.' He turned back and looked up into the blossoms on the tree above his head. Again there was silence. Virginia didn't want to fill the void. If there were details he wanted to hear, then he deserved to hear them, but he'd made it plain he didn't want her to volunteer the information, and she wasn't going to. What had it been anyway but a moment of weakness with a man she'd only encountered professionally, and with whom it was never again mentioned.

'Did he . . . does he know?' he said after a while.

'No.'

As Piers contemplated the mug in his hands, Virginia remembered a meeting at Greg's offices in London soon after she'd gone back to work from maternity leave. Derek and the chairman had been there to look over design boards. Greg had greeted her with a kiss on both cheeks and had said 'how are you?' politely and warmly, but there hadn't been a hint of complicity. He hadn't even realised she'd been on maternity leave—and why would he?—and in his expression was nothing to suggest that night in Harrogate had been anything more than two people, a bit drunk, who'd made a bad judgement call.

She had to ask. 'Why didn't you say something before, if you knew?'

He shrugged and laughed dryly. 'Because I'm your classic ostrich. It's my worst weakness, but then you know that. Your difficulties made it easier somehow because I could put the blame on you.'

'But we managed it once!'

'I know and I just held out hope it would happen again. But, Gin, I've been a coward about Mum too. I should have been on your side earlier. I shouldn't have waited until she bought that sodding pony before I waded in. You had a right to my support and Scarlett shouldn't have been put in the position of having a present like that taken away.'

'Well, Judy's not the easiest, I have to say, but I can't tell you how relieved I was when you saw my side of things.'

'Took me long enough,' he mumbled, then he leaned forward, resting his arms on his knees. 'I've even been a coward about the book. I should have pulled my finger out earlier.'

'Come on, love, stop the self-flagellation.' Tentatively she touched his leg, not sure if he would reject her, but he put his warm hand on hers. 'I am the one here who has done a bad thing. A very bad thing, and the fact that you knew the truth and yet carried on being Scarlett's dad is amazing.' She

363

could feel tears on her cheeks and he looked into her face. 'I don't deserve it. She's so precious and I was so frightened you would reject her, and me, if you knew.' He put his hand up and brushed a tear from her cheek. 'She's yours, Piers, in every way.'

'I know, darling. I know.' He leaned over and kissed her on the mouth.

'Does your mum . . . do you think they know?'

'I've wondered that sometimes, but no, I don't think they do. They've treated her exactly the same as their other grandchildren. They've always been good at being fair with their affection.'

'And Piers,' she swallowed. 'Scarlett must never know. Not ever.'

'No, I know she mustn't. It's weird when I notice some of her characteristics and I wonder where they came from. Traits I don't see in you. At first it used to make me ache with jealousy. There would be times when I'd have to take myself away in case I punched someone. It was as if a huge part of the jigsaw was missing, but I kidded myself that she only came from *you*—like some sort of immaculate conception—and I think, after all this time, I've persuaded myself that those traits are unique to her. They're not from someone else. It's just Scarlett's character.'

Virginia marvelled at the generosity of his spirit. Was it genuine? Would he be comfortable for ever with this knowledge? This revelation?

'I wonder that with me and Rosie too,' she said weakly, and sniffed. 'I can't see her character in either of my parents, and I hope to God there's none of her anger and resentment in me.'

'No, darling. I think Rosie is unique!'

They both laughed at this just as Scarlett came

through the French windows. 'Dad, can you . . . Mum, have you been crying?'

'No, Mum's been laughing,' Piers lifted Scarlett onto his knee, her gangly legs hanging down to the grass. 'You're too big for this now.'

'What were you laughing about?'

'About you, Miss Nosey. We were laughing about how much we love you.'

Scarlett frowned. 'That's an odd thing to laugh about.'

'Yes, isn't it?' Piers replied, kissing her neck and blowing a raspberry against her skin. 'But then people can be very odd at times.'

Chapter 48

October 2010

Frowning and tense, Alice called the school, trying hard to keep her voice even as she discovered that, as far as they were concerned, Scarlett had left as normal. The teacher she spoke to sounded more concerned than she would have liked. It seemed this wasn't such a common occurrence after all, girls not turning up on buses. 'Are you aware of any arrangement Scarlett might have made to go and see a friend? Sometimes Mum is the last person to know.' Alice didn't bother to put her straight. 'Try calling her friends, and her mobile, of course,' the teacher advised. 'I'll contact her form teacher and I'll call you back in ten minutes. All right?'

Alice's hands were trembling as she hung up. She checked her mobile again. Nothing from Scarlett.

Nothing even from Greg. He must have got the message. She supposed she was relieved. She tried hard not to panic. There was no need for anyone else to know yet, really. Not Bill and Judy, certainly. The last thing they needed was more worry. And the last thing Alice needed was for anyone to realise what a poor excuse for a guardian she was, not even able to keep track of an eleven-year-old girl. But Scarlett would be bound to be home soon, wouldn't she? Alice called her mobile again, but was put straight through to the answerphone without it even ringing. What did that mean? Had she turned it off? Had she run out of credit or had the battery given up?

She flung off her coat, hot now, almost stifling. The awful, unthinkable thought was nudging its way into her mind. What if . . . ? Forcing herself to think rationally, she located the list of phone numbers she had started to compile—Scarlett's friends' mums, both landlines and mobiles—and started calling.

Twenty minutes later, drawing a blank with everyone she called, but with plenty of promises to let her know if there was any news, Alice called Vince, got his answerphone, and left a tearful message. What could she do? She was trapped. She couldn't go out looking just in case Scarlett or someone else called. She needed help—and fast. She picked up the phone once again and called Walter. His gruff voice answered almost immediately and this time Alice didn't even attempt to suppress the sob that came as she explained.

'Don't fret, Alice. She's a sensible girl. Betty and I will be right over.'

With the elderly pair on their way round to hold

the fort at home, she could go out and look for Scarlett—though where she'd even start, she had no idea. Lewes, she supposed, then Brighton. Oh God. All she knew was that she had to find the little girl—*her* little girl—and make everything right for her. That was all that mattered now.

The door knocker sounded, and she rushed to answer it, not even bothering to wipe her eyes, relieved at Walter's rapid response. But standing on the doorstep, looking pale, tired and wary, was Greg.

The distance between them felt immense and for a few seconds they simply stared at each other.

'What's going on, Alice? What is all this?' he asked quietly, holding up his phone.

Alice was beyond caution. Nothing mattered now except finding Scarlett. 'She didn't come home from school. I don't know where she is.'

'Scarlett?'

Alice nodded dumbly. He stepped in and took her into his arms at exactly the moment she broke down in tears again. 'Oh, honey! You must be so worried. She called me last night,' he said. 'I missed her call because I was driving to the airport.' He shook his head angrily. 'If only I'd hooked the phone up in the car. I haven't been able to raise her since then. She left a message—I didn't understand it at first, but then I got your text.' He held her away from him and looked at her. 'I simply got back on a plane home—thank God I did. When did you last see her? Is there anything I can do?'

Until moments ago Greg had been the last person she wanted to see. Ever. But in spite of everything she knew, Alice had an immense feeling of safety, just having him there to support her. Haltingly, she

367

explained how badly Scarlett had taken her decision to end it with him and he looked at her searchingly, his eyes hollow. 'Look—I can't say I understand what's going on either. I thought—I really thought we had something good here. But the last thing we should be doing is talking about us now. We have to find her. Let's just try to think about the situation from Scarlett's point of view.'

Alice nodded, grateful that, for now at least, things between them didn't seem complicated at all.

Greg sat down at a careful distance from Alice and pulled at his lower lip, the way Scarlett did when she was concentrating. 'Did she take anything with her this morning, when she went to school? Anything that might indicate she had a plan in mind?'

Alice thought back. 'Well, she wouldn't eat anything. She was angry and I was too ... never mind. Then she went upstairs again. Yes! She doesn't have PE today, I know that—it's on Mondays and Wednesdays, but now I think about it, she took her sports bag. I wonder ...'

She ran upstairs and went into Scarlett's bedroom. There, on the floor, was her sports kit. A quick check under the pillow revealed that her pyjamas were gone and her toothbrush was missing from the bathroom. Her money box was empty, the cork stopper left to one side and the pink cat Vince had bought her was no longer sitting in its usual place. She heard Greg's footsteps on the stairs and turned to see him stop halfway up, a look of uncertainty on his face. 'She planned it,' she confirmed. 'At least we know she hasn't been ...' Alice broke off and looked down.

'But that's a good thing,' he reassured softly.

'She's angry. Upset, probably, because of ...
Well, maybe that's why she hasn't been answering
our calls. She trusted us and perhaps she feels let
down.'

It was what he wasn't saying that hurt her most.
Even though he seemed as baffled by her rejection
of him as Scarlett had been, he wasn't reproaching
her. A sudden thought occurred to Alice—what if
he *didn't* know he was Scarlett's father? That would
change everything. But she dismissed that for now.
All of her attention had to be focused on her girl.
And on bringing her home.

Greg was thinking out loud as they went
downstairs again. 'So she's angry with us. We have
to assume that. Where would she go to feel safe?
Who does she trust?'

At that moment, the phone rang and they both
jumped. Alice snatched up the receiver. 'Hello?'
she gasped.

'Alice,' came the whispered reply. 'It's me. She's
here. She's fine. Get over here now.' The caller
hung up and she turned to face Greg, relief making
her dizzy.

'She's at Vince's.'

Chapter 49

May 2010

Virginia stepped out of the shower and dried
herself with the warm towel. Piers finished shaving
and switched off the razor and, as she passed him
to go into the bedroom, she ran her hand across his

strong back. What was it people said about there being strength in recognising your weaknesses? Perhaps that was what she loved about him the most, his honesty, and now she felt that, because the truth about Scarlett had emerged finally, she could meet him halfway. No more secrets, no more lies.

'Don't do that,' he muttered.

'Why not?' she asked.

'Because it turns me on and we haven't got time and our daughter is downstairs.'

'Sorry,' she smiled, teasingly. 'Can I do it later?'

'You'd better.'

She dried her hair and made up her face with more care than usual, wanting to look her best for him. Needing to show him that she was *his* and that nothing that had gone before mattered. She slipped the new silk dress over her head and it fell down around her legs, feeling soft and sexy.

'You look beautiful, Mrs Waverley,' he said coming into the room, fresh and clean in his white short-sleeved shirt and shorts, his hair still wet from his shower. 'Is that new?'

'A Bicester bargain,' she smiled back, enjoying his approval. She twirled round to show him.

Scarlett had already packed her overnight bag and had changed into the floral skirt and top from Jigsaw. 'And you look beautiful too,' Piers kissed the top of her head. 'My beautiful girls. What a lucky man I am.' His face was relaxed. Perhaps more relaxed than she had ever seen him before; an expression in his eyes that she hadn't even appreciated was there had vanished. 'I feel quite jealous not having anything new to wear.'

'You hate shopping,' Scarlett answered, following him out to the car.

370

'True, but you could have bought me a new pair of socks at least,' he teased.

At that moment the phone rang. Piers picked it up from the side. 'Hello? Oh hi, Mum. No, it's OK. We're on our way out, but if it's urgent. . .'

Virginia and Scarlett exchanged a look and, sighing in resignation, they both sat down at the kitchen table and waited. Scarlett doodled on some paper and Virginia, looking over at her husband on the phone, pulled out a scrap of paper and started to write.

'Sorry, sorry,' Piers muttered five minutes later. 'She wanted to run through some stuff about their holiday. Can't think why it couldn't have waited. Never mind. We'll need to hurry though. Don't want to be late.'

Tucking the paper into her journal and picking up the bunch of roses she'd bought for Natasha, Virginia glanced back into the house to check all the windows were closed. There was a pile of newspapers on the floor. She'd clear them up tomorrow, she thought, and slammed the front door.

Chapter 50

October 2010

Within moments, they were in Greg's car, heading for Brighton. Alice sat beside him, in silence, thoughts teeming in her mind. But over all the others was just one, like the beat of her heart: Thank God. Thank God. Scarlett was safe, at least. And whatever it would take to make her happy as well, Alice was prepared to do. Anything. She glanced at Greg, concentrating hard on the dark country roads. Yes, anything. If it meant sharing Scarlett with him, if that was what Scarlett wanted, then Alice would agree and they'd find a way to manage. Because if the events of the last two hours—was that all it had been?—had taught Alice anything, it was that Scarlett was the most important person in her life. As they drew close to Vince's street, Greg spoke for the first time since they'd rushed from the cottage, not even bothering to switch off the lights and only taking a moment to scrawl a note to Walter and stick it on the door. 'I'll drop you right outside and I'll find somewhere to park. Do you want me to come in, or shall I wait?'

Alice looked at him, surprised. 'No—you come up too. She'll want to see you. It might help.'

He nodded, sombrely, as he pulled up outside. 'Whatever it takes. If you want her to think we're—you know—OK together, I can act the part.' He sighed heavily. 'If it makes her feel better.'

Without speaking or meeting his eye, Alice opened the door and ducked out, dodging the raindrops to get to Vince's front door and using her key to open it. She ran upstairs and hesitated outside the door to his flat, unsure if she was breathless because of the stairs, which she'd taken two at a time, or because of what lay ahead. Did Scarlett even know she was coming? She steeled herself and knocked on the door. Vince was there in a flash and hugged her tightly before ushering her into the sitting room. Scarlett was curled up on his sofa, still in her uniform, with both hands wrapped round a large, steaming mug. She looked up at Alice warily, then lowered her eyes.

'Thank goodness you're all right!' Alice had been wondering what to say all the way from home, but now it burst from her. 'Oh, Scarlett, I'm so sorry I made you miserable. I'd give anything to make you feel better. I'm just a stupid, moody cow and I'm not used to sharing my life with another person. Will you give me another chance?'

There was a moment of surprised silence and Alice was aware of Vince, off to one side, his hands clasped in front of him, and Krissy in the kitchen doorway. Scarlett frowned as if she hadn't heard properly. 'Aren't *you* cross with *me*?'

Alice shrugged helplessly and shook her head. 'To be honest, the only thing I really feel at the moment is huge, huge relief. I was so worried, baby! I was afraid that . . . Well, never mind about that now. And now you're here and I'm just so glad to see you . . .' She started sniffling and Vince came over, putting a comforting arm around her waist.

Scarlett looked down. 'What about Greg? Does he know I ran away? I tried to phone him, but he wasn't there.' Her voice, too, was starting to wobble and the effort she was making not to cry made Alice's heart ache with regret. 'I don't want him to go away. I don't want anyone to go!'

From the open door, came Greg's voice. 'I'm right here, Scarlett, and I'm not going anywhere. Would you believe I got off one plane in Dubai and got right back on another so I could come and convince you that, when I do go, I'll always be coming straight back.'

At the sound of his voice Alice felt her pulse race and realised that, try as she might to deny it, she was well and truly in love with this man. And

373

it would take all her effort to conceal the fact from him. Greg came over and stood with Alice, Krissy and Vince, an uneasy tableau, all looking down anxiously at Scarlett, who eyed them suspiciously. 'But are you two staying together?'

There was a beat of hesitation—just too long, and Scarlett's face started to contort with emotion. 'You've got to stay together. You've *got* to. Can't you see? I want you *both* looking after me—and Vince and Krissy, too. I need you all.' Her voice started to rise. 'I've lost ... It's not fair. I've lost everything. My mum and my dad. My house and my cat and my bedroom, and all my friends and all the things I thought I was going to do. Even Minty had to go back. That's enough, isn't it? I can't bear to lose any more!'

Alice made to take Scarlett in her arms, but Scarlett held up her hands defensively. 'No! You've got to listen to me,' she wailed. 'Don't just say everything will be all right. I don't believe that any more. Everyone keeps telling me things like that, but no one really listens to what I feel.'

'I'm sorry, Scarlett. Go on. We're listening. Truly we are.' Greg's voice was quiet and soothing as he crouched down in front of her, next to Alice.

Scarlett took a shuddering breath and pressed her lips together, as though preparing herself, as the tears fell. 'The thing is, no one else I know has lost their mum and dad. I'm the only one, and people don't know what to say to me. And I don't know what to say to them either. People try to be nice and comforting but they don't understand. I'm frightened. Every day, I think things are going to change and I don't want that. I want everything to stay the same. I know it can't for ever, of course.

374

But just for a bit, can't everything stay the same? I don't want to lose anyone ever again. Grown-ups just don't think. You shouldn't break up with someone just because you're a bit bored with them. That's stupid.'

Next to her, Alice felt Greg flinch and she cursed herself for the half-truths she'd told. Scarlett went on. 'I wouldn't break friends for a thing like that. It's stupid. You don't realise how important it is to other people. You can't just think about yourself all the time. I'm only eleven, and I can see that. Why can't you?' The little girl stopped, and her shoulders sagged. 'That's all really. That's what I wanted to say.' She let out a juddering sob. 'I expect you'll all say I'm silly and too young to know what I'm talking about. But I do know what I feel.'

There was a long silence. Then Alice put her hand on Scarlett's leg and rubbed it gently. 'You're right. I don't have any excuse to give you. You're absolutely right. You're not silly at all. In fact, I think you've got more common sense than the rest of us put together.' She paused and thought for a moment, then decided that all she could do was tell Scarlett the truth about how she felt. 'When you didn't come home today, it was as if my heart had been pulled out.' No point mentioning that her heart had been in a bit of a mess already following the bombshell of Ginny's letter. 'I realised then that you've become everything to me. I know I can never replace your mum. I never even thought I wanted to have children of my own. But now I've got you in my life, everything has changed. Making you happy and spending all the time I possibly can with you have become the main ambitions of my life. That's basically it. And if you want all of us around, taking care of you, then that's what's going to happen. I promise.'

'Yes, me too,' chimed in Vince.

'Absolutely,' added Krissy. 'It's an honour even being a kind-of aunt to you.'

Alice was aware she was holding her breath.

'I'm in,' said Greg firmly.

Scarlett looked from one to the other, nodding slowly. 'But will you stay together?' she asked, her gaze intent on Alice and Greg.

'We'll give it our very best shot. I promise.' Alice felt Greg's intake of breath beside her.

'Me too,' he added.

Scarlett seemed to sag. 'All right,' she smiled tiredly. 'Can we go home now?'

*   *   *

With Scarlett safely tucked up and in an exhausted sleep, Alice and Greg went downstairs. He stood awkwardly in the middle of the room, making it feel tiny with his height and the breadth of his shoulders in his dark-grey business suit. They avoided making eye contact—as they had since the moment at Vince's when Scarlett had harangued them. Alice felt immensely uncomfortable.

'Well, I should probably go. You must be exhausted,' he said at last.

'Thanks—so much. For helping, I mean. I'm not sure what I'd have done without you being there.'

He shrugged, still looking down. 'Well, I was glad I could help. Although it was all right in the end, wasn't it? I mean, she was safe.'

'But we didn't know that, did we?' She shuddered. 'I couldn't bear it if something happened to her.'

376

He raised his eyes slowly to look at her face, his expression guarded. 'You're really thinking like a mother. I think Scarlett's in exactly the right place now. So—are you going to be all right?'

Alice forced a smile. 'Yeah—fine.' This was what had to happen, she knew, but she didn't want to be alone. The trauma of the last few hours had shaken her up and she needed someone with her. And that someone had to be Greg. She sat down heavily. 'So, are you going to get another flight? Have you still got time to get to your meetings?'

'Alice, I promised Scarlett I'd stick around and I'm not going back on that now.' He scuffed his foot on the rug in a gesture that echoed Scarlett's when she was unsure about something and Alice's heart lurched. 'If it's all right with you, I was going to come over early to do the hens with her. I thought maybe—if it's OK with you, of course—I could drop her at school next week. Unless . . .'

Alice was torn between the promises she'd made to Scarlett only a few hours ago and the danger she felt in having Greg too close. She looked up at his face, so concerned and so hurt looking. Maybe he didn't know after all. Maybe . . .

He shoved his hands into his trouser pockets in a gesture of sudden resolution. 'Look, Alice—I'll do whatever you want on this. I don't really understand what's happened between us to change your mind and I wish you'd tell me. Scarlett said something about you being *bored*. I thought we were—well, never mind that now. But if you're not going to tell me, I'll try to stop guessing, though it's driving me half crazy. I'll go, I'll come back early. I'll be here for Scarlett, if you want me to, so she can think that everything's all right. But apart from that, I'll have to stay away from you. It's just too painful, to be honest.' He sighed and started to turn to the door. 'I can be here at seven—OK?'

'Why didn't you tell me you'd slept with Ginny?'

He spun round, the shock in his eyes not quite covering up the guilt.

'Oh.'

So it was true. Until that moment Alice had been nurturing a ridiculous hope that there was some mistake. 'Yes. Oh. You should have told me, Greg.'

He sat down heavily. 'I know, I know. And I've been debating with myself about it—particularly when it started getting serious with you ... Well, for me, at least. But there never seemed to be a good moment.'

'What do you mean? For you, at least?' She was stung by his comment and spoke instinctively, then frowned at her own response. It wasn't where she wanted the conversation to go at all.

He gestured upstairs. 'What Scarlett said at Vince's. About you breaking up because it was getting boring. That's what she said—and you can rely on Scarlett, at least, not to lie!'

Alice rubbed her eyes. 'Look—don't change the subject. Scarlett—she got the wrong end of the stick. I had to say something when I found out ...' She stopped herself in time and looked at him sharply. 'When I found out about you and Virginia.'

Greg's shoulders sagged. 'OK—I admit it, I was wrong not to tell you, I suppose. The fact is, I didn't want to. I didn't want *this* scene to happen. And I suppose I rationalised it with myself. I never asked you about any previous relationships—I wouldn't consider it my business. The fact that you and Virginia were such close friends—well, it was a

378

coincidence, or at least that's what I was clinging to. And, to be entirely honest now,' he spread his hands out in front of him and stared down at them. 'I guess I was hoping you'd just never find out. I know it was cowardly, but I thought if I did tell you, it would have made it seem like it had been a big deal. And the point is, Alice, it really, really wasn't.'

Alice took the chance to stare at him sitting there, looking so dejected. She realised he couldn't possibly know. He sighed and went on, raising his eyes now to meet hers.

'Nothing's a big deal except you. I'm so sorry, Alice. If I'd thought that just one night, years ago would make all that difference to us now, I'd have told you straightaway. I've never felt about any woman the way I feel about you, and I was frightened it would change everything.'

'Tell me now,' she said quietly.

'Are you sure? Do you really want to know? To be honest, neither of us comes out of this story very well.'

Alice shook her head. 'I don't know. I don't know. Nothing like this has ever happened to me before and I don't know the rules. Yes—tell me the basics, anyway.'

'Well, since it's over between us—for whatever reason—I don't suppose it can do any more harm. It was ages ago. Maybe thirteen years ago?'

Just over twelve, Alice thought to herself, but allowed him to go on, a bubble of hope forming inside her.

'I can't remember exactly, but I could find out, if it's important to you. It was at the opening of a hotel that the firm I was working for had refurbed.

No—hang on. It can't be as long as that because I started my own company up eleven years ago now. Anyway, I'm not proud of what I did. I was a bit drunk. She was a bit drunk, too.' He stopped and looked at Alice searchingly. 'Are you sure you want to know? I mean, she was your best friend.'

Alice nodded silently. He didn't know about Scarlett. She was almost sure now.

'And I really feel terrible about that—taking advantage of a girl I knew was married—I'm not making any excuses for myself. It was absolutely unplanned, I promise you, and very irresponsible, but it was a long time ago. I'd just had a bad break-up. I left in the morning before she even woke. Yes—I know—I'm not proud of that either. And I only saw her one more time after that. At a meeting in London. We both acted as though nothing had ever happened. So there you are. It was basically a one-night stand. But, honestly, Alice, I'm not that guy any more—I wasn't really then. I would never get with a woman just for one night now. And the fact that she was your best friend is—well, it's just bad luck.'

Alice breathed out, a sense of relief tinged with something else starting to edge its way into the misery and tension of the day. But he was looking at her carefully now, and she could see the questions forming in his mind. She spoke before he had time to ask them.

'I found out just recently. Well, yesterday actually. After you left. I was looking through some of Ginny's papers that I brought back that day from the house. And she'd kept a kind of diary.' Alice was aware she wasn't being as honest as Greg had been—and that might be something for her to think about later but, just for now, she had Scarlett to think about as well as herself. Scarlett—who had demanded that she and Greg try to make a go of it. Scarlett, to whom they had given their solemn word that they would do so. She chose her words with care. 'She wrote about what happened and I read it. She didn't say much—although she did say she was drunk too. She felt guilty but . . .' Alice paused. 'But in the long run it was OK. She was OK with it.'

And it had brought her heart's desire—that precious gift called Scarlett, sleeping safely and trustingly upstairs.

'This might sound weird, but I'm relieved now that I've told you. And, Alice,' he was searching her face now, his eyes expressing hope once again. 'Is that why you broke it off? Because you found out about what happened?'

Alice hesitated. She couldn't tell him yet. Maybe never. 'Yes, that was it. It was such a shock.'

'And now I've explained it. And now you've had time to think about it. And because Scarlett wants us to. Do you think we could give it a go?'

Joy and relief made Alice smile, in spite of his serious expression. 'If you still want to. You know I've got to put Scarlett first in everything. She's completely my responsibility now.'

His smile matched hers and he reached out and took her hand. 'Yes, I do understand, and I'll give you all the support you want, and I'll back off whenever you want. She's your daughter—or as good as—and I'll be here for you both. And the hens.'

They stood up and he pulled her into his arms, lifting her off her feet and swinging her round.

They both laughed until he stopped suddenly, and put one finger to her lips. 'Shhhh—you'll wake Scarlett.'

Chapter 51

Christmas 2010

Well, this was a pleasant change. Alice wriggled her toes on the sun-lounger and settled more comfortably into the cushions. The last time she had been to Marrakesh it had been on her gap year and all they'd been able to afford was a dodgy, unbearably hot hotel that smelled strongly of garlic across from the bus station. This was more like it. Five-star opulence, with its pillars and roof terraces. This riad exhausted even Alice's extensive vocabulary of travel superlatives. She was too relaxed even to bother opening the novel she'd brought with her.

'Has lunch tired you out?' Greg called across from the other side of the pool, where he and Scarlett were tipping each other off lilos. Each time he came up he pushed the hair off his face and the water ran down his tanned back. Alice peeped at him behind her sunglasses. He was utterly oblivious to how sexy he looked.

'Terribly,' she replied with mock exhaustion, 'and can you imagine? I've got to summon up the energy for my massage at half past three.'

He smiled back broadly and turned his attention back to Scarlett. This holiday had been exactly what Scarlett needed and it hadn't been until Alice had

382

acknowledged the dark shadows under her eyes that she realised what the last seven months had done to this little girl. And on top of everything, she'd had to cope with a new school, making new friends, and all in a completely new part of the country. Ginny had been right in her diary; she was an incredibly self-possessed little character and perhaps that had been her salvation.

Over the last few days since they'd arrived, Christmas fare still sitting heavy in their stomachs, Alice had watched Scarlett unwind in the sunshine. The tension had gone from her face, and the sound of her giggles across the pool lifted Alice's heart. With just the three of them, she'd chatted about holidays she'd had with Ginny and Piers, and even talked about the trip to Turkey that had been snatched from them. She was slowly returning to the lively girl Ginny described in her journal.

Christmas itself had been a mixture of joy and trauma. Scarlett had decorated the house with Alice, something Alice had never bothered to do before. Last year, when Ginny, Piers and Scarlett had turned up on the doorstep, refugees from The Gables and the pony disaster, she hadn't had anything in the fridge, let alone a single strand of tinsel. But this year the fridge had groaned under the weight of delicious things to eat, and the sitting room had looked like Santa's grotto by the time Scarlett had finished with it. Alice was assiduous in making sure the decorations salvaged from the loft at the Oxford house were given priority—even over Vince's garish contributions—and with each one, there was a story from Scarlett about it. It was a cathartic process that was both painful and moving. Tears came from Scarlett more easily these days and she let them fall, and Alice hoped it was a measure of the trust and safety she was growing to feel. More often than not, Alice joined her, and Greg would come home and find the two of them red-eyed and cuddling, their heads resting against each other and a pile of tissues on the table in front of them. He wouldn't comment but would simply put the kettle on and wait until they recovered.

It was a wrench taking her over to Judy and Bill's for a Waverley Christmas lunch—more than Alice imagined it would be—but it meant that she and Greg had time to themselves to relax and enjoy roast pheasant—a rather unexpected present from Walter who'd also allowed them to pick their sprouts from his veg patch. It wasn't until they were on the sofa with a glass of wine that they realised they'd talked about little else other than Scarlett as they had eaten.

'Bloody hell,' Alice had laughed, sniffing with emotion. 'I'm turning into a proper mum!'

Christmas lunch at The Gables had been an emotional affair and tears had obviously been shed by everyone. The whole family were there, surrounded by wrapping paper in the drawing room, and they'd greeted Alice with genuine warmth when she came to collect Scarlett later. Scarlett had been spoilt rotten with gifts but if anyone deserved it she did. And not a pony in sight. Judy, despite red eyes, was as keen as ever to play the hostess, and tried to press some leftover Stilton on Alice but the excuse that they were leaving first thing for Heathrow saved her from having to accept the smelly thing.

'But it'll keep for ages!'

'Why don't you keep hold of it and we'll

have some when we come back?' she replied diplomatically, amazing herself with her new ability to say "no" to Judy. She had come on, and she knew Ginny would have appreciated it. She felt a wave of loss for her friend.

On the way back, Scarlett chatted about the lunch and how Stone had sneaked outside for a cigarette before his mother caught him and raked him over the coals. They laughed about how everyone had studiously avoided eating Maggie's nut roast which Scarlett described as looking like horse poo.

'Oh,' she added as an afterthought as they pulled up outside the cottage. 'I told Granny that I wouldn't mind having riding lessons next year. Do you think that was the right thing to do?'

Alice smiled her approval. 'I think that's the kindest, most thoughtful thing you could have done for her and, who knows, you might enjoy it.'

As Greg had finished off the packing and Scarlett had soaked in the strawberry-scented bubble-bath Alice had put in her stocking, Alice had read the last of Ginny's journal. The final entries were painful to read, full of excitement about their forthcoming holiday and Ginny's new assistant, but her description of Derek and his management-speak had made Alice laugh.

As she closed it, she noticed a small piece of paper tucked into the back flap of the journal and she slipped it out and opened it. It was dated May and was enigmatic and unfathomable, no matter how many times Alice read it.

My darling Piers. What a man you are. I feel closer to you now than I have ever done and I never believed I could ever love you more than I do already. You understand me so well and we're so strong together, you, me and Scarlett. Our beautiful daughter. Our blessing.

Alice looked over at Greg and Scarlett again, lying side by side now on their lilos, floating in the pool and chatting quietly to each other. Had Piers ever found out? And if he had, had it changed anything? Alice thought not, his love for his daughter and his wife was so strong. And what of Greg? Alice was not ready to tell him yet—perhaps not ever—and she certainly wasn't going to defy her best friend's wishes. But what if he found out the truth somehow? Would it change everything?

Who knew? What Alice thought she understood now, though, was the strength of a love that had made Ginny so happy the day she wrote the note. Because Alice was fairly sure she was feeling it too.

Acknowledgements

We'd like to thank the following for their help and advice with what has been quite a challenging and emotional book for us to write. Dr Helen Gunton, Dr Penny Shearman, Florian Combe from the City of Oxford Rowing Club, Gaye Hillier, Olivia Okell, Lindsay and Alex Fox, the London Sperm Bank, Julia Silk and Sara O'Keeffe and all at Orion, and Mary Pachnos as ever. But most of all to Mike and Elaine Nicholas for their immense generosity which gave us the germ of the idea.